THE LAND ARMY GIRLS ARE HERE

Kay Snow

The Land Army Girls Are Here © 2023 by Kay Snow. All Rights Reserved.

All rights reserved. Kay Snow asserts the moral rights to be identified as the author of this work. No part of this book may be reproduced in any form or by any electronic or mechanical means including information storage and retrieval systems, without permission in writing from the author. The only exception is by a reviewer, who may quote short excerpts in a review.

Cover designed by Kay Snow

This book is a work of fiction. Names, characters, places, and incidents either are products of the author's imagination or are used fictitiously. Any resemblance to actual persons, living or dead, events, or locales is entirely coincidental.

Kay Snow
Visit my website at kaysnow.co.uk

Printed in Great Britain by Amazon

First Printing: May 2023

ISBN- 9798392407477

To all that served, to all who are and to all that will – God bless you all.

Calf's Lament

My name is Pat, I am a calf,
My Land Girl often makes me laugh.
The way she thinks she knows just how,
To bring me up to be a cow.

Why won't she let me eat all day,
And guzzle luscious meadow hay?
Or fill my tummy up with swede?
Life should consist of one long feed.

Outside this yard I'd like to run,
To chase a hen would be such fun.
She seems to think I'd do some harm,
Investigating round the farm!

Thank heaven for the day-to-be,
When all my grief shall turn to glee.
For when she milks me in a pail,
I'll love to lash her with my tail!

—M Baxter 62953

Poem from the book, 'Land Army Days: Cinderellas of the Soil' by Knighton Joyce.

1

Striding across the room to the door, the small red-haired girl checked her stride and stood uncertainly for a moment before turning back with a toss of her head. Then going to the little oak wardrobe which stood by the bed, she opened the door and lifted out a battered shoebox. Sitting down on the bed, she lifted the lid and brought out a cigarette packet. Flipping back the lid, she emptied it onto her lap. She smiled with satisfaction on seeing the one lone woodbine and three matches which lay there. She broke the woodbine in two and put half between her lips, struck a match on the side of her shoe, then lit the tobacco. As she inhaled deeply and slowly, she gave a sigh of contentment, the forbidden pleasure always gave her a feeling of playing with fire, as her parents' did not approve of anyone smoking. Her Mam said that it was a most unladylike practice and common. Dad could not understand why anyone wanted to look like a smoking pit chimney. She stood and looked into the mirror which hung on the wall, not a beautiful face, but an interesting one, with large hazel eyes, a firm mouth with a hint of stubbornness lurking in the corners, a skin that glowed with health and red-gold hair which hung to her shoulders in loose curls, complementing her eyes. She smiled at herself as her thoughts went racing ahead to her big day, as tomorrow she was going to join the Women's Land Army. Fancy her, April Thornton, a Land Girl! No more fancy frocks, silly hats and make-up for her; she would be wearing the Land Army uniform with pride, it would be lovely to be meeting and working with girls her own age. She had learned that the work would be hard from the Land Girl who sat behind the desk at the recruiting office down in the Ministry of Labour, and that she could be posted to the wilds of Scotland, the bottom end of England, or even Wales. She had told the girl that she would not mind where she went, if she was doing her bit for the war effort. Tomorrow was her D-Day, she would sign up, *then* tell her parents', they would be distraught, but it could not be helped, it was her life to do with as she liked.

"Well, April," she said, "time to turn in, up with the lark in the morning."

She drew the curtains closed and undressed for bed.

* * *

Her interview day was beautiful and warm, with a bright blue sky and fleecy white clouds sailing lazily on their way. The river shone like a silver mirror in the distance, and the smell of cut grass hung in the air along with the indescribable fragrance of early summer.

This is the first day of the rest of my life, even the Thrush must know as he sings his head off in the old Apple Tree, April thought as she caught the bus into Doncaster. She had slept poorly last night but felt much better now that she was in the summer sunshine.

As she came to the dingy building that housed the Ministry of Labour office and Recruitment Centre, she had a sudden qualm of what she was about to do, then with a toss of her head, she muttered.

"In for a penny, in for a pound," and hurried down the dimly lit passage, whose peeling wallpaper was decidedly unpleasant.

Coming to a door marked 'Office' in large bold print; she opened it and entered a sparsely furnished, gloomy room which contained a couple of well-worn, comfortable chairs with stuffing poking out in places. Seeing a bell on the shabby desk with a notice saying, 'Please Ring For Attention', she crossed the room and pressed it twice. Almost immediately, the door opened to admit a tall, slender, slightly masculine-looking woman in her early forties. She smiled at April, then sat down behind the desk, shuffling through a pile of papers which she carried.

"Hello, you must be, April Thornton," she said pleasantly. She stood, then said, "come with me, April, we'll have a chat before you put pen to paper, and make sure that you know just what you're signing up for."

April rose and followed the woman into an adjoining room, which again contained a desk and two canvas chairs. She sat down and gripped the chair arms tightly; her heart beats blaring in her ears. She told herself to relax, stay calm and make a good impression.

Still smiling pleasantly, the Recruitment Officer said.

"Now, Miss Thornton, I am Miss Barr, so, we'll get on with it, shall we? I hope that you've thought very deeply about joining the Land Army, because it's no job for the squeamish, the weak or the lazy. And I must tell you that we have little time to give you any training, as the farmers are crying out for help. So, in a word, Miss

Thornton, you'll be thrown in at the deep end. What you're signing up for can be a delightful job in the spring and summer, although backbreaking at harvest time. In winter you'll be called upon to work long hours in all weathers, fog, rain, snow and storm. You may be working with animals, muck spreading, clean out pigsties, milk cows, stand knee-high in dirty ditches, handle machinery such as tractors and threshers. Dig, hoe, plant and uproot, in short, do every job asked of you. Your lodgings may be uncomfortable, bad, nasty, or first class. Food can be poor, your wage small, and some farmers wives will see you as a female enticement, out to run off with their husbands, and therefore treat you like the dirt on your boots. You must be able to stand the sight of blood, there's no time for fainting fits. Walk for miles across fields, ride a bike in the dark, climb a five-barred gate at speed if dealing with a temperamental bull. You'll roll a full milk churn, heave a bale of hay onto your shoulders, have mice running up your legs while haymaking, and use the hedge bottom as your toilet.

These, Miss Thornton are just a few of the things you'll have to do. Oh, I forgot to mention, you'll have to be up at the crack of dawn before the birds start singing sometimes. It's a tough, hard job you're putting yourself up for, it's a man's job you'll be doing, but, the other side of the life is, you'll meet, and have fun with other girls who are away from home doing their bit like yourself. You'll make good friends, laugh together, even I suspect cry together, and go dancing on your time off if you're lucky enough to get any. You can't be homesick, but I rather think you'll be working too hard to even think about home.

You must remember, Miss Thornton, that the WLA is an essential band of women. Although it's not classed as a fighting force, it *is* doing its bit for King and country.

You may think that I've waffled on a bit, but it's my job to make sure that you understand just what you're letting yourself in for. The job is no bed of Roses, but I think that you're the type who is foolish enough to think that it is."

April took a deep breath, then said.

"Is that all? You make me feel tired before I begin the job."

"Why pretend?" laughed Miss Barr. "Sometimes I've to be really hard with some of the girls who wish to join the WLA because they think life down on the farm is going to be glamorous, just because they don a uniform."

There was a short silence as April thought about all Miss Barr had said, then she said thoughtfully.

"You told it as it really is, Miss Barr, I'll give it my best shot. I can't say fairer than that, can I."

"Good girl," Miss Barr said as she handed a pen to April. "I've a feeling that you're going to be an excellent Land Girl!"

"I think that I'm going to enjoy it," April said with a smile. "Give me a pen, I'll sign on the dotted line."

"Good girl," Miss Barr repeated as she handed April a pen. "I'll send your papers and uniform, also your posting, along in a few days. Leave your measurements with the girl in the small office by the door where you came in, and remember, Miss Thornton, you could be sent anywhere, please be prepared for that won't you." As she stood, Miss Barr patted April on the shoulder as she said kindly with a smile.

"Goodbye, and good luck, Miss Thornton."

April squared her shoulders as she strode jauntily along in the bright sunshine. *She* was going to be a Land Girl, and was looking forward to it, but *not* telling her parents', who would dither and moan, beg her to change her mind. Then knowing how stubborn she was, give in with a good grace, tell her to be a good girl, write home at least twice a week, and not to go near any of those no-good G.I's. April smiled at this, might as well tell the moon to stop shining, the G.I's could not be as bad as they were painted. She would find out for herself, she certainly intended to!

* * *

April glanced out of the window as the train sped along the winding track, which was set among a monotony of green, which now and again was broken by white and purple Rhododendron bushes, which grew in wild profusion. Her hazel eyes widened in excitement as she saw the vast expanse of open country before her and said aloud.

"This is lovely!"

The last two days had been one long goodbye to family and friends, who had been eager to wish her luck in her new job as a Land Girl. Her posting was near Skipton in North Yorkshire, on a lonely farm about a mile and a half from the town. The farmers two sons had been called up, so he was short-handed and had asked for help from the WLA, which was she.

She smiled to herself as she propped her feet onto the seat opposite where she was sitting and thought how lucky she was to have a carriage all to herself, and therefore had no need to pretend to concentrate on the magazines which her Mam had tucked under her arm as she had boarded the train in Doncaster. She had not been sorry to leave the pit village where her Dad had spent the best part of his life working like a mule underground, nor had she been sad to leave her job in the shoe shop once she had made up her mind to answer the call for girls to work on the land. Mam and Dad had been upset at the thought of her leaving home, but her twin brothers, Barry and Harry, had thought it hilarious that their five-foot four-inch sister was going to do a man's job. They had made comments like, 'You don't know one end of a cow to the other or which teat to pull first!' Her Dad had roared with laughter at this, then had put *his* two pennyworths in by saying. 'Our little April mucking out pigs, that'll be the day!' She had tutted at them and gotten on with the packing. Later, she had told her Mam that she would take things as they came, in wartime a new job was a milestone in anyone's life, and she would be doing her bit for her country. Lads who were called up had not been given a choice, but were fighting for a peaceful, happier world. So, you could say that the WLA fought the enemy of starvation. It was 1944, and the end of the war could be in sight, but until then, she would do her best in her new job and learn as she went on.

Her thoughts came to a sudden halt as the train pulled into busy Skipton Station. As she stepped down onto the sun-baked platform, the heat which met her had a ferocious dry quality that made her long for a cold drink. Putting down her suitcase, she pulled out the paper she had received from the Ministry of Labour and read the directions to Linderhome Farm, where she was hired as a Land Girl. She glanced around her, but no one seemed to be there to meet her, so she pushed the papers back into her pocket and said aloud.

"Shanks pony then. What's a mile and a half in this heat?!"

Setting off in good heart, after twenty minutes the countryside began to unfold before her, she had breath-taking views of the hills and fields spread with wild summer flowers. The air was filled with the scent of Dog Roses, which merged with wild massed blossom, and the lazy murmuring of the bees mingled with the whirr of the airborne grasshoppers. Soon, the sun felt like a gentle caressing hand on her head as she walked on through tangled green growth, littered with clumps of Dog Daises. In a field to her right was a large herd of cows which stood together, their hides glowing in the sun that shone through candyfloss clouds piled like castles on the horizon, ever-changing. The relentless heat had continued for the last few weeks' and rain could not be far away, but to April's eyes, the crops looked healthy enough, so the farmers must have a way of keeping them well watered.

Her case was getting heavier with every step she took, and she longed for a glass of water or a cup of good strong tea like the way her Mam made it.

She was now walking on a Buttercup covered grass verge towards a sea of golden Corn, surrounded by a thick Hawthorn hedge, and there, a dozen yards away, was a sign that read 'Linderhome Farm'. Sighing with relief, she started up a path that wound steadily uphill, then gave another heartfelt sigh as she saw the farmhouse, with numerous outbuildings surrounding it. As she drew nearer to the farm, she could see that she was going to be confronted by a small, portly male figure that was hurrying towards her, waving his arms wildly in the air. As the figure rushed towards her, April could see that the man was in his late fifties, with prominent eyes bulging from their sockets at the sight of her. He wore the old-fashioned knee breeches, a khaki shirt which had seen better days, and a battered flat cap on his head.

"I say, you there, what are yer doing on my land?!" he called.

"If this is Linderhome Farm, and the signpost says that it is, I'm your help from the WLA, a Land Girl for whom you asked."

"What's that yer say?!" he bellowed.

April took a step closer to him, saying.

"The WLA, I'm from there. You sent for help, remember?"

The farmer gave April a hard stare.

"Aye, I remember, gal, but I sent for a Land Girl, not a bit of a kid straight out of school. The works hard here and the hours long, you'll never stand up to that by the look of yer."

"I don't know how old you think I am," April returned angrily, annoyed that she had coloured under his scrutiny. "But I won't see my eighteenth birthday again, *and I'm stronger than I look!*"

The farmer looked startled, gave a curt nod of his head, and said acidly.

"If yer as quick with your hands as yer are with your tongue, yer'll do. Any road, the Mrs will weigh yer up in a crack, she doesn't take any claptrap from nobody, especially from young whippersnappers like you, so come on up to the house and we'll see what she meks of yer."

As the farmer marched off, leaving April to carry her suitcase, it struck her that really, he was a pathetic little man, and it sounded as if the Mrs of his wore the trousers. Maybe his bark was worse than his bite?

She was soon to find out how wrong she was.

As he marched ahead, he called over his shoulder.

"How much training did they give yer?"

April took pleasure in saying.

"Hardly any, no time, but I'm a fast learner. I'm sure I'll soon pick it up."

The farmer stopped and turned to face her, saying.

"Sod it! This is a fine how do yer do I must say! No training?! Not going to be much use are yer?! Any road, where do yer come from?"

"South Yorkshire coalfields," April said.

"By, but yer a raw recruit and no mistake, the Mrs will soon have yer jumping through hoops, so it's a good job yer a fast learner in't it, for I can tell yer, the Mrs is a good teacher!"

On hearing this, April smiled to herself, for she knew that she had a charming personality which most men, and some women found appealing, but she could also be very forthright, which was going to come in handy with this Mrs of his by the sound of things.

As they came to the farmhouse, whose door stood open letting in the still hot sunshine, April followed the farmer into a large kitchen, which had cupboards on every wall, but even these were overshadowed by the most extensive kitchen range she had ever seen. Polished with blacklead, it winked and gleamed in the sunshine which straggled through the open door, reflecting both her and the farmer's figures in it. Then she was struck by the sight of a beautifully built Spanish galleon which stood on top of the mantelpiece, with on either side of it, two chipped china dogs. The white-washed walls complemented the yellow chintz curtains, which hung at the large window, under which stood a battered oak sea chest piled high with newspapers. Three old armchairs with filling poking out in places stood on well-scrubbed stone flags which covered the floor, but in command of these, held the most enormous wooden table April had ever seen. Behind this, sat a large-boned woman shelling peas. She looked at April with shrewd mahogany brown eyes, which were also cold and cynical. She had a broad double chin and a dingy complexion under a mass of thick iron-grey hair, which was scraped back into a bun at the back of her head. She gave April a cold, keen look, then asked sarcastically.

"Well, Miss, and who are you?"

"I'm your Land Girl," April said politely.

"Oh, you are, are yer? Yer not the size of two pennies worth of copper. What good do yer think yer going to be for us?"

"What you see is what you get," April said scathingly. "I was brought up to never judge a book by its cover, and," she went on, "you'll just have to take me or leave me."

The Mrs made no reply, and went on shelling peas, then suddenly said grimly.

"As things stand at the moment, we'll have to take yer, we don't have much choice, and before we start, I'll have less of yer lip or yer'll end up with a fat one!"

April looked shocked, then said calmly.

"I don't think the War Agg would like that, in fact, I'm *sure* they wouldn't."

The Mrs gave her a disapproving look, then with a crease between her brows, said.

"I know all about the War Agg. Now, why did yer join the Land Army?"

April gave a tight-lipped smile.

"To be part of the war effort, see more of my country, and meet a different class of people."

"Oh, aye," the Mrs said. "Well, yer've met me, and I'm a force to be reckoned with, as yer'll soon find out. And as for seeing more of yer country, there's lots of it here, and yer'll be seeing it in all weathers. Yer'll be sick of the sight of it before yer much older."

The farmer had stood silent throughout the exchange, and now he cut in.

"She's had no training either, Mrs."

"No training?!" the Mrs said, horrified.

"No training," he repeated.

"Well, Mr," she said commandingly. "Yer going to have yer work cut out, aren't you?! Starting from tomorrow at five, see how she frames milking the cows."

The farmer nodded while the Mrs began once more to shell the peas, then she said.

"And you being a redhead, I don't suppose that hair of yours is no lie, so we'd better start as we mean to go on, hadn't we?!" She paused to draw breath. "Yer'd better know also, the Mr might be the Boss in the fields, but in here I'm the kingpin, and what I say goes. Everything runs like clockwork, meals on time or yer don't get any, no cheek from yer, and yer keep your room clean."

April smiled as the Mrs went on.

"I don't know what yer smiling at, but yer won't be smiling at the end of yer first day."

April smiled again, then said sarcastically.

"I comprehend."

"Oh, yer do, eh?!" the Mrs said sneeringly. She sniffed loudly and went on sharply. "I'll bet yer don't dig out a potato bigger than a walnut, and yer'll peel a carrot instead of scraping it."

April gave a toss of her head, then said jauntily.

"Makes no difference to me carrots being peeled *or* scraped, as I won't be doing either. I've been sent to work on the land. I was told to do no kitchen work or housework."

"Yer'll do as yer told, Miss." snapped the Mrs angrily. "What I say goes, the sooner yer learn that the better."

April did not have red hair for nothing and could feel her temper beginning to rise. She turned to the farmer, who had been stood mute throughout the battle of words between the two women.

"Well, Mr?" she asked. "What have you to say about me working in the house? Because I want it understood here and now, I'm going down the road to the nearest phone box, and I'll report you both to the Labour Exchange and the War Agg. The result of that will be no help on your farm. I suggest you both make up your minds now. While you do that, I'd be glad of a sit down and a cup of tea if it's not too much trouble."

The Mrs smiled calmly while her husband stood speechless, then slowly she put down the basin of peas, rose, and placed her large hands on the table. Then leaning toward April, said.

"Before yer get any further on your high horse, I can see yer can stand up for yourself, I like that. But understand, this is a working farm, which means yer have to work till yer drop. Yer'll have realised that we're isolated out here, so there's very little to do on what time off yer'll get."

"Yes," April said. "I'll just have to make the best of a bad job, won't I."

"Enough of yer cheek, girl, the Mr will show yer to yer room, such as it is, but it's the best we could do. I'll send yer a mug of tea and a beetroot sandwich to put yer on until suppertime."

Turning to the farmer, who stood looking preoccupied, April said with an ironical smile.

"Lead on, McDuff, I can't tell you how much I'm looking forward to that beetroot sandwich, even though I've never been a lover of beetroot."

"Well, yer'll get plenty of it here I can tell yer, and yer can call me Mr Whiteman," the farmer said casually. "Mr is the wife's pet name for me. It would seem funny yer calling me Mr all the time."

"Really?" April said. "Do you always call her the Mrs?"

"Always have done since the day we wed, so does everyone else. Truth to tell, I've forgotten what her name is!"

"Do you have any family?"

"Two boys on active service, one in the army, the other in the navy on the subs."

"Oh," April exclaimed. "You must worry about them."

"Yes, we do, who wouldn't? But so far, they're okay, we hope, although we haven't heard from Bruce, the one in the navy, for a few weeks', no news is good news, so they say." The farmer changed the subject quickly. "If I were you, I'd get myself to bed straight after supper. We rise at five-thirty for the morning milking. Yer can watch, then have a go, yer'll soon get the hang of it, nothing to it really, cows are gentle creatures."

"Getting up at five-thirty?!" April gasped. "That's the middle of the night."

The farmer chuckled.

"Not on a farm, love, early to bed, early to rise is our motto."

"But what about breakfast?" April asked.

"Oh, breakfast's at eight, a good time by wartime standards, that's when all the milking and swilling down the floor in the milking barn's done, but don't worry, the Mrs sends yer out with a good strong hot cup of tea."

"I should hope so. Fancy having to start the day on a cup of tea."

"Oh, yer'll get used to it."

"I don't have much choice, do I."

"Oh, and, April," the farmer said casually. "Don't let the Mrs get yer down, she's just testing yer, and really she admires anyone who stands up for themselves."

"Really? You could've fooled me."

During their chatter, they had walked down an extended ground floor passage, the walls of which were hung with photos of cattle, sheep, cats and dogs. Stopping at the last door on the left, the farmer pushed it open. It creaked loudly on the unoiled hinges.

"I'll get that door seen to for yer. We thought this ground floor room would suit yer better than the attic, which is a bit damp."

He stepped aside to allow April to enter the small room, which contained an uncomfortable looking bed, one chair badly in need of a coat of paint, and a well-scrubbed white wooden dressing table. Behind the door was a square wickerwork table on which stood a china washbowl and jug. The wooden floorboards had no covering, only a hand pegged rug which stood by the bed. A tiny alcove was curtained off to serve as a wardrobe. The small, but clean window looked out onto the side of the barn; its windowsill covered with dead flies due to the heat. The room smelled stuffy as if it had been shut up for weeks', due again to the weather. April flung open the window to let in the fresh air; the draft causing the dead flies to tumble to the floor.

Grinning, the farmer said.

"I'll bring a dustpan and brush later so yer can get rid of that lot, but there's always clouds of flies about on a farm due to the animals yer see." He turned to the door where he said. "Well, lass, I'll leave yer to get on with things, I hope yer'll be comfortable. See yer at supper, which is rabbit stew, the Mrs is a dab hand at cooking as yer'll soon find out."

Alone at last, April sat on the bed, which was more comfortable than it looked. She gazed around the room which desperately needed a coat of distemper. I'll do it myself, she thought, if they provide the brush and distemper, there's nowhere to go on my time off, so it will give me something to do.

Then reflectively, life is going to be no bed of roses, but then, did I really expect it to be?! Oh, what have I let myself in for? Up at half-past five in the morning, I'll never do it, but I must! I have to start by watching smelly cows being milked. Oh well, it has to be done; I'll see worse than that before I'm done, I'm sure!

2

It was a hot, sunny day in July that found April sat on the back of a mowing machine enjoying the bright sunshine. As she listened to the drone of the engine and the clicking of the connecting rod, it was like a lullaby to her, while all around came the sweet smell of Honeysuckle and Dog Roses, which were scattered in the hedges. White fluffy clouds trailed along in a delicate eggshell blue sky, and a lark trilled merrily overhead.

Suddenly realising her concentration was slipping, which would never do, she saw that it was necessary to calculate how many more turns it would need to finish off the field. Soon the last swath would be laid, and the four village helpers and she could finish for the day. It was no good working the volunteers too hard, excessive overtime would not do their health, *or* hers any good, as the time they put in was never wasted, they worked jolly hard with only three breaks all day. They always arrived on time, and never stopped to gossip in the middle of a job. They had done ten hours today; she had done twelve, with a half-hour lunch break and two fifteen-minute tea breaks.

The end of the war was not in sight, and food had to be put in everyone's mouth. The last few years had been bitter for everyone, who knew how many more were to come. Another half-hour would see the job done, the workers on their way home, and she would be back at the farmhouse, dusty and hungry, but happy.

She had taken to the job straight away; a matter of weeks' and she was an old hand. Farm work was excruciatingly hard, but to her, wholly absorbing, but oh how she enjoyed it, loved it in fact! Her twin brothers would never believe the amount of work she could get through in a day, and she was quite proud of herself. Having said that, she had her first winter to get through, so she had better not count her chickens before they hatched!

Things were looking up though, the farmer was getting another Land Girl to help and live in, she was due any day now, then maybe I'll get a day off, I could certainly do with one. It would be lovely to have a lie-in instead of getting up at five-thirty to help with the milking, washing endless milk bottles, mucking out sodden straw litter and sluicing down the sheds. Cows had to be milked on time as the animals rapidly filled up again.

She had been getting extra pay for no days off, but really it was no compensation for the loss of liberty. Her thoughts came to a sudden halt as she came to the end of the field, cut the engine, and called.

"Alright lads, time to knock off. Thanks for your help, you've all done well, see you tomorrow bright and early."

As April made her way back to the farmhouse, the sun on the horizon was becoming a huge molten ball surrounded by a beautiful sapphire sky. It seemed to rest on top of a group of stunted trees in the distance. As she walked amongst swaying grass stalks, a gentle breeze sprang up, bending the heads of the Dog Daises which grew in wild profusion along the winding path.

Once in the yard, she stood at the pump, tucked her aertex shirt into the waistband of her breeches, rolled back her shirt collar, then began to splash her face with cold water that gushed out. She did this until her skin tingled, and after the heat of the fields, she felt much refreshed and ravenously hungry. As she dried herself vigorously, the farmer appeared behind her and said mysteriously.

"Come on lass, don't be hanging around here too long, there's a nice surprise waiting inside for yer."

"For me?" April queried.

"Yes, for you, and yer going to be pleased with it, very pleased," he repeated while nodding his head.

"Go on, tell me," April begged. "I don't like sudden surprises, sometimes they can be more of a shock."

The farmer put his head to one side, then said.

"It's a female."

"A female?" April repeated, then gave a loud whoop.

"Aye," said the farmer. "A good looking one too, aren't I lucky, two pretty Land Girls!"

"At last, our extra help! Does she look strong?" April enquired.

"Strong enough, although I'd say she's a bit of a lady," the farmer answered. "With a name like Fay Bennett-Trent, she must be, but here she is Land Girl 470211. Anyway, bring yer self on to the house and see for yer self."

Throwing down the towel, April cried.

"I don't care how posh she is as long as she can work."

"It'll be a new friend for yer," the farmer said hopefully, pleased to be the bearer of good news.

"Maybe I'll get a day off now, eh?" April said pertly.

"We'll see, we'll have to see how the new girl gets on with things, how quick she'll be at learning."

"If she's as quick as I was, she'll do."

"Aye, yer was fast; I'll grant yer."

"Didn't have a choice *but* to be otherwise did I with you shouting and bawling at me the whole time."

"Less of yer lip and come on, tea's just about ready, it's a feast today to welcome the new girl, a slice of ham, tomato and spring onions, but she need not expect it *every* day."

"She's lucky; all I got was beetroot sarnies."

"That's all we had at the time."

"Oh well, we have to be thankful for small mercy's these days," April replied.

Walking into the kitchen, April saw a pretty girl of about twenty-four that was standing at the table with the Mrs. She was quite tall with lovely fair hair and blue eyes. The Mrs beckoned to April, saying as she did so.

"April, this is Fay from Harrogate, she's a little nervous, but I'm sure yer going to get along well together, although you don't have much choice do yer. Yer'll show Fay how to do things won't you, because the Mr can't be with her all day. All farm work is hard, as she'll realise on her first day, just as you did."

"I'm glad to know you, Fay," April said with a smile. "And really, the work isn't as bad as the Mrs paints it once you get the hang of it. I hope you grow to love it just as I do."

"Never mind the chit chat now," the Mrs cut in. "Sit down and eat your tea, you can get to know one another later, although by the looks of things, April could do with a couple of matchsticks to keep her eyes open."

To which April replied.

"It's been a hard day, and it's all this fresh air. I'm still getting used to it, there's nothing like it where I come from, so to me it's like wine."

Once at the table and sipping her tea, Fay asked April.

"What's it *really* like working on a farm?"

"Don't worry," April said with a grin. "Mr Whiteman will give you complicated instructions, but I'll explain it in more simple terms."

Fay looked worried as she put down her teacup.

"Oh, dear, I do hope I understand. I've had no training you know; I was told not to worry as I'd be shown what to do."

"Don't worry," April said calmly. "As long as you're willing, that's all that matters."

"And not afraid to get yer hands dirty," the Mrs cut in.

April put her elbows on the table, leant forward, and said seriously.

"The Mrs thought I'd be no use when she first saw me, but she couldn't have been more wrong. I proved my worth after I'd milked my first dozen cows in record time. I sing to them now when I'm milking, they love it. They all have names you know, and you have to watch out for Gert, she can be a bit naughty and cantankerous at times and isn't above kicking, but give her a good slap on the rump, and she soon settles down to the business in hand."

"Oh," Fay choked, looking shocked.

"Don't let slapping Gert put you off," April continued. "She's had many a slap from me. She expects it; life on a farm isn't all tiny calves sucking milk from your fingers, no matter *what* the posters portray."

"I didn't think it was," Fay put in.

The Mrs looked at April intently, sniffed, then said.

"Listen to her; you'd think she'd been working on a farm for years."

"It seems as if I have," April defended.

Standing, then beginning to clear the table, the Mrs said to no one in particular.

"Soft hands and weak muscles are no good for us. Town bred girls have a big shock coming to them. It's not sniffing Roses and Thyme, or hooing and cooing at new-born animals, no time for that, and it's not always peaceful in the country. Admiring a field of golden Corn is alright, but how many town-bred folks think about the complicated process which produces it? Yer look to be a good strong girl, Fay, but those lily-white hands of yours won't stay like that for long. Potato picking, cauliflower lifting, hoeing, digging out weeds and nettles will soon put paid to those. It's necessary to bend your back a lot of the time which yer'll have to get used to, then on comes the backache like yer've never known. It'll last for a week or two then yer'll be ok. Yer'll have got your farm legs as we say. Don't look so downhearted Fay, I'm only telling it as it is. Oh, and one more thing, yer'll have to cover up those golden locks of yours. April will lend and show yer how to wear a turban."

"A turban?" Fay repeated. "Whatever do I have to wear one of those for?"

"Yer'll see why after yer first day's work here," the Mrs retorted.

April stood, bringing the flow to a sudden stop. She pushed her chair under the table, turned to Fay and said.

"I'm sure you'll do alright, Fay. Anyhow, I'm ready for my bed, come on, I'll show you to your room."

"I'm sorry Fay, but I'm afraid it's the attic," the Mrs said kindly. "It's all we have now, but it's roomy and dry, it usually is in summer. In fact, yer could get two single beds in there if yer want to double up, but it's up to you. The other two rooms belong to my boys; I like to keep them empty in case they arrive home on leave. I'll wish yer both a goodnight and I'll see yer in the morning." Then, as an afterthought, she called. "Five-thirty Fay, breakfast at eight."

As the girls made their way out of the kitchen, Fay echoed.

"Five-thirty, did I hear her right?"

"Yes, you did," laughed April. "We're up with the lark here, and you'll soon get used to it." Picking up her case and laughing at her shocked expression, she said. "Come on, girl, follow me, time to turn in, tomorrow's another day, and it's going to be a busy one, so if I were you, I'd get my head down. You need all the sleep you can get in this job."

* * *

A few weeks' later and at six o'clock in the morning, April and Fay stood in the kitchen doorway of the farm, only half awake. The Mrs bustled up and put a mug of hot tea into their hands and hurried away, saying over her shoulder.

"Look lively girls."

"Just look at that," Fay said to April.

The beautiful wild scenery was spread out before them, the grey dawn slowly turning to a flushed pink by the rising sun. A gentle wind blew warmly around them as if surging with impatience for the start of a new day. The busy twittering of the hedge sparrows in the Ivy which grew up the front of the house, mingled with the cry of the goldfinches that flew around the Apple Trees, giving promise of being heavily laden with fruit. The woodpecker had begun his laughing notes, and in the distance came the monotonous call of the cuckoo. A barn owl flew quickly past, and Fay gave a startled cry. She soon learned that the country had many surprises in store. A gentle natured girl, she had taken to farm life, and everyone was pleased with her. Both girls were tanned and glowed with health. Fay would have been loath to admit it, but during the brief time she had been in the Land Army, she had acquired an extra vitality that she knew not from where.

The ever-down to earth April gave Fay a gentle push and said.

"Come on, gal, can't stand here taking in the sights all day, much as I'd like to. Let's get to the shed, the cows are waiting to be milked, and nature waits for no man nor beast."

"I know," Fay replied. "But will you do Cowslip this morning? She's always so crusty, *and* she's big and bony. I'm suffering from a painful kick she gave me yesterday, and my eyes are still sore from the lashing she gave me with her tail, which is all matted and smells horrible."

"Oh," said April, matter of factly. "Show her who the Boss is and give her a slap on the rump, and she'll behave."

"Into the bargain," Fay went on. "I knocked a bucket of milk over that swirled down the gutter, which didn't go down well with the Boss, *and* he called me a clumsy sod, how about that?!"

"Yes, he would," April laughed. "But to get back to the cows swinging tails, it's all part of the job."

"It's alright telling me to clamp my head into the side of the animal, I do," Fay explained loudly. "But I still got whacked."

"These things happen," April replied. "But people who have milk delivered in the mornings don't think of the poor farmworkers who have to be up at five in the morning to supply private houses, rural districts, schools and shops. Not to mention the Army, Navy and Air Force, and all the fighting forces, *and* not forgetting the dark winter mornings having to trail through snow, slush and frost to get the churns into the lorries, no, they don't. Let's enjoy the summer while it's here and not even *think* about winter."

"I won't moan about anything else, April, I promise. If I do, just give me a dig in the ribs," Fay said sheepishly.

"I will," laughed April. "Anyway, the lads should be here soon, you take Sid and milk down the left, I'll take Fred and go down the right, that's Cowslip's side. Remember me telling you how cows like to be sung to? It calms Cowslip down no end."

Fay looked downhearted.

"I can't sing for toffee, you're the one with the voice, it's terrific, you should sing with a dance band, you'd 'wow' them as the Yanks say."

"Well, at the moment, I'm only a 'wow' with the cows, but one day I'll tell you a funny story about my singing and playing boogie-woogie on the piano."

"You play the piano too?" gasped Fay.

"I do indeed, when I get the chance, but haven't played for some time so will be a little rusty."

"I suppose you dance as well?" Fay asked inquiringly. "You seem to be a girl of many talents."

"Yes, I do," replied April jauntily. "And although I say it myself, I'm rather good! I love dancing; I used to go to the Globe every Friday and Saturday night at home, and never sat a dance out. You're never short of a partner once the lads know you can dance."

As the sound of footsteps approached the barn, they each picked up a milking stool, and April said.

"Enough chatter, here come the lads, so we can get started, and about time too, these town lads hired to help with the milking can't get out of bed in a morning, can you lads?" She jokingly called to them.

"We're here, aren't we?" one of the lads said.

"Only just, so shall we start then?!" April snapped. Then turning to Fay. "Maybe on Friday we can get two or three hours off, and if we get done early enough, we could go into town and find out where the local hop is held, see what the local talents like. How does that sound to you?"

"It sounds just wonderful!" said Fay as she began to gently pull on the teats of the gentle cow named Dollywee. The hiss of the milk as it streamed into the buckets was a relaxing sound which came from both sides of the shed. It was oddly soothing, Fay thought as she tucked her head more firmly into Dollywee's side. Then as an afterthought, "I don't know what I'll wear."

"Wear?" April called over her shoulder as she gave a cow named Miss Millie a gentle pat on the head. "You wear your WLA uniform."

"Do I?" Fay asked hesitantly.

"Of course you do. I love going out in mine, and it makes us different from the other girls and sets most of the lads hearts aflutter, and you'll not be short of a partner or two I can tell you."

"But I'll be a wallflower, April, I told you, I can't dance."

"Don't worry about that, Fay, I'll soon have you going, all you need to know are a few basic steps, and the rest comes naturally."

The rest of the milking was completed in silence except for the swishing of the cows tails, and the odd bellow from one or the other. The clang of the milk pails sounded loud as a full one was exchanged for an empty.

Once the cows had been herded back to the fields accompanied by the barking of Cane, the sheepdog, snapping and worrying at their heels, the girls had some ditch clearing to do. It was a job they least enjoyed doing, for it was back aching work and boring, but the compensation was the lovely scenery around them. The valley in which the fields were situated was well wooded and sheltered by rugged slopes, and in the distance, a sparkling river meandered, where, the farmer had told them, moorhens and coots made their nests, and herons could be seen flying over the water searching for fish for their next meal. Also, he had told them pipits and stonechats could be seen.

"There are lots of rabbits around here, just look at them hopping and bobbing about; they don't seem to be aware of us, do they?" asked Fay.

"Oh, they know we're here, make a move towards them and they'll be off like lightening," April replied. "By," she went on as she laid her hoe on the ground. "It's grand round here; I want to stay forever. When you've lived in a pit village all your life you don't know that anything like this exists. My heart is full of contentment when I look around at the beautiful countryside. At the thought of leaving it all I want to weep! Can you imagine anyone not seeing this wonderful scenery? All those people stuck away in pit villages, not knowing this is only fifty or sixty miles away from them."

"Yes," Fay agreed. "I know what you mean, but most of all, can you imagine if the Germans took it into their heads to drop their awful bombs here and ruin everything, wouldn't it be terrible?!"

"It would, but most unlikely as they aim for the factories, docks and steelworks, but most of all, London. They have a terrible time of it. My heart goes out to all the folk who have lost their homes and loved ones. At least we're doing our bit, even though we're not a fighting force."

"I know," Fay nodded her head. "I understand now how crucial our job is and hope the government and people of England know this."

She picked up her spade and thrust it into a pile of moss and dead leaves to get to the weeds which had thrived healthily underneath, covering lots of large stones.

"Let's hope we'll be recognised when the war's over," April said as she energetically threw a spade full of sludge into the wheelbarrow which was gradually filling up beside her. "We'd better be, or I'll have something to say." She dug her spade into the earth, then turned to Fay. "I'll collect all the leaves and twigs to burn, you pick up as many stones as you can, then it should be time for lunch."

Some lunch, the beetroot sandwiches, and the cold tea in a bottle with no sugar, *oh* how she missed her sugar. Still, one could get used to anything, but after the war, oh boy, would she make up for it!

When lunchtime was over, the girls were in the stable admiring Rhett, who had to be geared up and taken to be shod, as one of his shoes was loose, and the Mr thought he might have a small stone wedged under it. The girls had to watch Rhett, as he was a large animal with a bad habit of galloping off and not coming to heel when called. Today he had a devilish gleam in his eye, and the Mr said he was more trouble than he was worth. Last year he had gotten loose by jumping a fence as high as the Chair in the Grand National, went into the field of a neighbouring farm and put in foal the neighbour's prize mare! Today, the girls had found it quite a struggle to get his tackle on in readiness for the blacksmith outing, and now he was getting a little jumpy and frisky. April was used to his little tricks and tried to warn Fay.

"He's going to get himself into a real old lather and try and get his gear off. He's tried that before, and he's got a mean old mood on him today."

"Maybe his foot is hurting him, should we take a look?" worried Fay.

"No, no, don't go near him, he's used to me. Watch and learn," snapped April.

The horse shook himself frantically from side to side, nodding his head violently, then started to buck and kick. April pulled Fay outside the stall and said quietly.

"Just wait a few minutes, you'll see what he can achieve when he's got the mood on him."

In no time at all, the giant horse had the band of braces twisted around his neck collar, causing him to pull back, putting him in a great deal of pain. On seeing this, Fay wrung her hands, and with tears in her eyes cried.

"Oh, poor thing! He's hurting himself, do something, April, *please* do something!"

"Calm down, Fay, remember, I've been through all this before, three or four times to be exact. I'm going to try and get near him and redo everything."

"He might trample you," Fay cried, concerned. "Be careful."

"Don't worry, Fay; I'm always careful where Rhett's concerned. I'll talk to him, calm him down; you keep quiet and don't say a word."

Fay, white-faced, nodded her head. Strolling towards the horse, April spoke soothingly.

"There now, boy, there, come on boy, come now, come on, there now. Be still and let me get that hurtful gear off you, come on my beauty, who's a nice boy then, Rhett? Come on, lad and be still."

April walked slowly forward, put out her hand and gently tried to touch the proud head, but the horse swung away from her. She tried several times to get near him, then just stood and talked to him in a gentle voice. Gradually the horse calmed down and allowed her to approach him. Once having managed to get near his head, she was able to remove all the harness, taking it very slowly and speaking quietly to him as she did so. Then turning to Fay, she gave a sigh of relief, then said.

"Thank goodness that's over! He really is a sod, isn't he?!"

Fay put out a trembling hand and touched April reassuringly on her shoulder.

"You were marvellous, simply great! I was so afraid you'd be trampled under his heavy feet."

"That wouldn't take much doing, I'm only a little un, but I'm going into the house for a cup of tea to steady my nerves, whether the Mrs likes it or not."

"I don't blame you, and I'm coming with you, one word from her and I'll tell her how brave you were," Fay said determinedly.

April linked her arm in Fay's.

"Oh, come on, girl, it's all in a day's work, part of the job. Being a Land Girl is no picnic, we'll have a cuppa then I'll take Rhett to be shod."

3

"Muckspreading has to be the most degrading smelly job ever invented by man!" Fay moaned as she gazed at the muck dumped in untidy heaps around the small field. "I mean, look at it!" she went on. "Do we have to do it all today?"

"Oh, this job isn't too bad," April replied. "Wait until you have to do the threshing, *that's* filthy work. The dust flies everywhere, and it's a lousy job, but it must be done," April sighed as she pulled her turban more firmly over her ears. Then went on. "Fred, the lad from the village, explained it to me like this... A belt's connected to the thresher to start the wheels, we feed the sheaves into the top, then the straw is gathered into a rick after travelling up a chute. All the waste comes out of the bottom somewhere, which someone must keep clearing so that it doesn't jam up the works. The grain is then funnelled into sacks which will weigh a hundredweight. It needs four of us to do the job."

"Sounds like arduous work to me," Fay grumbled. "And who may I ask lifts those full sacks? Not us, I hope?"

"We'll be expected to, after all, we *are* here to do a 'man's' job, can't let the side down can we," April said as she dug her spade into a pile of muck and began to spread it evenly around her.

"This can't be very good on the lungs," Fay commented harshly as she walked to the next pile of dung and began half-heartedly to smooth it out. "Oh, this stuff smells revolting!" she cried.

"It's a healthy smell," April called. "There's worse smells on a farm I can tell you. What about the pigsties?"

"Oh, shut up, April."

"You'd better pray the sun doesn't come out until we finish this lot. If it does it warms the manure up, it steams, and the smell is enough to turn the hardiest stomach! So far, it's dull today."

"Let's hope that it stays that way," Fay said, hopefully.

"Well, come on then, let's get stuck in, soon be break time," April chirped.

Both girls worked quickly and quietly, shovelling and patting the manure evenly over the ground. It squelched up and around their wellingtons, the smell mingling with the stiff breeze sweeping in from the hills, throwing its strong aroma far and wide.

April didn't think the smell was as unpleasant as Fay made it out to be. In fact, she thought it was quite a healthy smell, one that she could get used to. As she worked, her thoughts went on to the next job of the morning. The farmer had told them to get on with the stone picking, which meant walking up and down the fields with a bucket, picking up stones, which left, would break the cutting blade of the machine during haymaking. That time would soon be here, and was jolly hard work, but enjoyable if the weather went their way. Everyone mucked in, even the Mrs, now *that* would be worth seeing, she kept to the kitchen usually. The winter was going to be hard, and it filled her with dread, as the lads had painted a gloomy picture of life on the land. 'Soon sort the men out from the boys' Fred had laughed. You had to drag yourself out of bed on cold bitter mornings; walking through fog so thick you could not see your hand in front of you. Going to frost-covered fields and working with frozen fingers that refused to obey your command when digging out ice-covered sprouts. He had told her much more about the dreadful conditions and jobs that still had to be done regardless of the weather. People still had to be fed in war-torn England, as had the fighting forces. However, she would look forward to haymaking, even if it meant long hours, and surely, they could wear a sun top and get a nice tan.

As if reading her thoughts, Fay called.

"I know I'm going to regret asking this, but what do we do in winter?"

Thrusting her spade into the ground, April leaned on the handle and replied.

"I haven't had a winter here yet, Fay, but, as I understand it, it sorts the men from the boy's, meaning *us*."

Fay interrupted her.

"Stop, I don't want to know, let's not think about it. I'm going to enjoy what's left of summer, take things day by day."

"Yes," answered April. "In your case, that's the most sensible thing to do. Me, I don't mind, I love the job, and when the war's over I plan to stay. In fact, I'd love to have a small farm of my own, but there's little chance of that."

"Maybe you'll marry a rich farmer," Fay said softly. "Fate has a funny way of smoothing our paths for us."

April threw back her head and laughed heartily.

"Me?! Marry a farmer? I'll end up with a poor farmhand, and we'll live in a tied cottage."

"You never know what life has in store for you," Fay said seriously. "I'm from a money family and know that all the money in the world cannot make you happy if you're with the wrong man."

"No, I don't suppose that it can," April replied. "By the way, you haven't spoken about your family."

"No, I haven't, one day I'll tell you more about my background, it'll surprise you though."

"Nothing surprises me, Fay; it's a funny old world. Look at it, Germany bombing us, us bombing Germany, hundreds of people dying, and for what? Do they really know? Politicians make wars, not the common people, but it's common people who have to pick up a gun and bravely go out to face the enemy. Anyway, enough of this." She threw down her spade. "When you've lived in a pit village like I did, you get used to all kinds of things, but I will say this, the miners are the salt of the earth, working underground for hours at a time. My Dad and twin brother's all work in the pit, you should see the state they come home in, covered in coal dust, black from head to foot with only the whites of their eyes showing."

"Oh, April, that's terrible. I've never known a miner, living in a place like Harrogate, to us, people like that don't exist."

"Well, Fay, when the war's over, I'll take you to my pit village," April promised. "Let you rough it a bit, eh!"

"Yes, it would be nice to see how the other half live," Fay replied. "I'll look forward to it."

April put a hand on Fay's shoulder and gave it an affectionate squeeze.

"I won't forget, honest."

"Can we have a break now, April? I'm parched, I could really do with a drink, and my back's killing me."

"Yes, I think we deserve one, there's a nice big tree over there throwing its branches out, it has a good thick trunk which we can lean against. We're having half an hour, blow only ten minutes!"

"It'll be just our luck for the farmer to catch us," Fay said doubtfully.

"Oh, he'll be too busy with that new bull he's having delivered, the farm has been paying its way, and he's spent nearly all he has on it to enlarge his herd. Also, he can hire it out to other farmers."

The girls sank down onto the grass, which was heavily starred with Daisies; each had a bottle of cold tea from which they drank thirstily.

"Oh, I never thought that cold tea could taste like wine, but it does," Fay said with satisfaction. "A few weeks' ago, I was drinking the best wine that money could buy; now I'm a world away, sitting in a field drinking cold tea from a bottle without a care in the world. Mother would be horrified! I've encountered insuperable difficulties in my time, and this is all new and strange to me, but I'm really beginning to enjoy it. I know I moan a lot, but I thought that I was going to be totally unsuited to the life, but I've gained more confidence in myself I can tell you. It's better than being stuck away in Harrogate doing nothing worthwhile every day with the silver spoon brigade."

"Well," April began, "you'll be pleased to know that Mr Whiteman thinks you're okay. He's pleased with you so far," she suddenly cocked her head to one side, saying. "Listen, someone's coming on horseback."

"It's the Boss coming to check on us," Fay gasped, scrambling to her feet.

"He can check all he likes; we've done a good job on this field," April snapped angrily.

As the horse rider drew near, the girls could see that it was Mr Whiteman, sat astride Rhett, who pranced around tossing his head, full of himself. The girls waited silently for the farmer to speak. Something was afoot, as he never came seeking them out at this time of day.

"You, girls, come with me; there's something I want to show yer," he said abruptly.

The girls picked up their tools and empty bottles, then walked over to the farmer.

"Now?" April asked. "What's so important that we have to down tools?" Then as realisation dawned. "Oh, you want us to see your new bull, don't you?"

"Clever girl," the farmer said sarcastically. "Come along, I'll ride on ahead and meet yer by the new stall in the main barn." He laughed, then said jovially. "It's a good job I built it strong, this is one powerful animal." He slapped the reins across the horse's neck and trotted off, whistling merrily.

"Oh dear, I don't like the sound of that," Fay said anxiously.

"Now, why is he eager for us to see his new acquisition, I wonder?" April said thoughtfully.

"Sounds to me as if he thinks it's a new toy," Fay said nervously.

"No bull is a toy, Fay, I can assure you, and if he thinks we're going anywhere near a ferocious savage bull, he has another thing coming."

"Oh dear, I don't like the sound of that," Fay repeated.

As they approached the farmyard, they could see the farmer stood near the big barn waiting for them, and April had a vague presentiment that something was not quite right when she saw the Mrs stood gaunt and tall in the kitchen doorway. The two girls came to a halt as she called to her husband.

"Be it on your head!"

He ignored her and waved the girls, again, the Mrs called to her husband.

"Yer got yer way but don't expect those slips of lasses to go near that spawn from hell."

The girls looked at each other in horror, the Mrs lapsed into silence, and Mr Whiteman said.

"Come on," as he began to walk to the stable.

Just as the girls took a step forward, a loud, angry bellow filled the air, then again it thundered out, and a furious thumping and banging came from inside the barn. The noise was tremendous; Fay gave a loud scream and clutched April tightly, crying.

"Oh, my good God, what's that?"

"Mr Whiteman's new toy I suspect."

The white-faced Fay continued to hang on to April.

"I refuse to go in there."

The farmer looked around at them, then called.

"Move yer sens then."

April pulled Fay's clinging arms from around her, and tried to pull herself together, then dragged on the unwilling Fay with her into the barn. She was beginning to feel a wave of irrational anger towards the farmer as she called.

"Wait on then, we're coming."

As the girls entered the barn, Belle, a favourite cow of April's who had been off her food, kicked back away nervously.

"That's most unlike Belle," April commented.

As they drew near to the newly built stall, they could hear the bull's heavy hooves thumping and pounding on the concrete floor. By this time, the farmer was stood at the far side of the barn by the stall, which April saw had extra high walls around it; these were of bricks reinforced with concrete to keep in whatever manner of creature was in there.

"Over here, girls," the farmer called with a silly grin on his face.

Fay stood still and said stubbornly.

"I'm staying here, you go, April."

As April made to walk forward, Fay grabbed her arm to pull her back, shouting.

"No, stay here!"

"Let go of me, Fay, I'm not going to let that mad bugger think he's scared the pants off me, because that's just what he wants."

As Fay reluctantly loosened her hold, April walked towards the farmer, who caught her by the shoulder, saying as he did so.

"Quietly now, lass, we don't want to start him off again."

As she looked over the gate, which was securely fastened with a chain link, she could see why. When she saw the creature which stood there, her heart seemed to stop, and the blood to freeze in her veins. She stood rooted to the spot, closed her eyes, then slowly opened them again. No, it was still there, the largest, most powerful looking black bull she was ever likely to see. She was looking at his rear end, and he had the most impressive genitals that any beast would have been proud of. His coat shone like ebony, and as he swung his massive head round to glare at her, she saw the wicked gleam in his pink eyes. He began to toss his head from side to side, saliva dripping from his mouth in drooling strings while he pawed the ground in a fury, then once more rent the air with a roar. April jumped back in shock, her ears ringing, while the farmer smiled with amusement.

"He's magnificent, isn't he?!"

"He's quite a specimen, I grant you," April said acidly, looking the farmer straight in the eye. "And I wish you luck in handling him."

"Aye, we'll have a good crop of calves out of him."

"I reckon you will. If I were one of the unfortunate cows, you wouldn't see *my* rear end for dust."

"Breeding is nature's way, lass; I thought yer knew that by now."

"Of course I know, but I'm telling you, don't take risks with him, he'll kill someone. It's in his mean little eyes, and it's not going to be Fay or me, we're giving him a wide berth."

The farmer stood staring at her, angry at being told what *his* Land Girls were not going to do.

"Yer will do as yer told, Miss! You seem to forget that *I* give the orders around here."

"Within reason," April snapped back.

"Oh, it's like that is it?!" he said sharply.

"Yes, it's like that," April repeated.

"Look here," the farmer said authoritatively. "If you take my advice, yer'll start getting to know him now. There'll be a lot to do, he's going to be busy servicing the cows a lot of the time in the barn, and yer'll both be helping with that."

Fay's head jerked up, and she said in a polite voice.

"I'm sorry, but I don't even want to look at that monster, just hearing the noise he makes is enough for me."

"That goes for me too," April cut in. Then as an afterthought. "Anyway, what do you mean, we'll be helping him service the cows?"

Just then, the bull gave another ear-splitting bellow, shook his head and charged into the wall, thrusting the ring which went through his nose even deeper into the flesh. The chain, which was threaded through the ring grew taut, causing him more pain. As he stepped back, he realised that the chain gave off slack, and he was able to take two steps to the right or left, so, with his wicked-looking horns, began repeatedly head-butting the wall.

"He's crazy, completely crazy," April gasped.
Giving a loud cackle of laughter, the farmer said.
"I'll cure him."
"What do you mean? How can you cure a creature like that? He's a mean machine!" April paused, then said. "You're as crazy as he is, you should be in a stall next to him."
"Yer won't believe me, but there are ways and means of controlling him."
"I don't want to know, and you haven't answered my question yet," April reminded him. "How can *we* help with the servicing?"
"The Mrs will tell yer if you ask her, I don't want to go into the subject out here, I don't want any theatricals, haven't time."
"I don't think I like the sound of this," Fay said nervously. "I'm going for a cup of tea to calm my nerves."
The farmers face set into a strained smile, April's face had lost all its colour as she retorted.
"You can go to blazes, and your farm and the bull along with you! I don't care what you do, I'm not going to allow you to browbeat me into handling that devil, job, or no job, and I speak for, Fay too!"
There was a long silence; the farmer broke it by saying in a sanctimonious voice.
"I should've known better than to hire girls to do a man's job. When it comes to the tough stuff, yer haven't got the gall for it have yer?!"
April could feel her temper beginning to rise as she shot back.
"Don't you dare use that sanctimonious tone with me, you old sod! We've worked hard here, and you couldn't have managed without us. One Land Girl is worth two men any day! Anyway, do what you want, I mean what I say, Fay and I are *not* going near that mad creature."
"We'll see about that!" the farmer shouted, bringing his fist down hard on top of the gate. "You'll both do as yer told!"
"Are you thick, or just plain stupid?! Look at Fay, she's near to passing out, and she hasn't even looked at the creature yet. Once is enough for me, so, I'm going to kick up an almighty fuss, I'm going to send for the District Rep."
"Is that so?!" the farmer shouted at the top of his voice.
"Yes, that's so," April shouted back. Then she turned to Fay, who had stood silent throughout the heated argument. "Get the buckets; we've some stone clearing to do." She turned and walked away, Fay following her.
As they walked out of the yard, Fay asked apprehensively.
"Can he make us handle that bull?"
"Yes, he can if he's a mind to, but we're not going to let him know that. Anyway, the War Agg will have a fit when she sees that spawn from hell. She'll have us away from here fast, I can tell you."

"Oh, April, I'm scared."

"Don't be, it's not going to happen."

"But what if it does?"

"Straight after knocking off time I'm going to find the nearest phone and send for the Agg."

"But the nearest phone could be in Skipton."

"I don't care if it's in Timbuktu, I'm going, and I hope that you'll come with me."

"Of course I will, we're in this together."

"God, I hope we find a phone tonight." April suddenly stopped, then said excitedly. "I remember now, there are two bikes tucked away at the back of the small barn where all the hen feed is kept, they belong to the Mrs's two sons, we can borrow those tonight to look for a phone."

"Do you think we should? What if they're missed?" Fay asked nervously.

"They won't be missed. I've only ever known *us* to go in there; it's us that feed the hens," April explained calmly.

"Okay, we'll do it," Fay said bravely. "But did you see how dumbfounded Mr Whiteman was when you said you were sending for the War Rep? What exactly is her job?"

"As far as I know, each county with Land Girls has its own Organizing Secretary Committee and Local Representative, she is called a Rep for short. She has many jobs to do, including discipline, comfort, and help each girl in her numerous troubles and make sure they are happy in their job. In short, the Rep acts on behalf of the County office. You have to remember that the Land Army is not subject to military discipline."

"That's interesting," Fay exclaimed. "I'd like to know later on, but I say, April, what do think the Mrs will say about all this?"

"I think she'll be on our side. I know that she's outspoken, but she's honest, and I think that she'll speak out for *us*."

"Yes, but what will she say if we send for the War Rep?"

"Oh, she knows that the Rep is there to deal with a grievance or dispute we have with any unreasonable farmer, and we've got one here. The Rep is the eyes and ears of the County Office, in other words, she is the Liaison Officer, and if she doesn't do her job properly, the County Secretary has to send the County Organizer to deal with things, but I don't think that our grievance will go that far. The Mrs is a bit of a tarter, but she won't want us going near that mad brute of a bull, she's going to come down on Mr Whiteman like a ton of bricks, believe me, especially when she hears that I'm going to send for the Rep."

"Oh, April, I'm so glad you're here to stand up for us," Fay said in a heartfelt way. "I don't have the nerve you have."

"At a time like this," April replied gruffly. "I could wish myself miles away, even back in my pit village." Then looking up, she held her hand out, saying. "I don't believe it, it's starting to rain, that's all we need."

The rain began to pour down from an overcast grey sky, sending a fresh smell from the earth as the girls started to run towards the farmhouse. Once inside, they stood with their backs to the glowing fire, their dungaree's steaming slightly in the heat. The Mrs stood at the table making beetroot sandwiches for lunch, their usual fair, April thought ruefully.

Suddenly, the Mrs barked out.

"Well, you two, what's going on in that barn?"

April looked sombre; Fay nervous.

"Well, come on, spit it out," the Mrs asked again. "I'm not going to bite yer."

"I'd rather you heard it from Mr Whiteman," April answered.

"Oh, you would, would yer?" the Mrs replied abruptly. "Well, happen I know already, it's that mad bull he's bought, and it *is* mad, and he's expecting yer to help him with it, yer have refused, he's lost his temper, which doesn't take much doing, along with a few 'blasts' and 'damns'. Well let me tell yer both, that I don't intend to be a widow yet, and I will be if he doesn't get expert help to handle that creature. If I have *my* way, it'll go right back to where it came from. I'll handle the Mr, you two get off to yer work, it's stopped raining."

As April listened, it suddenly struck her that the Mrs did not have much of a life. It *was* rather an empty one, nothing but hard work, cleaning, cooking and helping on the land. She never went out of an evening, and with only her husband for company, life must be very dull for her. She must have had good looks in her youth, what on earth had she seen in Mr Whiteman, who was as plain as a pikestaff?!

The Mrs handed the girls a packet of wrapped sandwiches each, along with a rare smile.

"Off yer go," she said.

"So sorry about the trouble, but I'm glad you're on our side."

"Don't worry," the Mrs nodded her head. "It'll be alright," she said positively.

As the girls walked across the yard, a watery sun was trying to shine through, lighting the clouds which still scurried across the sky. A Speckled Breasted Thrush, perched on the old water barrel, began to warble his song. The rain had brought out the sweet, heavy scent of the Chrysanthemums which grew at the back of the house, while in the distance, the bellowing of the cattle floated up from the fields.

Turning to April, Fay queried gingerly.

"The Mrs is very annoyed, isn't she? If I were Mr Whiteman, I'd be cautious about what I said to her, wouldn't you?"

"Oh, he certainly won't have an easy time of it," April laughed. "But if I know him, he's going to retaliate."

"Then thank goodness we'll not be there to hear it," Fay returned. "Are you still going to call the Rep tonight?" she asked.

"No, I'll hang on; see what the Mrs can do about things," April said, then started to sing, 'Don't Sit Under the Apple Tree.'

"What's brought the singing on?" Fay asked.

"Oh, I just felt like it, if the birds can warble, so can I," April laughed. "Anyway, let's nip into the orchid and eat our lunch, such as it is. Maybe the wooden seat won't be too wet, it is under the tree's so should be fairly dry."

"I don't know about you, but after the war, I'm never going to look at beetroot again!" Fay said determinedly. "I always thought that it came out of jars, which it does, but you don't think that it has to be planted, grown and picked do you?"

As they came to the orchid gate, April released the sneck and swung the gate wide to allow them to walk through, then closed it carefully behind them. The old wooden bench stood underneath a large Apple Tree with wide-spreading branches which bore ripening fruit. It had protected the bench from most of the rain, and the girls sank gracefully down with a heartfelt sigh.

"I'd like to be a fly on the wall when Mr Whiteman goes in for *his* lunch, wouldn't you?" Fay asked.

"Yes, I think I would. She should've been consulted, she's worked the fields like a horse as hard as anyone, but that old sod of a farmer will try to bluster his way out of things... Anyway," April went on. "Let's change the subject, I've been thinking of having a change, moving from here, maybe up into the dales and working with sheep. I've been reading about what it entails, and it's interesting, I thought that once lambs were born, that was the end of it, but not so. Did you know that on hot days in summer, flies attack the sheep, lay eggs in the wool, which turn into maggots. If you don't treat them quickly, the sheep could die. There's foot rot, dipping and shearing, and lambing must be a joy. Then again, I wouldn't mind going down to Kent for the fruit picking, you know what they say, 'Golden September' and 'Brown' and 'Blue October.' Imagine, walking through orchards heavy with fruit, Laxton's, Cox's, Granny Smith's and Bramley's. Think of the lovely smell, and they'll be pears, plums and cherries; and the grading and packing. And if we want something really different, there's pest extermination, rabbit gassing and rat killing, oh, and mole trapping. I've been reading about rats, Fay; do you know that there are more rats in Britain than they are people? We eat to live, so do rats, and they like to eat the same things we do, they love Corn, a severe matter in wartime, *and* they are good at being able to camouflage themselves. A rat can hide in its own shadow, so you see, it's them or us. Another thing I fancy, is living in a hostel along with other girls, you get sent out to different farms every day, it sounds interesting, don't you think?"

As April paused for breath, Fay laughed, then said jokingly.

"If I could get a word in edgeways, yes, it *all* sounds interesting, where you go, April, I go, I'm not staying here on my own."

"Yes, I have rambled on a bit haven't I. Lunchtime's over and I haven't had a bite of my sandwiches, but never mind, the pigs are welcome to them." Standing, she straightened the bib on her dungarees, picked up the packet of uneaten food, then said. "Well, come on, girl, must get cracking, we've eggs to collect, grade and pack, or the Boss will be on our backs."

As the girls crossed the yard, the Mrs came to the door, a look of triumph on her face, she waved the girls over.

"Now, you two, I've had words with the Mr, to put it plainly, I've told him that the bull goes, or I do, until it does. It has to be chained up; I don't want you girls to go anywhere near it, do you understand? No matter what the Mr say's, yer don't go near it. If he insists, fetch me."

"Thanks for letting us know Mrs, that's a load off my mind," April said thankfully.

As the girls hurried away, Fay laughed.

"I bet she gave him a tough time, eh, April."

"I'll bet she did, oh to have been a fly on the wall," April said serenely. Then laughing, she caught Fay by the hand and cried. "Come on, race you to the field, *and* you have to jump the gate, not climb it."

The Mrs watched them, a smile on her face as she thought, what it is to be young, it will be a good job when the war's over and those girls, and others like them, can go home and get on with their life's, but until then, the land has to be farmed, the nation fed, and it was best foot forward.

* * *

April and Fay were giggling loudly as they set off down the lane, wobbling uncertainly on bikes that had seen better days. Only one of them had a lamp to light the way to the village, but both girls were in a cheerful mood, as they were on their way to the local pub for a glass of beer, and a singsong round the piano. Then they would go over the road to the church hall for a bit of dancing. They had missed the last dance, to which half a dozen G.I's had quickly visited, and by all accounts, a good time was had by all. They had handed out chocolate and nylons to the local girls, the village had been amazed.

'Trust us to have missed out,' April had commented when the barmaid, who had gotten off work early, and so had been one of the lucky ones, told her. 'Those Yanks can't half jitterbug!' she had said excitedly. 'One of them tried to teach me how to do it, but my feet got all in a muddle; still, it was fun, and he was nice, roll on the next dance.'

The girls wore their brown breeches and aertex shirts, on their heads set at a jaunty angle, was their Land Army hats. Their uniform always drew the eyes of the lads, which made the local girls jealous and resentful. 'We certainly put their noses out of joint, they look down at us. I'd like to see them work the land like we do, they would soon be crying for their Mummies,' April had told Fay. 'Oh, I can see why they don't like us, April, we're better looking with good figures.'

When the girls reached the pub, they hid their bikes in the long grass around the back, then walked to the front door.

"Come on," April said pertly, pushing her hat to the back of her head. "I like to make a grand entrance." As she pushed the door open, a wall of noise met them. "Blimey, it's packed in here, just follow me, Fay, I'm going to fight my way to the bar."

Someone was belting out, 'Beat Me Daddy, Eight to the Bar' on the piano, accompanied by many out of tune voices.

"Will you listen to that?" April shouted to Fay. "This is what I love to see and hear, people, enjoying themselves."

Fay nodded doubtfully.

"They can all forget about the war for a few hours, just like we're going to do. Come on, nearly at the bar, what are you having, Fay? I'm going to have a glass of cider to put me in the mood."

"I'll have the same," Fay answered as she grabbed hold of April's hand. "Don't lose me in here, April, I don't know anyone."

"Stay right here, don't move, I'll go to the bar and get the drinks."

"Okay," Fay nodded nervously as she glanced around the crowded room and saw two local girls staring at her. She looked away, embarrassed to be caught looking back at them. Her eyes searched for April and found her stood at the bar talking to a tall youth with protruding teeth.

April began to make her way towards Fay, saying as she did so.

"Excuse me, gangway, can I pass please?"

Suddenly, a tall, good-looking G.I said.

"Sure, honey, you can pass me anytime as long as you smile that beautiful smile of yours."

"I'm particular who I smile at. Would you please let me pass, my friend doesn't like being left on her own for too long."

"At once, honey, but say, aren't you one of those Land Girls we've heard so much about? You do a damn fine job, if I may say so."

"Thanks," April said as she turned away. "It's nice to be appreciated."

As she handed Fay her drink, she took it with a sigh of relief, then said sharply.

"April, the next time you go to the bar I'm going with you, I felt awful standing here on my own. People were staring at me. Who was that good-looking man you were talking to? He's a G.I, isn't he?"

"Oh," April said casually. "He made a pass at me, I soon put him in his place, but he did say the Land Girls do a good job, which was nice of him, I suppose."

"Yes, it was," Fay replied.

"The Yanks will tell you anything, Fay to get you into the sack, remember that won't you."

"I'll remember, but they all can't be as bad as they're painted, can they? I believe in giving anyone a chance."

"Do you?" April said, a mischievous look in her eyes. "You'd better be telling the truth then, because the tall, handsome one is coming towards us, with his mate right behind him, and the handsome one has got his eye on you if I'm not mistaken."

"Oh, my goodness," Fay said, almost choking on her drink. "Let's go, it'll look as if we're being picked up."

"Don't panic, it's our uniforms they go for, not what's inside them, at least I hope so," April said matter of factly. "Give me your glass, I'll put them on the nearest table as we go out, come on, look sharp or they'll be here."

As the girls hurried through the door, April glanced back to see the two G.I's shrug their shoulders and turn back towards the bar, but as they crossed the road to the church hall, April said.

"I'd laugh if those two came to the dance."

"Oh, they're probably lovable rogues," Fay replied. "Anyway, I don't think they'll be interested in us, after all, we almost ran out of the pub to avoid them."

"No, I suppose they won't, they'll go for the local girls and expect them to lower their knickers. After all, the local girls took their chocolate and nylons, didn't they?"

"You can't say that, April, it's not right, the village girls may be nice people."

"Are they? You'll see, my friend," April laughed. "Anyway, come on, I love to be on the dance floor, it's the greatest pleasure life can offer me. And anyway, I hope that some Yanks *do* come to the dance, I'd love to have a go at this jitterbug thing."

"April, you wouldn't," Fay cried.

"Just watch me," April laughed. "And by the way, don't be offended if they call you 'honey', it just seems to be their way."

"I hope they don't ask me to dance, I'm not a good dancer, as I told you before, April."

"If you get asked to dance, don't panic, just do your best."

"I don't fancy being dragged round a dance floor while trying to do my best."

"If you don't, you'll be sat like a wallflower all night, and that would be embarrassing now, wouldn't it?"

Fay looked crestfallen as she said.

"I think I want to go back to the farm."

"You'll do no such thing, I never had you down for a coward, we've come to enjoy ourselves, and that's what we're going to do, now come on, and I don't want to hear another word about going back to the farm."

The large church hall was almost full as people came from surrounding villages to enjoy a night's dancing, even though it was only to records: Glen Miller, Harry James, Benny Goodman, Artie Shaw among others, the American swing bands being trendy. As the girls joined the packed hall, Harry James was playing 'You Made Me Love You.' April joined her hands together, her eyes shining as she said.

"Would you listen to that sweet sound?"

"Yes, I'm listening," said a male voice in her ear. "May I have the pleasure of this dance Ma'am?"

Without waiting for a reply, April was swung onto the dance floor, clasped in the arms of a G.I of medium height, with laughing brown eyes and black curly hair. As they moved slowly to the music, April smiled and said.

"You're a bold one, aren't you; do you usually grab hold of girl's and drag them onto the dance floor?"

"No, honey I don't, but I saw you in the pub and fell for you on sight. The name's Tony by the way, what's yours? I have to know because I intend getting to know you like a second skin."

"Hmm, you have to be one of those randy G.I's I've heard so much about," April said sarcastically. "My Mam warned me about men like you."

"Okay, sugar, forget my rude remarks and tell me your name," Tony said.

"For two pins I wouldn't tell you for your cheek, but it's April."

As the music came to a stop, Tony whistled loudly and said softly.

"I should've known that a beautiful girl like you would have a pretty name. You remind me of a sun-kissed April morning back home."

"Do I now?" April said as she walked across the floor, Tony following her. "And where would home be?" she asked inquiringly.

"Kentucky, bluegrass country, my Dad breeds horses. Kentucky is beautiful like England, but the people here can be a little funny sometimes."

"Can they?" April said with a toss of her head. "Well, don't think I'm being funny when I say thanks for the dance, nice talking to you, I have to get back to my friend."

"April sweetheart, the night's still young, and I want to have every dance with you."

"Sorry, no can do," April laughed as she walked towards Fay, a smile of amusement on her face, while Tony called after her.

"You've just proved me right about English people."

He walked back to his friends, a sad expression on his face as he thought, oh well, you can't win them all. But if he saw 'April morning', as he thought of her in his mind, again, he would try a different approach. She seemed like a nice girl, these Land Girls certainly had something, and the way she wore that hat, oh boy, what a girl!

April stood near the bar looking around for Fay, then spotted her dancing with a good-looking G.I with a crew cut. Hmm, she thought to herself, he's not bad, good on you Fay, and she was doing the waltz okay, which was easy to do anyway, but that guy was holding her a little too close, and Fay didn't seem to be minding too much. The dance ended, and Fay was walked politely back to stand by April's side.

"Thank you, Fay," the G.I said, walked away, and stood at the end of the bar where he kept glancing at Fay as if to make sure she was still standing there.

"It looks as if you've made a conquest, Fay. Your dancing partner can't keep his eyes off you," April quipped.

"Can't he? I wouldn't know, I'm not going to stand gawping at him am I," Fay said crossly.

"He's very handsome; I'll bet he's broken a few hearts in his time," April said seriously.

"Well, he won't be breaking mine; I'm ready to go if you are," Fay said. "We've to be up in the morning at five-thirty." She glanced at her watch. "It's nearly ten, and it'll take us a good twenty minutes to get back to the farm."

April sighed.

"Yes, you're right, we'd better be off."

As the girls made their way to the door, a male voice called loudly.

"Goodnight, April Morning."

April tutted, then said.

"I'm glad I won't be seeing that Tony again, he could become a nuisance."

"Oh, he's just being friendly I expect, and you're not likely to see him again, are you?" Fay asked.

"No, thank goodness," April agreed. "Now, where did we leave those bikes?"

* * *

The next day the girls didn't get off to a good start, it was a dull morning with low cloud, it was starting to drizzle, the cows waiting to be milked were kicking up a fuss in the milking shed, and the Mrs was yelling up the stairs.

"Where are you, girls? Get down here pronto!"

"I wish she'd shut up; my head feels as if it doesn't belong to me," April moaned.

"Morning after the night before eh," Fay said quietly.

"No, it's not that, I didn't have much sleep, it took me ages to drop off," April said glumly. "And if those bloody cows start playing up this morning I'm going to be tearing a few teats off."

"You know you don't mean that," Fay laughed. "Now come on, although it's the last thing I feel like doing, let's get over to the cowshed."

As the girls entered the shed, thirty-two large heads swizzled round to stare at them mournfully, with large sad eyes.

"You take the right side, I'll take the left, and if that bugger at the end kicks out at me, I'm going to kick her right back," April said moodily.

Fay laughed as she said.

"You wouldn't do that." Then bent to pick up a small milking stool on which to sit. When settled, she clamped her head into the cow's fat side, and began to pull on the udders. The milk, a vibrant creamy colour, spurted merrily into the pail with a loud ping-ping.

"Tell you what," April called, sounding in a better mood. "I'm going to sing rude songs to my lot, they seem to like it."

"Do you know any rude songs?" Fay called back.

"Do I know any rude songs?" April repeated. "You don't come from a pit village and not know any rude songs."

"Well, I hope they aren't too rude, I'm not used to that kind of thing you know. Shall I stuff the cow's tail in my ears?" Fay said jokingly.

"Please yourself," April shouted.

"Anyway," Fay called back. "We won't be doing hand milking for much longer, Mr Whiteman's getting electric milkers soon, so that means we'll be getting breakfast a bit sooner."

Suddenly April gave a loud scream, then cried.

"Oh no, I've knocked the bloody pail over!" Milk flowed merrily across the floor. "The Boss is going to give me a right telling off," April moaned.

"He won't, it was an accident, and what's done is done," Fay comforted. "It's not the first time that's happened, and it certainly won't be the last."

"Well, he can say what he jolly well wants," April answered abruptly. "So come on, Fay, let's get done, I want my breakfast."

* * *

As the girls walked into the kitchen, the smell of frying bacon met them, the Mrs swung round from the cooker, a smile on her face. April was instantly suspicious, the Mrs never smiled in a morning, it took her all her time to be civil. When she saw the surprised look on the girls face's, still smiling, she said loudly.

"Come on, don't stand there looking dumbstruck, sit yerselves down. I thought I'd give yer both a treat, since I've something to tell yer that maybe yer not going to like. Now don't look so apprehensive, Fay, yer not going to be hung."

The girls sat down side by side. As they did so, April thought, I don't think I'm going to like this, she looked at the Mrs expectantly as the Mrs went on.

"Give me a minute while I put yer breakfasts out."

She slapped two rashers of bacon, along with two eggs, onto the plates set out in front of the girls, saying as she did so.

"April, you pour the tea, Fay would yer cut the bread. Don't bother putting any out for the Mr, he'll be having his later, I wanted to see yer both alone."

Something's definitely up, Mr Whiteman not being here for his breakfast, never had she known him not to be. She turned to Fay and pulled a face at her as if to say, 'what's coming'.

"Now eat up," the Mrs said firmly. "Then we'll talk."

"You can tell us while we eat, can't you?" April said as she picked up her knife and fork. "We've a lot to do this morning."

"Yes, I suppose I could," the Mrs answered. "Now, listen carefully. During yer time here yer've been good, hardworking girls."

I don't like the sound of this, April thought. She's praising us, giving us her stamp of approval, first thing in a morning too; she never had before, at *any* time, only if a job had been done very well would she thank them in a begrudging manner.

The Mrs went on.

"We've not always seen eye to eye, and I know that yer found the Mr to be a bit of a rum un, but it would not do for us all to be made in the same mould, would it? Now, what I've to say may come as a bit of a shock with the suddenness of it, but it's like this. My sister, who lives in London, as you know, is having a terrible time of it, what with the bombing and everything, poor London is taking a terrible pounding. Well, to cut a long story short, she's written and asked me to take her two boys for the duration. I could hardly refuse, could I? They are fourteen and fifteen, old enough to work on the farm and earn their keep. The Mr will soon have them trained as he did you."

April broke in here.

"You're telling us we have to go?"

"Well, yes," the Mrs said. "What else can we do?"

"I trust you'll be paying these two boys a wage?" April said grimly.

"That's up to the Mr, and nothing to do with you, April."

"I see," she answered. "Poor lads don't know what they're in for."

Suddenly Fay broke in.

"Well, I for one think it's a dirty trick, but I don't suppose we'll be out of work for long."

"No," said the Mrs brusquely. "I don't suppose that yer will, but we have to help our own, don't we?"

"I don't expect Mr Whiteman will pay those boys as much as he paid the WLA for us, will he?" Fay said.

"I bet the poor little sods get nothing while he's training them," April said knowingly, then stood in silence for a moment before going on. "I hope you and Mr Whiteman don't think that Fay and I are staying on while you train those boys, if so, you can forget it."

"Oh, they are bright lads, they'll soon learn," the Mrs said airily.

"I hope they're as strong as they are bright then because they'll need to be, the work is hard," April said sarcastically.

"That's not your concern," the Mrs said harshly. "Anyway, you won't be here when they arrive, I've been in touch with the War Agg, and as far as I know, yer'll be sent to a hostel somewhere."

"That was kind of you, I must say," Fay sneered, then said gaily. "On second thoughts, it'll be nice to get away from here, be with other girls in a hostel."

April gave a grin, then said happily.

"Yes, Fay it *will* be nice, a change is as good as a rest, so they say." She turned to the Mrs. "So, we'll go and pack and be out of your way."

The Mrs looked amazed, then shouted.

"Yer can't go now; I didn't mean now."

"Oh, didn't you?" Fay asked. "When *did* you mean?"

"I meant next week," the Mrs snapped.

"Next week," April repeated. "For your *own* convenience, eh? No, I don't think so; we're going today for *our* convenience, straight to the war Agg's office. And if she hasn't sorted anything out for us, well, we'll just go home until she does. But she won't want two good Land Girls sat at home, she'll find somewhere for us very quickly I think, and Mrs, I don't like being made a mug of, so I'll thank you for the good breakfast, although had I known what was to follow, it would have choked me." She took Fay's hand, then said. "Now, if you don't mind, we'll go and pack."

"If I were you, I should wait and see what the Mr has to say about this," the Mrs said, red-faced.

"It makes no difference what he says," April said airily. "He can rant until the cows come home; no pun intended. In fact, he'll be glad to see the back of us, he hasn't yet realised that one Land Girl is worth two men, but he will, oh yes, he will." She tugged at Fay's hand. "Come on, love, let's be off."

Once out of the room, Fay said, sounding worried.

"Can we really walk out just like that, April?"

"Who cares, it's what we're going to do, I was getting ready for a change anyway. After that row about that terrible bull, things haven't been the same, have they?"

"No, they haven't, I have to agree," Fay said. "Never will I forget my first sight of that terrible creature. Anyway, it'll be nice to be with other girls, won't it?"

"Yes," April said positively. "I quite fancy that, yes," she repeated. "I definitely fancy that."

"April, I'm really not happy about walking out like this, won't we get into trouble?" Fay said apprehensively.

"We'd be in more trouble if we stayed and had to get close to that bloody bull, most likely be killed, and I, for one, am not ready to pass on yet. Now, Fay, you either come with me or stay and be tossed around by that creature from hell." April shook her head, then went on. "Farmers and farmhands have been gored to death by bulls through the years you know, and Mr Whiteman is dicing with death if he tries to handle that creature. He paid a lot of money for it, and I can only think that the owner was glad to be rid of it. *I've* got nerves of steel, but when I clapped my eyes on that thing my legs turned to jelly, so," April went on determinedly. "We pack and go straight to Skipton, report all this to the War Agg, and if she does her job properly, she'll come out and see the situation for herself. Now, come on, Fay, stop your worrying, get packed, and let's be off, they'll be no lift to Skipton, so it's Shanks Pony."

"What's Shanks Pony?" Fay asked.

"In other words, our own two legs," April answered with a laugh, then said. "My word, you have led a sheltered life if you don't know that one."

"Yes, I have had a sheltered life, but to change the subject, where will we sleep tonight? And will we get another posting at such short notice?"

April sighed in exasperation, then said shortly.

"Don't start your worrying again, Fay, the War Agg will see to all that."

"I hope so, I don't fancy sleeping under a hedge, in spite of the lovely weather, and I hate spiders." She glanced around the tiny room. "I won't miss this 'cubby hole', but I *shall* miss some of the animals. I haven't been here as long as you, but you grow fond of them, don't you?"

"It's hard lines you having such bad luck in your first job, let's hope we have a change of district for our next billeting," April said hopefully.

"Wouldn't it be lovely to go down South, stay in a small village and go out to different farms every day. We can hope can't we," Fay said.

April slammed her case shut, locked it, then glanced around the room as she stood by the door, then carrying on the conversation, she said with a smile.

"It would be a nice change to be in a hostel with other girls, not too many mind you, just about a dozen, somewhere around Oxfordshire or Kent. Some of them have one or two large residences where Lord or Sir so and so lives. They grow their own vegetables and fruit, but a lot of it is commandeered for the forces. I heard *they* use the Land Girls."

"I remember Mother saying that there's a good hostel for Land Army Girls at Kingwood Common in Oxfordshire," Fay said.

"We've to go where we're sent, no picking and choosing I'm afraid."

"Well, one good thing came out of this job, I met you, and we must stick together, where one goes, so does the other,"

"Yes, Fay, I agree with that, now, are you ready for off? If we bump into the Mrs or Mr Whiteman, I'll try not to enter into any argument or trade insults with them."

"I'm ready, lead on, I'm right behind you," Fay replied, nervously.

The girls picked up their suitcases and walked out of the room, leaving the door open and swinging behind them where it banged into the wall, causing bits of plaster to fall onto the floor. Unfortunately, they had to walk through the kitchen and where the farmer and his wife were stood muttering angrily together.

On seeing the two girls, the Mrs turned towards them, folded her arms across her chest, and said through gritted teeth.

"Ah, there yer are. I hope yer both know that yer'll not get paid for today, and I hope you know that yer supposed to give a week's notice."

On hearing these words, April forgot her vow not to enter into an argument. Putting down her case, she said quietly.

"You can keep your days pay; we value our lives more than that. And in any case, the Agricultural Wages Board pay our wages, but I expect you don't know that, and I'll be sending the local representative to see for herself what the Land Girls are expected to deal with. When she does, I doubt you'll get any more help from the Land Army."

Purple-faced, the Mrs shouted furiously.

"Go on, get out of it yer, cheeky bugger!"

April calmly picked up her case, then said.

"I wish I could say that it's been nice knowing you, but it hasn't, so I'll just say goodbye." Then turning to Fay, she said. "Say goodbye nicely to Abbott and Costello, Fay."

At this, the Mrs stepped forward angrily, shouting.

"I'll bloody fetch yer one yer, cheeky monkey!"

Pale-faced, Fay grabbed hold of April's arm and dragged her out of the kitchen, saying as she did so.

"She would've slapped you, April."

April laughed.

"Oh, she wouldn't have dared, the Ministry of Labour would've had her guts for garters."

Fay groaned.

"April, what am I going to do with you."

"You'll never change me, kiddo, so don't try. I've never allowed anyone to walk over me. I had to be tough having twin brothers, but now I'm grown up I thank them for teaching me to rely on myself."

"I wish I had brothers and sisters; Mother couldn't have any more after she had me, she was what you call, 'sickly'," Fay said sadly.

"Oh, forget about that and let's enjoy the walk into Skipton, it's a beautiful day," April shouted.

The countryside around Skipton was stunning, with the air smelling pure and sweet. Across the landscape the hills stood out sharply, clear and green in the shimmering hot sun. skylarks swooped and sang in the bright blue sky, while along the hedgerows Dandelions and Dog Daisies nodded their pretty heads in the slight breeze.

"I wish we could've had more time to go for walks while we were here, April. It's charming. I thought where I lived was lovely, but this beats it hands down."

"Think of poor me living in a pit village. I thought I'd died and gone to heaven when I first saw the countryside round here; let's hope we're sent somewhere just as nice in our next billeting."

* * *

Late afternoon found the girls sat facing the local representative in a small, hot, dusty office. Her name she informed them, was Mrs Mayfield. With her penetrating bright blue eyes and grey hair piled high on top of her head, April thought with delight, she reminds me of Ethel Barrymore, the famous film star. Ethel was a lady; let's hope Mrs Mayfield is as well, if she was, they would get on famously.

"Now, girls," Mrs Mayfield asked in a posh, deep, vibrant voice. "What can I do for you?"

She sounds just like Ethel; April said to herself, I wonder if she's here in aid of the war effort? No, she'll be too busy in Hollywood making all those good films she stars in.

"Now, girls, I am waiting," Mrs Mayfield said softly. "Don't be afraid, I am here to help you."

April took a deep breath, turned to Fay, and asked.

"Shall I tell her?"

On Fay's nod of her head, April began, not stopping to draw breath until she had finished, with Mrs Mayfield adding in. 'I see,' and 'Oh, yes.' As April came to a halt, Mrs Mayfield's eyes began to twinkle, and she asked.

"You were going to be expected to help this bull mate with the cows I understand? I take it that you do know what that entails?"

"Of course we do, but if you'd seen that great big bellowing creature with his enormous tackle you would've done what we did, walk out. That stupid farmer thought he could make us go near that monster, well, he soon found out that he couldn't." April folded her arms, sat back, and asked Fay. "Isn't that right, Fay?"

The white-faced Fay nodded her head and whispered.

"Yes."

April continued.

"We were made very aware by one of the farmhands, who took great pains may I say, in telling us that sometimes the bull missed, and you'd get his load all over you. Poor Fay here hadn't the least idea what he meant. When I explained it to her, she nearly fainted." On this, April rolled her eyes at Mrs Mayfield, who was trying her best not to laugh, while thinking, oh, but I like this girl, she has guts, and will go a long way in life.

April went on.

"I slapped that stupid farmhand and knocked him into the middle of next week, of course, that was another black mark against me."

Mrs Mayfield changed the subject.

"It sounds to me as if this farmer is too big for his boots. I shall certainly be paying him a visit, without any warning too, and you *will* be paid for everything you are owed, girls, I shall see to that."

"The Mrs is a tarter, Mrs Mayfield," Fay said.

"So can I be, dear. I don't think that he will be having any more help from the WLA."

"At first, we got on okay, he was all sunshine and light. Then things started to go downhill when he sold one of his fields and got a lot of money for it, which he wasn't used to having, then bought that son of Satan," April finished.

"I see." Mrs Mayfield nodded her head.

"Farmers pay good money to have their cows serviced by a good pedigree bull, but on seeing that creature, I felt sorry for the poor cows. Can you imagine the poor things having to stand there and be…"

"Alright, April, no need to go on," Mrs Mayfield interrupted. "I get the picture."

Oh my, she thought, wait until she told her husband Jim about this tonight over dinner, he would die laughing. How she had not been in wild hysterics, she did not know. She put her hand over her mouth and tried to hold in her bubbling laughter. Pulling herself together, she asked.

"Should I see this famous bull for myself?"

"Yes, you should, then you'll know we're not lying," April replied.

"I should be very careful dealing with Mr Whiteman," Fay cut in. "He can be rather nasty, so can the Mrs."

Mrs Mayfield broke out into laughter, and her blue eyes twinkled mischievously as she said.

"My dear, Fay, there is not a man born that I cannot handle. I was brought up with four brothers and had three boys of my own, plus, a sometimes-cantankerous husband, so you see, Fay; I am fully qualified to deal with these people."

"Mrs Mayfield, where will you be sending us next?" Fay asked with a worried look.

"There is a nice little hostel down in Kent that has room for two more girls," Mrs Mayfield replied. "I think that you will like it down there, they are a nice bunch of girls in the hostel, and you will be sent out to different farms every day doing general jobs, which is a change from what you have been doing. Did you know that Kent is known as 'The Garden of England'?"

"Yes, I did," Fay answered.

"No, I didn't, you learn something every day don't you," April said.

"Now," Mrs Mayfield went on. "The hostel is called 'Whitmore'. I won't go into its history at this stage, but it is set in its own grounds and is quite a beautiful house."

"Have you seen it then?" April inquired.

"Oh yes, I happen to know the owners," Mrs Mayfield said. "I spent many happy hours there as a child, but meanwhile it's much too late to send you down there today, so, I shall take you round to Aunt Polly's who runs a B&B for females. She will put you up for the night and send you off in the morning with a good breakfast inside you. You will love Aunt Polly, everyone does, she waffles on a bit, but that's just her way."

"A good breakfast, what's one of those?" April asked mischievously.

"I shall be round first thing in the morning," Mrs Mayfield went on. "With your train tickets and instructions on how to get to 'Hazeldene', the housekeeper will be expecting you, whose name, by the way, is Mrs Twigg. She is adorable and has the hostel running like clockwork. She does have a set of rules, which she expects her girls to stick to. Remember, the WLA is not subject to military discipline as we are not a fighting force, but we, in charge, *do* like to keep an eye on our Land Girls. Now, do you both agree to all this?"

"Oh, yes," both girls said together.

"Girls, I want you to remember that you are an individual, not just a Land Girl, although at Headquarters you are just a number, one of many thousands. Wear your uniform with pride, but always remember that you must go without protest anywhere you are sent. Some girls prefer to be near certain towns and cities near home, but it does not work like that. If a girl is miserable, she can always write the

County Office a letter of complaint about a farmer or owner of a certain land who is not treating her right. Being sent without protest can mean doing general farm work including ploughing, milking, threshing, hedging, thatching, picking fruit in orchards, gardening, rating and a million other jobs."

"Rating?" April interrupted. "Now, that sounds interesting."

Fay shuddered and said.

"Don't even go there."

"You heard what Mrs Mayfield just said, if we had to do that, we would," April said abruptly. "Anyway, it's going to be nice to be with other girls, have a bit of fun and a laugh."

"Right you are then, let's be off, get you round to Aunt Polly's," Mrs Mayfield chirped. "You will be just in time for tea; Aunt Polly makes scones to die for, smothered in her own rhubarb and date jam, and chocolate cake which just melts in the mouth."

4

The day had become hot and sultry as the girls and Mrs Mayfield entered the ivy-covered, apple-pie cottage, to be greeted by a tiny old lady with bright blue eyes and rosy-red cheeks.

My, I bet those eyes miss nothing, was April's first thought as she saw the old lady.

"Hello, Aunt Polly, could you put these two up for one night? They move on tomorrow to a fresh posting," Mrs Mayfield asked. "As you can see, they are Land Army Girls. She pushed the girls forward. "The small one is April, the tall one Fay."

"I'll be happy to put them up," Aunt Polly said. "Land Army eh, and don't you look smart in your uniforms, send a lot of lads hearts aflutter I'll bet. I really admire the Land Army Girls; they're a plucky bunch, equal to men, if not better. Now, girls, you're just in time for tea, go through to the kitchen, which is straight in front of you, wash your hands then come and sit down."

The girls duly did as they were told, and after wiping their hands on a snowy white towel, April said softly.

"I'm going to like it here."

"Yes, I am too, isn't she a lovely old lady, really makes you welcome," Fay said. She leant over the sink to look through the window at the garden, which had a lush emerald-green lawn surrounded by a sturdy fence, covered with intertwined Honeysuckle and Passionflower, which made a pleasing picture. "This garden reminds me of home, but ours is much larger and sweeps down to a river," Fay said softly.

"Does it now? Sounds very posh," April replied as she folded the towel and laid it on the draining board. "Come on, stop stargazing, let's go and sample Aunt Polly's mouth-watering tea."

"Yes, we'd better; Mrs Mayfield will want to go," Fay agreed.

Aunt Polly bustled into the kitchen.

"If you've finished girls, I'll pop the kettle on and set things out, you go through and make yourselves comfortable. Oh, I'm so pleased to have some company, we'll have a bit of a chat after tea, and won't that be nice."

"Yes, indeed," Fay answered. "We'll look forward to it." She pushed April in front of her and out of the kitchen as Aunt Polly called after them.

"I'll tell you all about my Bert, he'll be so sorry to have missed you."

Mrs Mayfield was stood by the open door.

"Now, I must leave, girls, I am going to the station to collect your tickets, then I am going home, so I shall see you in the morning at about eight-thirty. I am sure there is a train to London around ten. Aunt Polly will look after you; she will talk your heads off but will entertain you with her chatter. You will hear all about her Bert, that's her husband. Now, I simply must go, goodbye, see you both in the morning." With a final wave of her hand, she was gone.

As the two girls sat down, they looked around the room with interest. It was small and cosy, containing two small settees covered in a gaily patterned flower material. A highly polished round table with two chairs tucked underneath. A china cabinet full of delicate china and a large bookcase filled with books. A very intricate wooden fireplace, highly polished, took up most of one wall, its shelf covered with photo frames and figurines. On its hearth, was a large glass vase filled with fresh Lilies, Lupines and Goldenrod, an unusual combination, but it worked, Fay thought.

Aunt Polly hurried back into the room, humming cheerfully, and pulled out a small coffee table which had been out of sight behind one of the settees. She set it down in front of the girls, hurried out of the room, and came back with a beautiful, embroidered tablecloth which she spread over the table.

"What a lovely piece of embroidery, so elaborate, and what lovely colour silks," Fay exclaimed.

"Yes," Aunt Polly said proudly. "I did that in my younger days, but sadly my eyes are not as good as they were. I used to enjoy it, buying the silks, looking for nice patterns, but all good things come to an end, so instead, I tend my garden."

"It's a credit to you, Aunt Polly; one can see that it's looked after. I used to spend a lot of time working in ours at home."

April turned and looked at Fay keenly as she thought, that's twice she's mentioned home in the last half hour, things are looking up.

Fay looked at her defiantly, then turned to ask Aunt Polly.

"Can I help?"

"No, thank you, dear, everything's ready, I only have to set it out then all you need to do is eat and enjoy."

She hurried out once more and came back to set a large tray filled with neatly cut teacake sandwiches, scones, chocolate cake, vanilla slices, a pot of butter and a dish of jam. She picked up and handed them each a knife.

"Now come on, get tucked in," Aunt Polly said. "I expect you to do full justice to my tea, growing girls like you need a satisfying meal, don't be shy, help yourselves. I'll away and bring in the teapot, you don't want to be claggy do you."

As she once more hurried away, Fay whispered.

"What does she mean, claggy?"

"It's an old Yorkshire word, it means thirsty," April whispered back.

Fay frowned.

"I come from Yorkshire, but I've not heard that word before," she said.

"It's more South Yorkshire," April replied. Then impatiently. "Now, if you don't mind, I'm going to get stuck in, like Aunt Polly said."

The two girls helped themselves to sandwiches.

"Oh," April exclaimed after her first bite. "Cheese and cucumber, lovely."

"Mines egg and cress," Fay cried.

April picked up another.

"My goodness, boiled ham and onion."

"I've got potted meat and tomato now," Fay said in delight. "How does Aunt Polly do it?"

"I don't know, and I don't care, I think I've died and gone to heaven! Pinch me so I can make sure I'm still here," April laughed in delight.

Aunt Polly came back into the room, carrying a large brown teapot, and on hearing the tail end of the conversation, asked.

"How do I do what, my dear's?"

"Have all this wonderful food?" April asked.

"Oh, it falls off the backs of the several lorries that pass through here, and you can't look a gift horse in the mouth can you, or is it in the eye?" Her eyes twinkled. "I accept what I find as gifts from the fairies. I've always believed in the little people, that comes from the Irish blood in me. Yes, the little ones are good to me. So, there you have it."

April had a mouthful of food and tried to stop herself breaking out into hysterical laughter.

"Aunt Polly," she managed to get out. "You're priceless, a woman after my own heart."

Fay was sat with a bewildered look on her face.

"I don't understand, off the back of a lorry. What does that mean?" She asked.

April looked at her dubiously, then said.

"I think that you've been living in the dark ages, Fay, I shall have to take you in hand."

"Oh dear, I've said something I shouldn't, haven't I," Aunt Polly cried, looking worried.

"No, you have not," April said reassuringly. "Our Fay here was brought up wrapped in cotton wool, but I'm going to teach her the ways of the world."

"Are you?" Fay asked abruptly as she helped herself to another sandwich. "Should be interesting."

April laughed.

"If you're going to string along with me, kiddo, you're going to learn a lot."

"Listen to her, Aunt Polly, you wouldn't think that I'm the oldest, would you? Thinks she's the Boss," Fay said.

"I am, kiddo, get used to it," April replied.

"Okay, I'll let you think so for now. Aunt Polly," she went on. "These scones are the best scones I've ever tasted, and the jam too."

"So glad you like it, dear. How about the chocolate cake, April? Enjoy it, did you?" Aunt Polly asked.

"I have no words; it was utterly delicious. I think I shall pack you in my suitcase and take you with us."

"I'm perfectly happy in my little abode, dear, lived here all my married life; I couldn't bear to live anywhere else."

"What time does your husband get home? I'd like to meet him," Fay asked.

"He doesn't come home tonight," Aunt Polly said sadly. "His job entails four nights on and three off, he's a lighthouse keeper on the coast, and of course, I'm not allowed to say more, the war you know."

"Of course, we understand, don't we, Fay," April said.

"That's why I take people in for B&B, gives me a bit of company at night, and lots to do."

"I expect people come back time after time, if only for your delicious baking."

"Yes, I expect they do."

"I'll bet you remember their names too."

"You know, I think that I do."

"Mrs Mayfield told us that you only take girls."

"Yes, I do, I feel more comfortable with girls when Bert's not here."

"When he's home, do you still take in B&B's?"

"Not often, we like our time together."

"He must look forward to coming home after being stuck in a lighthouse for four days."

"Bert loves his job, loves the sea, it's in his blood, all his family were fisherman, so he wouldn't want to do anything else."

"Have you ever wanted to live where he works either of you?"

"Oh no, my dear, both of us love it here, and you see, Bert has the best of both worlds."

"He's a lucky man."

"Yes, and I'm a lucky woman."

"Do you go out and about when Bert's home?"

"I should think we do."

"You have some lovely countryside around here; do you go off for days?"

"Oh, yes, dear."

"Do you have a car?"

Aunt Polly laughed.

"Bless you no, we have a motorbike and sidecar which we both love, we roar around the countryside as if we own it."

"It's been wonderfully kind of you to make us so welcome and give us such a scrumptious tea, and I loved your date and rhubarb jam. Mother would kill for that recipe," Fay said with a smile.

"Sorry, my dear, I promised my Granny to never tell a sole," Aunt Polly said regretfully.

"I understand. Now, can we help you clear away?" Fay said, rising to her feet.

"Yes, dear, we'll just put everything into the kitchen, and I'll wash up later. I want to hear everything about you, and I shall tell you about my Bert."

When everything was cleared away and the little sitting-room tidy again, the girls and their host sat down to chat.

"Now," Aunt Polly asked. "Who's going to be spokeswoman?"

"Me, I think," April answered. "As I've been doing this job longer than Fay."

"Why have you left your last job? Were you not treated right by the farmer?" Aunt Polly asked.

"He was alright in the beginning, so was his wife, although she was a right tarter, but I stood up to them both."

"I'll bet you did too," Aunt Polly said, smiling.

"I love the work, and did all that was asked of me, and more, so did Fay. There's nothing like being up at the crack of dawn and stood with a cup of tea in your hand by the kitchen door before you start the day, just listening to the bird song all around. I won't have to tell you what fieldwork entails, I'm sure Mrs Mayfield will have told you as she'll know it from A to Z. Everything was ticking along nicely until the Boss, that's the farmer, bought a bull. A *gigantic* black bull, a creature from hell it was, you should've heard the roars and bellows as it was trying to pound the stall walls down. I couldn't believe my eyes. It was the most frightening thing I ever saw, and poor Fay nearly passed out.

So, imagine our horror on being told that we would have to handle it. I won't go into detail about what would be expected of us, you wouldn't believe it. Anyway, I had an almighty row with him and marched Fay and myself right out of there. Our nerves were jangling, and Fay was white-faced and trembling like a leaf, so we went to the kitchen and demanded a cup of tea. But to give the Mrs her due, she did stand up for us, and told us to go nowhere near that creature, and that if she had her way 'it was going back to where it came from, and believe me, I always do get my own way' she said.

Then, the next morning after giving us the best breakfast ever, she dropped a right bombshell. Told us after next week we were not needed, her two nephews were coming up from London to escape the bombing, so they would be working on the farm. I had something to say about that I can tell you, what a cheek, but the woman thought we would carry on working until these boys arrived. You should've seen her face when I said we're going to pack and leaving now. 'But you can't', she said, watch us, *I* said. I told her we were going straight to Skipton to report this to the War Agg. Which is how we met Mrs Mayfield, who is going to the farm tomorrow to see how things are for herself. We were a bit worried at first, but Mrs Mayfield has fixed us up with another job."

"Well, April, that's quite a story, you did right to walk out. Our Anita will sort this farmer and his wife out, and I don't think that they'll be getting any more help from the Land Army, they certainly don't deserve it, do they?"

Fay, who had been sat quietly listening, said.

"I only hope some other poor unfortunate girl won't be faced by the sight of that bull like we were, I shudder to think of it."

Aunt Polly shook her head.

"Don't worry, my dear, our Anita will sort things out, she's good at her job."

"She'll have to be, taking those two on. Now, enough about that, I want to forget about it all, I want to hear about your Bert," April said pertly.

"I do wish you could've met him. My Bert's a lovely man," Aunt Polly said with shining eyes.

"He must be to put that sparkle in your eyes at your age," April laughed.

"Oh, my Bert and I are forever young, to me, he looks just the same as the day I met him."

"How did you meet?" Fay asked softly.

"I'll bet it was love at first sight," April said dreamily. "Although I've never really believed in that."

Aunt Polly clasped her hands together and said excitedly.

"Oh, but you must, April."

"It can happen, and it happened to me a long time ago," Fay whispered.

"Really?" April said, looking at Fay keenly. "You become more of a mystery woman every day."

"You'll know all when I'm ready to tell you, April, now, can we please get back to Aunt Polly's love story." She turned to Aunt Polly. "Where did you meet the love of your life?"

"We met at a garden party the vicar was giving for the church folk in our little community. It was a beautiful bright sunny summer day in July 1900. I remember the birds were singing, butterflies were swooping all around the flowerbeds, mingling with the bees who were buzzing happily around collecting their pollen, and somewhere in the distance, I could hear a band playing. We were all sat at little round tables drinking tea and eating fancy cakes, chatting amongst ourselves like young girls do, stopping to cool ourselves with our fancy fans which we carried in those days, it was so hot. I remember I wore a cream muslin dress dotted with small pink roses; my hat was pale pink with a band of cream ribbon around the brim. I must say, I felt very posh as it was my best dress. Then suddenly, a tall, manly, handsome young man was striding across the lawn. He was dressed in cricket whites. My friends Bella and Olive saw him the same time I did. My heart did a summersault, and I heard Bella say, 'my God, he's mine.' 'No,' Olive said, 'mine.' I was speechless and couldn't say a word, but when I'd pulled myself together, I knew deep down inside that this was the love of my life. I was instantly in love, so I stood, and saw that he was being handed a cup of tea by a silly young thing that was making sheep's eyes at him. Gripping my parasol firmly in my hand, I made my way over to him, contrived to bump into him accidentally, dropped my parasol and exclaimed, 'I'm so sorry, how clumsy of me.' He bent and picked it up, handed it to me with a smile, and I looked straight into his eyes which were twinkling with merriment, blue, blue eyes, how handsome he was with his fair wavy hair and small neatly trimmed moustache, I hardly came up to his shoulder. As I stood gazing up at him, I began to feel a little faint, so stammered, 'If you would excuse me, the heat you know, it gets to one.' 'Yes, it does, but before you go my darling, let me set your hat straight for you; it has become a little tilted due to our accident.' He reached down and straightened my hat. I felt myself blushing and hoped that he would think that it was the heats doing. I tottered away on legs like jelly, feeling such a fool."

"So, you knew he was the man for you the moment you clapped your eyes on him," April said seriously. "But what about him?"

"Ahh, I'm coming to that," Aunt Polly said softly. "As if I could forget. When I sat down again with Bella and Olive, I got a right old earful from them about my daring and boldness, 'but you had the chance to do the same', I retorted, they didn't reply to that. As the afternoon ended, I kept an eye on him, without him knowing I hoped, but imagine my surprise and delight when we rose to go, he strode over, and directly looking at me he said, 'could I walk you home?' I was speechless and could only nod my head. 'I shall take that as a yes', he said thoughtfully. 'And I'm not usually so bold, my name is Bert Jackson, and I'm going to marry you.' I could hear the girls gasping in shock, but I felt only delight and slightly dizzy, then, my boldness returning, I said loudly, 'I should hope you are, because I knew I'd marry you the moment I saw you.' 'Good', he said, 'we are both in agreement then are we not.' He took my hand and tucked it into the crook of his arm while Bella and Olive looked on horrified. 'Have you taken leave of your senses?' I heard Olive gasp. 'No,' I said, 'I've just met the man of my dreams, and I hope that one day you will too.' Then we marched off. We were married four months later."

"Wow," April declared. "You didn't let the grass grow under your feet, did you?"

"Why wait? We were madly in love and had to be together," Aunt Polly smiled.

"But what about your parents', what did they have to say?" Fay asked.

"They were shocked, but could do nothing about it, I was nineteen and didn't need their permission, but anyway, they really liked Bert, and in the end gave their blessing."

"Did you have brothers and sisters?" Fay asked.

"Just one sister who died at six years old, so you see, I was an only child."

"Did you have a nice wedding?"

"Yes, I had a lovely wedding. Bella and Olive were my bridesmaids."

"Here in Skipton?"

"Where else? It's where we met."

"The church where the garden party was?"

"No other."

"How lovely."

"I remember feeling very proud as I walked down the aisle to where Bert was waiting for me with love shining out of his eyes."

"Did you have any children?" Fay asked.

"No, my dear, I'm afraid we didn't, we would've loved to, but it just never happened, it wasn't meant to be, so we had to accept it. Apart from that, Bert and I have been, and still are blissfully happy, although I don't see as much of him as I'd like to. His lighthouse duties you see, he watches the sea. It's wartime isn't it, and that's his job and duty."

"Well, I'm not bothered if I never get married," April said crossly. "I love my work on the land, and when the war's over, I shall remain to work the land."

"Never say never, April, one day it could happen to you, just like it did to Aunt Polly," Fay said.

"I'll see that it doesn't, I'll be far too busy," April said firmly as she stood and stretched her arms above her head. Then, after a loud yawn, glanced at the grandfather clock that stood at the bottom of the stairs. "Goodness, look at the time, I think we should get a good night's sleep, Fay. Do you mind if we turn in, Aunt Polly?" she said.

"Mind? No, I'm ready for my bed; I'm up with the lark every morning at six-thirty. I do hope you find the beds comfortable."

"I'm sure we shall," Fay answered as she patted her on the shoulder. "If they are anything like your tea, they will be super."

Aunt Polly led them up a narrow-carpeted flight of stairs to a small landing and opened a door on the left.

"Here we are, girls, this is your bedroom, the bathroom is the door opposite. Now, I'll say goodnight, sleep tight, oh, and breakfast is seven-thirty, hope that's alright."

"Aunt Polly, that's fine, we're used to getting up at the crack of dawn remember," April said. "And thanks for the wonderful tea."

"You're most welcome, you've already thanked me enthusiastically like the nice polite girls you are. Now, go to bed and have a good night's sleep." She hurried away once more, humming happily to herself.

The girls were delighted with the charming tiny bedroom. It had pale pink emulsion walls with a large picture of Skipton Castle hung between the twin beds, whose counterpanes were a pretty flowered cotton. A mahogany single wardrobe with a chest of drawers to match, and a small chair painted red completed the room.

Fay drew back the counterpane and felt the mattress.

"I thought so," she cried. "It's a feather mattress, oh this is heaven. I have one like this at home, so we're in for a good night's sleep."

"Do you now? *Why* doesn't that surprise me?" April said sarcastically.

"A lot of my past life would surprise you April, but now is not the time to be telling of it." There was a short silence. "Shall I use the bathroom first?" Fay asked casually.

"I can't wait to hear about this life of yours," April said. "And yes, use the bathroom first, by all means, ladies first."

5

After a hearty breakfast the next morning, the girls and Mrs Mayfield were stood on the station platform waiting for the nine-thirty train. As they did so, Mrs Mayfield was explaining to them about a change of plan. They were now going to Essex to a place near Tiptree.

"Never heard of it," Fay exclaimed.

"I expect it's in the back of beyond," April said glumly. "Places like that usually are if you've never heard of them."

"I have had good reports about it," Mrs Mayfield said firmly. "And while you are in the Land Army you will have to appreciate that variety is the spice of life."

"If it doesn't kill us first," April commented.

"I have not heard of anyone dying yet, April, so cheer up."

"There's a first time for everything, Mrs Mayfield."

"Now that's enough, April. Have you got your papers and directions I gave you?"

"Yes, we have thank you, and I don't like the thought of changing trains in London."

"That's the way you have to do it, and mind you don't lose one another; it's a bustling station teeming with all walks of life."

"I wouldn't like that to happen," Fay said, a look of dismay on her face.

"We're too grown up to be getting lost on railway platforms, and if we do, we have a tongue in our heads and can ask a porter," April said impatiently.

"That would be the thing to do," Mrs Mayfield put in.

"What with having to change at Leeds, then getting on the London train, I don't know if I'm on my head or my heels," Fay cried, distressed.

"I'm in charge, Fay, so you have nothing to worry about," April said in a voice of authority. "So, just calm down, and I'll make sure we get there safely."

"Now, girls," Mrs Mayfield said. "When you are settled in, please drop me a line and let me know how you are getting on."

"We will," Fay said with a smile. "It's nice of you to bother about us as we'll be out of your jurisdiction. We've promised to write to Aunt Polly too."

"You seem to have been a hit with Aunt Polly," Mrs Mayfield said with amusement.

"She was a hit with us too," April replied.

"She told you her life story I expect."

"She did, and we loved listening to her, we found her fascinating."

"I'll bet she told you the story of the great love of her life and how they met, and a few other romantic things."

"Oh, yes, it was lovely."

"She mentioned her Bert?"

"Of course."

"Aunt Polly tells her stories to anyone who will listen, that's how she tries them out."

"Tries them out. What do you mean?"

"My dear, Aunt Polly is a writer, published, but, before it is, she tries out the plot on someone. Heaven help us if she ever decides to write murder mysteries."

The two girls stood with their mouths open in shock. April was the first to speak.

"I'm bloody gobsmacked," she waved her arm in the air. "That old lady a writer."

"I'm not so surprised really," Fay said quietly. "She was very lucid and expressed things well. Does she write under her own name?"

"No, she doesn't."

"Do you know what name she uses?"

"I'm afraid not."

"I'd love to read her books."

"She won't tell anyone her pseudonym."

"Lots of authors use a fictitious name."

"That is their choice; it's certainly Aunt Polly's."

"You never know, we may have read her books."

"Yes, we may."

"Well, I can only say this, Aunt Polly is a mystery woman, *but*, I say, has she *ever* been married?" April asked.

"No, never wanted to be, always said she has been delighted with her life the way it is," Mrs Mayfield replied. Then, "here comes your train, you should get a good seat here, there's not too many people waiting to board."

The large black train pulled into the station puffing and hissing clouds of steam.

"No wonder they call these trains the giants of the railways, they certainly live up to their name, just look at the size of the wheels," Fay said in amazement. "I'm going to enjoy my ride."

"Let's begin it now then and get on the train," April said sharply.

"Mother took me around in the car, so train riding is a treat for me," Fay said in explanation.

"Ha, another snippet from your life's files," April said sharply.

"Now, April, Fay's business is her own." She swung open a door and beckoned the girls inside. "On you get, make yourselves comfortable." She shook each girl's hand. "God speed and good luck to both of you."

When she slammed the door closed, April let down the window as the train pulled away with a mighty hiss of steam. Both girls leant out and waved energetically to Mrs Mayfield, who waved back as the Queen would until the three lost sight of one another.

As they sank back onto their seats, April said gloomily.

"There ends another chapter of our lives. I wonder what the next will be like?"

"I'm more worried about finding this hostel at Tiptree, wherever that may be, and I can see us arriving at midnight. I only hope that it's not too far out in the country. If it's dark, there won't be any lights to guide us," Fay ended nervously.

"Whatever faces us, we will handle," April replied diplomatically. "So, stop worrying."

"What do you think about Aunt Polly?" Fay asked. "About her being a writer. I wonder if she'll put us in one of her books."

"I hand it to her, she had me fooled."

"I can hardly believe it."

"She's a very clever lady."

"I'll say."

"All that about her Bert."

"Most ingenious."

"Maybe she had a love affair that went wrong?"

"Yes, maybe."

"And this is her way of getting it out of her system."

"Could be."

"If only we knew her fictitious name."

"Well, we don't, so that's that."

Fay pulled a face.

"There's ways and means of finding out anything you want, you know, *if* you know the right people."

"And I suppose *you* do," April said sarcastically.

"In a way, yes, I do," Fay said softly. "But I'm not going into it yet."

"No, I didn't think you would; now why does *that* not surprise me," April said. "Anyway, I'm going to get my head down and have forty winks, you should do the same, won't be long before we're in Leeds, then we've to get onto the Kings Cross train." She laid her head back against the seat rest, sighed contentedly and closed her eyes. "The sound of the wheels on the track will put me to sleep, listen to how they go click-clickety-click."

As April nodded off, Fay leant her head back, then turned to face the window. She saw how lush and green the fields were, and in the distance, the hills covered with a purple haze. Rabbits darted about, and at the sound of the approaching train, darted off, their bobbed tails twitching. Birds flew in clouds from the trees, startled by the noisy sounding train. Cows stood still, swishing their tails lazily to ward off the persistent hordes of flies that were in abundance in the hot, humid heat.

One would not think that there was a war on when you could see such beautiful countryside like this. It looks so peaceful, Fay thought, so sweet smelling and fresh.

As she saw the cows so still, she wondered how on earth she had ever managed to milk them, she had been so frightened of the large, cumbersome beasts; she must have hurt them as she fumbled about, pulling and squeezing their teats, but she had mastered it and felt quite proud of herself. The fieldwork was heavy, but she had not let it get her down, but now, her hands were calloused and rough, her nails short and unkempt. For a time, she had suffered from severe backache and had been only too glad to roll into an uncomfortable bed at night feeling like a wooden life-sized doll. She would not have gotten through without April's help and her cheerful good humour. Yes, April was a friend indeed.

I shall forget about the uncomfortable times and remember the happy, pleasant ones.

She felt her eyelids begin to close and was lost in sleep.

She awoke to find April shaking her and saying.

"Come on, girl, we're here at Leeds, grab your case and let's depart, we've to find a porter and ask about the London train to Kings Cross."

The girls alighted onto a very crowded platform that was heaving with people wearing the many different uniforms of war apparel.

A young sailor bumped into Fay, then tilting his hat jauntily forward onto his forehead, said.

"Sorry, love," in a South Yorkshire accent.

Fay smiled and nodded her head in acceptance of his apology.

A tall, middle-aged man with a head that was too small for his body, and wearing the army uniform, shouted for all to hear.

"Look here, lads, the Land Army!" Every head turned to look the girls way. He went on. "They do a man's job do the Land Army, but under that uniform, they don't look like men, all that digging will keep them in shape!"

A course looking type with a nose that filled his face, called.

"All that digging will give 'em good tits."

Fay blushed to the roots of her hair, while April called.

"You, big mush, any more of that and I'll squash it all over your face like a bad rotten apple."

There were cheers at this, and some of the lads started to clap and chanted.

"Come on the Land Army!"

April bowed from her waist and called.

"Thanks, lads, much appreciated."

Fay pulled at April's shoulder and said loudly to be heard.

"This is getting embarrassing, there'll be a riot soon, let's go."

"I'd love to, but to where? You tell me?" April shouted back.

They stood, undecided, while the crowd milled around them, pushing and shoving in every direction.

One girl wearing the uniform of a Wren said disdainfully.

"If I were you, I'd move before you get trampled underfoot, I've never seen such a crowd before; everyone's going back to base after leave."

"Oh, I see," Fay said.

"Where are you headed for?" the Wren asked.

"We want the London train to King's Cross," April replied.

"Oh, that's very easy, the next platform, the London train leaves in ten minutes."

"Thanks very much," April said

"If I were you, I'd hurry, it's a packed train, you'll be lucky to get a seat, and you don't want to be standing all the way to London. I did once; it nearly did my back in."

With a grin, April said.

"We're used to standing in our job you know, often for hours, all weathers."

"Yes, I know, my sister's a Land Girl, that's why I stopped to help you," the Wren replied. "I must go, or I'll miss *my* train, goodbye." She sped off with a wave of her hand.

April took hold of Fay and shook her arm.

"Now, hold onto me and hold on tightly to your case, I'm going to bulldoze my way through this crowd if I can. If there's any complaints and cursing, pretend that you're deaf."

As the girls fought their way to the train, they did so to shouts of.

"Nar then, who does tha thinks tha's pushing?!"

"Steady on, girls were all trying to get out of this crush."
"Yer nearly 'ad mi over then, and yer trod-on mi bloody foot!"
A very tall A.T.S girl called.
"You're not working in the fields now, slow down!"
A young, red-haired sailor who held his crushed hat in his hand held it out.
"You'll be jolly lucky to get out of this mob in one piece; look at my blooming headgear, the Petty Officer will have my guts for garters!"
As Fay stopped to commiserate, April yanked her on, shouting.
"No time to stop."
Suddenly an R.A.F Officer said loudly and clearly.
"Let these girls through, don't you know we rely on the girls in the Land Army to put food in our bellies. Make way now."
Miraculously, a path appeared before the girls, and they fled while shouting thanks over their shoulders.

6

After a very tiring train journey from Leeds to Kings Cross, where the girls had no choice but to sit on their suitcases in the narrow train corridor, amid catcalls, insults, cheers and whistles, with the forces really enjoying the girls discomfort, they found themselves at last stood on Tiptree Station, fed up and lost. Fay, who very much felt like crying, looked around her. There was nothing much to see, only a dozen or so people waiting for trains, but down the far side, she saw a café sign.

She tugged April's sleeve.

"Look, a café, come on."

"Thank God for that," April said. "I'm dying for a drink; I'm not going away from here without a cup of tea inside me."

As the girls reached the café, they saw a notice which said, 'Free Drink To Serving Forces.' As April pushed open the door, she said.

"That's nice, a free cup of tea, it'll be like nectar to me."

As they walked into the room, a wave of noise met them, and every table seemed to have been taken.

"My goodness, not much room in here, where are we supposed to sit?" Fay asked.

"You wonder around and find two seats; I'll get the teas."

"How can I do that? This place is packed."

"I don't know, just go and look." April snapped impatiently. "Go on, don't just stand there."

April made her way to the counter where a small queue had formed, as she slowly moved up, she could hear the woman serving being pleasant and polite to everyone she helped. As it came to April's turn, she asked.

"What can I get you love?"

"Two cups of tea please, one with no milk."

"Two cups of tea coming up, that'll be two pence."

As the woman poured the teas, April looked puzzled, and said inquiringly.

"Two pence, but I thought the drinks were free?"

"What?" the woman said with a frown on her face.

"It says outside that the drinks are free."

The woman plonked the mugs down heavily onto the counter, causing them to slop over, then crossed her arms over her chest.

"The sign *does* say that, it means what it says, the fighting forces. *You* are hardly that are you."

"I beg your pardon?" April said politely.

"*You* are only The Land Army; you are *not* the fighting forces."

April felt her temper begin to rise.

"Only the Land Army?! How dare you, we do our bit, and more besides, if it weren't for us, you'd starve."

"I'm not giving you any tea unless you pay for it."

"If I don't get that tea, I'll pour it over your head!" April shouted angrily.

A man's voice shouted.

"Go on, lass, do it."

'Don't encourage me', April thought.

"Do I get those teas?" she said quietly.

"No!" the woman snapped. "No, means no."

The same man's voice shouted out.

"Report her."

"Yes," April said. "I shall report this to The War Department, it's an outrage."

"Good for you, lass! My daughter's a Land Girl," the man's voice called out.

"You can do what you like." the woman said cockily. "I have my orders, and I am doing my duty by carrying them out."

"Right!"

April reached forward to pick up a cup of tea with every intention of throwing it over the woman, when an arm reached over her and pulled her away from the counter. She looked up to see a tall, grey-eyed, handsome G.I smiling down at her.

"Excuse me, sweetheart, but that is not the way, I'll deal with this." He turned to the startled woman who had stood back from the counter. "Excuse me, Ma'am; I couldn't help overhearing what you said to this little girl. I thought that England treated its workers better than this, I'll see to it that this matter is reported to the authorities."

"Oh, you will, will you?!" the woman snapped. "You Yanks think you can do what you want in our country."

"*We* Yanks as you call us, are helping you to fight *your* war, but I don't intend to stand here exchanging insults with *you*. By the way, you will address me as Captain."

The woman looked red-faced with mortification.

"And," the Captain went on. "You cannot refuse to serve *me*, I would like two mugs of tea please, and given pleasantly,"

The woman poured the tea without a word and handed them to the Captain with shaking hands, who then handed them to a grateful April.

"There you go, sweetheart, have these on the good old U.S of A. I'm Captain Silverton, Bomber Command. May I say how much we admire and respect you girls of the Land Army, you do a mighty fine job. One of my gunners has just married a Land Girl, fine girl too."

"Thank you so much for getting my friend and me a cup of tea, it was kind of you to help," April said gratefully

"Glad to, but you girls shouldn't be treated like that, I'll report it, you bet I will."

"Oh, I don't want any trouble over a cup of tea," April cried.

"My dear, *what is* your name?"

"April Thornton," she stuttered.

"A pretty name for a pretty girl, nice to have met you, April." He looked at his watch. "Must go, I may be a Captain but can still be in trouble for being late back to base. Enjoy your tea, April, goodbye." He strode off towards the door.

April turned to the sour-faced woman behind the counter and stuck out her tongue, then said.

"See."

The woman pulled a face back at her, sniffed, and with a disdainful look on her face repeated back.

"*See.*"

April stood for a moment looking around for Fay. At last, she caught sight of her sat at a table at the back of the room with three G.I's. She made her way over to them, trying not to spill the mugs of tea which she had such trouble getting. With a loud sigh, she sat down on the vacant seat.

"You won't believe the trouble I had to get this bloody tea, if not for a knight in shining armour I would've come back empty-handed."

"We saw something was going on, but before you tell us, let me introduce you to these gentlemen who kindly let us share their table," Fay said. She pointed to a small broad-shouldered young man with large blue eyes. "This is Tommy, he has the gift of the gab and has kept me entertained while you were gone, he's from San Francisco."

"Glad to know you, April," Tommy boomed out.

He had a deep voice for such a small person, April thought.

He went on.

"Been hearing about how hard you gals work." He turned to a man who sat head and shoulders above him; he had a high forehead and a scar below his left eye. "This here is Tiny, you can see why we call him Tiny, everyone does, he's six-six and a very nice guy."

He leant across the table and shook April's hand, saying.

"Hi there."

April looked at the third G.I and felt her heart give a little flip.

"April, this is Glenn, he's from New York same as Tiny, they went to the same school and grew up together."

Glenn had black hair and midnight blue eyes, his nose, April thought, reminded her of Basil Rathbone's, the actor who played Sherlock Holmes, and his mouth she thought, oh, imagine being kissed by that!

"Hello, April," he said, with a smile Clark Gable would have died for. "Glad to meet you, I've heard about you Land Girls."

"All good, I hope," April replied.

"Fay," he went on. "Has been filling us in on the work you do on the land, it can't be easy."

"She hasn't had time to tell you much; it would take a month of Sunday's," April said shortly.

"A month of Sunday's? What does that mean?" Tiny asked.

"It means an awfully long story, too long to tell," Tommy said knowledgeably.

All three men wore G.I uniforms and had crew-cuts.

I can see why the girls fall for them, but not me, April thought.

"Say, April, you were helped out by our dashing Captain," Tommy said.

"Yes, I was. I was just about to throw the tea she wouldn't let me have, all over her, the bloody woman insulted the Land Army, so I was thankful your Captain stopped me. She was going to charge me for the tea."

"But I thought the tea was free to all the forces?" Glenn said.

"The Land Army is not classed as a fighting force."

"That's a bit mad, isn't it?"

"Yes, it is, but tell that to Churchill."

"You got your tea in the end though," Tiny said.

"We did, there's nothing like a good cup of tea."

"You English and your cup of tea."

"Cures all ills, Tiny."

"We Americans love our coffee."

"So I've heard."

"I need a gallon before I start to play, keeps me awake," Tiny said with a laugh.

"That sounds interesting, what do you play?" April asked.

"What does he play?" Tommy laughed. "Only the meanest trumpet next to Satchmo."

"Oh, how wonderful!" Fay gasped with shining eyes. "How I'd love to hear you!"

"He's the best," Tommy said. "The best."

"If we ever meet up again, maybe at a dance or something, I'd love to hear you, Tiny."

"And *I'd* love to play for you, Ma'am."

"Please, call me Fay; I don't reckon much to this Ma'am business."

"It's our way of being polite, I notice you English people call everybody 'love'."

"If you went into South Yorkshire, you'd be surprised at what they call you down there," April said with a wink at Fay.

"What would that be?" Tommy asked.

"I prefer not to say if you don't mind," April said firmly. "Every county in England has its own dialect, different in its own way. You'll have noticed that Fay talks very posh, while I'm broader."

"Really, April, I'm not posh; it's just the way I was brought up," Fay protested.

"It doesn't matter how a person talks," Glenn said. "We're all the same inside."

"Tell us about your job, from what I've heard; you girls are badly done to," Tommy said.

"Some are, some aren't," April answered. "It's potluck, you get onto a good, or onto a bad farm, but I love the life, and I never want to do anything else."

"One day you'll get married, April, a pretty girl like you," Glenn said.

"I'd never find anyone who would put up with me, I like to be my own Boss, but I must confess, I *have* to do as I'm told when working, but some of those bloody farmers rub me up the wrong way."

"You should see April in a temper," Fay laughed.

"I can imagine," Tommy said with a chuckle.

To change the subject, April said.

"It's good of you boys to help us win the war, and we *are* going to win, although the end is utterly uncertain. They won't need the Land Army then I expect."

"You'll get a gratuity, surely?" Tiny said.

"I don't know about that, Tiny, as you now know, we're not classed as a fighting force." April said, shaking her head. "We're mistreated *now*, as regards to wages, time off and poor food. A lot of us survive on beetroot sandwiches."

"You've got to be kidding?!" Tommy cried.

"I kid you not," April said seriously.

Glenn suddenly jumped up and picked up from the floor a small handheld army bag and upended it onto the table. Bars of chocolate, chewing gum and cigarettes cascaded all over the table.

"My goodness, look at the chocolate!" Fay cried.

"All for you, girls, help yourself," Glenn said.

"Do you mean it? Can we have it? All of it?" April said in amazement.

"It's all yours, little one," Glenn laughed.

"Where will you put it?" Tiny asked.

April stood, then put their five empty mugs onto the next table, then bending down; she picked up her case from the floor, placed it onto the table, opened it, then said to Fay.

"Don't sit there like a startled chicken, get your case opened and put some of this stuff in before these boys change their minds."

"Are you sure?" Fay asked the G.I's bashfully.

"Of course we're sure, honey, pack it all away, there's plenty more where that came from, America looks after its own," Glenn said commandingly.

The girls began to throw their booty willy-nilly into the cases, each thinking that their birthdays had all come at once.

"I can't thank you guys enough," April said.

"Me neither," Fay said as she shut her case and placed it back onto the floor. "Every time I eat a chocolate bar, I shall think of you three boys."

"I hope we meet up again some time," April said softly.

"If we make it," Glenn said sadly. "We're losing our flyers every day; some of them are our best buddies."

"That must be heart-breaking," Fay said sadly.

"It is, honey, it is. Every time you go up, you wonder, is it going to be my turn." Glenn paused, then said. "It's heart-breaking when you see one of the boys shot down in front of you." His voice broke. "And know that it was your best buddy, who you used to laugh with, be sad with, talk about home with and drank with." He fell silent, and Fay felt tears spring to her eyes.

"Now, let's not get morbid, what is the time? Surely we should be on our way, although which way I don't know," April said cheerfully.

"Gee, it's almost six o'clock," Tommy said, looking up at the large clock on the wall over the counter. "We've to push on, guys, our train leaves in ten minutes."

The three rose to their feet, as did the two girls. The boys hugged and kissed the girls, saying how nice it was to have met them, and how much they had enjoyed their company, with the girls returning the compliment.

Before leaving, Glenn pushed a piece of paper into Fay's hand, saying.

"Ring me sometime, honey, I'd love to talk to you again."

Then, they were gone.

"What was that he gave you?" April asked.

Fay opened her hand to reveal a small, folded piece of paper. On it, was a phone number.

"It's a phone number," she gasped. "He's given me his phone number."

"Hmm, you certainly impressed him, he was attracted to you," April said.

"Go on, he wasn't."

"You liked him, didn't you?"

"He *was* rather nice."

"Ships that pass in the night."

"I suppose so."

"We'll meet lots of people in our job, Fay; you just have to keep your head screwed on the right way."

"I know that *you'll* see that I do," Fay said brusquely.

April shook her head as if dismissing the matter.

"Now, let's get down to the business of getting ourselves to this damn hostel." She slapped down the papers Mrs Mayfield had given them. "It says here, 'walk to the very end of the village when you come out of the station, keep to the main road, follow it for a mile and a half until you come to a lane on the left, it's called Cherry Tree Lane, follow this for another mile, then still bearing to your left, you will come to a tall pair of iron gates, do not try to open these, there is a small gate on the right which is used to get in and out. In front of you will be the hostel, it stands in its own grounds. You may be able to get a bus from the village. Good luck girls.' Well," April said dubiously. "It seems to be clear enough, although I hope we *can* get a bus, it sounds as if it's nearly a two-mile hike."

"I don't fancy that in a strange place," Fay said.

"Come on then, let's be off and see if there's any buses about," April said firmly as she picked up her case. "Heck, this case is heavy now with all that stuff the G.I's gave us."

"That was so kind of them," Fay said.

"Yes, it'll come in handy if we're on a starvation diet in this hostel," April said, nodding her head.

"Oh, I hope not, surely we'll get fed well in a hostel!" Fay exclaimed in dismay.

"You never know, we have to take it as it comes," April answered.

As they made their way towards the door, the cocky serving woman shouted after them.

"Good riddance!"

"Well, the cheeky bugger! I'll soon sort her out," April said infuriated as she dropped her case onto the floor.

Fay pulled her back, saying as she did so.

"Don't, April, the woman has no manners, don't put yourself on her level."

"Alright, but if you hadn't been here to stop me, I would've put that face of hers back a mile!" April shouted furiously. So instead, she screamed. "You want to get out into the fields and do our job, you whey-faced bitch!"

Fay pulled April out of the door.

"Don't take on so, she's not worth it," Fay begged.

"I can't help it, people like her get my back up! I hope I don't meet up with *her* if I'm ever in this village again."

"*I* hope you don't either."

"Well, I just hope *you* aren't with me."

"Look, there's a bus stop right outside the station," Fay said thankfully. "I vote we stand there for ten minutes or so, see if a bus comes."

"It'll be just our luck for there not to be one," April said moodily.

"Well, our luck seems to have changed," Fay laughed and pushed April playfully. "Look, there's a bus coming."

"Thank god for that, we'd better stick our arms out; we don't want it to go past us do we." She stuck out her arm and waved it wildly about.

The bus pulled up with a loud clatter and a shriek of brakes.

"I don't like the sound of that," April said as they lifted their cases ready to board.

The conductor suddenly appeared, and April went on in a whisper.

"And I don't like the look of him."

He was a steely-eyed broad-shouldered man with dark hair flopping into his eyes; he kept throwing his head back to see more clearly.

"Now, what have we here? More Land Girls, as if we haven't enough running amok in our village."

This put April's back up straight away.

"Stop the clap-trap and put our cases onto the luggage rack."

"You're supposed to be strong tough girls, put them on yourself!" he snapped. Then, reconsidering, he said, "I'll do it; I don't want reporting for bad manners."

"Thank you," Fay said politely.

"Anything for you, beautiful," he said, giving her a saucy wink. "But I don't know about your friend."

"Don't worry about me, I'm a strong tough Land Girl remember," April said sarcastically.

"You're a lippy one into the bargain," he shot back.

April pulled a face and wondered why he was not in the forces. Looks strong and healthy enough, probably has flat feet or knock knees, maybe both. She smiled at her thoughts as he rang the bell to send the bus on its way. It set off with a jerk, and Fay, who was in front of April, was sent catapulting at speed down the aisle, while

April just managed to catch hold of a seatback. As Fay sank onto a seat by the window at the front of the bus, feeling shook up, she turned and looked for April.

The conductor had caught hold of April and grasped her upper arm to hold her upright. As he did so, his ticket holder clouted her shoulder hard.

"That hurt," she said with a grimace.

"It was only a little bump," he grinned. "I thought you were tough?"

"Tougher than you, evidently, or you'd be in the army doing your bit, not an easy issuing tickets job like you *are* doing."

"Why I'm not in the army is *my* affair, so don't comment on something you know nothing about."

"Likewise, don't call the Land Army *or* its girls."

"It was a joke."

"A joke we don't like."

"Oh, shut up you lippy young bugger and go sit down."

"I'd better, or I'll end up on the floor."

As April made her way down the bus, she took note of the few passengers who had been listening avidly to the exchange of argument between herself and the conductor. On the right was an old man wearing a brown trilby, he was wiping his eyes with a snow-white hankie, April wondered why. Had he been laughing at her? Next to him was a middle-aged man with a few grey hairs combed over his gleaming bald head. It looked silly, why not face the fact that his youth had gone, and had the remaining few hairs removed?

Two seats down from the two men, was a woman sat by the window, she was looking straight ahead, and seemed lost in thought. She had a plain wool turban on her head, poking out of the front, over her forehead, were curling pins, but she had a good profile April thought, must have been a looker in her day, and look at the lipstick, bright red! By her side sat a boy of about eleven. He had white-blonde hair, which stood up in spikes all over his head as if he had had an electric shock. As April passed, he looked up at her with large brown eyes, which had lashes any girl would die for. She smiled down at him and winked, he smiled shyly back, and she saw that his two front teeth were missing. In front of them was a teenage girl with almost black hair curled into a bang on her forehead. She wore no make-up and was looking out at the passing scenery. As April passed; she looked up at her and rolled her eyes towards the conductor.

April sniffed and mouthed.

"Yes," In acknowledgement.

The girl turned back to the window.

As April sat down next to Fay, she saw that two women sat in front of them, both wore shabby hats with grey hair peeping from the back. The hat the woman wore who was sat in front of April, was a monstrosity. It was a bilious purple and shaped like a dented basin. A long, dirty, white dilapidated feather stood up in the middle.

April nudged Fay.

"Look at that."

Fay nodded her head to signify that she had seen it, then said.

"We'd better get our money out ready to pay our fair."

"We'd better, and I hope we don't get any more claptrap out of him. I got a right clout off that ticket rack of his, my shoulder is still hurting."

Suddenly he was there, holding out his hand. Looking down at April, he said grimly in a no-nonsense voice.

"Now, Miss Lippy, what can I do you for?"

April gave him one of her famous dirty looks.

"You couldn't afford it," she said loudly.

The man looked blank, then realised that he had said the wrong thing. He breathed in slowly, then said.

"No need for a remark like that, it's smut."

"You asked me, and I told you. Do you ask all your passengers what you can do them for?" April said with a straight face.

There was a smothered giggle from the girl sat behind them.

"What's your name?" April asked.

"Why?"

"I can't keep addressing you as conductor."

"Most people do."

"I rather think we'll be using the bus service a lot on our nights off."

"Heaven forbid."

"There must be more than you doing this job."

"There is. I must warn them about you."

"Don't forget to tell them my name is Miss Lippy."

"Oh, I will, you can be sure of that." He looked at Fay and gave her a lopsided smile. "Maybe I'll get more sense out of your beautiful friend." April pulled a face, which he ignored. "Now, Miss," he asked Fay gently. "Where you getting off at?"

As Fay opened her mouth to reply, April said.

"The terminus, same as me."

"I don't know where *you* come from, Miss Lippy, but we don't have a terminus here, only a last stop," the conductor said cockily.

"Okay, two tickets to the last stop then."

"Two pence each," he snapped.

April handed him the money, which he took with a forced thank you.

Again, he ignored April and asked Fay.

"You'll be going to Whitmore then?"

"Pardon?" Fay said politely.

"He'll mean the hostel," April said.

"Go to the top of the class!" he snapped angrily.

"*You* evidently were not, or you'd not be doing *this* job," April said with a grin.

"Were not what?" he asked.

"The top of the class, of course," April said.

The young lad sat with his Mother, gave a loud giggle, his Mother dug him with her elbow and said angrily.

"Stop it, Norman."

April leant towards Norman and winked, and he winked back.

"I don't have to stand here and take insults from an ignorant Land Girl," the conductor said.

"No, you don't, you can always sit down and take them," April laughed.

Oh, but she was enjoying sparring with this stupid man; he couldn't see that she was playing him like an old fiddle. Fay could, and she believed young Norman could too.

"You could learn some manners from your beautiful quiet friend here," the conductor went on.

"Could I now? I'll think about it. Now, why don't you give me the tickets I've just paid for, we can't have you falling on the job can we," April said sweetly.

He handed her the tickets and walked away.

There was silence for a while on the bus, which was trundling at a steady thirty miles an hour on the main road. Fay was looking out of the window, and April began to feel bored. She felt the pen which she had, digging into her leg, so she took it out and twirled it between her fingers, then caught sight of the upright white feather in the obnoxious hat in front of her. She leant forward, and carefully with the pen, started to move the feather from side to side.

Young Norman watched goggle-eyed. She shrugged her shoulders at him then beamed a mischievous smile. He stared at her, fascinated as she started once again to move the feather, then clapped a hand over his mouth in order not to laugh aloud. The woman in the hat continued to sit silently and still, which made it seem all the funnier. Then, becoming more venturesome, April slipped the point of the pen underneath the bottom of the hat, and slowly started to push it upwards. She heard Norman gasp at her daring. As she pushed a little faster, the hat slid forward onto the woman's forehead. She turned to her friend and said.

"It's rather close in here don't you think?" Then pushed her hat back into place.

"No more than usual," the friend replied.

April looked at Norman and mouthed.

"Shall I?"

He nodded vigorously.

She began the process again, and Fay, who had suddenly realised what was going on, hissed.

"Stop it," while giving April a dig in the ribs.

April took no notice but continued with a smug grin.

By this time, Norman could not contain himself any longer and howled with laughter. His Mother turned to him and said.

"What on earth's wrong with you?! Just wait till I get you home, showing me up like this!"

Norman could only point at April helplessly, and continued to laugh, tears pouring down his face. Behind them, the old man in the trilby still had his hankie in his hand and appeared to be wiping his eyes while giving deep belly laughs. The man who was with him, his son, was saying.

"Now, Father, calm yourself, you'll make yourself ill."

"Make myself ill?" he stuttered. "This is the best laugh I've had in years; I haven't laughed as much since you took me to see Laurel and Hardy fifteen years ago. That girl should be on the stage."

"I don't think it's funny, I think it's stupid," the son replied.

"Oh, *you* would," the old man said grimly. "You never did have a sense of humour, just like your Mother."

"Let's leave Mother out of this."

"She never could stand to see me have a good laugh." He pointed at April, then said. "That girl's a hoot."

"Father, you've been spending too much time in the pub with those G.I's, you're picking up their slang. A *hoot* indeed."

April, upon hearing this, leant towards Norman and asked.

"What's a hoot, Norman?"

"It means that you're funny, Miss," he answered. "*I* think you are too, Miss."

"Why thank you, Norman, I'll take that as a compliment," April said with a smile.

By now, the woman with the hat had turned around to face April, her face the colour of purple to match her hat, which had slid sideways to cover one eye. This was a comical sight, and Fay was biting her lips in order not to laugh.

"Young, woman," the lady said angrily. "I believe you are trying to make a fool of me."

"I've no need to do that, Mrs, you *look* like one with your hat cockeyed over one eye," April said, trying not to laugh.

The woman pushed the hat straight, then said.

"I don't appreciate being spoken to like that, you're a bad-mannered, ignorant girl, and I can see why you work on the land, that's where you belong, with the animals."

April's dander was up.

"I was only..."

"I don't want to hear what you were *only* doing!" the woman snapped, cutting April off.

"There's no need," April persisted, "to class me with the animals, although you have a right to your opinion, but on second thoughts, I'd rather be in the company of animals than yours."

At this, there was a loud giggle from Norman, and his Mother said.

"Mrs Gadd, I'm so sorry that Norman is finding all this so funny, I must say that *I* don't."

The outraged Mrs Gadd said.

"Your son's been doing a lot of laughing at this girl's antics. I suggest you give him a leathering when you get him home, teach him not to think other peoples' downfalls are funny."

"It'll be worth it," Norman had the cheek to say.

Mrs Gadd tutted in outrage, and Norman's Mother clouted him on the back of his head, which caused him to bang his forehead into the seat in front. He rubbed it vigorously, winked at April, then said.

"It didn't hurt."

The conductor by now had realised that commotion was taking place and stamped down the bus angrily.

"What the blazes is going on here?" he shouted.

Mrs Gadd pointed at April.

"She's the cause of all this, I demand that she's put off the bus."

He glared at April.

"I might have known. Well, Miss Lippy, you've blotted your copybook now, I'm putting you off at the next stop, you can walk to wherever it is you're going, I won't have my passengers upset like this." He looked at Fay. "I'm sorry, beautiful, although you can stay on if you wish."

"No thank you, where April goes, I do too," Fay replied.

"You don't want to let this Madam lead you off," he pointed to April. "She's a load of trouble."

"Do your job, I want her off *now*," Mrs Gadd said.

He reached up and rang the bell, thinking as he did, Roy will wonder what's up; he was one of the bus companies most lazy drivers and would not get up off his fat backside to see what was going on.

April put a determined look on her face.

"We're *not* getting off; you ring that bell as much as you like."

"Oh, are you not, we shall see about that," the conductor said through gritted teeth.

"I think we should go, April," Fay said nervously.

Norman bit his lip, oh crumbs, he thought, this is going to get nasty. April was only a little un, the conductor wouldn't hurt her, would he?

April stood, then moved aside to let Fay pass.

"Go get the cases, Fay, put them and yourself onto the pavement, and wait there."

Fay looked apprehensive as she asked.

"What are you going to do?"

"I warn you, Miss Lippy," the conductor said firmly. "I shall put you off bodily."

Crumbs, Norman thought, I think he will.

April sighed, then said.

"You'll put me off bodily, will you? Tell me, pray, who is going to help you?"

Gosh, but she had guts, standing up to the conductor! He was bigger than her, Norman thought as he clenched his hands together.

"I don't need any help."

"But *I* think you will."

"Oh, you do, eh. I've dealt with people like you before, *and* drunks, and never found it a problem."

"I think that you will this time."

"Come on; get off under your own steam."

"No."

"Be sensible."

"No."

The old man at the back of the bus shouted.

"Stand up to him, lass, stand up to him."

"Shut up, Father," his son said in horror. "I don't like the way this is going, you're embarrassing me, and please remember your position in the village."

"You're a bloody wimp, and don't tell me to shut up," his Father said acidly.

Mrs Martin, Mrs Gadd's friend, said hesitantly.

"Let it go, Edna, sit down."

"No," Mrs Gadd snapped. "I want her off."

April turned to Norman and asked.

"How far to the hostel, lad?"

Norman looked out of the window.

"Keep on the main road, then first turning on the left, which is Cherry Tree Lane, straight up, and you'll come to it, can't miss it."

"Thanks, Norman, you're a good lad," April said with a smile. "Now, Norman, I think that you're about to see something you've never seen before."

"Oh, what, Miss?"

April turned to the waiting conductor.

"Come on; let's see what you can do."

He broke out into loud laughter, which was suddenly cut off as April, quick as lightening, bent down and effortlessly hoisted him onto her shoulder.

There were gasps of amazement from the passengers.

"Wow, look at that!" Norman said.

April walked down the aisle painlessly; after all, she *was* a Land Girl, used to strenuous physical work on the land. When she came to the back seat, she plonked him down unceremoniously where he landed in a crumpled heap.

She said triumphantly to the shocked conductor.

"Never underestimate us Land Girls, buster, we heave sacks of potatoes and bales of hay heavier than you, it's part of our job. You men think you're better than us, well, you can think again!"

"Gosh! I wish my mates could've seen that!"

"Shut up, Norman," his Mother croaked, shocked.

Mrs Gadd dropped onto her seat, nearly fainting; refusing to believe what she had just seen. That chit of a girl, heaving that man over her shoulder with no effort at all! Her friend was panting in shock as if just having run a ten-minute mile. The young teenager, who had been sat silent and goggle-eyed, leant towards the old man, and called.

"You enjoyed that didn't you, Judge Bentley."

He nodded, then said.

"It's shut my son up, he's speechless."

"I think I shall join the Land Army."

"You should, girl, you should, teach you a lot about life, you couldn't do anything better," the Judge said firmly.

April turned to face them all, and bowed from the waist down, she grinned mischievously.

By, but she had set this village on fire and hadn't been here a day yet, she would love to be a fly on the wall in some of the houses when word got around.

Meanwhile, the conductor was laid, stupefied by what had happened to him, he could not believe it, and could not muster the energy to lift himself up.

He would never live this down with his mates, the whole village in fact, everyone knew everybody, and the pub, could he go into the pub without everyone laughing at him? And his girlfriend, he could hear it now what she would have to say, most likely would pack him in. Fancy that girl, the size of two pennyworths of copper, lifting him like that, with no warning, and dumping him like a sack of coal. He would never live it down, may even have to give in his notice.

Meanwhile, April and Fay stood, and looked down the road they had to take, then Fay asked.

"I see he didn't put you off then. What happened?"

As April launched into the tale, Fay kept interrupting with, 'oh no's', and 'you didn't', and 'how could you.' As April ended, Fay said resignedly.

"What *am* I going to do with you, April." She sighed, then went on. "Not here two minutes and your name will be mud."

"I don't think so, young Norman enjoyed it and will tell all his mates at school, I'll be a hero, *and* the old man at the back, is, would you believe, a *Judge*."

"How do you know that?" Fay asked.

"Because that young girl sat behind us addressed him as Judge Bentley."

"I hope you don't ever end up in court in front of him then, he'd throw the book at you."

"I don't think so."

"Why?"

"Because he was egging me on."

"What do you mean?"

"He was shouting 'stand up to him gal.'"

"He never was."

"He was."

"A Judge doing that?"

"Maybe he's a retired Judge."

"I somehow don't think so, all Judges are old aren't they, and he was."

"Sometimes, old Judges can be unfair."

"What makes you say that?"

"A lot of people I know have come across it, unfairness I mean." She stopped and picked up her case. "Let's get going shall we."

"Yes, we should, it can't be so far, Norman gave me directions, and he knew what he was talking about. I must give the lad some of the goodies the G.I's gave me."

"He seems like a great kid," Fay said. "Where are you going to see him to do that?"

"I'll go to the school in the village some time, that is if I get any time off."

"I don't know about that; it could mean more trouble."

"There you go again; you worry too much."

"I know, and I can't help it."

"Have you not learnt by now that trouble is my middle name?"

"You know that old saying, never trouble trouble, till *it* troubles you."

"Everybody knows that one. If it finds *me*, I can handle it, and I always do, don't I?"

"I must admit that you do."

"Well, shut up then and let's get going." She paused, then said proudly. "One more thing, the Judge said how much I'd entertained him, wasn't that nice of him."

"Yes, it was, and most unusual, my Father wouldn't have been entertained, and would have said so."

April came to a halt, put down her case, and pulled Fay to a stop.

"You're Father? He was, or *is*, a Judge?" she said, utterly amazed.

"Forget I said that," Fay exclaimed, "It was a slip of the tongue, and I don't wish to discuss it." She began to walk. "I mean it, April, so don't go on, I know what you are when you get the bit between your teeth."

"I'll just say this one thing, kiddo," April said angrily. "One day I'm going to sit you down and make you tell me about your life, after all, you know all about mine, no secrets withheld about me, and if you're not forthcoming we're going to fall out, and I wouldn't like to do that, after all, we're best mates aren't we?"

"I hope we always shall be," Fay answered.

She began to walk on, with April following slowly, her thoughts flowing through her mind.

By, she is a dark one our Fay, more to her than meets the eye, fancy her Father a Judge, by the way she talks she has no love for him, it's all her Mother. It's evident they did not get on; it makes you wonder if she left home willingly or was made to go by this Father of hers. What had she done? Had she committed some sin? Married a German? Had a child out of wedlock? No, I could not see Fay doing any of those things. I shall just have to wait until she is ready to confess all. Whatever it is, I shall stand by her. That's what mates are for. Look at her, striding along without a care in the world, it just shows that you never know anyone as well as you thought you did.

"Hey, Fay," April called. "Slow up a bit, will you."

"Sorry, April, am I going too fast for you?" Fay said, amused.

"Not really, but this road's going on forever, although the scenery is nice, isn't it? Rather flat, not like the hills we had around Skipton," April commented.

"No, but look at the rich brown soil, field after field, all cultivated, there's going to be a lot of work here, April."

"That's what we're here to do, kiddo, work."

"It's tranquil isn't it; I hope that it's always like this."

"What time do you think it is? Fancy, we don't have a watch between us," April said.

"The sun hasn't gone down yet, so I'd say around seven, but I may be wrong," Fay said doubtfully, then cried. "Listen, someone's coming, maybe we'll get a lift."

An American jeep was tearing towards them. As it came alongside the girls, the driver stomped on the brake, bringing the vehicle to a screaming halt, spinning it round to come to a standstill before the startled girls.

"Well," April shouted at the driver. "Do you always drive around the English country lanes like a bloody maniac? You're not in America now you know."

"I'm real sorry, Ma'am," the driver said, red-faced. "But we're late getting back to base."

"Better to be late than kill someone getting there," April fired back angrily.

One of the two men sat in the back, said loudly.

"Well, bless my cotton socks, if it ain't the Land Army! We've heard a lot about you lot, like a good time don't you."

"Do we?" April asked as she stared at him.

He had a huge nose, a small mean mouth and short ginger hair.

He went on.

"Why don't you climb up here and sit between my buddy and me, we'll show you a good time." He touched himself between the legs suggestively. "Your good-looking friend can sit with Ray, our driver. You'd like that, Ray, wouldn't you, buddy," he leant over and gave the driver a prod in the back.

"Knock it off, Carl, I'm a married man," the red-faced driver said. "And I think you should stop harassing these girls." He paused, then said. "Don't draw me into your dirty little games, I think we should move on, we're late enough as it is, and it's me who'll get it in the neck for being late."

"Shut your trap, Ray, you're only the driver, and we move on when I say!" Carl snapped.

Fay stood, a terrified look on her face as April said acidly, a determined look on *her* face as she took a step nearer to the jeep.

"Tell you what, Carl, why don't you play with *yourself*, that's if it's big enough to hold in your hand, from what I've been hearing from these so-called easy little village girls, you 'big brawny Yanks' have now't to call ought down below."

She stood defiantly with her hands on her hips as the three men flushed a deep red.

Suddenly Carl made a move to get out of the jeep, but the so-far silent young G.I who had been sat alongside Carl, said pleadingly.

"No, don't, Carl, it isn't worth it."

"The boys right, Carl, it isn't," April said, a note of warning in her words. "Do yourself a favour and stay where you are."

Carl had a malevolent look on his face as he said.

"Do *myself* a favour? Lady, I'd be doing *you* a favour, we Yanks like a bit of pussy, and you English village gals will do anything for a pair of nylons, and, honey, we have plenty of those."

Fay gave a gasp of horror and moved closer to the wall.

"Would they indeed?! Well, my friend and I are not that way inclined, nylons don't bother us, the old cold tea is just as good, so, don't lump *us* with the village girls!"

"That's rubbish, honey; all the girls we've had are all alike," Carl said insultingly.

"Okay, Carl, pack in the insults and be on your way before I *do* climb up to join you, you insignificant little man, but it'll be to spread that big nose of yours all over your mush!"

Carl broke out into loud laughter.

"Hear that you, guys, this little girl is a real toughie!" He turned to April. "Think a mighty lot of yourself don't you little, Miss, I'd like to see you try."

"Alright," April said matter of factly. "Shall I come up, or will you come down?"

Carl began to look uncertain, while the driver was starting to look white-faced. The young G.I was shaking his head and mumbling.

"Oh God, no, Carl, no."

Fay, at last, found her voice and said firmly.

"If I were you, Carl, I'd stay where you are, because April here, can do what she says she can. How are you going to explain a broken nose to your friends? Tell them that a pint-sized Land Girl did it? You'd be the laughingstock of your base. You picked on the wrong one when you picked on our April here."

The driver had by now pulled himself together.

"Right, that's it, we go *now* before things get out of hand," he said firmly. As he made to drive off, he said, "would you have done it, girl?"

"Oh, yes! You bet your bottom dollar!" April said.

"We'll meet again, small fry; you bet we *will*. I won't forget you in a hurry," Carl shouted jeeringly.

"Carl, *you* are very forgettable, goodbye!"

The jeep took off, leaving behind a trail of exhaust fumes.

Fay breathed out loudly and said.

"Phew!"

April laughed uproariously as she got out between laughs.

"Those G.I's were really entertaining; I really enjoyed that little spat!"

"Enjoyed it?!" Fay said in horror.

"Yes, really, it was a great finish to the day, but I shall have to watch out for that Carl, he could be trouble."

"Really, April, you do push things to the limit. What if he had got down? What would you have done?"

"You forget, Fay, I was brought up with two rough and tumble twin brothers who taught me how to look after myself, they were boxers, and good ones. Yes, I could've handled that Carl, no bother."

Fay started to smile.

"April, you never fail to amaze me."

"Kiddo, you ain't seen nothing yet," April said happily. "Look, about two hundred yards up the road, there looks to be the lane we're looking for."

The girls quickened their steps, almost running in their eagerness, but there was no sign to tell them the name of the lane.

"We'll just have to take a chance that it *is* Cherry Tree Lane. So far, the directions that Mrs Mayfield and Norman gave us are correct," April said.

"Remember, all the road signs and street names were taken down at the start of the war so that if the enemy landed, they wouldn't know where to go," Fay said.

"There doesn't seem to be any other Lane insight, so we'd better go up this one," April replied.

"I wonder how far we've to walk from here?" Fay said as she stopped and set down her case. "We seem to have been walking for a long time."

"Just a bit further, I think I can see the spikes at the top of the iron gates over the treetops to the left. Our directions were to keep to the left," April answered.

"I do hope you're right; I've just about had enough," Fay said resignedly as she picked up her case. "My feet are killing me."

"Land Girls feet are not *supposed* to kill her," April said sarcastically.

"Well, at this moment in time, *mine* are," Fay snapped.

As the girls walked on, the fields to their right were flat and cultivated, giving the impression of stretching out for miles. The ones to their left were partly hidden by a tall hedge, which was covered in wild, pink, sweet-smelling Roses, which threw out a mild summer perfume. A small dike trickled lazily underneath the hedge as water flies flitted slowly over it, and a lark could be heard trilling his happy notes in the clear blue sky.

"There," April cried. "There are the gates, and just look at the height of them, the owners of the house don't intend anyone getting in do they. Hitler *himself* couldn't get in!"

"Yes, they give that impression don't they," Fay agreed.

Standing as high as a modern house, they were elaborately patterned and bore a coat of arms.

"The people who own this house must be important to have their own coat of arms," April said firmly. "*And* must be the Lord and Lady of the manor and parish."

"I suppose we'll be finding out soon enough, but could we please get inside, April, I'm dead on my feet, it's been a long day."

April nodded, then stepped back to look up at the house.

"It's a lovely house, Fay, warm brown brick, sorry, stone, lots of not over-large windows with nicely hung curtains, can't see any blackout blinds though."

"If you don't mind, April, I want to get inside the place, not stand admiring it," Fay moaned.

"Alright, moaning mini, but first, we've to find the side gate Mrs Mayfield told us of in her directions." She walked alongside the gates to her right. "No, nothing here, must be on the other side." She turned and walked to the left. "Yes, here it is, Fay." As she lifted the latch, she said, "by but it's heavy!" She pushed, and the gate opened with a loud un-oiled squeak. She held out her hand. "Come on, kiddo," she called to Fay.

"Thank goodness for that," Fay said.

When the girls had stepped through, April pushed the gate and closed it with a loud clang, then made sure that it had correctly closed. They turned to face the house, then gave a gasp of amazement at what was spread out before them.

"Would you look at that," April said quietly.

Smooth well-cut green lawns stretched right up to the house; these were surrounded by flower borders so well-tended that one would be forgiven for thinking that the many-coloured flowers were plastic. It was an incredible display. A long full drive led up to the house which had an extensive half-moon frontage.

"If this is really our billet, I think I've died and gone to heaven," Fay whispered. "Do you think this is the right house, April?"

"Of course it is, didn't you see the sign on the gate? It said 'Whitmore' in a fancy scroll," April snapped.

"No, I didn't," Fay snapped back.

"You never notice the important things do you, Fay, it's a good job you have me to look after you, come on, let's go and see about getting into this little palace."

As the girls set off up the long driveway, Fay said dreamily.

"I feel like Judy Garland walking up the yellow brick road."

"Only it's not yellow, is it," April laughed.

"It was a lovely film though, April, so real, you felt that you were there too, and I loved those little munchkins. It's a film that will go on forever. In the future, Judy Garland will be immortalised, and we'll be taking our Grandchildren to see it at a very modern up to date picture house."

"That's if I get as far as having Grandchildren," April said. "But look at that front door, very grand, solid oak, and a lion's head for a doorknocker, solid brass too, clean, done every day by some caring person."

"Don't you think that we should go to the back door?" Fay asked apprehensively.

"No, I rather fancy knocking with that lion's head," April said mischievously.

"Don't, let's go to the back," Fay begged.

"I'm going to knock," April said determinedly. "If anyone answers, and they should, and tell me to go to the back, then I'll go."

"Why do you always have to make things hard for yourself?" Fay asked tearfully.

"Because nothing is easy in this world, kiddo, get used to it. You may have had a namby-pamby upbringing, but you're now in the real world, with me may I add, who likes to do things the hard way. That way you're not disappointed."

She walked up the four steps that led up to the front door, Fay stepped two paces back as April took hold of the doorknocker and gave a resounding rat-a-tat-tat.

The door remained closed.

"Looks like nobody's home," April said loudly. "But there must be, I'll knock again."

"Do you think you should, April? That noise is enough to waken the dead," Fay said, twisting her hands together nervously.

"Of course I should, unless you want to stand here all night?!" April snapped.

"Have you thought that the front door may not be used at all during wartime? We should go to the back," Fay reasoned.

Ignoring Fay, April raised the knocker and banged three more times, then stood back, staring at the door, as if expecting it to open by magic, which it seemed to do. It opened suddenly and noisily, to reveal a tiny stick-thin woman, who was stood on two pencils for legs. But it was her feet that April's eyes were drawn to, they were large and broad, and as April stared in fascination, she said to herself, 'they look as if they were just plonked onto the ends of her legs on an assembly line in a factory!' With an earnest effort of will, she tore her eyes away and investigated the face that was glaring at her with ice-blue eyes, above which were bushy white eyebrows that met just above her nose. Those matched her snow-white hair which was cut short like a man's. But it was the mouth which also caught the eye. It was large with thick colourless lips, and beneath these, a giant mole sprouting two or three hairs.

Golly, if she opened that mouth, I swear she could swallow me whole! April chuckled to herself, talk about the thing from outer space, she *is* it! But I'm being unkind thinking like this, she can't help her looks, maybe she's a nice woman, we shall soon see.

April's illusion was soon shattered as the woman bellowed in a voice much too loud and piercing.

"What the devil do you think you're doing banging on the door like that?! Go around to the back!" She banged her fist on the door frame. "This door is not used by such as you, Land Girls indeed!" She said 'Land Girls as if it were a dirty word, then gave April a cold penetrating stare. "Well, what are you both waiting for?! Are you deaf? Go around to the back," she yelled.

April returned her stare with narrowed eyes, then asking in a warning voice.

"Who are you, pray tell? Don't shout at me, *and* don't bark orders at me either!" She stepped into the hallway, which brought her face to face with the woman, who said.

"Get out!"

I'm two inches bigger than this midget, which is a change for me, *I'm* usually the tot, so this should be fun!

"Step aside if you please, my friend, I would like to come in, this is our billet as I understand."

On April's words, the woman spat out in a fury.

"Don't you speak to me like that you little chit, I'll have you know I am the housekeeper here; I keep the girls in order, and as you two seem to be the two I've been told to expect, that means I keep *you two* in order too."

"Really? Well, let's start as we mean to go on shall we," April smiled.

'Oh God', the silently watching Fay thought, she's got April on the raw, now there'll be fireworks.

April pushed the woman out of the way none too gently and walked into the hall where she turned and beckoned to Fay.

"Come on, kiddo, take no notice of this woman with no name, enter the dragon's lair." As Fay made no movement, April shouted, "well, come on."

Fay moved slowly toward the door, keeping a wary eye on the woman, giving her a wide berth as she did so.

The housekeepers face had drained of what little colour it had, she turned and slammed the door closed, then said aggressively.

"Well, it hasn't taken long to get your measure, Miss! You'll regret your attitude; I can promise you."

"Will I," April said sweetly.

"Oh, yes, you will," the housekeeper answered in something like a normal voice. "I'm to be addressed as Miss Topp at all times. I demand and *get* respect from my girls."

"Really," April said with pursed lips. "I can understand the Miss bit," she said sarcastically. "But we'll have to see about the respect, in my book, respect has to be earned, then you get it back."

"I knew you were trouble the moment I clapped eyes on you," Miss Topp ground out.

"How very perceptive of you," April said. "Now if you don't mind, Miss Mopp, showing us to the kitchen, we'd like something to eat and a cup of tea, we've been travelling all day."

"My name is *Miss Topp*," the housekeeper barked out furiously.

"So sorry, *Miss Topp*, now, do the job you are paid to do and get us some food."

"You're pushing it, April," Fay whispered.

"You ain't seen nothing yet." April laughed as Miss Topp stormed angrily away, leaving the girls to follow her.

They entered a large kitchen which was light and airy, owing to the pale-yellow painted walls. A large stove stood against one wall, while taking up another, was a dark, oak welsh dresser holding fancy plates, cups and saucers to match. Cupboards ran around the other walls, these painted light brown with dark wooden handles. An extra-large wooden table stood in the middle of the floor, scrubbed almost white, with twelve chairs tucked neatly underneath.

"This is a lovely kitchen, Miss Topp, and so clean," Fay said softly.

"Oh, it speaks, does it?!" Miss Topp said sarcastically, glaring at Fay with eyes like chips of ice.

Fay blushed bright red in embarrassment.

"My friend's name is Fay," April said, quietly furious. "Don't you dare address her as *it*."

Miss Topp sighed as she folded her arms across her non-existent chest, then said to April.

"What is *your* full name?" she asked. "Although I could think of many more appropriate names that would suit you."

"Ditto," April said.

Miss Topp sniffed.

"I'm April Thornton, and I *too* could think of many more names to fit *you*, most of which I don't think you have the intelligence to appreciate, which is why you're in the lowly job of a housekeeper. Any fool can clean, cook and bash orders out." She pulled out a chair and sat down, then continued. "And before we go any further, I want no cracks about my April name. Now, food please for my friend and me." She turned to Fay. "Sit down, kiddo; don't be overawed about *Miss Mopp*." She paused, then continued. "You may as well realise, *Miss Mopp*, that I don't suffer fools gladly, we're here to work, serving King and country, we work hard, long hours, and I don't want to be coming back here at the end of a long hard day listening to your claptrap."

Miss Topp stood speechless as April went on.

"I'm prepared to call a truce, try to get on with you, if you're not agreeable so be it, but it would be in your best interests to try."

"Are you threatening me?!" Miss Topp said, warningly.

"As time goes on, you'll learn that I don't threaten, I *do*."

"Really, well, we must see what time brings."

"Yes, we shall."

"The first thing I'm going to do is report you."

"Good, I have a bit of reporting to do myself."

"You can't report me; I'm only doing my job."

"You've yet to prove that haven't you, now, I suggest you get some food on the table before my friend and I pass out from hunger."

Miss Topp chose to ignore April's remark and turned away towards the cooker.

"Oh, by the way, *Miss Mopp*, I trust that you'll be regaling us with all your house rules, I can't wait to hear *those*," April called.

Miss Topp ignored this as April continued.

"Maybe tomorrow when we're not too tired to take it all in."

Miss Topp turned around, a triumphal look on her face.

"After you've done a day's work at where you're being sent to tomorrow, you'll be lucky to have the strength to walk into here. That will shut you up I can tell you."

"I've yet to be defeated at any job that is set me," April said jauntily, giving a grin at Fay. "Isn't that right," she asked.

Fay nodded her head.

"That's right," she replied.

"Miss Thornton, let's get one thing straight, I'm the Boss here, my word is law, and I rule with a fist of iron," Miss Topp said.

"Well now, *I* would like to get one thing straight, Miss Mopp, I know a lot about fists, you see, I have twin brothers who are both boxers, good ones too, and they taught me a lot about fists and boxing."

"I'll have to watch my step I see."

"It would be advisable."

"You won't be here long; I'll do my best to have you removed."

"Dear me, giving up so soon?" April laughed.

"It's not a question of giving up."

"What *is* it a question of?"

"I don't like you; I don't want any of my girls upsetting."

"I don't intend to upset the girls, I would hope that they have a mind of their own, that is unless you have brainwashed them to fear you."

At April's words, Miss Topp stood threateningly over her, her hand raised as if to strike. April stood up and faced her, then said.

"Be my guest, it'll be the last time you hit anyone."

Fay hurried to April's side and said anxiously to Miss Topp.

"I wouldn't if I were you."

"You're not me!" she shouted at Fay.

April sat down and pulled her chair up to the table, rested her chin on her bent arms, then said.

"Miss *Mopp*, sorry, Miss Topp, something to eat and drink please." Then turning to Fay. "Sit down, kiddo; don't let her get to you, she works for the government just like us, only *we* work harder and longer."

Miss Topp clattered plates, cups and cutlery onto the table with a heavy hand, while the girls sat silently. Suddenly the kitchen door burst open to admit too healthy-looking Land Girls. On seeing the kettle on the stove about to boil, the taller of the two girls said.

"Oh good, just in time for a cuppa."

Miss Topp swung round angrily.

"What the hell are you doing rushing in like that?! You're supposed to be ladies, act like one!"

"I do apologise."

Miss Topp gave her a formidable scowl, then said ungraciously, pointing at April and Fay.

"These two are the new Land Girls, introduce yourself, but I warn you, the little red-haired one is hard to take."

"The woman's mad, take no notice," April said reassuringly.

The tall girl looked surprised at April's words as she held out her hand, saying.

"Hi, I'm Jane."

She pulled off the turban she was wearing and hung it on the chair back, then shook out her shoulder-length blonde hair.

"I'm April, and this is Fay."

Jane smiled at them with large, baby blue eyes.

"I can't tell you how welcome you are here." She rolled her eyes in Miss Topp's direction, then went on. "We've been shorthanded for a few weeks'; I thought the powers that be had forgotten all about us."

"I'm pleased to know that *someone* welcomes us here, we had a poor reception from Miss Mopp there." She pulled a face in Miss Topp's direction, then went on as if Miss Topp were not there. "We committed the cardinal sin of banging on the hallowed front door and barging through it into the hall."

Might as well tell it how it is, April thought, while Jane looked amazed at her words.

Miss Topp swung round.

"Don't bother getting to know her, Jane; Miss Thornton won't be here long."

"Your housekeeper seems not to have taken to me, but I'm hard to get rid of," April said. She turned to the other girl who had been stood silently by Jane's side. "Hello, what's your moniker love?"

This girl was just a little taller than April, but plump, with eyes set too close together, a large nose that looked too big for her face, and a small prim mouth. Pale ginger hair was sticking out of the front of her turban.

"What do you mean, what's my moniker?!" she said angrily. "I hope you're not trying to be funny."

"Why would you think that? I've only just met you," April replied, puzzled.

"Because my name really *is* Monica!" the girl snapped.

"I'm really sorry," April exclaimed. "You see, where I come from, South Yorkshire, that's a way of asking someone's name."

"It's a damn silly way if you ask me," Monica snapped.

"Maybe, but that's our way," April said firmly.

"I've put this April person in my little black book, girls," Miss Topp said bitingly to Jane and Monica.

Fay tittered as April said in amusement.

"Are we supposed to be honoured at that?"

Miss Topp glared at Fay angrily.

"I don't know what you're tittering about, lady, you're in it as well."

"Oh, shut up, Miss Topp, oh, I've got it wrong again; it's Miss Mopp isn't it!" April laughed.

Jane and Monica looked stunned at April's daring to speak to Miss Topp that way.

"April apparently thinks she is a comedian," Miss Topp commented sarcastically as she banged down a plate each in front of the girls, on which was four slices of beetroot, some wilted looking lettuce and one slice of dry bread.

April looked at it in amazement, then said.

"What's this? Surely you don't expect us to eat this after we've been travelling all day."

"That's all there is, like it or lump it," Miss Topp said, giving April an unpleasant smirk for a laugh. "You can't just stroll in here and demand food."

April stood, picked up the slice of coarse grey bread, then, with contempt in her voice, gave Miss Topp a crushing response.

"I choose to lump it."

She dropped the bread back onto the plate and looked at Miss Topp defiantly, then walking to the rubbish pail which stood by the sink, she tipped the food into it.

"There, pig muck goes to the pigs, does it not?" Then turning to Fay, she called. "Bring your plate, kiddo, yours can join mine."

Fay apprehensively did as April asked, then April dusted her hands together as if to say, 'there, a job well done!'

The other two girls stood wide-eyed without saying a word until Jane said softly.

"April Thornton, I think I like you."

Wearing a triumphant look on her face, Miss Topp placed her hands on her hips as she said.

"Well, Miss, you'll go hungry until morning."

"Oh, I don't think so," April retorted airily as she walked back to the table. She sat down, then asked Fay. "Do we still have those sandwiches the old lady put up for us this morning?"

"Yes, I think we do," Fay said, surprised.

April pushed her chair back and hurried into the hall where she picked up her suitcase, then, returning to the kitchen, she dropped it down onto the table with a loud thump.

"Get that dirty thing off my clean table!" Miss Topp yelled at the top of her voice.

"Of course it's dirty!" April retorted. "It's been all around England with me, what do you expect." She unfastened the clasps and lifted the lid. "Now for some *edible* food." She took out two well-wrapped packets and handed one to Fay. "Get those down you, kiddo; you'll feel a lot better."

"Thanks, April, I'm really going to enjoy these."

"So am I, kiddo," April replied. As she unwrapped the sandwiches, the smell of raw onion wafted around the kitchen, she breathed in deeply, then took a large bite of the teacake sandwich.

"Mmm, lovely, cheese and onion, this is what you call food, not that swill that *you* served, Miss Mopp."

April was so hungry that she ate with a careless voraciousness, while Fay ate with tiny ladylike bites.

"Look at her, eats as if she's been starved all her life!" Miss Topp said savagely.

"I apologise if my eating offends you," April answered aggressively.

Jane spoke with authority to Miss Topp.

"Leave the girl alone; let her get on with her food."

Miss Topp stared at her frostily.

"Just who do you think *you* are talking to?!" she asked.

Jane shrugged her shoulders.

"Apparently, someone named 'Miss Mopp'," she said.

Miss Topp's eyes narrowed.

"If you think you can behave like this stupid Miss Thornton, don't try it."

Jane gave her a contemptuous look with dislike in her eyes, and Miss Topp stormed out of the kitchen.

Jane sat down heavily onto a chair.

"Well," she said.

"You might well say that," Monica piped up, then fell silent as April glared at her.

"If I hadn't seen with my own eyes and heard with my own ears the way you stood up to Miss Topp, I wouldn't have believed it. But, April, she's not the kind of woman you make an enemy of, she can be real nasty, so watch your back, it's best to follow her rules," Jane said, anxiously.

April leant forward.

"Thanks for the advice, Jane, but I don't need it. I had Topp weighed up the moment I set eyes on her, and that gorilla mouth of hers is a clever one. But my, she *is* ugly isn't she!"

Monica, who had not sat down, stepped forward.

"You shouldn't talk about Miss Topp like that, she can't help her looks, and besides, your no oil painting yourself, are you?!"

"We have a Miss Topp fan here I see," April laughed.

Monica nodded her head.

"I happen to get on with Miss Topp."

"That's interesting," April said softly.

"And I'll thank you to stop calling her Miss Mopp."

April grinned.

"I could call her a lot worse; you should hear me when I really get going."

Monica looked up at the ceiling.

"I'll pass on that thank you."

"It seems to me that you and Miss Mopp are tarred with the same brush," April said with narrowed eyes.

Jane slowly nodded her head in agreement with April.

"I don't know what you're implying, and I don't like you, but I think you've been very rude to Miss Topp."

"Ha, I see that you're a do-gooder, Monica, but as the great Al Jolson said, you ain't seen nothing yet." April flapped her hand at Monica as if swatting away a fly, then said. "Miss Mopp's favourite are you, Monica? Her talebearer?"

Monica flushed a deep scarlet and hurried out of the kitchen.

Jane breathed a sigh of relief.

"Thank goodness she's gone! Now I can tell you about the rules around here, and there's lots. You were right about Monica, watch what you say in front of her, she *is* a tittle-tattle and tells Miss Mopp everything," she broke off as she laughed, then continued. "You've got *me* calling her Miss Mopp; I must say that it suits her! But to go on, it didn't take us long to work out that Monica gets the best and easiest jobs at the best farms."

"Haven't you said anything or complained?" April interrupted.

"No point, it wouldn't get us anywhere."

"We'll have to change that," April said.

"Like I said, April, no point, we had a girl who tried, but she didn't last long, somehow Miss Topp got rid of her."

"How did she do that?" April asked, puzzled.

"We never found out."

"Sounds to me as if she has friends in high places," Fay said.

"Maybe, but to go on, we have a cook, Mrs Wilkinson, we call her Wilkie, she's not a bad old stick. When there's food to cook, she cooks it, and does some cleaning. She comes in five days a week for a few hours."

"Who's in charge of the food?" Fay asked.

"Miss Topp, she doles it out as she sees fit."

"From what I've seen of Miss Topp, she'll guard it like the crown jewels," Fay said.

"Do you get what you're supposed to get, like sugar and tea, for instance?" April questioned.

Jane thought for a moment.

"We hardly see any sugar or tea, in fact, not much of anything; we're always at work when the stores are delivered."

"It's your right to see your own rations; it's paid for out of your wages," April said furiously. "I smell a rat here!"

"Meat is non-existent; we almost live on beetroot sandwiches, that's our daily pack up." Jane went on. "If it weren't for the farmers wives feeding us, we'd be walking around like skeletons."

"What about breakfast?" Fay asked, hopefully.

"From here, just a cup of tea, we get a bit of breakfast from the farm we go to," Jane replied. "It's better really to be able to live in on the farms rather than a hostel. I'm afraid this one may give other hostels a bad name."

"I'm interested in the rules," April said. "Can we get back to them?"

"Yes, of course," Jane said. "I must warn you that Miss T is very cantankerous in the mornings, she sees that we almost throw our cups of tea down us, if you can call it tea. It's too weak to come out of the pot. She insists we make our beds before we go to work, and tidy our rooms, which she inspects, if they're not up to her standards she soon lets you know about it and gives you a good telling off. We're expected to thoroughly clean our room once a week in our off-duty time, she can't stand untidiness. No loud singing, noise or drinking is allowed. Family can visit on certain days, with a time limit, they can't be fed here, they must bring their own food, which is only fair, I suppose. If you don't stick to her rules, she has ways of making you suffer, as you'll soon find out."

"Anything else?" Fay asked apprehensively.

"Oh yes, no boyfriends to be allowed inside, unless given permission by her."

"I wouldn't *want* any boyfriend of mine to meet her; he'd get the shock of his life!" April laughed.

"Don't whatever you do slide down the bannister, she'd go mad, it's her pride and joy, polishes it every day. Although I must admit, we have one at home which I slid down every day, so the one here is *most* tempting!"

"We shall remember, won't we, Fay, or at least, I'll *try* to. Sometimes I may forget," April said, smiling mischievously.

"See what I've to put up with, Jane," Fay said in exasperation.

"Sometimes *we* forget all the rules, we're so tired after a day's work, we fall into bed and are asleep as soon as our heads touch the pillows. Monica and I are on a cattle farm this week to help with milking, but I don't enjoy it as I'm nervous deep down about cows. I've been told that they like to be sung to, but I've a voice like a corncrake! One of the girls told her that I didn't like milking, what did she do, Miss Topp that is, sent me out of spite, you should've seen the malicious look on her face."

"Hmm, we'll have to do something about Miss Topp; she has no personality at all and has a Jekyll and Hyde character I shouldn't wonder," April said musingly.

"What do you do on your time off?" Fay asked.

"We get little of that now summer's here. Not much entertainment in the village, there's a pub, a small park you can wander about in, and on the weekend the village hop, or dance, whichever you want to call it. There's a G.I base about three miles away, they come to the dance, all the ones I've met treat you like a lady, one asked me to dance in the jitterbug contest with him, I did, and we won! I got four pairs of nylons which are like gold to me."

"How nice," Fay said, a gleam in her eye as she clasped her hands together in delight. "Can we go to the next one with you?" she asked.

"Of course you can," Jane replied.

"We will go, won't we, April?"

"You bet we will, it's been a few weeks' since I did the jitterbug, but let's forget about dancing for now, I'm ready to hit the sack. Could you show us to our room please, Jane? First though, how do we find out about work in the morning? Miss Mopp wasn't very forthcoming was she."

"Follow me, I'll show you," Jane said, striding briskly away and heading for the hall. "The notice board is fixed to the wall; all details about work are listed on it."

As the three girls entered the large hall, Fay stopped abruptly, bringing the other two girls to a sudden halt.

"I say, look at this, how lovely!" she exclaimed as she looked up at the ceiling.

It was a work of art, having elaborate featured angels, cherubs wearing angelic smiles, roman maidens semi-naked, and a small boy firing into space a wicked-looking pointed arrow. All painted gold with a deep frieze in pale blue surrounding them.

"Yes, it *is* lovely; I have to agree with you," April said.

"Look at all the doors," Fay went on. "There's lots of rooms, Jane, do we use them all?"

"No, I'm afraid not, most of them are locked up, we have two sitting rooms, a reading room where we write our letters, and we have use of the library room. It's a rich family who owns the house, they only agreed to let the government use part of it you see, that's why most of the rooms are locked up, and this is only half of the house. When you go upstairs, you'll see on the first landing that the doorway on your left is bricked up, the other side of that is the rest of the house."

"I don't blame the family for doing that, if I owned a beautiful home like this, I'd protect it too. Where are the family by the way?" April asked.

"Do you know, I don't really know, somewhere abroad, out of England I expect," Jane replied.

April continued looking around her: the cold, very pale green painted walls covered with expensive landscape oil paintings, the mosaic-tiled black and green floor, the huge crystal chandelier which hung from the ceiling. Then, her eyes were drawn to the far wall, hung there was a massive portrait of an extremely handsome man.

"Gosh, look at him!" she cried. "He was a looker! Who is he, Jane?" she asked.

"Lord Langdown, one of the past owners of the house, died young in a riding accident. One of our girls claims to be psychic, and says that she's seen his ghost, but I don't believe in that kind of stuff." Jane shook her head.

"There's more in this world than man ever dreamed of," April said reproachfully.

"Yes, I agree with that," Fay said softly as Jane ran her finger down a list of girls names and work details.

"Here you are, bottom of the list obviously as you're new, there's one more girl to come tomorrow. By the way, you three will be sharing a bedroom. Fay, you're at Bellows Farm, you too, April, which is about three miles from here, not too bad for your first day. If Miss Topp had met you before she put the list up, she would've sent you on a ten-mile hike."

"No doubt she would. How do we get to this Bellows Farm?" April asked.

"We use bikes for short journeys, longer ones, the farm's wagons, or lorries pick us up. We have to sit in the back which isn't very pleasant as they smell awful, no one has time to clean them out. Uncomfortable but it can't be helped," Jane pulled a face, "I think they like to see us moaning to each other, we're not well-liked you know," she finished.

"Yes, we know," April smiled. "You see, Jane, the men know we do a good job but are not man enough to admit it, and their wife's think we're going to run off with their men. From what I've seen of the men, I'd be running *from* them, not *with* them!"

"What time do we have to be up?" Fay asked.

"Five o'clock, off at five-thirty, you haven't far to go; otherwise it would be earlier," Jane said, regretfully.

"Why did I join the blooming Land Army?!" April moaned.

"What is Bellows Farm like?" Fay asked. "Have any of you worked there?"

"Connie and Binnie did a couple of weeks', said it wasn't too bad, but had to insist on taking break times, so watch that," Jane said, warningly.

"When do we get to meet the other girls?" Fay asked.

"Now, there's a question, we're never all in together, so it'll be a lucky dip. We're all nice girls, except for a couple, but you, April will pick them out straight away."

"I know without a doubt that one of them is Monica," she pulled a face. "I don't like her, can't stand talebearers, so I've got her measure, like Miss Mopp. Now, Jane, lead on, let's see this bedroom of ours. How many bedrooms are they?"

"Six, all large, three girls to four of them, one for Miss Topp made into a bed-sitting room, one for the cook, also a bed-sitting room.

As the girls trooped across the hall, a loud shout of, "Hello, anyone home?" came from the kitchen.

"Well, speak of the devil, it sounds like this is Connie and Binnie, they like to work together as I expect you too will also."

As they entered the kitchen, a tall, sturdy girl was taking off her boots, she looked up inquiringly.

"Hi, Jane, how are things? New girls hey, Topps not around I see. Hello, girls, what's your name? I'm Binnie, they tell me I never stop chattering, talk in my sleep even. I'm glad this day is over! That bloody farmer wants strangling, might do it tomorrow if he calls me 'Hi you' once more, and his wife is as bad, that's if she *is* his wife or a bit on the side, she can't make a decent cup of tea can she, Connie?"

Connie shook her head.

"Nope," she replied.

She shook her head so emphatically that her brightly coloured turban fell, covering her eyes, she pushed it back then introduced herself.

"Excuse me, hello; I'm Connie, pleased to meet you."

"Hello, I'm April, this is Fay," April said as she looked admiringly at the willow shaped figure of Connie, who had large violet-coloured eyes, set in a heart-shaped face. It was a beautiful face with a heart-warming smile.

"Have you just arrived?" she asked in a voice as pure as crystal.

"Yes, a couple of hours ago, although we had quite a job finding it," Fay answered. "But it's a lovely house, isn't it. Aren't we lucky to be able to call it our billet!"

"Yes, we are," Connie said as she pulled out a chair and sat down. "Rather we had it than the G.I's; they would've wrecked it in no time."

"Oh, that would've been awful!" Fay cried. "At least we girls respect where we live."

"Met our Miss Topp, have you?" Connie asked grimly.

"I should say they have," Jane said. "April and Miss Topp had a real old ding-dong; things are going to get very entertaining around here. Miss Topp has met her match in April. I can assure you."

"Don't be too sure about that," Connie said seriously, then pointed at April. "You may be tough, but she's the housekeeper from hell sometimes, so you'd be well advised to try and get along with her."

"Hmm, we'll see. I don't let myself get pushed around by anyone," April said firmly.

"You do right; I wish I were so brave," Connie said, sadly.

"Time to get moving, come on, April and Fay, I'll take you to your room," Jane said.

"Nice to have met you both," April said to Connie and Binnie as she left the kitchen. "We'll have a good natter later."

"I second that," Fay called over her shoulder.

Connie and Binnie, now alone in the kitchen, looked at one another in silence for a moment.

"I think," Connie began in anticipation. "That we're going to have some fun around here at last, we seem to have someone who's going to stand her ground with Topp."

"It's about time," Binnie said loudly.

"Really, we should be ashamed," Connie went on, "taking all that vicious sarcasm from Topp as long as we have, not one of us daring to say a word back to her, and her knowing that we wouldn't. Well, I think she's about to get her comeuppance. What a show it'll be."

"I know," Binnie said, rubbing her hands together gleefully.

"Don't say anything to the other girls, let's surprise them," Connie said, mischievously.

"Okay, I can't wait to see the looks on their faces!" Binnie answered with a laugh.

Meanwhile, Jane, Fay and April were making their way up the wide, dark blue carpeted staircase. At the top, a large window let in the evening sunset, which threw a vibrant red glow across the landing, which had seven doors leading off it. Stood against one wall between two of the doors was a magnificent highly polished mahogany dresser, its reddish-brown wood brought to life by the polishing it had received. A large blue patterned china dish stood on top.

"Say what you like about Miss Topp, but she keeps everything sparkling clean," Fay remarked.

"Yes, you have to give her that," Jane replied as she pushed open the door nearest to them. "This is the girls bathroom, we take turns using this, to wash I mean, not using the lavatory, we have rules about that which I'll explain later. The people who own the house didn't use this as it was for the staff only." She closed the door. "The other rooms are ours, Miss Topp's and the cooks."

"The cook lives in, does she?" Fay asked.

"Most of the time," Jane replied. "She has a daughter in the village and sometimes stays with her on weekends, if she does, it's cold meals for us."

April pulled a face.

"So, what's new, we're used to cold meals."

Jane opened the door opposite the bathroom.

"This," she said with a flourish, giving a dramatic wave of her hand, "is your abode, I hope you'll be comfortable, we are, the beds are okay, better than some places we stay in." She allowed April and Fay to step in front of her. "Not bad, is it?" she asked.

It was a large room, its walls painted a pale primrose, except the one facing them which had wallpaper patterned with large pink roses, this surrounded a small back iron fireplace. Rose patterned curtains hung at the little window frame facing them, this also had a blackout blind, which spoiled the effect. There were three single beds covered with pink counterpanes, three two-drawer chests of drawers, and a bedside cabinet stood by each of the three beds.

"It's set out like an army barracks, but we can soon change things around," April said.

"Not tonight, I hope," Fay said anxiously. "Those beds look very inviting, and I'm exhausted."

"Of course not tonight, kiddo, don't panic, I'm tired too." She turned to Jane and gave her a beaming smile. "Thanks, Jane, the room's fine, very comfortable, and thanks for your help, we'll see you in the morning. One more thing, where are the bikes kept? We'll need one in the morning."

"Round the back of the house, bottom of the garden in the shed. Goodnight both of you, sleep tight, mind the bugs don't bite, although there are none of those here, Miss Topp would have a fit if there were. You may hear the other girls coming up, but they do try to do it quietly."

"I won't hear them; I'll be asleep as soon as my head hits the pillow," Fay said, giving a loud yawn.

April nodded her head.

"Me too."

As Jane closed the door quietly behind her, she thought, 'two nice girls, but April could mean a peck of trouble, better to give her the benefit of the doubt.'

Downstairs in the kitchen, Binnie and Connie had been cornered by Miss Topp, who began.

"I take it that you've met the new girls."

Connie sighed and put a firm expression on her face.

"We have," she replied.

"That April person is a truly terrible girl, she started giving me lip as soon as she put her foot over the threshold, she won't last long here," Miss Topp said promisingly.

"Really?" Connie replied.

"That type always ends up the same way, she's cheap and common," Miss Topp said.

"I don't think that's a nice way to speak of anyone, I liked April, she has her head screwed on the right way," Connie said angrily.

"She's got you on her side already I see, and her not here two minutes."

"I like to judge people for myself," Connie said, tolerantly.

Miss Topp shook her head.

"You're easily taken in, Connie," Miss Topp sniffed. "Girls like you always are."

"Girls like me?" Connie said politely, raising her eyebrows inquiringly. "What do you mean?"

"I mean that you're gullible. I take it you know what gullible means?"

"Of course I do," Connie retorted.

Binnie smiled to herself, 'if only Miss Topp knew about Connie', who gave Miss Topp a condescending look.

"If you don't mind, I shall take my gullible self to bed." She turned to Binnie. "Are you coming?" she asked.

"Yes, I am," Binnie replied.

Connie made to walk out of the kitchen, then turned back to look at Miss Topp, saying as she did so.

"We could all take a few lessons from April, I for one shall be."

She paused expressively, expecting Miss Topp to say something. She was not disappointed, and Miss Topp smiled maliciously as she spoke.

"I should think twice if I were you, I think this April is the type to go snooping around, others tried that and got nowhere."

"Have they not," Connie said softly, looking at Miss Topp scornfully. "People who snoop around, as you put it, usually have something to snoop around *for*." She paused. "*You* must have if you fear April will do that."

Miss Topp's eyes opened wide, she sighed, then said.

"You girls live in a dream world, I've nothing to hide, you see too many rubbish films. Go on, take yourselves off to bed," she waved her hand, dismissively.

As the two girls climbed the stairs, Binnie said.

"That woman, she's getting on my nerves, maybe we should put in for a transfer?"

"No, we don't want a transfer, not now; things are going to be changing around here."

"She did sound nervous though, didn't she?"

"Yes, she did, it makes you wonder if she *has* anything to hide."
"What if she's a German spy?"
"If she was, how would we find out?"
"There are ways and means."
"We shall watch her closely."
"How exciting!"
"If she knows, she may shoot us."
"She wouldn't know how to fire a gun."
"How do you know?"
"Her type, I wouldn't put anything past her."
"*I* know how to shoot."
"Do you?!"
"Yes, my Dad taught me."
"Really?"
"He said that I was pretty good."
"Really."
"I used to enjoy it, noisy though."
"You didn't shoot any wildlife, did you?"
"No, of course not."
"What did you shoot?"
"Tin cans, empty bottles."
"I'm impressed."
"If there *is* anything to find out, I'm sure April will find it."
"Do you really think so?"
"Yes, I do, I also think April is a good judge of character, we must listen to her." Connie looked encouragingly at Binnie. "She's going to become our leader, which will be no bad thing, she'll have us standing up to Miss Topp, you mark my words." She nodded her head and repeated. "You mark my words."

* * *

In their bedroom, at last, both April and Fay gave a sigh of relief as they sank down onto one of the beds.

April patted the mattress.

"Seems comfortable enough, although I'm so tired I could sleep on a clothesline."

"Yes, so could I," Fay answered as she looked around her. "Oh, look, April." She pointed to the corner of the room. "Look behind you, there's a curtain pulled across, concealing something I'll be bound."

"I didn't notice it, kiddo, let's have a look."

April strode across the room and pulled back the curtain which revealed a marble top unit, on top of which stood a large china bowl decorated with a blue china willow pattern. By its side stood a tall jug to match, which was filled to the brim with cold clear water.

"This is where we're expected to wash in the mornings I take it, I wonder who lugs up and empties this lot?" April said.

"Maybe we are?" Fay said dubiously with a frown on her face. "One of the girls will fill us in, I'm sure."

"No problem about emptying the bowl, we just sling it down the lavatory across the landing, although it'll be heavy," April said.

"Yes, we can take turns at doing that," Fay answered as she stuck her fingers in the jug of water. "Oh, that's freezing!" she cried.

"We'll be scurrying around like ants in the mornings," April grumbled. "And have you thought about the lavatory, it must be first there, use it, then get out of the way, charming, I'm sure."

Fay shrugged her shoulders, then began to pull off her boots, when off, she gave a sigh of relief, then tugged off her heavy woollen socks.

"Why do we have to wear the regulation Land Army socks? They're much too warm in this weather; would anyone know if we wore our own?"

"Better stick to the rules," April replied.

"Blinking stupid rules. Now, I'm going to get a good strip wash down, after all that travelling today I feel grubby. I'll sleep better for it," Fay said positively.

"If that water is as cold as you say, it'll invigorate you, then you won't sleep at all," April exclaimed. "And, to go back to the lavatory problem, Jane said that there was an outside loo, in other words, a flushing lavatory."

"No, you've got that wrong, April, the flushing one is down the hall. It's an old primitive one that's outside," Fay corrected.

"Well, it isn't so bad is it, three lavatories between twelve of us, fourteen counting Topp and the cook. One would hope that somehow Miss Topp would get flushed down one of them, headfirst," April said with dry humour.

"April don't be awful," Fay said with a grin.

"Awful nothing," April said gaily. "Now, I'm off, get on with your wash, you have ten minutes."

She slung her case onto the bed, opened it and took out a toilet bag, nightgown and a pair of fur-lined slippers. She held the slippers in the air, waved them at Fay and cried.

"A Christmas present from Mam."

"Posh," Fay said. "Now go, let me get on."

As April left the room, she thought, 'so far so good, the next hurdle would be meeting the other girls, and by the sound of it, some of them are clumping up the stairs now, I'll wait and introduce myself, it would be the polite thing to do.'

The first girl that came into sight was of medium height, she held her turban in her hand, and it looked as if her deep brown hair had been recently permed as it was a complete mass of frizz. It stood up around her head as if she had received an electric shock. Her face was plain, and would not be noticed except for her hair, but she wore a friendly look as she saw April.

"Well, hello," she said. "Who are you?"

"I'm April, one of the new girls."

"Ah, an uncommon name like mine, I'm Belinda," she said in a strong Scottish accent. "And, you may as well know from the start, that I don't like abbreviations, I hate them, I'm not Bell or Linda, I am Belinda."

"You do right to insist on your correct name. Belinda is a lovely name, rich sounding, it rolls off the tongue. I've never met a Belinda before," April said, surprised at Belinda's outspokenness.

"Thank you very much, April, as you can tell from my accent, I'm a Scott."

"Oh, beautiful Scotland, what part are you from?" April asked.

"Oban, it's a base for the ferries that go to Mull, Iona and other islands, but Oban itself is a tourist holiday spot. I've been to most of the islands as my Dad's a member of staff on one of the largest ferries. When I was a kid, I was well travelled." She said this proudly as she nodded her head. "Yes, I was so lucky, but now of course with the war, everything is at a standstill, but, enough of that." She took the arm of the girl who had been stood by her side, quietly listening to the conversation. "This," she said, "is Anita."

While talking to Belinda, April had not looked at the other girl, now as she did; she stared at her with pity. Anita stared steadily back at her, but disdainfully, she shrugged her shoulders, then said bitterly.

"People often stare at me in shock and pity the first time they see me, but soon get over it, they learn to live with it just as I have. I have this face for life you see, so I've no other choice. I loved horse riding, and one day my horse suddenly went mad, threw me, and trampled all over me. As you can see, he left the imprint of his hoof on my face, along with two broken arms, broken ribs, ruptured spleen, abdominal injuries, and oh, a broken nose. The doctors healed me, but no one in the world can give me a new face. I wanted to die, really wanted to die, but I must have something inside that wanted me to live."

As Anita spoke on bitterly, April looked at her face, part of the hoof print stood out in sharp relief on the left side of her face, the right bore a long-jagged scar, purple, where the marks of the stitches could be seen, while along the length of her forehead, a livid white scar stood out.

"We later found out that Spike, my horse, had stinging nettles put under his saddle, which *would* send any horse-mad, which it did. So, you see, Spike lived up to his name, he well and truly spiked me."

"What a terrible thing to do!" April cried, horrified. "Did you find out who put the nettles there?"

"No, there was an intensive police inquiry, but no one could be found, no one knew anything. So, here I am in the Land Army, hidden away in the country, hiding from the world. What I will do when the war's over, I shall have to think about."

"What about your family, do you have one?" April asked, curiously.

"Oh yes, I have one of sorts, a Stepmother who couldn't care less if she never saw me again, a Father who allows her to henpeck him, and a brother who's in the African jungle trying to convert the natives into Christians. No one has seen him for years; fortunately, I have money of my own left to me by my Mother, so I'm independent. When this war's over, I shall take myself off to some godforsaken spot and wallow in my own misery."

"I never judge a book by its cover, Anita; it's what's inside a person that counts," April said softly.

"You're the minority, but as I said, I've learned to live with it," Anita replied.

"On that note, we must toddle off to bed; we've to be up at five in the morning," Belinda said, giving Anita a push towards the bedrooms.

"Goodnight, April, nice to have met you, we like you, don't we, Anita."

Anita nodded.

"You're a good listener, April, thanks."

"No thanks needed, see you tomorrow."

7

The next morning found the girls cycling happily down the lane, which led to the main road. The sun had already begun to throw its heat down out of a brilliant blue sky, heralding a beautiful day to come. Sparkling cobwebs laced the hedges, gently swaying in the soft breeze, the early morning dew sparkling and glittering as it clung on to natures wonder. Bob-tailed rabbits raced around fields having a game with themselves, in and out among the grouse and pheasants that were grubbing in the fresh dew grass in the hope of finding breakfast.

"Tell you what," Fay called out. "I'll race you to the church."

"Not a good idea," April called back. "We can't go speeding through the village, we'll get arrested."

"Nonsense, there's no one around at this time of the morning." She paused. "Come on, ready, steady, go!" Fay shouted at the top of her voice as she set off, peddling briskly.

'Oh well, here goes', April thought as she set off in pursuit. 'Oh, I love this, it's like we have the world all to ourselves, I could go on forever, and I'm gaining on Fay!' Then, she suddenly realised that Fay was slowing down, 'the main road must be coming up, so after all, I *wasn't* gaining on her.'

As she came alongside Fay, who was checking both sides of the road for traffic, which was clear, April called.

"Alright, kiddo, I'm off." She began to peddle, then called over her shoulder. "See you at the church." She took tight hold of the handlebars with one hand, and with the other, gave a backwards wave.

"That's cheating; you should've waited for me!" Fay called, angrily.

April was out of earshot; her thoughts were busy. This took her back to when she used to ride with her brothers, pell-mell down country lanes around the pit village, often falling off, ending up with grazed knees, cut elbows and a torn dress. Sometimes she would beat her brothers and wonder if they let her win out of kindness. They used to tell her 'never let anyone beat you April, go all out to win, and you will.' They had taught her how to mend a wheel and change a tyre. Her Mam always used to say, 'our April should've been a lad.' One day she had bust her nose and gone home covered in blood, Mam had nearly passed out, but the next day her brothers had her back on the bike.

She glanced behind her and saw Fay was only a short distance behind her, so she picked up speed, as she did so, the breeze that had been gentle a moment ago, blew strongly into her face, lifting her turban almost off. She had an uplifting exhilarating feeling and peddled faster as she came to the village, zoomed past the church and saw the bridge looming up. She slowed down and dismounted, leant the bike against the wall and looked over at the river.

It was quite shallow and flowing lazily over the glistening white stones which lay on its bed. Green trees ran down to its bank and dipped their branches into the water.

Fay pulled up alongside her.

"Look at this," April said softly, pulling her to the wall. "It's lovely. Sometime on our day off we'll come and walk beside the river."

Fay was silent.

"It's an enchanting spot," April went on. "Maybe secret fairy dells are hidden amongst its banks, with fairy rings and the little people dancing to fairy music."

With a queer look on her face, Fay said.

"Don't be silly."

April stared at her, then asked.

"Why are you looking like that?"

"Never mind!" Fay snapped. "Let's get on; we don't want to be late on our first day do we." She climbed back onto her bike and peddled off, leaving April to follow.

'Well, it's true what they say, there's now't as queer as folk', April thought musingly as she followed Fay.

They rode in silence for a few moments until Fay slowed down and called.

"Here it is." She pointed to a large hand-painted sign that read 'Bellows Farm' in bold white letters. "Thank goodness," she said. "We've come a good three miles I should say."

"More like four," April answered.

They followed a well-worn track that led up to sprawling barns and the farmhouse. The loud bellowing of cows waiting to be milked came to their ears, along with a cockerel crowing and the clucking and honking of geese and ducks.

"Gosh, this is a heck of a noise first thing in the morning," April called to Fay as both girls got off their bikes and pushed them into the yard. "Better knock on the door and let someone know that we're here."

Suddenly, a large honking gander with a wicked gleam in his eye made a beeline for April and pecked her hard on her leg.

"Get away you nasty bugger!" she shouted as she swung her bike and knocked it over onto its back, its legs kicking in the air. "Go and attack someone else!"

The farmhouse door swung open to reveal a tall, heavy built woman, regarding them in some amusement.

"Hello," she called. "You did right to boot Freddy, he does that to all newcomers, don't be afraid of him, he'll be alright with you now."

"I hope so, that came right out of the blue," April said, then. "I'm April, and this is Fay, as you can see, we're your Land Girls, I do hope we're not late, we've biked it here and it was much further than we were led to believe."

"No, you're not late. I'm Mrs Bellows, and we're glad to have you, we really need your help, but come on in, I have some breakfast for you. I don't suppose you've had anything have you?"

"No," both girls said together as they followed Mrs Bellows into a large roomy kitchen.

The smell of frying bacon wafted towards them from the extensive kitchen range at the far end of the room, which made both girls mouths water. They looked at each other as if to say, please let her offer us some of that delicious bacon.

As if Mrs Bellows had read their thoughts, she said.

"Sit yourselves down while I make some bacon sarnies, I'm sure that you're both very hungry."

"Starving," April said loudly as Mrs Bellows took a sizeable brown teapot from the range and poured two mugs of tea. She pushed one to each of the girls, saying as she did so.

"Help yourselves to sugar and milk." As she set about making bacon sandwiches, she went on talking. "As I said, it's good to have some help at last, we've been without for three weeks', we lost our two good workers, a brother and sister, Paul, and Pauline Winterbottom. Paul went into the Navy, and Pauline into the A.T.A, so we're left with three young lads from the village, good workers, but they can't do everything that needs doing around here, you know what it's like on a working farm don't you. I can't help as much as I'd like to as I've my hands full indoors. Mr Bellows will be waiting for you in the milking shed; he's a hard taskmaster, but a fair one. He does sometimes live up to his name, but his bark is worse than his bite. He misses our kids a lot."

"How many do you have?" Fay asked.

"Five, two in the R.A.F, one in the navy and two girls are nursing the wounded in a military hospice, so we don't get to see very much of them," Mrs Bellows said sadly.

"Nursing is a worthwhile profession," April said softly. "But I couldn't do it."

"The Land Army is a good, worthwhile job, the country couldn't do without you girls, you're needed to feed the nation, you serve beneath the flag like all the other forces, and don't let anyone tell you any different."

"Now, that's a lovely thing to say," Fay said proudly.

"It's true. Now here you are, get this lot down you," Mrs Bellows said as she set a plate piled with sandwiches in front of the girls.

"You bet we will," April said gleefully, taking a sandwich and a large bite. "Oh, lovely!" she said happily.

"I've died and gone to heaven," Fay mumbled between bites.

There was silence in the kitchen as the girls made short work of the sandwiches, with Mrs Bellows stood at the sink peeling potatoes.

April stood, patted her stomach and said.

"I feel better now, thanks, Mrs Bellows."

"Yes, me too," Fay said as she pulled her turban straight. "We'll do a good days work now."

"You'll see me at twelve o'clock with a bit of lunch for you," Mrs Bellows said with a smile. "No hot drink though, only cold."

"That'll be great; we'll look forward to it," April said in surprise. "But now we'd better be off and find Mr Bellows."

"Go to the large shed straight in front of you, the cowshed, he wants you to milk," Mrs Bellows said. "See you both later."

As the girls walked across the yard, Fay said.

"What a nice woman isn't she, I think we've have fallen on our feet here, April, don't you?"

"Don't count your chickens, we've to make the acquaintance of her husband yet, and she did warn us that his bark is worse than his bite. Anyhow, we can milk, and it sounds as if that's going to be our first job, which I'm happy with."

Suddenly, a loud wolf whistle came from behind them.

"Don't look round," April said commandingly as she pushed the shed door open and walked quickly through, Fay following, when suddenly a large male arm stretched past her to hold open the door, and a voice said.

"Okay, I've got it, love."

Fay glanced over her shoulder and said.

"Thanks."

In front of them stood a middle-aged man, tall, wearing a dirty flat cap and horn-rimmed glasses. He sported a large grey moustache with pointed ends, which, April thought, he must be proud of.

There were no polite introductions as he bellowed.

"I see you've all arrived en-mass."

April had not seen the two boys who had followed Fay in.

"What a bloody time I've had, the cows wouldn't come in this morning, just stood huddled under the hedge by the stream, I swore and cussed at them until I saw the reason why. One of the carves had got stuck in the stream sideways on, I managed to get it out by brute force." He came to a halt, then pointed at the girls. "Come on, let's be having you then, what's your names?"

"I'm April, this is Fay," April said shortly.

Then waving his arm over his head, he shouted.

"Come on lads; let's be having you an all."

Two young men stepped past the girls.

"Yes, Boss, shall we get cracking then, are these girls with us on milking?"

"Yes, they are," he replied. He narrowed his eyes as he looked at the girls, then said brusquely. "You can milk, I hope?"

"Of course we can," April snapped. "None better."

"We'll see about that," he said, smiling smugly. "You know about taking the foremilk first?"

"Of course," April said, nodding her head.

"And about harmful bacteria?"

"Yes."

He looked at Fay.

"You an all?"

Fay nodded her head.

April looked around the cowshed; it was spotless, airy and light, with white glazed tiles halfway up each wall. Washed often April noticed, with a hosepipe. The other farm they had just left did not have tiled walls, but walls which had to be lime-washed every six months according to regulations. She saw that the cow stalls here were correctly placed back-to-back with a very wide passage so that carts could get through to collect the manure. When they had finished milking, there would be a big scrubbing down.

"Hold out your hands," the farmer asked. He took a close look. "Hmm, clean I see, also your nails, I'm very particular about hands." He pointed to where smocks and caps hung on nails hammered into the wall near the window. "Get your gear on and get cracking. These lads are Barry and Dennis, they'll look after you, they know their job and are good workers. My lad and lass worked with us but have now joined up, you won't be as good as them, but I can live in hope."

"Well, thank you for your touching faith in us, Mr Bellows," April said sarcastically.

He raised his bushy eyebrows at her remark.

"You're one of them are you, titch, a bit gobby, one of those who think that they're as good as a man," he laughed loudly.

"I am, we all *are* in the Land Army; otherwise, you wouldn't want our help would you," April said with a smirk plastered all over her face. "Well, would you?!" she demanded.

The farmer chose to ignore her question and said.

"Get on with it," and stamped out of the shed.

The tall, thin lad, who had wavy fair hair falling into his eyes, bent down and tugged his wellingtons more firmly onto his feet.

"I'm Barry, and we'd better get started, listen to the buggers crying out to be milked." He swept his arm along the two sets of stalls.

"Aye, that's right, we better had," the other lad agreed, who was just as tall as Barry, but heavily built with a short crew cut and brilliant blue eyes. "I'm Dennis by the way, pleased to meet you, girls; we certainly need your help, no matter *how* poor."

"You'll find out we're as good as yourselves," Fay said indignantly.

The four put on the white milking overalls and caps to cover their hair, Barry having trouble to fit his cap over his mop of thick curls.

"I hate this bloody silly cap, I'd leave it off, but if I did, the Boss would catch me out."

"Get your hair cut, then you wouldn't have trouble with it," April said.

"No fear, my hairs my pride and joy, and nobody's getting near it!" he said abruptly as he pulled off the cap and tried to flatten his hair with both hands.

"If you went into the army or any of the forces, they'd soon lop it off," April said, enjoying the little spat.

"No fear of that," Dennis said determinedly. "I won't be joining up, and they can't call *me* up, farmworkers are exempt."

"So they are, end of story," April said disgustingly. "Now, where do you start?"

"You work with me on the left, start at the top, and I'll start at the bottom. Dennis will work on the right side with Fay. It should work out ten each." He handed April a clean shining bucket. "Here you are."

"What about a stool?" she asked.

"You'll find those down at the end where you're starting, bring me one would you?" Barry asked.

"Nope," April said firmly. "Get your own, it means me walking up and back again, might as well start as we mean to go on."

Barry grunted and stamped off to the bottom of the shed, April following with a grin on her face.

She put the bucket under the cow's udders, sat on her small three-legged stool, flexed her fingers then firmly pulled on the cow's teats, taking the foremilk first into a small can; then commencing to the actual milking, which hit the bucket with a loud ping.

She liked milking, resting your head against the cow's side, your head moving slightly with the movement of its breathing, who now and again would swing her head round to look at you with large, soft eyes.

The loud bellowing had stopped as the cows realised that milking had begun, so stood patiently awaiting their turn.

She would like to get more into the agricultural side of farming, have a go at rat-catching, fruit picking and more work with horses, she loved to feel the softness of a horses nose. Medicinal herbs would be fascinating to work with, such as Deadly Nightshade, Henbane, Valerian, Foxglove and Thornapple. All these grow wild in the country. She knew that Deadly Nightshade is poisonous, sometimes confused with Woody Nightshade, a common hedgerow plant. You must know when to harvest the crop, only done when the leaves are fully grown, yes, that would be interesting. So far, she and Fay had been lucky, but now with this terrible Topp woman, was she going to be fair in allocating rotten farms fairly? She got the paperwork from the War Agg and said who went where. Topp hated her, so would send her out to rotten farms. She had heard that some of the hill farms were awful, hardly civilised, and you could catch impetigo, which meant being in an isolation hospital. Anyway, my dreams will most likely come to nothing; I may be sacked if Topp has anything to do with it. But, before that can happen, I would have to go before The War Agricultural Committee, and if that happens, I shall certainly be telling them about Topp.

Her thoughts ended as she realised that she had a full bucket of rich, creamy milk. She stood and called to no one in particular.

"Where do you want this full pail?"

"At the top of the shed in the large churn," Barry's voice rang out.

She carried the full pail as carefully as she could, trying not to let any slop over. She walked slowly and cautiously up the aisle, then emptied the pail carefully into the churn. She went back, patted the finished cow on the rump, picked up her stool and started on the next one, which seemed a little restive, moving her back legs around so that April could not get a grip on her teats. After trying a few times and failing, April thought sod it; I know what you want to settle you down, a song from Aunty April.

She began to sing softly, then a little louder as the cow became still. Oh, you like me singing do you; the cow released a tender moo as if in agreement. Both boys began to whistle along with her singing, and the cow flicked her tail in time to the song, but that was impossible, April thought in amusement. Soon all the cows were milked, and, in record time the boys informed the girls, admiration in their voice.

"You'll do for us," they said.

"You've a good voice, April; you can really belt it out," Dennis said, putting his hand onto her shoulder. "I've really enjoyed working with you; let's hope we get you two every morning."

"All being well, you will," April answered. "Now, what's next, swilling out and getting the cows down to the field I expect?"

"Yes," Dennis replied. "Barry and I will take the cows; you and Fay do the swilling. There's a tap in the yard with a long hosepipe attached, one of you spray the water, the other scrub with the hard brush. You have to shovel the cow shit into the manure cart first, which I'll bring you before we start."

"Thank you, Dennis," April said in a knowing voice. "We've worked in cowsheds before you know."

"Of course you have, silly me," Dennis said with a laugh. "Shift yourselves; I'm going to open the stall doors."

He picked up a long, stout looking stick that was leaning against the wall, then walked down one side of the stalls and opened the doors, while Barry did the other.

The girls stood well back as the cows lumbered out, hurrying to the wide-open double doors, eager to get out to the field, with now and again both boys calling.

"Get on, Gert, go on, Bluebell, gerr-up, Cleo, shift yersen, Minnie."

When the shed was quiet at last, Fay said.

"Now for the clearing up, what do you want to do? I'm easy."

"I'll scrub, it's good for the hips," April said as she picked up a dense looking yard brush, then laid it down again. "But first we've to take all the plops out of the stalls." She paused, then said. "Here comes the manure cart."

Barry entered, pushing a large cart.

"Here you are girls, it's all yours," he said as he set it against the first stall. "And Mr Bellows says when you've done here would you go down to the bottom field."

"Yes, we would, if we knew where it was," April said pertly. "Don't forget it's our first day and we're not mind readers."

"Through the yard, down the lane, it's the last field on your left; it's next to the wood."

"Thanks, Dennis, we'll find it," Fay said with a smile. "We shouldn't be too long here."

"If I were you, I wouldn't be, the Boss likes fast workers, although when I told him about your milking speed he had a huge grin on his face, put him in a good mood for the rest of the day I hope."

"Okay, off you go and let's get on," April said, pleased at Dennis's words.

As he went off whistling cheerfully, April said firmly.

"Right, kiddo, you wheel the cart, I'll shovel the shit."

"April!" Fay said in disgust.

"Well, that's what it is, no good dressing it up in fancy words," April laughed. She picked up the large shovel that was laid in the cart. "Come on."

"Make sure it goes into the cart, I don't want it all over me."

"If you have the cart where it should be, they'll be no problem."

"I will, just go steady."

April stepped into the first stall.

"Not too bad in here." She scooped three shovels full of plops up and threw them into the cart. "I love the smell, it's so wholesome."

"I think it's awful," Fay said in disgust, a look of disdain on her face.

"You don't think that when it's helped to grow the food you eat," April snapped.

"Well, you don't do you."

"You should when we work on the land."

April worked her way quickly up one side, then down the other. When the job was done, the cart was almost full, and the girls shoved it into the yard and left it by the barn.

Now for the swilling. They crossed the yard to the pump and fixed the nozzle of the long hosepipe to the tap.

"I'll go and get the brush ready; you turn on the tap then come into the shed with the pipe, I hope the pressure's strong," April said as she hurried away.

Fay turned the tap onto full, then raced to the shed, the hosepipe uncurling quickly behind her. Just as she reached the shed door, water gushed out in a raging torrent.

"Here it comes, April," she shouted.

"Hold it down nearer to the ground you fool, or you'll wet me through."

"Sorry," Fay called, realising her mistake.

"Come towards me, we'll start at the top end and work down, I'll give the stalls a good brush then sweep the water into the channel."

This they continued to do until the stalls were clean.

"Now, I'll just give the channel a scrub. I think we've done a good job," April said, pleased with herself.

Fay agreed wholeheartedly and swung around towards the door, saying as she did so.

"I'll go turn off the tap."

At first, she did not see the figure stood in the doorway, and as she still had the gushing hosepipe in her hand, held at waist height, the water cascaded like a waterfall all over the figure, which suddenly came to life and exploded like a volcano.

"You bloody fool! Lay the pipe in the channel! You've drowned me, I'm soaked to the skin! And who the bloody hell are you? And what are you doing playing around with the bloody hosepipe?!" The figure, a man, shook himself like a dog. "Well?!" He bellowed. "Are you deaf as well as daft?!" He walked towards the terrified Fay, who was numb with shock, and glared at her for a second, then shouted. "Who the hell *are* you?!"

By this time, April had thrown down her brush, which landed with a loud clatter into the channel, and stepped to Fay's side. She glared angrily up at him.

"And just who the hell do you think *you* are shouting at my mate like that?! For two pins I'd turn the hosepipe on you again and flush you into the bloody yard. And for your information, *we* are Land Girls come here to help Mr Bellows, and don't even think about making any sarcastic or funny comments about the Land Army or I'll flatten you! You didn't get a soaking on purpose, it was an accident, but my mate is too terrified to apologise, yelling at her like that, you should be ashamed!"

To April's surprise, he didn't say a word, but turned and walked to the farmhouse. The girls watched him in silence as he opened the door and walked straight in.

"He must be well known here, he didn't even knock on the door, just went in," April said. "What a horrible man though."

"Be fair, it will have been a shock being pelted by a stream of freezing water and drenched to the skin," Fay said, distressed.

"Granted, but he had no need to shout and swear at you like that," April said angrily. "Anyway, I hope mine and his paths don't cross again. *Men*, they get on my nerves."

"Maybe he works here."

"Heaven forbid."

"We'll just have to grin and bear it if he does."

"You might, I shall avoid him."

"That'll be hard to do if we're given a job to do together."

"I'll work in silence."

"That will be impossible for you, April."

"Why would it?"

"Because you've never worked quietly as long as I've known you."

"There's a first time for everything."

"I can never see it happening."

"We'll see. Anyway, he may not even work here, he could just be a visitor."

"Could be, but why was he coming to the barn in the first place?"

"He could be one of the sons home on leave."

"I don't think so, Mrs Bellows would surely have told us."

"Yes, you'd think so."

"Could be a man looking for a job."

"Could be, but he wouldn't walk straight into the house would he."

"Look, let's stop playing Sherlock Holmes and get on down to the bottom field, time is getting on, it must be nearly lunchtime."

"I'm sure Mrs Bellows will find us wherever we are, I hope so, I'm hungry. I wonder what lunch will be." April said.

"I'll be glad of anything as long as it's not beetroot sarnies," Fay said.

"No, Mrs Bellows wouldn't serve beetroot sarnies up," April said firmly, then pointed. "Look, here we are, there're the lads and Mr Bellows."

The girls climbed the five-barred gate with ease and hurried up to the waiting men.

"Hope we haven't held you up," April said cheerfully. "But we had a bit of a spat in the cowshed."

"A bit of a spat? What was that about then?" Mr Bellows asked curiously.

April laughed, then said with shining eyes.

Fay here drenched some man with the hosepipe, not on purpose, but she didn't see him stood in the doorway as she turned to say something to me. Any road, he got a right soaking and played hell with Fay. You should've heard the way he spoke to her. I wasn't having that and gave him a right gob full, threatened to smack him in the gob I did, and he didn't like that, he stormed off into the farmhouse."

"What did he look like?" Barry asked.

"What do you think he looked like?! A bloody drowned rat, I'd say," April replied.

"Oh-oh, sounds as if it were Larry," Mr Bellows said abruptly. "*And* he wouldn't appreciate being hosed down."

"Who's Larry?" Fay asked, apprehensively.

"He's my other farmhand, a good one too. I'm sorry you had to make his acquaintance in that way, he's really a nice chap," Mr Bellows said.

"Oh, he'll get over it," Dennis said firmly.

"You'll both probably fall for him like all the other girls in the village have, they all give him the glad-eye, but he doesn't give them one back."

"Well, there's one here who won't be falling for him I can assure you; I think he's a clever bugger, *and*, he had better not shout at us again, or I'll be rearranging his face for him," April said angrily.

"There's fighting talk for you," Mr Bellows laughed. "Five-foot nothing and she's going to take on our Larry."

"Really," Fay said seriously. "She could."

"Enough of the chit-chat, let's get to work," Mr Bellows said firmly as he handed them each a hoe, then went on. "I want this field of cabbages hoeing." He pointed to little seedlings which had large weeds around them. "Start off in rows, and mind you don't hoe the seedlings up instead of the weeds."

The girls nodded their heads, and the lads smiled.

"Okay, Boss."

"I don't want any bald patches so watch what you're bloody doing, it's dig, twist and pull, the weeds I mean. As you go along, you'll get into a rhythm," Mr Bellows said bossily. "Any road, Mrs Bellows will be along in half an hour with lunch, so get on, get those weeds out."

As he hurried away, he glanced back to make sure that everyone was working, he sighed with satisfaction as he saw hoes digging and backs bending. He did not envy those two girls, he instead thought that there would be complaints about bad backs tomorrow, but they seemed to be good grafters. That little April was a live wire though. Now, he admired a lass that could stick up for herself, she'd had a go at Larry, and he would have liked to have seen that! The days ahead looked promising.

As the boys and girls worked busily, Dennis began to whistle.

Barry called to the girls.

"Done this before have you?"

"No, there's a first time for everything," Fay called back.

"I like it, being out in the fresh air, gets the stink of the cowshed and muck out of the nostrils, although there's something to be said for the sheds in bad weather," April shouted.

"Done hedging and ditching?" Barry asked.

"Yes, I liked that, did it on my own," April called back. "Now, if you don't mind, I'll save my breath for the job in hand."

The four worked at a steady pace until they heard Mrs Bellows voice calling.

"Hi there, ready for some lunch?"

She beckoned them towards her, so the four laid down their hoes and hurried to her. She gave them a cheerful smile and handed the basket to Barry, as she did so, saying to the girls.

"Come along, you two, let's feed you, I've some goodies in my basket."

They followed as she led them through the gate into the lane, where a swiftly flowing stream ran under the hedge, and onto a vast expanse of grassed area which was shaded by a large Oak Tree which cast out a dappled effect, it looked cool and restful.

"Here we are, this is a lovely spot. Everyone sit down," Mrs Bellows said as she took the basket from Barry. "I hope you're all hungry."

"Starving," April said as she sat down with crossed legs.

The more lady-like Fay sat with her legs stretched out in front of her and rubbed the bottom of her back.

"My aching back," she moaned.

"Mr Bellows has got you hoeing I take it, not an easy job that, you'll feel it when you climb into bed tonight, but it soon wears off," Mrs Bellows said as she opened the lid of the basket. She knelt and took out a snowy white linen tablecloth, then spread it out onto the grass, along with five plates, knives and napkins. "Now," she said firmly. "You must all have dirty hands, so." She took from the bottom of the basket, a plastic bag which contained a wet tea towel, she held it out. "Here you are, all of you give your hands a wipe with this, get the dirt off then get tucked in."

When all hands had been inspected, lunch was started.

"The cornish are still warm, they're Mr Bellows favourites, he can shift three at one sitting," Mrs Bellows said happily as she laid a jar of pickled onions onto the cloth. "These are my own; I do all my own pickling." Then, realising what she had said, flushed a deep red.

April burst out into mischievous laughter, then said.

"I should hope you do, Mrs Bellows."

"April," Fay said, her face as red as Mrs Bellows. "Trust you to come out with something like that."

"Well, you have to see the funny side," April replied, still laughing.

"This will shut her up," Mrs Bellows said as she handed April a still warm cornish pasty, from which April took a large bite.

"Mmm, totally delicious," she mumbled as she pulled the jar of pickled onions towards her, fished out two, and put them onto her plate. She bit one in two and crunched slowly. "Shop-bought ones don't hold a candle to these," she said through a full mouth.

"Why thank you, April," Mrs Bellows said in delight. She turned to Fay. "How about you, Fay? Are *you* enjoying your lunch? I've no need to ask the boys, they know what to expect at Bellows Farm, don't you, boys."

Fay smiled happily.

"Best meal we've had in days, you should've seen the so-called rotten meal Miss Topp expected us to eat yesterday. April threw it into the pig swill."

"That won't happen here, I can assure you," Mrs Bellows said sharply as she took a fruit cake out of the basket. "We think more of our pigs."

"That Topp woman is a nightmare, I've had a dust-up with her already, and I expect to have more," April said abruptly before she popped the last of her cornish into her mouth.

"I've heard about her," Mrs Bellows said, nodding her head. "There's been talk in the village about her, the Land Girls go into the local shops saying she doesn't feed them enough. She goes into the shop at odd times and is very abrupt in her manner, Mrs Cook, the shopkeeper, hasn't a good word to say about her, and is thankful that she has her large order delivered every week."

"I don't know about a large order being delivered every week, the girls in the hostel don't see much of it from what I can gather," Fay said bitterly. "We could do with *you* and your excellent cooking, Mrs Bellows."

"If ever I need a job, Fay, I'll bear that in mind," Mrs Bellows laughed. "But can't you report her or something?"

"When I have more facts, I shall do just that," April said, a determined look on her face.

"I took one of the Land Girls out a couple of times, she's left now, and she used to tell me tales about Miss Topp, from what I could gather, most of the girls feared her. If they stood up to her, she made life very uncomfortable for them," Barry said, knowingly. "If one girl got too brave and stood up to her, Miss Topp would discredit her to the War Agg, then suddenly the girl was moved. Although I think she was glad to be away from the place, so the story goes. Nothing happens that the villagers don't know about."

"That's a long speech from you, Barry," Mrs Bellows said in amusement.

"It's the truth, cross my heart," Barry cried.

"Yes, we believe you, but it sounds to me as if this Miss Topp knows, and is friendly with someone high up, someone with authority, a relation maybe," Mrs Bellows said musingly.

"I shouldn't be surprised," April answered. "But we'll learn more when we meet the rest of the girls, hopefully tonight."

"On that note, lunchtime is over, better get back to your hoeing or my husband will be on the warpath." She rose and began to gather plates and knives. "Oh look, no one's had any fruit cake, I'll serve it tomorrow."

"I'm full, and thank you for a lovely lunch," Fay said as she handed the jar of onions to Mrs Bellows.

April stood, then said hesitantly.

"Has anyone realised that we haven't had a drink?"

"My goodness!" Mrs Bellows cried out in horror. "What a fool I am." She shook the tablecloth furiously and pushed it into the basket. "I'll send Larry straight down with something for you all straight away."

Dennis laughed.

"Don't upset yourself, Mrs B, there's always the stream, it wouldn't be the first time we've drank its water, it's clean and cold on a hot day."

"I had two bottles of cherryade out ready to bring and I've left them on the table," she said as she hurried away.

"Do you really drink from the stream?" Fay asked. "Won't there be creatures swimming around?"

"Yes, but you make sure you don't swallow any," Dennis smirked at the look on Fay's face, then went on. "In the hot weather, we strip off our boots and socks and have a paddle."

"Yuck! Then you drink it?!" Fay cried in disgust.

"Take no notice of him, Fay." April said, giving Dennis a push as he walked in front of her. "He's having you on."

"We pee in it an all if we get taken short," Dennis said softly, thinking that the girls wouldn't hear. "Kind of flavours the water."

"Oh, you are disgusting," Fay cried.

Barry laughed.

"Don't listen to him, he wouldn't do that, his Mam has brought him up proper."

"Don't let *me* catch you," April warned. "I'd push you in and hold your head under."

Dennis roared with laughter.

"I should like to see you try, little un."

"One day, you just might," April said casually.

"Yes, you'd better listen to her, she just might," Fay cautioned as they got back to the field. "Anyway, back to the blessed hoeing, the Boss will be along soon to check our progress."

* * *

Six o'clock saw the two girls cycling slowly back to the hostel, tired but happy.

"Phew, what a day, but I enjoyed it, what I did notice though, Fay, and I don't know why I haven't before, you're left-handed. That could be a problem if we ever have to stand with three or four workers working across the field. If you ever develop a good rhythm and good swing, it would be a bit scary for the person working next to you."

"Do you think that I haven't thought of that, April, I would just have to swing the scythe in the opposite direction. I was the only child in my class at school who was left-handed; they made fun of me and called me cock handed. My teacher tried to make me use my right hand, and I'd go home in tears. This used to upset Mother, and one day she stormed up to the school and complained. It was a little better after that."

"One of my twin brothers is left-handed, but did you know that left-handed people are supposedly more intelligent?" April asked.

"No, I didn't," Fay replied, surprised.

Suddenly changing the subject, April said.

"We're coming to the village, let's push the bikes and walk through."

"Why do you want to do that? I'd much rather get back to the hostel," Fay queried.

April came to a halt and dismounted.

"If there's any villagers about, might as well let them have a good look at the WLA new girls, from what I've heard, we're a good topic of conversation for them."

Fay unwillingly got from her bike and ambled behind April.

"I say, why don't we go the whole hog and nip into the village pub and have a shandy?" April said enthusiastically.

"No, I'm not doing that," Fay decided firmly.

"Okay," April said, just as firmly. "You sit outside and wait for me, spoilsport; you'll probably be picked up by one of the village lads who thinks he's God's gift to women."

"Alright," Fay said resignedly. "I'll come."

April smiled at getting her own way.

"Come on, we'll leave our bikes at the back of the pub, they should be safe there."

They saw in surprise that the back of the pub was delightful, with chairs and tables holding sun umbrellas, a small, grassed area with a riot of flowers and a slide and swings for the children.

"This is nice," Fay said. "Mother and Father can sit and have a drink and keep an eye on the kids enjoying themselves."

"There's more to this village life than meets the eye," April summed up. "This place is for drinking parents', a bus conductor who thinks he's King Kong, a Judge who enjoys any trouble on the local bus, and the spider-faced Miss Topp who thinks she's a female James Cagney, but maybe I'm insulting Mr Cagney."

"April, you get some daft notions in your head."

"True ones though, think about it, Fay."

"I will, later, now come on, let's get into the damn pub, the sooner we do that, the sooner we get home, and *don't* get into a conversation with anyone, and *don't* get into rows either, now, April, I mean it."

"I don't know what you mean, Fay, I don't cause any rows, I just stand up for what's right."

"Yes, I have experienced you doing that."

"Fair comment. Now come on," April said firmly. "Lean your bike against mine; they'll be okay by this wall."

As the girls came to the open door of the pub, Fay pushed April forward.

"You go first," She said nervously.

Without looking around at Fay, April laughed, pulled her turban a little back so that a good deal of her red hair fell onto her forehead, then said loudly.

"Get your head up, kiddo, walk in as if you own the place, let them know The Land Army Girls are here."

Fay sighed, then said under breath.

"Oh, my God."

As they walked into the pub, which was large, with a bar taking up one wall with brass holdings shone to a gleaming gold supporting the beer pumps, sudden silence reigned, and the atmosphere could have been cut with a knife.

April glanced around keenly and saw two old men sat as if turned to statues, their dominos held mid-air as they gawped at the two girls. There were only four other men who were stood at the bar, and as the girls entered, the conversation at the bar ceased. They turned around, hoping to see more of the locals, at the sight of the girls, two of the men turned back to the bar with a shrug of their shoulders. The other two stood leering at the girls.

"Well, well, what have we here?" said one of the men, who had broad shoulders, a goatee beard and a shiny bald head that looked as if it had been polished with furniture cream. He narrowed his eyes. "If it ain't the Land Army gracing us with their presence, to what do we owe the honour?"

April looked at him as if he were a foul-smelling rat, ignored him and strode to the bar; her head held high; Fay followed unwillingly.

Boldly he went on.

"Seems we've a couple of deaf un's here lads, the cows must be glad a that."

April turned around, leant over towards him, and called.

"I hope you mean the cows in the field and not my friend and I."

"There's now't to choose between yer from what *I've* heard, love a good roll in the hay the Land Girls do."

"Really? Have *you* had a good roll in the hay with one?" April asked, incredulously.

He bit his lip.

When April saw this, she laughed.

"I can see that you haven't, one of the unlucky ones eh. Who would want to roll around with an ugly big gobbed gorilla like you?! Really, you must fancy yourself."

Fay stood mortified as she thought 'Oh God.'

The other man, who had been stood silent, now spoke.

"Really, girls, it might be better if you went."

"Would it?" April asked haughtily. "We'll go when we're ready, which won't be until we've had a drink, which is," she turned determinedly to the waiting barman. "Two beer shandy's please."

He gave a wink.

"Certainly."

As he worked the pump, he began to whistle 'April Showers.' As he put the drinks down in front of the girls, April asked quietly in a calm voice, but inquiringly.

"Tell me, why were you whistling 'April Showers' particularly?"

He sniffed, gave a grin, then said.

"We know, or should I say, *I* do, who *you* are, you're the one the Judge told us about."

"You'll mean Judge Bentley I take it?"

"Yes, Judge Bentley, he really admires you, you should be honoured."

"If I knew what I had to be honoured about, I would be," April said as she picked up her drink and took a large swallow.

"He told us all about you man-handling Perkins."

"Who may I ask is Perkins?" April said.

"Perkins is one of our bus conductors," the barman said.

"Ha, I begin to see," April said with a grin. "The one who thought he could throw me off the bus."

"That's the one. The Judge was most amused! And it takes a lot to amuse him; he thinks you're quite the bees-knees."

"I've been called many things, but never the bees-knees, I think I like that, don't you, Fay?"

"Yes," Fay mumbled as she took a sip of her drink, then said, "let's go."

"It seems I'm becoming notoriously known for my strength, your conductor soon learned that it was a mistake to mess with me. I hate men who try to throw their weight around, the sooner they learn women are as good as, if not better, especially the Land Army Girls, the better off they'll be, then we girls will respect them more."

Everyone was so intent on April's words; they hadn't noticed the silent figure stood in the doorway until it began to clap.

The Judge strolled into the pub, then said.

"Here, here, April, I endorse everything you said! The WLA is an excellent band of women! And I had better not hear anyone say other. In fact, I've been lurking in the doorway for quite a while and have listened to all the conversation." He pointed at the bald man. "You, Smedley should be ashamed, bad mouthing this young lady, at least she's doing her bit for her country, which is more than can be said for a great hulking excuse of a man like you, getting out of it because you have flat feet! I get types like you in my court every day, I just hope that one day you'll put a foot wrong and end up before me." He rubbed his hands together, then said, "I live in hope." Then turning to the girls. "Hello, you two, can I buy you a drink? It's so nice to see you again."

"Thanks, Judge, it's nice of you to offer but we must get back to the hostel, we've had a tough day and look forward to relaxing, and I've to write to my Mam and Dad, let them know where I am, they worry about me something awful."

"You're a good lass, April, some other time, eh? And in the meantime, if anyone in the village gives you a tough time, let me know," the Judge said firmly.

Smedley, who was leaning up against the bar, gave a grimace, and underneath his breath muttered.

"Gibberish."

April smiled and patted the Judge on the arm.

"Thanks, that's quite a manifesto, Judge. Hope we see you again soon, goodbye for now." Once out of the door, April turned and called, "ta-ra the rest of you poe-faced buggers."

Fay looked stricken and said.

"Oh, God."

The Judge broke out into laughter and shouted.

"That's my gal."

As the girls peddled out of the pub yard, Fay said exasperated.

"Well, that went down like a damp squib, why do you do it?"

"Do what?" April asked.

"Find trouble? I just knew we would, going into that pub at this time of the day."

"*I* didn't start it. Did *you* like being likened to a cow? Because that's what that ugly-faced bald hulk was inferring."

"You should've taken no notice; I was prepared to."

"Oh no, I wasn't going to let him get away with that."

"You've made an enemy there, April."

"I agree, I have, he's a nasty piece of work, but we mustn't class all the villagers the same."

"We seem to have met the bad ones."

"Yes, we do, but there must be some amiable people around, and it's unlikely that I'll have another run-in with Baldy." April said seriously. "If I did, I could handle it."

"There might come a day when you can't," Fay said apprehensively.

"If it does, I'll have had my chips," April laughed. "Now, put all that out of your mind, here we are, back at dear old Whitmore, I *don't* think."

"I can't say I'm not sorry, maybe we'll meet some of the other girls tonight," Fay said.

"Remember what Jane said, we're never all here together, and I don't know as I would want to meet them all at once. I wouldn't be able to remember all their names, and it would be nice to have some peace and quiet. Imagine what it would be like to have twelve girls talking all at once, *and* remember, we've that new girl sharing our room tonight, we must make her welcome, get to know her."

"We can't get to know her in one night, April; it takes ages to get to know a person."

"It didn't take you long to get to know me, but then, I am a very open person, not like you, who's very deep."

"What do you mean, very deep?"

"I don't really know anything about your life, you know all about *mine*."

Fay did not answer as she got off her bike and opened the gate into the back garden.

"Well?" April said.

"I told you; I'll tell you everything when I'm ready."

"The other girls will be asking you stuff."

"I'll tell the other girls what I tell you, nothing."

"Alright, keep your hair on," April snapped as she stomped angrily up the path. As she came up to the closed back door, she came to a standstill and said to Fay. "Listen."

A gabble of voices came from behind the closed door.

"Sounds to be quite a few girls in there, sounds like a bit of an argument going on," Fay said.

"Only one way to find out," April said firmly.

She opened the door and stepped inside, and April being April, with her sense of humour, said.

"Hello, you lot, are we entering the third world war and need our tin hats on? Or are you just having a friendly heated discussion?"

Five heads with startled eyes swung round to look at April and Fay. Jane was the first to speak.

"Hi, you two, no, we're not having a row, or an argument, just talking about the unfairness of the allocating of jobs."

"Knowing that Topp woman, you can count me in on that," April said as she pulled out a chair and sat down, "Fay too."

The sullen-faced Monica muttered.

"Trust you to be in on it."

"Were you speaking to me?" April asked.

Monica remained silent.

"Thanks for your support." Jane went on. "But you haven't met Joan and Nancy."

"Hi, Joan and Nancy, you'll have heard about me already I'll bet," April laughed. "And about how big a fan I am of Miss Topp."

"Oh yes, Monica soon filled us in on that," the plain-looking, well-built Joan said, casting a dirty look in Monica's direction. A roly-poly figure, with a fat face and twinkling bright blue eyes, she stood and walked around the table to April and

Fay. "Hi," she said with a smile, showing dazzling white teeth. "I'm Joan; I'm from Haworth in West Yorkshire, pleased to meet you." She shook the hands of both girls.

"Haworth, that's Bronte country, isn't it?" Fay asked.

"Yes, we are rather well known, we get visitors from all over the world, too many sometimes, but we get used to it," Joan smiled happily, then beckoned to a woman sat at the other side of the table. "Meet Nancy."

The woman stood, nodded her head and spoke.

"Hi." She sat down and waited for someone to speak. When no one did, she said in a deep contralto voice. "As you can see, April and Fay, I'm older than you other girls, I've been in the WLA for two years, I was thirty-six when I joined, it was the best thing I've ever done. I love the life and can't ever see me doing anything else. I've done many jobs, but my favourite one is rat-catching, I hope to go back to it, what a grand job it is. I'm from Blackpool, and worked in a boring dress shop. I didn't want to spend the rest of my life stood waiting for boring women to make up their minds whether to buy or not. When I saw posters appealing for women to join the Land Army, that was it, I was off."

"But rat-catching, yuck. How awful, how can you do that?" Fay said with a sick look on her face.

"There's nothing awful about it."

"I couldn't do it."

"Someone has to."

"Were you not afraid?"

"No, rats are pests you know."

"Yes, I know, the farmers hate them."

"I was sent to Dorset and was trained by a trapper who certainly knew what he was doing, it takes a lot of patience, but I got there. We had lots of farms to clear."

"Every day?" Fay asked.

"Sounds interesting, I'd like to have a go," April said.

"We caught thousands of the buggers by trapping and poisoning, there's many kinds of poison, we don't use the same kind twice, rats are cunning creatures, clever, and some get wise to the same poison."

"My brothers told me about rats, they get them down the pit you know," April put in.

"Yes, they do," Nancy agreed. "And it's the breeding rate that worries the farmers, it's fast, but that's a long story, too long to go into now."

"Is that why you're here?" Fay asked. "Going around local farms ratting?"

"We've a two-legged female one here that could do with putting down," April exclaimed with a malicious look on her face.

"That's a nasty thing to say," Monica cried as she threw herself from her chair. "Miss Topp is an okay woman; you want to watch your mouth."

"Ha, Monica, so, you know to whom I'm referring, no flies on you are there!" April laughed.

"Miss Topp's got your measure, she's reporting you and I don't blame her," Monica spat out.

"I shouldn't be too complacent if I were you, I'll see that she goes first, and you along with her."

Monica stood for a moment glaring at April, until April said softly.

"Well, run along and tell Miss Topp what I've just said, she has to put it in her little black book does she not. I've been here two days and know already that you're the informative spy in our little band. Off you go."

Monica turned and slammed out of the kitchen.

"There, now, where were we?" April asked, turning to Joan. "What did you do before the Land Army, Joan?"

"I worked in a wool shop, I liked it, but wanted something different, so, like Nancy here, when I saw the posters in Keighley calling for Land Girls, I knew that was for me. Mum didn't want me to leave home, she cried buckets, but it didn't change my mind, so here I am, and I love it, although I'd like to live in on a farm, but a good one."

"I think that there's a good mixture of good and bad," Jane said, matter of factly.

"I've enjoyed today though," Joan said happily. "I spent all morning mixing cow grub, and the afternoon in the back garden of the farmhouse weeding the vegetables for the farmer's wife. She also has a small, beautiful flower bed, and I found a Robin's nest in the hedge. The cat was lurking around, so I chased him off, I do hope that the Robin doesn't become the cat's breakfast, I'd be distraught. I simply love birds. There are two pairs of Thrushes who the farmer tells me has been around for several years. Blackbirds build nests in the Honeysuckle against the house, Wrens build too in the Buddleia, and, I say, girls, have you ever seen a Garden Warbler? They're a lovely soft grey-green colour. I saw a Greenfinch, they're lovely birds, and did you know that Yellowhammers spend hours on telegraph wires? *And* I've seen a female Redstart. We've a pair of Tawny Owls in the yew, and there are lots of Kestrels. Isn't nature wonderful?!" As Joan paused for breath, April said.

"Wonderful, most interesting, Joan, but do you know what would be more wonderful? A good cup of tea."

"Oh, sorry, you should've stopped me," Joan cried dismayed. "I'll put the kettle on at once."

"I think that we can take it that Joan loves birds," Nancy laughed. "I know how she feels; I feel the same about rats."

"A bit of difference between the two though, Nancy, one is sublime, the other a horror," Jane said, pulling a face.

"Granted, but each to our own," Nancy replied.

"I love horses," April added.

"I quite like milking now," Fay put in.

"I like to stand looking at a field of waving Corn, knowing that I'm going to harvest it," Jane said.

"What about the hard work involved?" Nancy asked.

"There's nothing easy about farm work, but, like you said, Nancy, each to his own," Jane reminded.

The door opened quietly, and a beautiful looking, tall, thin girl came into the kitchen. As she did so, she pulled off her turban, revealing light brown hair that fell in waves to her shoulders. She had large green eyes with long curling lashes, arched smooth eyebrows, a small perfectly formed nose and naturally red lips. She smiled at the girls, showing a dimple each side of her mouth.

April caught her breath, she reminds me of Vivian Leigh, Scarlet O'Hara in 'Gone with the Wind'.

Nobody should be so good-looking April thought.

The 'vision' asked in a soft musical voice.

"Am I in time for a cuppa?"

Joan walked towards her and pulled her nearer to April and Fay.

"Katrina," she said. "These are our two new girls, April Thornton and Fay Trent."

The two girls nodded and said.

"Hi."

"And this," Jane said with a flourish, as if introducing a Queen, "is Katrina."

Katrina gave them a devastatingly, beautiful smile, which lit up her whole face.

"Hello," she said. "Welcome, glad to have you, I hope you'll be happy here."

"I don't know about being happy here, in this hostel I mean, but I love my work," replied the ever-honest April.

"I can see that you've met our Miss Topp," Katrina said. "Don't let her get to you; she loves to think that she has."

"Thanks for the advice, but it's a little late," April said ruefully.

"Oh dear, you've had a run-in with her already?" Katrina said in dismay.

"I'm afraid I have," April said abruptly.

The kitchen door swung open to reveal the figure of Miss Topp.

"Ah, speak of the devil and it's sure to appear. Have you been listening outside the door? I wouldn't put it past you," April said.

"If I wanted to listen outside the door, I would!" Miss Topp snapped back, flashing April a malicious look.

"Listeners don't hear any good about themselves, you know," April said politely as she winked mischievously at Fay.

"*You'd* better not start the habit; you'd curl up black and be shrivelled to a cinder," Miss Topp said triumphantly, then smiled at April evilly as she waited for April's reply, which wasn't long in coming.

Fay cast her eyes heavenwards, then muttered.

"Oh, God."

"Would I? Well, the first person I'd make for while I was being burnt to a crisp would be you, Miss Topp. I'd clasp you to my chest as tightly as I could with my burning arms." Here, April stood and began acting the part. "We would burn together, the ground would open, and we would drop down into hell. Just think, Miss Topp, you and I, together forever. They do say that the devil looks after his own."

Miss Topp glared at April, her face a pasty white and her eyes standing out of her head.

"You heathen you," she began. "You're not a Christian, you shouldn't be allowed in a decent society. I will not allow you to corrupt these girls."

April laughed.

"These girls have a mind of their own." Then, in a deep sonorous voice, she said. "I would like you all to know that I'm an atheist, and I don't discuss politics or religion."

"Oh God," Fay whispered.

"See, I said she was a heathen!" Miss Topp shouted.

"If that's how you see me, I must be, but it's a state I enjoy," April said, happily. Then, changing the subject swiftly, she turned to Katrina. "You must be parched, and still waiting for a cup of tea, as are we all. Nancy, as you are the nearest to the stove, bang the kettle on, there's a love."

"Of course, we could all do with one after that spat, which was enlightening," Nancy said. "Joan, get the mugs out ready, would you?"

Joan was sat in a daze and had to be asked again by Nancy.

"Would you get the mugs out please, Joan?" Nancy shouted. "*Now*, Joan."

Joan gave herself a little shake, then whispered to Katrina, who was sat next to her.

"Did I really hear all that?"

"You did," Katrina whispered softly back. "I quite enjoyed it; April's something else isn't she."

"She is, but what, I don't know," Joan agreed.

Miss Topp had been stood silently with her arms folded across her chest; she cleared her throat, then asked.

"How many of you want tea?"

"April and I don't, we had ours at Bellows Farm before we came away," Fay answered.

"I don't, I had mine at the farm," Jane said.

"So did I," Nancy and Joan said together.

"Looks like there's just me," Katrina said softly.

"One it is then," Miss Topp snapped.

"May I ask what *is* for tea?" Katrina said.

"Scragg-end stew," Miss Topp answered with a toss of her head.

Katrina gave a grimace of distaste, then with disgust in her voice, said.

"I don't think I'll bother, thank you, Miss Topp."

"Suit yourself," Miss Topp snapped. "But they'll be nothing else until morning."

"If things run true to form, there'll be nothing *then*," Nancy said, discontented with her lot.

Miss Topp chose to ignore this.

"If, none of us here aren't having anything to eat, *by choice*, what happens to our rations?" April asked reasonably.

"That's a good question," Nancy said. "What *does* happen to them?"

Miss Topp turned a lighter shade of pale, then blustered.

"What do you mean?"

"You're paid board every week for each girl, now, if girls aren't eating here every day, where is the surplus food? Although, from what I've seen in the last couple of days, what you serve up is fit only for the pigs." Miss Topp remained silent, so April went on firmly. "I've been given to understand that we've the right to see our rations on the day they're delivered, but of course, none of us are here. That means you can do as you like with them, Miss Topp," April ground out, an angry glint in her eye.

Fay rested her elbow on the table, then putting her hand over her mouth, she groaned.

"Oh, God."

"What are you inferring?" Miss Topp asked.

"I don't infer; I say straight out what I think," April shot back.

"You can say that again," Fay groaned quietly.

"I've had my belly full of you!" Miss Topp said in a fury.

"Now, that's a rude word, *belly*, only the low born use that word," April said calmly.

Miss Topp turned, then stormed out of the kitchen.

"You've done it now," Nancy said regretfully. "She'll do all in her power to get rid of you. She got rid of young Rita last year; she was like you, stood up for her rights, called a spade a spade, but she was out in a matter of days. If I were you, I'd start packing."

"Who removed her? Did she get a letter of dismissal?" Fay asked.

"No, the War Agg came for her, we didn't see her go, I was sorry for her, she was a nice lass and a good worker," Nancy explained.

"That's rather odd, a Land Girl must work one week's notice and *should* be given one week's notice. Something doesn't add up here," Fay said puzzled. "Is there a phone in Miss Topp's office?"

"Yes, there is," Nancy replied.

"I see," Fay said, nodding her head slowly. "Tomorrow when I'm back from work, I shall make a phone call."

"Who are you going to call?" April asked curiously.

"Never you mind," Fay said mysteriously.

"Okay, it's your business," April said, miffed.

The girls sat silently for a while, drinking the tea which Nancy had made and poured.

Suddenly, April asked.

"How many of us take sugar? There are six of us."

Three arms rose in the air.

"Have you got sugar in your tea now?" April went on. "If you haven't, where is it?"

"Good question, yes, where is it?" Jane said, puzzled. "You don't think Topp's keeping it from us and hoarding it do you?"

"I wouldn't be at all surprised if she is," Nancy said. "But how would we find out?"

"There are ways and means. We have to wait until she's out of the house and only we are in," April said quietly, laying a finger onto her lips.

"I hope you're not thinking of doing anything unlawful," Joan said, a worried look on her face, "my Uncle's a policeman."

"I thought you said you came from West Yorkshire?" Nancy demanded.

"I do," Joan said.

"How the hell is your Uncle going to find out about anything you do down here?" April asked. "Not that you're going to do anything, I shall do what must be done, so stop worrying. It's between us six in this room, no one say anything, I've a plan but will keep it to myself."

"Whatever plan you have, I think you should forget it," Fay said worryingly as she stared at April with startled eyes.

"I wouldn't ask anyone to do anything that I wouldn't do myself," April said firmly. "Now, subject closed. I'm going to retire and hope to get a good night's sleep, so, I'll say goodnight to you all."

Fay rose.

"Me too," she said.

Goodnights were said all round, along with shouts of.

"Sleep tight, see you in the morning."

Then Jane's voice.

"Transport is picking up those who need it in the morning at five-thirty."

There were groans all round.

"Not us," April called. "We're biking it."

"Lucky you," Nancy called back.

As April and Fay climbed the stairs, Fay said.

"They were three nice girls we met tonight."

"Yes, we're lucky to have such a good crowd."

"I really like Joan; doesn't she know a lot about birds."

"Yes, she does, she's fascinating to listen to."

"I'm going to start and take more notice of the birds," Fay said determinedly.

"Yes, you should. I'm more interested in the animals."

"But I say, April, isn't Katrina a beautiful girl?! I wish I had her looks."

"What for? You're good looking yourself. It's me that could do with having been blessed with good looks; I must have been at the back of the queue when they were being handed out."

"You're a pretty girl with a bubbly personality, so don't put yourself down," Fay said firmly.

As April pushed open the bedroom door, she replied.

"Thanks for saying that, Fay, my Dad is always saying that about me."

"Your Dad is right, and so am I."

As they walked into the room, the third bed was now occupied; blankets tumbled into a heap, hiding the figure that lay there.

"Oh look, the new girl, I'd forgotten all about her, poor thing, she must be feeling very alone," Fay said quietly as she went up to the bed and gently began shaking the figure. "I say, hello, we're your roommates, can we talk to you?"

The girl threw back the blankets, swung her legs out of bed and fumbled around on the bedside cabinet for the horn-rimmed glasses that Fay could see lay there. She handed them to the girl, who quickly put them on.

"Thanks, I can't see a thing without them."

She stood. A small pathetic looking figure, dark straight hair, slightly prominent teeth and a birthmark which lay on her right cheek, which was the size of a half-penny, it stood out from her face as if it had been carelessly glued on.

"Hello," April said gently. "What's your name? How long have you been here?"

The girl sniffed and said nervously.

"I'm Tina, from Bath." She bit her lip. "I got here at two o'clock."

"Have you been up here since two o'clock?" Fay asked.

"Yes."

"I take it the housekeeper, Miss Topp, gave you something to eat?" April inquired.

"Some soup, yes," Tina replied. "It wasn't very nice."

"No, it wouldn't be," Fay agreed.

"I left it," Tina gulped.

"Did Miss Topp say anything?" Fay probed.

"No, and I was too scared to ask for anything else," Tina said, clasping her hands together.

"Yes, you would be, but don't worry, Tina, Fay here and I will look after you. Did Miss Topp say where you'll be working tomorrow?"

"No. Oh dear, what should I do?" Tina moaned, almost in tears. "Shall I go down and find out?"

"No, you'll come with Fay and me to the Bellows Farm, we can use the extra help," April said bossily.

Fay looked startled.

"Can she do that?" she queried.

"We're not going to leave her here in the morning stood around like a lost soul, you know what it's like, sometimes Topp isn't around."

Fay looked dubious.

"Don't worry, I'll take full responsibility," April said reassuringly.

"Oh dear, I don't want to be a problem or cause any trouble," Tina said, almost in tears.

"Now stop worrying, everything is going to be fine, we'll look after you. Have you had any training by the way?" April asked.

"Very little, but I'm willing to learn," Tina said nervously.

"Good, you have the right attitude," April said. "Is this your first job? How old are you?"

"Seventeen, and it's my first job. You see, I was brought up in a children's home all my life, and as I was growing up I helped with the little ones. The lady who ran the home wanted me to stay on, it would've been a job for life, but I wanted something different, so, chose the Land Army. I'm good with children but frightened of adults."

"Oh, you poor kid! You'll certainly learn about life in this job. You have to stand up for yourself, that's the first lesson."

"Oh dear," Tina moaned.

"And," April went on. "You have to stop saying 'oh dear'."

Tina put her hand up to her mouth as she started to say 'oh dear' again.

"Can you ride a bike?" Fay asked.

"Yes," Tina replied.

"Good, in the morning we bike to work, it's not far, about three or four miles. We leave at five-thirty."

"I've never ridden that far."

"You'll be fine," Fay said reassuringly.

"Oh dear," Tina said, then looked at April apprehensively. "Oh dear, I've said it again."

"You have to stop being such a mouse," April said firmly. "In this job you've to get on with things, life can bite you on the arse, but you turn around and bite it right back."

Tina flushed a bright red, then said.

"Oh dear."

"If you're going to be under my wing, you'll learn fast, isn't that so, Fay?" she asked grimly.

Fay nodded her head in acknowledgement.

"Starting tomorrow, you work with us, the day after I can't say; Topp will most likely take you off us out of spite."

"Isn't she a nice person then?"

"No, she's not human," April said firmly. "You'll find out for yourself, but the other girls here are a good bunch and will make you very welcome, although you won't get to meet them all at once."

"How long have you both been here?" Tina asked.

"Two days."

"Only two days? You talk as if you've been here weeks'."

April laughed.

"Oh, by the way," Fay said as an afterthought. "We're so busy grilling you, Tina, I am Fay, and this is April."

Tina pushed her glasses further up onto the bridge of her nose.

"I'll try and remember; I'm not particularly good with names," she said doubtfully.

"No problem. Now, me and Fay are going along to the bathroom for a wash, I take it you found it okay? Then bed-e-byes, we've to be up early, five o'clock," April said as she yawned.

"Oh dear, I don't think I'll sleep, a strange bed, you know," Tina said with a worried frown.

"Program your mind to sleep, I do, it works for me," Fay said with a laugh.

"I'll try," Tina replied as she climbed back into bed, took off her glasses and laid them onto the bedside cabinet. "Goodnight." She turned towards the wall, pulled the blankets over herself and prepared for sleep.

Out in the corridor, April commented to Fay.

"We have a very timid, nervous girl there, we've to see that she isn't bullied, she seems to be frightened of her own shadow, poor thing'"

"Life on the land is going to be completely different for her," Fay answered.

"As long as she's willing to learn, she'll be okay," April said firmly. "Now, Fay, you use the bathroom first, I'll sit on the stairs until you're finished."

8

As April, Fay and Tina wheeled bikes out of the shed, Tina said dubiously with a worried look on her face.

"I haven't ridden a bike for ages; I'll be a bit wobbly."

"Don't worry, we won't go too fast, we'll give you time to get used to it, get into the swing of it again, won't we, April?" Fay asked.

"Of course, climb on, Tina, I'll give you a push off," April said as she took hold of Tina's arm. "Up you go."

Once on the bike, Tina said in dismay as she tried to sit on the seat.

"Oh dear, I'm too little, my feet won't reach the pedals."

April stood back with her hands on her hips.

"Only one thing for it, we'll have to lower the seat, that's if there's any tools in the shed. Or is there another bike in there? Go and look, Fay."

"Yes, Boss," Fay said sarcastically.

"Oh dear, I am a trouble to you aren't I," Tina moaned. "I'm sorry, April."

"You're not a trouble, and for God's sake, stop saying 'oh dear'."

As Fay re-joined them, she said.

"No more bikes in there." Then added. "No tools either."

"Only one thing for it then, Tina sits on the seat, you stand and peddle, I'll jog along beside you, I'm not biking today."

"You can't do that; you'll be too tired to work," Fay cried in dismay.

"Nonsense, I've been running around all my life, and anyway, I'm fitter than you two," April said with a cheeky grin.

"But it's nearly four miles," Fay pointed out.

"We haven't got time to stand arguing the toss, we'll be late, and Mr Bellows won't be pleased, so off you go," April said, her mind made up. She stepped forward, took hold of Tina, and set her more firmly onto the seat of the bike. "Come on, Fay, cock your leg over."

Fay stood, legs astride the bike as April went on.

"Tina, put your arms around Fay's waist and hold on tight." She gave a grunt of satisfaction. "That's right, now, Fay, push off," she ordered.

After a slightly wobbly start, the girls were off, with April jog-trotting behind.

She began to enjoy her mode of travel, the start of a beautiful day, the slight breeze, the bird song and the gurgling of the river as she came to the bridge. On seeing Fay come to a halt, she slowed her pace until she joined them.

"Isn't this wonderful, I'm really enjoying it," she cried.

"I'm glad you are because I'm not," Fay complained. "My legs are killing me. Change over, I'll run, you peddle."

"As you wish," April replied, disappointed.

"We'll try and get a lift back," Fay said.

"What on? Shank's pony?!" April snapped.

"Shank's pony? What's that?" Tina asked timidly.

"An old Yorkshire saying, I'll explain later. Now, we've to get to work."

She took hold of the bike with one hand, and helped Tina on with the other, then throwing her right leg over the right peddle, she stood upright and began to peddle madly.

"Hold tight, Tina, I'll show you how to ride a bike," April called gaily. "We'll be at the farm before Fay."

Tina clung on for dear life as April zoomed along up the lane, through the gate which stood open, and into the farmyard.

As April climbed off the bike and helped a frightened-looking Tina to stand upright, Tina said breathlessly.

"Never in my life have I experienced anything like that, I did enjoy it."

"Good, because you'll be experiencing a lot more like that, I can tell you," April replied firmly, then, looking up and seeing Fay hurrying into the yard, she laughed loudly and cried. "Here comes the straggler."

"I'm not having this carry-on tomorrow morning I can tell you."

"Oh dear, I do seem to have caused a fuss, don't I," Tina said dismayed.

"Don't be silly, of course you haven't," April admonished. "You're one of us now, and *do* stop it with the 'oh dears'. Now, come on, let's get breakfast then me and Fay will show you around the farm, best foot forward, Mr Bellows won't stand for slow coaches."

"Oh d..." she was cut short by April's disapproving stare.

"Come on," Fay called as she ran past April and Tina. "I'll race you to the farmhouse, who's the straggler now, eh?!" she laughed.

* * *

"You'll have realised that this is a mixed farm, Tina," April began. "Cows, a few sheep, chickens, hen's, even a goat, and a few cultivated fields, also two working horses, one is in foal, but I haven't seen them yet, I look forward to that as I love horses. I understand that a farm a few miles away rears chicks, about thirty-thousand, now *that* would be interesting."

As they came up to the hencoop, Tina said

"What a din."

April laughed.

"It's even worse when you start throwing the feed to them, just stroll among them and throw a handful of feed at a time."

"Don't they peck your legs?" Tina asked.

"No, they're more interested in what you have in your hand," April replied. She swung open the gate, then went on. "See the old washtub stood in the corner, the one with the lid on, that's where the feed's stored; throw a handful around as far as you can."

"But don't some get more than others?" Tina asked with a worried look on her face.

"They don't starve, as you can see, they all look well-fed," April explained.

"Oh, yes, they do," Tina said with relief.

"You really are green when it comes to country life," Fay remarked.

"Of course she is," April said angrily. "What do you expect?! She *has* been thrown in at the deep end after all and will learn as she goes along, as you had to."

"I hope I do," Tina said fervently.

"There, I think that's enough food for them," April said as she placed the lid firmly onto the feed tub. "We've to come back later and collect the eggs, which we've to pack at the end of the week ready to be taken to the railway station. From there they get delivered to wherever it is they go."

"Do you know where they go?" Tina asked nervously.

"I haven't got a clue; I just collect them and help with the packing," April answered.

"Maybe Mr Bellows will give us one for our lunch out of the kindness of his heart," Tina said shyly.

April pulled a face, then said warningly.

"Don't push it, just be thankful; we get bacon sarnies here, some farms are really mean and give us a bit of bread and jam." She paused, then said. "Not fit for the pigs." Then, her face clearing, she cried, "now for the pigs.

"Pigs," Tina repeated. "I don't like pigs, nasty smelly things."

"Well, you'd better *get* to like them because that's one of the jobs on a farm, mucking out and feeding," April said with a big grin on her face.

"It's not one of my favourite jobs," Fay said.

"Nor mine, but we have it to do, so come on," April said bossily.

As they neared the pigpen, loud squealing rent the air.

"Oh no, it sounds as if the farmer's having one killed for his own use, they always squeal and kick up a fuss. I think that they know, or sense what's about to happen," April said.

Fay looked apprehensively at Tina; whose face had gone drip white.

"I think I'm going to faint," Tina mumbled.

"Don't you dare, you'll come across worse things than that on a farm, so toughen up!" April shouted angrily.

"Bend down and put your head between your knees," Fay ordered as she saw that Tina was about to pass out. "Now, take deep breaths slowly, in and out, in, and out."

Tina did as she was asked, then stood slowly upright. She held her hand over her mouth and coughed loudly before she said.

"Thank you, I feel a little better, but the smell is horrible."

"It is," Fay agreed. "And the hot sun doesn't help."

"You'll soon get used to it, Tina, all pigs smell, all they do all day is eat, shit, and breed, it's a fact of life, accept it."

Tina groaned at April's blunt words as she slowly followed her, squishing her way through the mire, glad to be wearing her wellingtons and not boots.

The sow and her ten piglets milled around the girls feet as they made their way towards the large pig bin, the closer they got, the more obnoxious the smell, as waste food, anything at all, was thrown into the bin, nothing went to waste on a farm. They tried not to tread on or fall over the piglets as they swarmed around their Mother, ever hungry.

Two buckets stood by the bin, April filled each in their turn and handed one to Fay and Tina.

"Empty it into the trough, and watch the sow, she likes to take a bite out of you – so Mr Bellows told me. If she tries it, hit her on the snout with the bucket."

"Oh, I couldn't do that," Tina cried.

"You'd be glad to if she took a bite out of you," April laughed.

"Why didn't you tell us that before we got in here?!" Fay cried angrily as she swatted at a wasp that flew around her head.

Suddenly a voice shouted out.

"Hi there, girls."

Three figures came into view.

"Here's Barry and Dennis, someone else too," Fay said. "I wonder what they want?"

"We're soon going to find out," April said.

As the men came up to the girls, Dennis began.

"Message for you three from Mr Bellows." He paused for a second. "But first, you haven't had a proper introduction to Larry have you." He turned to the silent man stood next to him and put his hand onto his shoulder, then said with a flourish, "this is Larry."

Larry was devastatingly handsome with black, curly, long hair which fell onto his forehead in tight, thick curls. Almost black eyes and a long Roman nose. He suddenly smiled, which lit up his whole face.

In a smooth, vibrant voice, he said.

"So, I get to meet the Land Army Girls at last." He turned to April. "You must be the little firebrand, April."

April nodded her head, then said.

"That's me."

Larry went on.

"Dennis has told me all about you."

"Has he now," April said. "I would've liked to have been a fly on the wall."

"It was all good, I promise you." He took hold of April's hand, shook it, then said. "Pleased to know you."

To herself, April was thinking, 'are you now, I'll make up my mind about you later.' Before he could speak to Fay, she said sarcastically.

"So, you're the one who's supposed to be God's gift to women according to the village girls, well, I can tell you now, you wouldn't be *my* gift."

"Now, why doesn't that surprise me, you're not my type either, April, so no sweat eh," Larry said politely.

April turned to the boys.

"What's the message from Mr Bellows?"

Dennis gave a grin.

"He wants you down in the middle field, hoeing I should think."

"What? Just before lunch?" April questioned.

"That's what he said," Dennis laughed as if it were a joke.

"I'll take your word for it." She turned to Fay. "Do you think that you could tear yourself away from 'God's gift to woman'? We've work to do."

Fay looked at April without really seeing her and said.

"Yes."

"What's hoeing?" Tina asked.

"Oh, you'll love hoeing," April answered sarcastically.

"When you say it like that, I think maybe I won't," Tina said dubiously.

"On your way, girls," Barry shooed them away. "Aren't you lucky, us doing the mucking out for you."

"It's so kind of you, see you on the muckheap," April called as the girls hurried away.

"I'm glad we've gotten out of the mucking out, I'd rather hoe, although it's not easy, but first, I have to go to the toilet. I'll use the one in the stable, you two go on, I'll catch you up." She came to a halt and looked closely at Fay. "You've not fallen for that Larry, have you?" she asked. "I hope not; I'm not putting up with a dreamy dewy-eyed maiden whose miles away working next to me."

Fay gazed at April, not having heard a word.

April shook her head and said.

"Bloody hell! Go on, I'll catch you up."

On the way to the stable, April had to pass a billy-goat which was fastened to a chain on an iron stake in the stable yard. For some reason, he seemed not to like people, and so was chained most of the time. He was an aggressive creature, so April gave him a wide berth, and, once in the toilet, shut the fragile bolt behind her. As she dropped her corduroy trousers to her ankles, she heard a noise like a fast-travelling express train, then, a loud bang at the toilet door. She stood listening, her heart beating madly in her chest, then the door rattled on its hinges as the blow was repeated. She quickly realised that the goat had gotten loose of his chain, and after repeated runs back, was determined to break down the door and get at her. So far, the bolt had held, but it wouldn't for much longer.

Finally, it gave and clattered to the floor. Hampered by her trousers heaped around her ankles, she managed to climb onto the toilet rim just as the goat charged in and head-butted the porcelain pedestal, sending splinters flying in all directions. He then ran back deliberately, turned, and resumed his attack. April managed to reach down quickly and pick up the lavatory brush, not much of a weapon she thought, but she belted the granite forehead of the goat every time he charged.

I can't keep this up much longer, I'd better start screaming, this mad bloody goat certainly has it in for me.

It seemed like almost at once, Mrs Bellows came along and took the goat by his collar, calling him a naughty boy and laughing at April's plight.

"Are you alright, April? It must have been a shock for you, Sidney going for you like that; we'd better strengthen the stake in the yard."

"Yes, you'd better. Call him Sidney, do you? Well, he's going to have one hell of a headache after the belting I gave him with the toilet brush."

Mrs Bellows laughed at the furious look on April's face.

"He's a tough old billy-goat is Sidney, he'll get over it, he's a pet really."

"Is he? Well, he's certainly never going to be my pet; I'd rather have a boa-constrictor," April replied as she none too lady-like yanked up her trousers.

"Excitement over with for now, we'd better get down to the fields, I've got lunch with me. You and the others must be hungry. I'm just going to shut Sidney up in the shed for a little while, serves him right for being so naughty."

Bloody naughty?! He wants strangling with his chain, April thought as she made her way to the fields. Blow me, I didn't have a pee! Oh well, I'll get behind a hedge.

9

"Okay girls, time to knock off, it's six o'clock, home-time, but call in the farmhouse, Mrs Bellows has some tea ready for you," Mr Bellows called across the field. As the three girls trooped towards him, he said happily. "You look to have done a good job, not a weed in sight."

"I should hope not," April commented. "We've been at it for five hours; my back's killing me." She put her arms above her head and stretched upright. "There, that's better." She looked keenly at Tina. "How are you feeling? It's been hard for you on your first day."

"I'm numb with pain all over," she moaned. "I just want to creep into bed and stay there for a week. Why did I join the Land Army?!"

Mr Bellows gave a ringing laugh.

"A few more days and you'll be as right as rain."

"I won't last a few more days," Tina said moodily. "I should've stayed in the home and looked after the kids; it would've been easier."

"You can stop the defeatist attitude right now," April said angrily. "Now come on, I'm hungry."

Once in the farmhouse kitchen, Mrs Bellows had the meal already for them. Cold pork, pickled onions, and fresh, crisp lettuce. Home-made bread was cut into slices and buttered, ready on a plate.

"Oh, this is quite a spread, Mrs Bellows, you do us proud!" April said with shining eyes.

"I'm pleased to, now sit yourselves down, I want to see three cleared plates."

The girls needed no further telling and got stuck in with a will. When every morsel had disappeared, April patted her stomach.

"That was lovely, thanks so much, Mrs Bellows."

"Yes, thank you," Fay and Tina echoed.

"We'd better get off, see you tomorrow bright and early, but I hope it's a little cooler, we'll wear our dungarees and boots, wellingtons make our feet sweat too much."

As the girls ambled down the lane, Fay holding the vacant bike beside her, they each took off their turbans and shook their hair around their heads. There was a slight breeze blowing gently into their faces, and each gave a sigh of contentment as the rich fragrance of Dog Roses drifted around them, along with the wildflowers from the hedgerows.

They each thought how lucky they were to be here in this beautiful part of the world, untouched yet by the war, but, for how long. They only heard by word of mouth what was going on in the outside world. They did not get a paper, did not listen to the wireless, indeed Miss Topp hogged that, but it was really for the use of the Land Girls.

April's thoughts ended as they went into the village.

"Why don't we walk into the village?" Fay suggested. "We don't have to rush back to the hostel, it's a lovely evening, let's make the most of it."

"Yes, that would be nice," Tina said. "I haven't seen the village yet. It looks quite charming."

"Maybe you're hoping to see 'God's gift to woman', is that it, Fay?" April said with a smirk on her face.

"No," Fay snapped back. "I've already arranged to meet him later on in the week."

"Good for you, that's another one fallen at his feet," April said abruptly.

Fay chose to ignore this remark.

As they came to the small village shop, a group of boys were stood looking into the window. As the girls came abreast of them, all the boys turned and looked at them in admiration; one gave a cheeky wolf-whistle, while April tried not to smile.

Suddenly, one of the boys stepped forward.

"Hi, Miss April," he said with a broad smile on his face, "remember me? The lad on the bus, Norman."

"Hello, Norman, of course I remember you, did you get into trouble when you got home? If I remember rightly, your Mam was going to belt you for enjoying my little escapade with the conductor."

"She gave me a couple of cracks, they didn't hurt, my Dad asked why she was mad at me, when I told him, he laughed and said he wished he'd been there to see it.

I told all my mates about you; they think you're wonderful! They had me showing them how you wrestled the conductor in the playground. These are my mates."

The other four boys were stood goggled-eyed, gazing at April in awe.

Norman gave them a half-hearted introduction to April, not wanting to share her with anyone else. He waved his hand towards the boys, calling out their names.

"This is Sammy, Billy, John and David."

"Hello, Miss," they mumbled shyly.

"Hello, boys. Shouldn't you be doing something other than hanging around shop windows?"

"Nothing to do, Miss April, too hot to sit in the pictures, and the park is full of silly girls," Norman replied.

"I'll bet you all like gobstoppers, don't you?" April asked with a gleam in her eye.

"Oh yes, when we've got some money, but spending money day isn't until Friday, and it's only Tuesday," Norman said sadly.

"Come on, boys, into the shop with me," April said suddenly.

If these boys thought of her as their hero, she would give them a treat.

April walked into the shop, the boys teeming around her and chattering non-stop. She could see that the little old lady that usually managed the shop wasn't stood behind the counter; instead, it was a very plump lady with dark grey hair. She stood with the flat of her hands placed on the counter, a pleasant smile on her face.

"Hello there, can I help you?" she asked.

"I really hope you can and will," April said.

"That's why I'm here, to serve and please. Just for today anyway, my Aunt's feeling a little off-colour and is resting."

"Oh, I'm sorry to hear that," April said sadly. "I need a massive favour."

"Anything I can do for the Land Army I'll do, my niece is a Land Girl and has told me how hard you work, I take my hat off to you."

"Well, thanks; it's nice to have a bit of praise for a change."

"You deserve it. I'm Mrs Birch by the way, and you are?"

"April Thornton."

Mrs Birch's face lit up.

"The April who threw around that no good conductor last week?"

"That's her," Norman cried with pride.

"What a sight for sore eyes that must have been! It was the talk of the knitting circle; a right laugh it gave us; I thought old Mrs Hartley would die laughing! She's ninety-four you know, you must go along and meet her, I know she would love to meet *you*."

The boys were starting to shuffle around impatiently, on seeing this, April began.

"It's like this, Mrs Birch, I want to give these lads a treat, and I've no money on me, I've just come from work. Could they all have a gobstopper each? I'll drop the money in tomorrow night, I'm very trustworthy."

"My dear, of course, it's very nice of you. I'll leave my Aunt a note to that effect, I'm sure she won't mind at all."

Mrs Birch turned away from the counter and reached down a large glass jar from a shelf behind her. Lifting the lid, she took out one at a time, a large smooth gobstopper, and handed one to each boy.

"Now, you lot, say thank you to Miss April."

"Thank you, Miss April." the boys said in chorus.

"You're welcome. Now off you go, and no more bragging about my exploits," April sang out'

"What's exploits?" Sammy asked.

"You don't know anything. Come on, I'll explain later," Norman said bossily.

At this, both April and Mrs Birch laughed merrily.

"Kids," Mrs Birch said.

"Do you have any family?" April asked.

"Yes, twin girls, both married, and I'm a Grandma to four boys."

"I have twin brothers, unmarried; my Mam keeps saying there's hope for them yet," April said with a smile. "I must be off, I've two friends waiting outside for me, and thanks for your help and understanding, Mrs Birch."

"Anytime, April. Goodbye for now."

Outside, Fay was shuffling around impatiently.

When April joined her and Tina, she said abruptly.

"Have you finished all your good deeds for the day? I've a phone call to make."

"Sorry, you should've said, I wouldn't have taken so long," April said, just as abruptly.

"There's a phone-box across the road, I'll use that, you two go on."

"I've never known you make a phone call before; it must be important," April said.

"Yes," Fay replied, looking mysterious. "It's imperative, so I'm off before someone else nips in to use it."

"Hmm," April said, pulling her face into an uninterested look.

As the two weaved their way down Main Street, Fay hurriedly crossed the road and stepped into the phone box; she picked up the phone and dialled the number for the operator. When a voice said, 'number please', she said loudly.

"Could I have a call, and collect please."

"What number do you require?" the voice came back.

"Harrogate, 3074," Fay replied.

"Please hold the line, I'll connect you shortly."

Fay tapped her foot slowly as she waited.

"I can connect you now; the receiver will accept the call."

Her Mother's voice came over the phone loud and clear.

"Fay, my darling! How are you? It's lovely to hear from you! There's nothing wrong, is there? You are alright? Not working too hard. Don't wear yourself out; I'm so proud of you doing the job you're doing."

"Mother, I'm fine, and I love the job."

"Do you get enough to eat, dear?"

"Yes, Mother, we don't do too badly."

"Would you like me to send you a food hamper, dear?"

"No thanks, Mother, as I said, we don't do too badly. How are you? How is *he* treating you? Let me know if he puts a foot wrong. Do you need any money? You must let me know if you do."

"I don't need money, dear, what I need is to see you, it's been so long."

"I don't have any leave coming up; when I do, I'll let you know."

"We'll have a party when you do."

"Please, Mother, no party."

"Silly, girl, all your friends will want to see you."

"Now, Mother, no party."

"Alright, dear."

"Mother, I want you to do me a very big favour."

"Anything, darling, just ask."

"With your title, you carry a lot of clout don't you."

"I like to think so, dear."

"Do you still have friends who are part of The Ministry of Agriculture, The Ministry of Labour and Local Representatives?"

"Why yes, dear, I do."

"Listen carefully, Mother, I have an absolute best friend whom I work with, she looks after me, you know, sticks up for me. Well, at the hostel where we live, we have this truly awful housekeeper that is supposed to oversee us. She's wicked, bossy and cruel, and has taken a dislike to my friend April. Mother, April is a straight-talker, afraid of no one, so stands up to this housekeeper, which only makes her hate April more. I know for a fact she's making plans to have April removed when *she* is the one who should be going. None of the girls like her, except one who's a tale carrier. And we're almost sure that she's keeping part of our rations, so, what I'm asking is, can you have this housekeeper removed, whose name is Miss Topp. April calls her Miss Mopp. I've been with April since I started in the Land Army, she's taught me all I know, so, Mother, dear, can you do anything? Straight away before she gets rid of April?"

"Fay, my darling child, consider it done, this Miss Topp sounds a terrible person, not fit to oversee girls. I'm certainly not going to allow her to make *my* little girl unhappy. Leave it with me, darling, I'll fix things."

"Oh, thanks, Mother, you're a pip!"

"What's a pip, darling?"

"The best, that's what you are, the best."

"I must meet this April of yours. When you come home on leave you must bring her with you, she'll be very welcome."

"I hope that *he* won't be around, I've a feeling April won't like him."

"I'll see to it that he isn't, so don't worry, Fay darling."

"Thanks, Mother, I must ring off and get back to the hostel, I want to have a bath, only six inches of water are allowed, isn't it awful, trying to get a bath in six inches of water."

"Yes, it is, dear, but that's the rule. I'll be glad when the war's over, but we don't get much trouble with bombing over here. I hear that you've lots of G.I's near you that are very over-sexed. Do keep away from them won't you, dear."

"Yes, Mother, I'll try. Good-bye now, I love you."

As Fay replaced the phone back onto the hand-rest, she felt relieved. Mother would see to getting rid of Miss Topp, when Mother set her stall out, no grass would grow.

As she peddled happily away, she was content, knowing that Mother was dealing with things. Bless all Mothers.

10

April was more well-liked and respected than she knew: having a run-in with the village bus conductor, flying at speed through the village on her bike, standing up to the hated Miss Topp, buying the boys gobstoppers, had all increased her reputation – all knew who April Thornton was. Her fame was about to be spread a little further this morning at the village school.

Norman, who had first seen and met April during her fiasco on the bus, was on this bright sunny morning surrounded by a crowd of his mates, bragging of how he knew April, and demonstrating how she picked up and disposed of the unpopular bus conductor.

"She did it like this."

Norman bent and picked up a small boy who was stood next to him, heaving him onto his shoulders, he then threw the lad onto the ground.

"Oww!" the lad wailed, "that hurt!"

"That's what Miss April did, and that bus conductor was twice her size and weight."

"Cor, I would've liked to have seen that!"

"Miss April's marvellous! And I saw her first; in fact, when I grow up, I think I'll marry her," Norman said, sticking out his chin.

"She wouldn't look at you with *your* spotty clock," a tall, thin-faced boy said in contempt.

"Who're you calling spotty clock?! I'll put you one on," Norman said angrily.

Just then, a small squat man, middle-aged, who wore milk-bottled-topped-glasses perched on the end of his long thin nose, appeared in the open double doors, and loudly rang a handbell.

The children filed in an orderly manner into one of the two classrooms, this was for boys only, aged eight to ten years old.

The boys stood quietly behind their desks, waiting for the order to sit. When the command came, it was like a military one, snapped out in a no-nonsense voice.

"Sit."

The teacher, Mr Simms, pulled the register towards him.

"When I call out your names, answer 'yes'." When roll call was completed, Mr Simms sat looking at his class over the top of his glasses. "You, McMasters, why did you pick up, and then throw to the ground a boy smaller than yourself? Turning into a bully, are we?"

Norman jumped, then gave Mr Simms a startled look.

"I was demonstrating Miss April's lift, Sir."

"Whom may I ask is Miss April?"

"She's a Land Girl, Sir, and my friend."

"Is she indeed? And where did you meet your friend April?"

"On the bus, Sir."

"On the bus, is it? Land Girls don't ride on buses, they walk, McMasters."

"This one doesn't, Sir, and there were two of them."

"Really?" Mr Simms pushed his glasses further up onto his nose. "And whom may I ask was this April lifting?"

"The bus conductor, Sir."

"The bus conductor?! But he is a man, there are only two conductors, and both are big men."

"Yes, Sir, but Miss April lifted him off the floor and threw him onto a seat."

"This is very interesting, astonishing even; you are an excellent liar, McMasters."

"I'm not lying, Sir, Miss April's an exceptional girl – Judge Bentley said so, I heard him."

"Come out here, McMasters." Mr Simms gestured towards Norman.

Norman obeyed nervously.

Mr Simms swayed back onto his heels, then said.

"I think that you are casting a slur on the good name of Judge Bentley, he would never countenance behaviour like that. How you thought that one up with *your* pee-brain, I will never know, McMasters."

"I haven't thought it up because it happened," Norman answered cheekily. "You ask him."

"You are asking for three lashes! Where do you get them, McMasters?" Mr Simms thundered.

Throwing caution to the wind, Norman said calmly.

"On the arse, Sir."

"*What did you say?!*"

"On the arse, Sir." Norman bravely repeated. "And he said he hadn't enjoyed himself as much for a long time, not since he saw an old black and white Laurel and Hardy film fourteen years ago."

Mr Simms chose to ignore Norman's speedy response, instead, repeating with his raised and readied cane. "Yes, on the arse *indeed*, McMasters!!" Three quick strikes with the cane whooshed down onto Normans posterior. "I'll say this for you, you are a good exaggerator!"

"I don't know what exaggerator means, Sir, but I'm telling the truth," Norman said, red-faced and breathless.

"Let's take your fairy story a little further, McMasters, what pray was the other Land Girl doing while her friend was throwing the conductor around?"

A loud snigger came from the back of the classroom.

"If that boy sniggers again, he will be bent over a chair and given three lashes, just like our McMasters here!" Mr Simms called out, his eyes never leaving Norman's face. "Pray, do go on, McMasters," he said. "I cannot wait to hear more of your fascinating story."

"I don't think I can remember any more, Sir," Norman said apologetically.

Mr Simms eyebrows shot up, almost to his hair.

"Cannot remember?! Now, why does that not surprise me. Are you wasting my time, McMasters?"

Norman smiled.

"No, Sir, I've just remembered."

A smothered giggle came from the back of the class, and a voice said sarcastically.

"He's just remembered."

Mr Simms narrowed his eyes and glared at the class.

"I am warning you all, if I hear another giggle, snigger, or voice, you will all be kept in after school for one hour. Go on, McMasters."

"The other Land Girl was called Fay." Norman paused.

"Go on," Mr Simms said sharply. "What did this Fay have to say during all the shemozzle?"

Norman looked blank as he thought, what the hell does shemozzle mean?! It was a new one on him.

"I am waiting."

"She went white, then said, 'oh God', and put her hand up and held her throat."

"She said, 'oh, God'. Are you sure, McMasters?"

"Yes, Sir."

"I am beginning to change my mind about your story, McMasters, someone as dumb as you could not possibly make all that up."

"I told you it was the truth, Sir."

"Who else was with you?"

"My Mum, Sir."

"What did she say to all of this?"

"She told me not to look, and gave me a leathering when we got home, for looking that way."

"What did your Father have to say about the matter?"

"He thought it was funny and would love to have seen it."

"Well, I tell you this, *I* don't think it funny, there can't be anything ladylike about this Land Girl."

"Oh, but there is, Sir. She's pretty and kind, she bought me and my mates gobstoppers, and I'd love to marry her when I grow up."

"Don't talk so stupid, McMasters."

"Can I sit down now, Sir?"

"Yes, and before I bring an end to this enlightening story of yours, I tell you now, I will be having a word with Judge Bentley."

"Good, Sir, he'll tell you what I have."

"I hope that you are not trying to be sarcastic, McMasters, or are you becoming cheeky?"

"No, Sir, not at all, Sir."

"Good, now, all of you take out your maths books and let us get on with some work."

* * *

Back at Whitmore, Miss Topp was stood, hands-on-hips, confronting some of the girls.

"Now, how many of you are going to the village hop tonight? I want you all in at the same time, and don't try to sneak in any boyfriends, I don't stand for that."

"Put your hands up like good little girls," April said sweetly.

Miss Topp smiled maliciously.

"Carry on, April; I haven't much longer to put up with you."

"You don't say, have you called the troops in," April laughed.

"You'll be laughing on the other side of your face when you're marching down the road, suitcase in hand," Miss Topp replied calmly.

Fay smiled secretly to herself, little did Topp, *or* April know what wheels had been set in motion.

Miss Topp went on.

"How many are going to the hop then?"

"I'm not, I've had a gruelling day, it's an early night for me," Jane replied.

"Me too," Connie said.

"And me," Binnie added.

"I'm going to have a bath, *if* there's any hot water, and write some letters home," Belinda said loudly.

"I've some sewing to do, although I hate sewing, but it has to be done," Anita put in.

"I'm no dancer," Katrina said sadly. "I've two left feet, me and Joan are going for a walk in the woods, we hope to hear the Nightingale sing. Are you coming too, Nancy?"

"Oh, I'd love to!" Nancy answered happily.

"That means only me, Fay and Tina for the hop then, Miss Topp," April said.

Miss Topp fixed April with a cold stare.

"So it does. You won't be welcome there you know, the village girls hate you lot."

"So I've heard, I wonder why?" April asked.

"Because you make out you're better than them, or so I've been told," Miss Topp said jeeringly.

"We *are* better than them, any fool knows that. Why are *they* not in the forces?" April asked.

"I don't know, I don't really care, ask them," Miss Topp shot back. "Aye, you'll not be able to be clever with them; they won't stand for it, make mincemeat out of you they will."

April gave a ringing laugh.

"Do you think so?! I'd like to see them try. We aren't going looking for trouble, Miss Mopp, just for a night out, have a dance and a drink, maybe some sensible conversation. Hopefully a few G.I's will be there, and *I'll* show those village girls how to jitterbug."

"Ha, G.I's! That's all your type deserves."

April felt her anger rising as she lifted her head high, sticking out her chin.

On Fay seeing this, she said.

"Oh, God."

"My type?" April said quietly. She stood, then moved closer to Miss Topp, then repeated. "My type, what *is* my type, Miss Topp?"

Fay pulled Tina towards her, and both moved to stand near the door.

Miss Topp stood her ground and glared at April disgustingly as she ground out through clenched teeth.

"You're a common little upstart from a common pit village, cheap mining stock who can't speak the King's English properly, you're all raggedy-arsed, snotty-nosed uneducated whelps. I could lay my tongue to a lot more, but I think you get my meaning."

Fay felt near to fainting, while the other girls were dumbstruck.

Tina held fast to Fay's hand, white-faced, as Fay said.

"Oh, my good God."

"Oh, you think that do you?" April said calmly. "Have you ever graced a pit village with your presence?"

"No," Miss Topp snapped back. "Nor do I ever intend to if its people are all like you." She narrowed her eyes. "Common ragamuffins, the lot of you."

"Really? So, that's what you think is it? Well, here's what I think of your opinion."

She pulled back her left arm, and with the back of her hand, swiped Miss Topp across the mouth, the blow knocking her onto the tabletop where she lay moaning in shock.

April laid her hand on Miss Topp's chest, pressing her down, then said quietly.

"I don't allow anyone, not *anyone* to call the mining folk, *my* folk, or their villages, you're not fit to lick the pit muck off their boots. And as for me being a type, *this* is the type I am, and proud of it!" Leaning down, she pulled Miss Topp into a sitting position, then said. "Now, you ugly-faced bitch, don't ever forget that the miners are the salt of the earth, always have been, always will be!" She shook Miss Topp as she would a rag doll. "The salt of the earth, understand?!"

At that moment, Monica came into the kitchen. Taking in immediately what had happened, she launched herself at April, screaming like a banshee.

"Get off her, you bitch!"

April knocked her away with little effort, as Monica continued to scream.

"*Stop that!*" April shouted. Then more quietly. "Take your Miss Topp to her room, and she should think herself lucky she's an older woman; otherwise, I would've hung her out to dry."

The now silent Monica gave April a look of hate, then turned and helped the still dazed Miss Topp from the tabletop.

The two left the kitchen in silence.

Fay pulled herself together and pushed the terrified Tina away from her; to April she said.

"I think that you went a bit too far, April."

"Do you," April replied. "I don't let anyone call the South Yorkshire people, so don't say another word."

"I don't intend to. I'm going to take Tina upstairs and calm her down," Fay said shortly.

"Yes, do that, protect her from the real world why don't you."

"She's only a babe."

"She has to grow up."

"But not your way."

"She has a choice; it'll make or break her."

Fay chose to ignore this and lead the silent Tina from the kitchen.

"Well, after all that, I think its cups of tea all round! When I signed on, they didn't tell me about all the excitement you get in the WLA!" Katrina laughed as she set the kettle on to boil.

"April did right to stand up for her people. I'm a rat catcher, and Topp's a female rat if ever I saw one. She got what she deserved, I'm glad. And another thing, I think that she's been keeping some of our rations, we never have sugar, and the tea's like water, so, I've made up my mind to report her. I hope you lot will support me," Nancy said.

There were nods of agreement and cries of.

"I will."

"Everything happened so fast, I still can't take it in," Belinda said. "But I wouldn't have missed it for the world!"

"You didn't seem as if you had really lost your temper though, April. I thought that red hair of yours was no lie," Katrina said puzzled.

"I held on to my temper. She's an older woman," April said abruptly. "And my Dad always said my red hair was my downfall."

"I wouldn't want to be around when you *do* really lose your temper," Connie laughed.

"Never mind about temper," Katrina called as she handed around cups of tea. "I can't find any sugar, plenty of milk, and I'm afraid the tea is like witch water."

"She means witch piss," April said mischievously. Everyone laughed. "But we'll find out about the shortage of tea and sugar, I promise you."

"Tina was really scared during all the trouble, wasn't she? Do you think that she'll go to the hop tonight?" Anita asked.

"I hope so; it'll take her out of herself," April answered. "That's what she needs, she's been stuck in a children's home for years looking after kids, she needs to grow up, get used to adults."

Belinda had a faraway look in her eyes as she said apprehensively.

"Tina must be watched; she doesn't have a long life in front of her."

"Here we go again, bloody 'Gypsy Rose-Lee' predicts," Anita moaned. Then sharply. "Shut up Belinda!"

"What the hell do you mean?" April asked anxiously, a worried look on her face.

"I can't help what I see," Belinda defended. "It's her fate, it's all mapped out I'm afraid, as it is for all of us."

April took hold of her by the shoulder.

"Don't ever say anything like that about Tina again."

Belinda frowned and pulled away from April.

"I'm a seer, it's a gift I have, I didn't ask for it. I've had it all my life, as did my Mother and Grandmother before me, it's handed down."

"Whatever you see, you should keep to yourself," Anita interrupted.

"Tell me what you mean about Tina," April insisted. "Go on, I want to know."

"Do you believe in the second sight?" Belinda probed.

"I have an open mind; I've come across some strange things in my time," April answered. "Now, tell me about Tina."

"Do you think it's wise? Knowing I mean," Anita said.

"I need to know, if I think that there's any truth in what Belinda tells me, I can look after Tina, both me and Fay," April said firmly.

"This goes no further than this room, understood?" Belinda said quietly. "It's between just us few here."

Heads were nodded.

"Against my better judgement, I have to tell you to listen to her, April, she's never wrong, as I've learnt to my cost," Anita said softly.

April nodded her head, then said.

"Go on."

"This is going to sound terrible, but I saw it the first time I met her. I saw her in a field being attacked by two men, she's fighting, screaming, one holds her down while the other..." She broke off.

There was utter silence in the room until April banged her fist on the tabletop.

"Are you mad?!" she screamed at Belinda.

"No, you asked what I saw, and I told you."

"I don't believe you."

"That's your choice."

"My choice?"

"Yes."

"What kind of a choice does Tina have?"

"She doesn't, that's the pity of it, we can't change fate."

"From now on, she'll be with me every minute of the day."

"It doesn't work like that."

"I'll change it."

"Fate is all-powerful."

"Is it?"

"The best advice I can give you, April is to accept it."

"Is she going to die?"

"No, but it will change her life completely."

"Oh."

"I'm so sorry to have told you, April, but you did insist."

The by now white-faced April said.

"Do me a favour, Belinda, if you ever see anything for me, don't tell me, let me remain in ignorance, then I can handle it as it comes."

"I haven't known you long enough, April, but I know that you can, and will," Belinda said softly. She picked up her cup of tea, drank the cup empty and set it carefully down on the table, then she stood, ready to leave the kitchen, until April asked.

"Tell me, Belinda, did you see me slapping Miss Mopp with your second sight?"

"Now, that would be telling, wouldn't it?" she said over her shoulder as she left the kitchen.

There was silence as everyone looked at each other.

April was the first to break it.

"Well, you lot, how good is she?"

"Very good," Anita said firmly.

"I never used to believe in that kind of thing, but since meeting Belinda, I do," Connie said.

"I'm going to take it seriously," April said fervently.

"Do you really mean that? If so, you're going to have your work cut out," Connie said, dubiously.

"Of course I mean it; nothing's going to happen to Tina while I'm around," April cried.

"You can't watch her every minute of the day," Anita put in. "And besides, she's bound to notice."

"You can't fight fate, or change your path in life, so, it's better not to know, or listen to predictions," Connie said, determinedly. "See the upset Belinda has caused with her latest one?"

"To be forewarned is to be forearmed," April said abruptly.

"This has upset everyone; I think we should let it drop," Anita insisted.

"I agree," Connie said, apologetically.

April shook her head.

"Actually, this has put me in the mood for the local hop! We need to get out, listen to the music, meet people and forget our troubles for a couple of hours, try to enjoy ourselves. And above all, see that Tina enjoys *herself*, although she says that she can't dance, but I'll get her around the floor, there's only one way to learn, and that's to try."

"I must warn you; the village girls don't like us going to their hops," Connie said, warningly.

"Don't they, well, they'll just have to get used it because I intend going to a lot more," April said.

"I wonder why they hate us so much?" Connie asked.

"We're better looking, have good figures, look smart in our uniforms, get the men and can dance. In a word, leave *them* standing, and don't forget, Fay has captured the village heartthrob, 'The Lord Larry'!"

"No! You don't say!" Connie cried. "Not that good-looking farmhand with the face of a Greek God and the figure of Adonis?!"

"That's the one, love at first sight it was," April laughed. "Although he wouldn't be my type in a month of Sunday's."

"He'd be mine," Connie moaned.

"Oh well, it's a good job we don't all like the same isn't it. I'm off now to get ready for this hop thing. No dithering around deciding what to wear, we're going in our uniforms."

"That means trouble, the village girls hate to see us in our uniforms," Anita warned.

April grinned, then strolled out of the kitchen singing 'Jealousy' at the top of her voice.

"I'll tell you what, April has a good voice, had some training if *I* know anything," Anita said seriously.

"April's good at everything as far as I can see; I wish I were more like her," Connie said firmly."

"We couldn't do with another April; we've enough with the one we've got thank you very much," Anita snapped.

11

The three girls leant their bicycles on the wall at the back of the village hall to the sound of 'Boogie Woogie Bugle Boy' being belted out by the band inside.

"Wow, listen to that, it's loud, isn't it?" Fay said.

"If you think that's loud, wait until we get inside," April laughed.

Tina stood silent, nervous at the thought of walking into the hall and having people stare at her.

Oh, she wished that she hadn't let April talk her into coming, why couldn't she have been firm and said no, but *who* could say no to April?!

Seeing the apprehensive look on Tina's face, April gave her a firm look, took her by the hand, then said.

"Come on, Tina, don't be a mouse, we're going to walk into there as if we own the joint, aren't we, Fay." She turned to Fay. "Isn't that right, kiddo?"

"That's right," Fay answered with a smile, although she had her doubts.

"Come on, times a wasting."

As they came up to the shabby looking door which had its paint peeling off, April first in line, gave it a good push and walked in, head held high, and hat set at a jaunty angle, Fay and Tina crowded in behind her. Just at that moment, the music ended, and, at the opening of the door, all eyes were focussed on the three girls. April brought her head up higher and saluted smartly with a sarcastic grin on her face.

A girl's voice called.

"Look out, *they're* here!"

There was a loud titter.

THE LAND ARMY GIRLS ARE HERE

As April lowered her arm to her side, she thought, like that is it, so be it. Then turning to Fay and Tina, she said.

"Come on, girls, follow me, we'll find somewhere to sit."

Just then, a male voice called out.

"Please take your partners for a foxtrot."

The three-piece band struck up 'Moonlight Serenade', and the couples took to the floor.

As the girls made their way around the room, most of the chairs had handbags and coats on them until April saw three together which were not taken.

As the girls seated themselves, they looked around with interest. It was not a large hall, but it was already crowded with young people dressed in their finery, brightly coloured dresses, ankle-strap shoes, hair brushed until it shone, and large chunky earrings of many colours. The girls far outnumbered the boys, who wore baggy trousers, white shirts and smart ties. Most of the boys had their hair smoothed back with brill cream, giving them a gangster look. Only the Land Girls were different, they wore their uniform with pride, their hats pushed to the back of their heads. They stood out in the crowd, which pleased April.

There were several groups of local girls stood around the floor; most were giving the Land Girls scathingly dirty looks, on seeing this, April grinned smugly. 'Maybe there'll be a bit of a scuffle tonight? It looks as if some of these fair village maidens have it in for us, they don't want us here, that's certain. Well, we're here, so they can lump it.'

She leant towards Fay and asked.

"Have you seen all the dirty looks we're getting?"

"I have," Fay replied. "Just ignore them, we don't want any trouble, dirty looks don't hurt anyone."

Tina caught Fay's last few words.

"Is everything alright? I do feel so out of place here, I do wish that I hadn't come, it's not for me, this dancing thing."

"Now, Tina, stop moaning, you've to try everything once, until you do how can you say that you don't like a thing?" April said sharply. "Now, when they play another foxtrot, I'll get you up."

"Oh no, I couldn't," Tina panicked. "Everyone will look at me."

"Don't be silly, there's lots of couples on the floor, no one will even see you," April said firmly.

The music stopped, and all the couples on the dance floor clapped in appreciation just as the door was flung open to admit a group of smart, handsome G.I's.

Some of them called out.

"Hi, folks!"

These were the boys from Bomber Command, stationed three or four miles down the road. They had been in the pub across the street, had a few drinks and lively conversation with some of the old-timers in the pub, heard the music and followed the sound into the hall. At their entrance, a wave of excitement could be felt in the air; the girls patted their hair into place, smoothed down their dresses, and put on an enticing smile on their faces. The village boys resented their presence and murmured.

"Oh no."

The G.I's stood on the edge of the dance floor looking around with interest as the band started to play a slow waltz. One sauntered across the floor, his eyes on Tina. He was small and could see that Tina was also. As he reached her, he held out his hand.

"Dance with me, chick?" he queried.

Tina's face whitened as she sat tongue-tied.

"Will you dance with me honey?" he asked again.

"I'm sorry, my friend doesn't dance," April said pleasantly. "But thank you for asking her."

"No sweat, sweetheart, how about you?"

"I'll give it a whirl," April said.

The G.I took her hand and led her onto the floor, which by now was crowded. He put his hand nearer to her backside than was necessary, and pulled her up tight against him.

April put her hand on his chest and said.

"Loosen up; we're dancing, not in a loving clinch."

"Sorry, sweetheart, I don't know my own strength." He released her a little. "Say, you're a Land Army chick ain't you?"

"Yes, I have that honour, hence the uniform."

"You English do have a quaint way of speaking."

"Really? We think you G.I's have too."

"We've heard a lot about the WLA."

"All good, I hope?"

"Baby, I can assure you that you're very much admired."

"That's nice."

"How about you go out with me one night? I'll show you a good time."

"Thanks, but no."

"Come on, baby."

"In English, we spell no, N, O."

"I get you, baby, not interested, eh?"

"You got it in one, buddy."

As the dance came to an end, April thankfully sat down and said.

"Phew."

"That bad, was it?" Fay asked.

"I've danced with worse, but Tina couldn't have handled that guy. He held me so tight I felt every bit of him, and I *mean* every bit, no underpants if you get my drift," April laughed.

Fay looked scandalised.

"Where is your sense of propriety?" she asked.

"I don't have any; you should know that by now," April replied.

The band struck up a quickstep, and a tall, fair-haired G.I asked Fay to dance. For a moment she hesitated, then rose and allowed the G.I to whirl her away onto the dance floor.

April looked at the unhappy Tina, who sat with her hands clasped in her lap. An amused smile played around April's mouth as she said.

"I'm sorry I dragged you here, Tina, you're really hating it, aren't you?"

Tina nodded, her eyes brimming with tears.

"Because I'm an accomplished dancer myself, I expect everyone else to be too, but I can see that you're not, and are never going to be the type to be pitchforked into the arms of amorous males."

"I'm so glad you realise that, April. I really don't care for males, they frighten me."

"Some frighten me, but I've learnt how to handle them," April laughed.

Suddenly, a tall, swarthy looking G.I was stood in front of April, he held out his hand.

"Would you dance with me, Miss?" he asked.

"I'm so sorry, but I can't leave my friend, she isn't feeling well," April answered.

"So sorry about that, Miss, could I get her a glass of water?" he asked politely.

"No thank you, I have things under control," April said gratefully.

As he walked away, the music ended, and Fay sank breathlessly into her chair.

"Thank goodness that's over! I hope *he* doesn't ask me to dance again, my nose was buried in his chest, and I could hardly match my steps with his. Why do they have to hold you so close?!"

"It's their thrill time," April said with a smile.

"What do you mean? Thrill time," Fay asked.

"If I say ramrod and holding you close..." April said mischievously.

"Really April." Fay's face went a brilliant red.

"I should've thought it was obvious, not just the G.I's, *any* man," April retorted.

By a curious coincidence, loud laughter came from the group of G.I's, and a tall, dark, plain-looking G.I detached himself from the group and approached Fay with a knowing grin plastered all over his face.

"Hi, sweetheart, I hear you like being held close. Would you like to try *me* out? My name's Holt."

Fay sat speechless, lost for words as she realised the implication.

April had an uncontrollable urge to smack him in the mouth, but instead, she said quietly.

"My friend would not, but I would."

She smiled sweetly as she stood, made as if to put her arms around him, then dug her first finger into a spot to the left of his neck.

He jumped back with a cry of pain.

"What did you do?!" he cried.

"Me? Nothing," April said surprised. "There's a lot of wasps about this week, can be nasty little buggers, can't they."

The G.I stamped off.

"April, what did you do?" Fay cried.

"Me?" April said. "Absolutely nothing."

"I know that innocent look you wear when you've been up to something," Fay said, a worried look on her face.

"Forget it, he won't bother us again."

"I hope not, I didn't like the look of him."

"I don't believe it." Hot colour suddenly flushed April's face as she repeated. "I don't believe it!"

"What's wrong?" Fay cried.

"Tony, that's what's wrong, Tony's here."

"The Tony you met at Skipton?" Fay cried.

"Yes, the Tony I met at Skipton." She bit her lip. "Oh, bloody hell he's seen me! If he calls out April morning, I'll crown him!"

Tony came at a run, his face lit up like a Christmas candle, a beaming smile for April alone.

"April morning, my one and only, April morning!" he cried as he pushed a couple out of the way which blocked his path to her. As he reached her, he bent and pulled her to her feet and gave her a hug and a kiss on the cheek. "I knew I'd find you again my April!" he cried. "And still as beautiful as ever."

April tried to detangle herself from his embrace.

"Let me go, you, idiot."

Tony laughed.

"Still the little firecracker I see, don't forget, you're going to marry me!"

"Marry you?! Are you nuts?!"

"Yes, nuts about you."

"Tony, I hope you're not going to be a nuisance and a pest all night."

"Now, would I be either?"

"Yes, you would. Now, be a good little boy and go back to your buddies and I may, only may mind you, have a dance with you."

"Do you promise?"

"Yes, I promise, now off you go." She pushed him in the direction of his friends. "Thank goodness for that," she said in relief.

"He never said hello to me," Fay said.

"It's spoiled my night I can tell you," April moaned.

"That lad is clearly besotted with you," Fay said quietly. "More than besotted."

"Well, I'm not besotted with him, and that daft notion he's got in his head that I'm going to marry him, well, he's away with the fairies."

Fay sighed heavily.

"He can't help his feelings."

"I can't help mine; I just want him to keep away from me." She pursed her lips. "All this silly 'April morning' stuff, it gets on my nerves. I'll have one dance with him, and one dance only, then that's the end of it."

Tina, who had been sat quietly listening, now said.

"He seems to know you well, April, how did you meet?"

"I'll tell you later, my night's been spoiled enough without going on about Tony," April snapped.

"No need to snap at Tina," Fay said angrily.

"You're right, there isn't. Now, I could do with a drink, I'll go to the snack bar and get three lemonades, how's that? It's getting hot in here," April commented.

"I need the toilet," Tina said, embarrassed.

April pointed to where the band was seated.

"It's over there in the corner, second door; will you be okay on your own?"

Tina nodded.

"She's not a child," Fay said.

"You're being very picky tonight, Fay, is it because your love Larry isn't here?" April asked.

"Leave it, April, go and get the drinks," Fay said shortly.

April shrugged her shoulders and marched off, accompanied by loud wolf-whistles from Tony. She set her hat onto her head at a rakish angle, and swinging her arms as if on parade, strode into the snack bar.

She elbowed her way to the counter and accidentally barged into a large fat girl with dyed black hair.

She turned and said to April.

"Did you do that on purpose?"

"No," April said loudly.

"I think you did."

"Think what you like, want to make something of it?!" April snapped.

Seeing the dangerous look in April's eyes, the girl turned away and muttered. "Bloody Land Girls!"

Holding three full glasses of lemonade between her hands, April made her way to the door, she glanced around, hoping to get some help from Tina or Fay, but could see neither one. The quickstep the band had been playing, ended, the floor cleared, and Fay walked back to her seat.

April looked around for Tina; 'surely, she wasn't still in the toilet?! Maybe there was a queue.' As she made her way to Fay, she saw a group of five girls surrounding a small girl – Tina, who stood with a terrified look on her face. One of the group was holding Tina's arm and shouting out something.

April turned around to two girls who sat behind where she stood, and thrust the three glasses of lemonade at them, saying as she did so.

"Here, have these."

The two girls looked startled but took the drinks from her.

April took her hat off and handed it to one of them.

"Here, look after this for me." She ran towards the group of girls and pulled two of them towards her. "Get out of my way," she cried, pushing them to one side.

A tall, unpleasant looking girl held Tina's arm in a vice-like grip, a malicious look on her face, shaking Tina, who was paralysed with fear and unable to move. The bully hadn't yet seen April, until April dug her in the back.

"Take your hands off my friend," April ground out.

The rest of the group moved slowly away.

The three band members, sensing trouble, did not announce the next dance, and the young drummer chewed furiously on his chewing gum.

The bully looked at April, a grin on her face, her smile showing a missing top front tooth.

"I won't tell you again, take your hands off my friend."

"Or you'll what?" said the bully.

April stepped forward and pulled her hands away from Tina.

"Go and sit down with Fay," she said sharply.

"But, April," Tina stuttered.

"No buts, do as I say."

"Yes, do as your Mother tells yer, Tina four-eyes!" the bully shouted.

By this time, silence had fallen over the room, everyone waited expectantly. What would this little Land Girl do? Rita, the girl who had been pushing the other Land Girl around, was known as the village ringleader, no one messed with her, but here was a five-foot Land Girl breasting up to her. The people who were sat down, stood and moved closer to the troublemakers.

Meanwhile, Tina was giving a garbled story to Fay, who said.

"Stay here; I'll go see what's happening." She pushed her way through the crowd and saw April facing three girls.

April was saying.

"You want to know what I'm going to do?"

Fay stood white-faced, her hand clutching her throat while moaning.

"Oh God, my God, this isn't good."

"Yes, I want to know what you *think* you're going to do to *me*. Well, come on, we all know what the WLA is good at doing don't we?!" Rita laughed. She looked around at the crowd. "Don't we?!" she repeated.

"*I* don't. Why don't you tell me," April asked.

Fay began to tremble, this was bad when April spoke quietly in a row, it was terrible.

"I'm waiting," April said.

"Ha, WLA, we know what that stands for don't we girls?" Rita cried.

"I don't, tell me," April said calmly.

"We Love Airmen, We Lay Around, We Like Attention," Rita sang out.

Fay gasped.

April's face did not change.

The group of G.I's who were Bomber Command seemed to be enjoying this row. One said.

"Wow, this little Land Girl's got some spunk."

"Gee, this is so English," another said.

"It's not right, there's three on her."

"I'll take bets on the land lassie."

"Yes, she'll wipe the floor with 'em."

"She's sure got a good kisser on her."

"Do you think it's true, she likes Airmen?"

"She's sure not the type you take home to meet Mom is she," a rich voice said.

"Shut your cake-holes buddies; let's listen to what's happening," another said.

"Yes, all of you shut the hell up," Tony said.

They all fell silent.

April slowly looked Rita up and down from head to toe, then said acidly.

"If I were you, which I'm not, thank God, I'd close my mouth and walk away."

Rita smirked.

"You are not me, and I've no intention of walking away," she laughed loudly. "Walk away from a little jumped-up pipsqueak like you?! I don't think so."

April narrowed her eyes as Rita went on adding fuel to the fire.

"You're dealing with me now, not your dirty, smelly animals."

"Really? I wasn't aware of the difference, but since you've pointed it out, there's one thing about my animals, they're better looking than you," April smiled.

One of the G.I's stamped his foot on the floor and said.

"Nice one."

Fay breathed in and out slowly and began to sweat, her heart banging in her chest. This was bad, April would wipe the floor with all of them, she wouldn't need any help from her, or anyone, even Tony, who she could see was looking on with all his friends.

Rita went on pushing her luck, if only she knew it.

"You, doing a man's job, look at you, a pound bag full of shit!"

"A pound bag full of shit that's going to explode and rearrange your nasty face!"

One of the G.I's laughed aloud.

"I like it, a bit of Jimmy Cagney!"

A small rotund girl with breasts like melons, stepped forward and said nervously to Rita.

"If I were you, Rita, I'd back off; she's the one who threw Perkins all around the bus."

"You've got to be kidding me!" Rita laughed.

Another small, stick-like girl said.

"I'm not getting involved, I'm off."

"That's right, go on," Rita said scornfully.

"It's your trouble, you handle it," the girl said as she turned away.

"Oh, I will, don't you worry," Rita cried.

Two other girls, obviously sisters, cried.

"We're with you, Rita! Bring it on!"

"What did I tell you, three onto one," a G.I said. "The odds are stacked against the Land Girl."

Tony's brown eyes began to twinkle; he smoothed back his hair, then pulled himself upright.

"This Land Girl's going to marry me, boys, there's nothing April doesn't know about self-defence, she can take those three on with one arm tied behind her back, believe me!"

"Oh, you know her. And well by the sound of it," the rich voice said, surprised.

"I'll tell you all later, now hush," Tony said happily.

As Fay saw April move and stand with her legs slightly apart, she thought 'oh God', this is it.

April bunched her fist, then fast as a striking snake, smashed Rita on the nose. Blood splattered and sprayed all around, the force of the blow knocking Rita onto the drums, setting the symbols clanking and crashing, while Rita lay with her head between the horrified drummers thighs, leaking blood down his legs. He swallowed his mouthful of chewing gum whole and began to cough and choke.

The G.I's clapped, cheered and called out.

"Hey, April, do you want to join the United States Air force?!"

April was so angry that she didn't hear the calls; the other two friends of Rita's were coming at her, one of them shouting.

"You, bitch, doing that to our Rita!"

As the first girl reached her, April brought her foot up, then with all her strength behind it, kicked sideways at the girl's ankles. The girl went down in a heap and lay on the floor moaning.

The G.I's cheered and roared April on.

She faced the next girl, saying.

"Come to Mama."

The girl looked confident, she shot her right fist out, but April was ready, she took hold of the girl's wrist, yanked her forward, then pulled. At the same time with her other hand, she punched the girl hard on the shoulder with the knuckle of the first finger. This was an old fighting trick, not in the Marques of Queensbury rules. It made the girl scream, but this girl was willing to fight back, she kicked out at April, catching her on her knee, but was only a glancing blow.

I must finish this now, April thought, she stepped to the side of the girl, held her by her hair, then with the first finger on her left hand, pressed on the girl's neck, making her shriek.

"Hurts, doesn't it?!" April said.

"You, bitch!" the girl screamed.

April pressed a little harder.

"Stop it, stop it!" the girl moaned.

Suddenly, one of the men in the crowd who had been watching, stepped forward.

"Let her go," he said. "I'm a trained self-defence expert, and that point in the neck that you're touching is dangerous, too much pressure can lead to death."

"I'm aware of that," April said softly. She let the girl go, saying. "Don't ever call the Land Army or its girls again, *any* of you."

"We love the Land Army!" one of the G.I's called. "A great bunch of girls!"

A spotty-faced youth walked quietly towards the door, opened it, stepped outside, then closed it behind him; he hurried down the street to the police station.

Most of the crowd who had been stood watching the fight, moved away, realising that the show was over.

Someone had untangled Rita from the set of drums, sat her down on a chair, and held a wet, cold tea towel to her broken nose, trying to stop the flow of blood. The other girl, whom April had knocked onto her back, was moaning that her back was broken and that she couldn't go to work on Monday.

Tina was sitting as if in a daze, not ever having seen anything like it before in her life.

Fay looked devastated, she had seen April in action before, but not like this, she had thought at the start of the trouble that it was going to be an unfair fight, three against one, she had felt that she would have to help April. Just shows how wrong you could be. Those twin brothers of April's knew a thing or two teaching her to fight like that! But she had a feeling this was not over yet, and she wasn't wrong.

The door opened, and in walked the village bobby with the spotty-faced youth who looked proud of himself.

The room fell silent.

April walked to the girl who held her hat and took it from her, set it on her head, then turning to the constable she asked.

"Anything wrong, Constable?"

Fay thought, 'oh God', can't she leave well alone?!

"From what I've been hearing from this lad here, *everything* is wrong. Someone fighting and rolling around the floor."

"Yeah!" a G.I called out. "And it was something! Worth coming to England for!"

One of his mates hushed him, but, before the G.I finished.

"You English bobbies sure are cute! And we love that helmet thing you wear on your heads."

The constable chose to ignore this comment and snapped out.

"Which one of you Land Girls is April?"

He looked surprised when April held up her hand and spoke.

"I am, Sir."

He had been expecting to see a big strapping lass. He made as if to move towards her, but April stopped him with the words.

"Stay where you are, I'll come to you." She walked across the dance floor to stand facing him.

He was six-foot-four and looked down at April, surprised.

"We don't want these good people to miss what you're going to say to me, do we?"

He narrowed his eyes, then sniffed as if he had a cold.

"Oh, you're one of those are you?" he asked.

"One of those? I don't know what you mean. What's *your* name?" April asked, raising her eyebrows in inquiry.

"Just a moment young, lady. I'm asking the questions, not you."

April pushed her hat to the back of her head.

"Ask away," she said calmly.

"I want to know what in tarnation has been happening here. This young lad..." he nodded his head towards the spotty-faced youth who had dragged him away from his supper. "Says that all hell has been let loose."

"In a way, I suppose you could say that it was," April said loudly and clearly.

"It sure enough was!" a G.I shouted.

The policeman looked toward him and held up his hand for silence. Then looked down at April.

"Are you going to tell me why you were fighting? And who started it all?" he asked. "And, all the other girls involved, come here!" he snapped.

When no one made a move, he looked around the room.

April smiled.

"Well?!" he shouted. "I'm waiting!"

The two sisters walked across the floor, one turned and called to Rita.

"Come on, Rita, it was your fight in the first place."

Rita reluctantly walked forward, holding the blood-covered tea-towel to her face.

"Let me look at you, remove that cloth," the policeman said.

As Rita did so, he gasped.

"Did you walk into a steamroller?!" he asked. "That looks bad, it's broken, you have to go to the hospital." He paused. "Who punched you?"

Rita pointed to April.

"She did."

The policeman looked shocked.

"You've got to be kidding," he gasped.

"She's not kidding, Mr, little April packs a mighty punch!" a G.I shouted, then gave a loud whistle.

"Whoever did what to who isn't the point right now. Who started it, and who struck the first blow is." He turned to April. "You, Miss, seem to have come out of this unscathed, what's your story?"

The unhesitating April plunged right in.

"What *is* your name?" she asked.

"I am PC Humble," the policeman said proudly.

"Hardly the name for a copper, is it? Humble," April laughed.

A few titters sounded round the room.

"Well PC Humble, I have to be honest, I struck the first blow, and unfortunately Rita here got in the way of my fist."

A loud laugh came from the group of G.I's.

"Why did you have to aim a blow at Rita in the first place?" PC Humble asked seriously. He drew a note pad and pencil from his pocket, licked the point, then said. "Continue." He paused a moment, then asked the two sisters. "You two seem to be alright?"

"We may look to be, but we're not," Maud, the eldest said. "I've hurt my back, and my sister has a dislocated shoulder, I think."

Her sister, Sheila, nodded her head.

"They do seem to be in the wars," April said sarcastically.

"Why was it necessary to aim a blow at Rita?" the policeman asked again.

"Rita and her friends were making disparaging remarks about the Land Army and its girls, singing rude ditties and comparing us to animals, and that I take from no one. But what started it was, Rio Rita here was bullying my friend and had put her hands on her. My friend is a quiet, shy girl and was clearly terrified. I asked Rita in a polite voice to take her hands away from my friend; *she* foolishly asked me what I was going to do about it if she didn't. To cut a long story short, when she didn't, I belted her one."

"Ha!" the policeman said. "You struck the first blow, and from the state of Rita's face you used undue force."

"You could say that, yes," April said calmly. "But I did warn her I'd rearrange her face, which I did, and is an improvement don't you think. Her nose is like a squashed tomato that's gone off."

There were loud titters around the room again, Rita was not well-liked.

Two or three of the G.I's cheered, then Tony called out.

"That's my April morning!"

When April heard this, she thought, that's another one that's going to end up with a squashed mush!

"I don't think that's funny," the policeman said, an annoyed look on his face. "Rita needs medical treatment, and this is a serious matter."

The drummer boy piped up.

"Never mind about her face, she fell onto my drum kit and damaged my symbols, who's going to pay for that?"

"Shut up, Simkins!" the policeman shouted. Then looking at April, he said sternly. "You young, lady have given the Land Army a bad name tonight, fighting like a fish-wife."

"PC Humble, I was defending the good name of the WLA, or are you too dumb to see that?!" April shouted angrily. She stuck her hands into her breeches pockets and lifted her head high. "And may I remind you, although I shouldn't have to, that these three girls have *slandered* the Women's Land Army. They made a false statement, maliciously, that was damaging to our reputation."

Rita removed the tea towel from her face and cried out.

"Rubbish! Arrest her! Look what she's done to me!"

"And us!" the sisters shouted.

The policeman chose not to hear, concentrating instead on April.

"What is your surname?" he asked.

"Thornton," April answered.

"Well, Miss Thornton, I think that you're most disingenuous. In case you don't know what that means, it means giving a false appearance of candour."

One of the G.I's whistled loudly.

April was becoming angry.

"Don't you use big words at me and think I don't know what they mean, you stupid man." She took an angry step towards the policeman.

He stepped back, a startled look on his face.

"Don't you take that tone with me, young lady."

"Really?!" April said aggressively, an angry glint in her eye. She took another step towards the policeman. He backed away.

The G.I's looked on in amusement.

Fay was beginning to feel apprehensive at the way this was going. If April planted one on the PC, she really would be in trouble.

She walked up to April, took her arm, and urged.

"Come on, love, time we were going, work in the morning."

April pushed her away none too gently.

"You go if you want, I'm seeing this through." She took a determined stance.

"I've had enough of this," the PC said. "April Thornton, I'm arresting you."

"Arresting me? For what?" April asked quietly.

"Yes, Mr Plod, what for?" all the G.I's called.

Tony marched across the floor.

"No one is arresting my gal," he said angrily. He fumbled in his pocket for his cap, found it and set it neatly onto his head.

"I will thank you not to interfere, Sir." the PC said sternly.

"April belongs to me; I'll not stand by and see her falsely arrested."

"Oh, you won't, eh?" the PC said, surprised.

"No, we of Bomber Command will not," Tony replied firmly.

The PC was beginning to look flustered.

"Just one moment, Tony you're out of your mind," April said angrily. "*I don't belong to anyone*; I'm not a bloody parcel, so just shut up!"

The PC held up his hand for silence.

"Right now, she belongs to the policeman," he said firmly. "I'm arresting her on several charges, so, if I were you young, man, I'd go back to my friends and keep quiet, better still, go back to your base."

A small blotchy-faced, stocky G.I stepped forward and said.

"I'm Stoll Stevenson of the United States Air Force Bomber Command, so listen here, *buddy*, police or not, stop bullying April here. *And* we'll go back to our base when we're ready, comprehend? Now spit out what you're charging this little girl with, but, before you do, remember that there were three other gals onto April here. She defended herself pretty well."

"With undue force, it seems." the PC said. He waved the G.I away then turned to April. "April Thornton, I'm arresting you for committing grievous bodily harm, assault, disturbing the peace, causing an affray and using threatening behaviour."

"Is that all?" April asked, straight-faced.

Everyone laughed.

The PC flushed a bright red.

A figure was stood in the doorway, who was dressed in pyjama bottoms, a knee-length tweed coat and had a flat cap on his head. He had been standing listening for the last two or three minutes. He suddenly stepped forward and strode over to the group stood in the middle of the floor.

"Most interesting," Judge Bentley said.

"Judge, how did you get here?" the PC gasped.

"I walked you idiot, how the hell do you think I got here?!" He paused, then said. "You're quite a fool, Humble, always have been, how you manage to keep law and order I'll never know."

"But Judge," the PC began.

The Judge held up his hand.

"Don't waste your breath telling me about tonight's happenings, I already know."

"You know? How?" the PC said, surprised.

"By carrier pigeon, you fool," the Judge said sarcastically. "And you three." He stared at Rita, Maud and Shelia. "*You* started the trouble with your big mouths." He pointed at Rita. "You're always at the root of any trouble, the village bully aren't you! Well, this time you met your match, it's been a long time coming. And I can tell the three of you, I'll be seeing your Mother's first thing on Monday morning!"

"Old fool," Rita muttered.

He turned to the PC.

"Clear the room, Humble, send everyone home."

The PC started to usher everyone from the room, calling.

"Everyone out, come on now, time to go home."

The crowd filed slowly out of the door.

Meanwhile, the Judge put his arm around April's shoulders and asked kindly.

"How are you, my dear? You seem to have come out unscathed, it's nice to see you again, but it could've been under better circumstances."

"They asked for it, Judge, they really did, I can't have anyone belittling the Land Army."

"Of course you can't, my dear. You did right to defend it, the Land Army has a fine bunch of girls."

"Can we go now?" Fay called. "Tina's still distraught and I'd like to get her back to the hostel."

The pianist called out.

"I'm responsible for locking up, I'd like to do so and get home if you don't mind."

"Of course," the Judge said. "Come along you, girls, on your way."

"Thanks for your help with the PC, I think he would've arrested me you know."

"If he had, and you'd come to court, I would've thrown it out, it would've been a silly trumped-up charge. The man's a fool, full of his own importance. God forbid any real crime happening here, he would be floundering!"

At the door, good nights were said, and everyone went on their way, the PC, knowing he had been talked down, the Judge to a cold supper, and the girls peddling slowly along the lane.

"I'm glad that nights over, I'll never go there again. I wonder why they hate us so?" Fay called.

"Who cares," April called back.

"I wish you'd try and keep out of trouble, April; I'm fed up with it," Fay shouted.

"You're not being fair; I was sticking up for us."

"I'd love to be like you, April but know that I never will be," Tina's breathless voice called.

"You're you, Tina, always be yourself."

"I'm afraid that I don't have a choice."

The conversation was ended as the girls approached the hostel.

"That's strange," April called out, breaking the silence. "All the lights in the house are on, something's wrong."

"Looks like it," Fay said, worried.

The girls rushed through the side gate, round to the back of the house, threw down their bikes willy-nilly and ran to the kitchen door. April pushed it open to reveal all the girls sat around the table, they all looked up as April, Fay and Tina rushed in.

"Thank goodness you're here to hear the good news!" Binnie said, her face glowing.

"Thank god it's not bad news, every light in the house is on; it's a good job it's still light outside!" April shouted. She turned to Tina. "Be a love and go around and turn all the lights off quickly, we'll be a sitting target if the Germans fly this way, are you all nuts?!"

"We're so excited we didn't think," Jane said.

"If those lights had been seen up in the air none of you would've been here to be excited at any bloody thing, I can't believe how stupid you all are!"

"You'll never guess what's happened," Anita said with shining eyes.

"No, never in a million years!" Katrina cut in.

"For God's sake, tell them," Nancy pleaded.

"I'll tell them," Belinda shouted. "I saw it coming in the cards!"

"Will you shut up about your fortune-telling!" Connie said loudly.

"All of you pipe down," Jane said bossily. "I'll tell them. The most unexpected and wonderful thing has happened."

"The war's ended?" Fay cut in.

"No silly, Miss Topp's gone!" Jane said in a sing-song voice. "She's gone, just like that!" She clicked her fingers.

"Gone? When, and how?" April asked, amazed. She pulled out a chair and sat down. "Don't all gabble at once, one of you tell us."

Fay still stood by the door, not saying a word.

"I'm the eldest and the calmest, I'll tell you," Nancy said, nodding her head. "Are we all agreed?" she asked.

Heads were nodded.

"To begin with," Nancy began. "We all trooped in in penny numbers, I was the first, I found Mrs Wilkinson sat here at the table like a stone statue, I think she was in shock, I couldn't get a word out of her for a while. When she did start to talk, it was like ants scurrying out of a nest, all jumbled up and not making any sense. When I calmed her down, the gist of it is this; the War Agg came to see Miss Topp and told her that they had received a phone call from an important person in North Yorkshire, complaining of Miss Topp's treatment of the girls in her charge, especially one by the name of April. This person also said that Miss Topp withheld the girl's rations, didn't feed them properly and expects the girls to do some of the housework, in a word, treating them like children. This person who complained had it in their power to relieve the War Agg of her job if she didn't resolve this matter straight away. The War Agg confronted Miss Topp, who blustered and carried on alarmingly, saying it was all lies, and that someone had it in for her, she named that someone as April. The War Agg insisted she had to look in all Topp's cupboards which were locked. Topp said no, she had no right, so the War Agg said that if she didn't unlock the cupboards, she would ring for the police, so Topp had no choice. The cupboards were stuffed with sugar, tea, butter, a few eggs, tinned milk, dried eggs, bottles of wine, and soup among many other things. The war Agg said pack your cases, I'll wait here and see you off the premises, charges will be brought against you. I'll be having a word with the police, those poor girls being deprived of their rations, you should be ashamed."

"Did Mrs Wilkinson hear and see all this?" Fay interrupted.

"Of course she did, how else would we know?!" Nancy said scornfully.

"Well, I'm tickled pink!" April laughed. "I would've loved to have been here."

"Wouldn't we all," Katrina said.

"That's all very well, but who will we get next?" Binnie asked.

"Oh, I think that they'll choose the right person for the job next time," Joan said.

Tale bearing Monica had been sat listening, not saying a word.

April turned to her.

"I'm surprised to see *you* still here; I would've thought you'd go with Topp."

"You thought wrong then, didn't you! Any-road, I think you had something to do with all this."

"I didn't, but thanks to the person who did."

"I don't believe you, Miss Topp never liked you, and you hated her."

"True, and I suppose you knew about the food she stole from us?"

"No, I didn't."

"Now *I* don't believe *you*."

"Please yourself."

"You were always her little spy, Monica," Nancy said. "I always did find you detestable, sneaky, sly and underhand. I think you *did* know what Topp was up to."

Monica smirked.

"Prove it."

April stood up angrily and shouted.

"Get out of here or I won't be responsible for my actions."

Fay stepped forward.

"Don't soil your hands on her, April, she isn't worth it."

"No, she isn't," a lot of the Land Girls cried.

"I expect to find you gone tomorrow," April said threateningly.

"Yes, we all do, and good riddance!"

All the girls started to slowly clap, making Monica rush out of the kitchen.

"Start packing!" Anita called after her. "*And* only what belongs to you mind!"

"Didn't the cards tell me about her?!" Belinda called.

"You and your ruddy cards," Jane laughed.

April pushed back her chair and stood, saying as she did so.

"If you'll excuse me, I'm going to bed, it's been a very traumatic day what with one thing and another, but there's one thing about it girls, we don't have to look at Topp's ugly mug in the morning!"

"No thank goodness," Connie cried. "No Topp pretending to supervise."

The ever-placid Joan gave the sign of the cross, then said.

"Thanks be to God."

April beckoned to Fay.

"You coming, kiddo?"

"Yes, I'm coming, April."

April looked at Fay piercingly, somewhere in her mind a bit of suspicion was beginning to take shape that there was a link between the mysterious phone call she made in the village and the removal of Miss Topp.

Who could Fay know that was so important that had the power to move mountains? Still, what did she really know about Fay's home life? Nothing, she would never talk about it, but she would tonight if I have to lock the door and throw away the key. There was more to this than met the eye. The War Agg would know who the important person was, wouldn't she? But maybe she had been told to say nothing? It all had an air of mystery about it. Topp had thought that it had been me that had her removed, but I thank the person who did from the bottom of my heart.

When April and Fay walked into the bedroom, Tina was just getting into bed.

"Hi, you two, what's been happening?" she asked.

"I'll tell you all about it later," April said shortly. "Right now, I have to talk to Fay."

Fay frowned.

"Now? It's bedtime, I'm tired."

"Sorry, kiddo, but this won't wait."

Fay looked apprehensive.

"What's wrong? What have you done now?"

"Nothing, it's what *you've* done that I want to get to the bottom of."

"That sounds serious," Fay said with the flicker of a smile.

"I wouldn't call it serious, unexpected is a better word," April said firmly. "Now, sit down." She pushed Fay onto her bed and sat by her side. She turned to face her, then began. "Fay, you made a phone call from the village phone box."

"Did I?"

"Yes, you did. Who were you calling?"

"That's nothing to do with you, April."

"Oh, I think it is, because you see, I think you had something to do with the sacking of Topp."

"You do get strange notions in your head, April." After a long pause, Fay said, "can I get into bed now?"

"Without a wash? I think I've got you flummoxed, Fay, now come on, spit it out, I'm not going to leave you alone until you tell me the truth. As long as I've known you your home life has been one big secret, you've let things slip yes, but nothing that I could put together. Now talk. If we must sit here all night, we shall."

"If I tell you, you'll not believe me," Fay said with a sceptical expression on her face.

After a short pause, April said.

"Try me."

"Very well."

Fay began sturdily enough; she had just completed three sentences when April held up her hand.

"Your Mam and Dad are Lord and Lady Trent?!" she cried incredulously. "I've heard of them!"

"Most people have," Fay said. "We can't help who are parents' are can we."

April ignored her and went on.

"Lord Trent is a big noise in North Yorkshire, he owns a string of racehorses, it's a wealthy family!"

"Very," Fay said sarcastically.

"Why do you say it like that?" April asked.

"There's only one way to put this. It's me who owns the racehorses, it's me who owns the land, the house, the farms, the money – a lot of money. I should think millions by now."

April was speechless and Tina gasped in shock.

"Now you know," Fay said abruptly.

"But why are you working on the land?" April asked curiously. "Does the War Cabinet or the Ministry of Labour know who you are?"

"No, of course not, my real name is Francis by the way; I choose to call myself Fay. As an only child, it's great to work with and get to know other girls. I went to a posh private school to please Grandmother; I hated it, so left at sixteen, then was expected to stay at home attending afternoon teas and being polite to the rich and famous – all to please my Father, whom I hate by the way. He never forgave me for being a girl; he'd set his heart on my being a boy. Life changed for Mother from then. But I'd better start at the beginning.

Father was an only child, his Father was well off, not rich, but as a good businessman dealt in stocks and shares. He spoilt Father, who believed in wine, women and song, *lots* of women, two of whom he got in the family way, who were paid off and were never heard of again. When Grandfather realised how far the rot had set in his son, he cut him off without a penny."

"What about his Mam? You haven't mentioned her," April cut in.

"She died when Father was nine years old," Fay said casually.

"When the will was read on the death of Grandfather, Father had got nothing, so he set about looking for a rich girl whom he could marry."

April broke in again.

"But what happened to your Grandfathers money?"

"That went to various charities; apparently. Father went crazy and tried to contest the will, but to no avail. Then enter Mother, after a whirlwind courtship they married, Mother told me she was very much in love with him at first, he was a handsome man and such a gentleman. Grandmother, Mothers parent, didn't like him on sight and tried to warn her, telling her it was money he was after, for

Grandmother was a wealthy lady. Her husband had owned mills in West Yorkshire, but when his health began to fail, he sold them, hence pots more money into the bank. Grandmother owned lots of land, farms which she rented out, houses and shops."

"Where did your parents' live when they got married?" April asked curiously.

"With Grandmother, she lived in a huge house, it had twelve bedrooms. You see, she wanted Mother near her, to keep an eye on her, she didn't trust my Father. Her fears were justified, after one year of marriage, I was on the way, and tales started to run around the village of Father being seen with other women. He liked the thought of becoming a Father, and oh, what he and his son were going to do together. Then along came me, the biggest disappointment of his life. He hated me on sight and wouldn't have anything to do with me. Poor Mother was devastated at his attitude, Grandmother wasn't, she expected it, said you can't make a silk purse out of a sow's ear, and he was a sow's ear. All during my childhood he would avoid me, I hated him. Then one day I found Mother crying, her face was bruised, I was seven years old, but she sat me down and told me about my Father, why he hated me, and that Grandmother had said she was going to have part of the house partitioned off for Father to live in on his own. She felt nothing but contempt for him. He took this on board, as Grandmother gave him a weekly allowance to keep out of our way. Things went on like this for a few years; he and I passed each other like strangers. I went to school, Grandmother and Mother looked after each other, and I was the centre of their world. Mother was happy with her church meetings, garden parties and afternoon teas. Then in later years, *he* became a Lord, Mother a Lady, to the eyes of the world Mother's marriage was fine and dandy. Grandmother went into racing, bought horses, and got a good trainer, her ambition to own a Grand National and Derby winner. She came close before her death; she got second in the National. Do you know what she said to me, 'Francis, watching my horse fight to finish second in the National was the biggest thrill of my life! The money does not count, it's the thrill of it all that does.'"

"But how come everyone thought those horses were his?" April asked.

"To aid his reputation, and for my Mother, Lady Trent."

"Do you still have racehorses?"

"No, I sold them when my Grandmother died; they were her hobby, not mine."

"Can you ride?"

"Of course, I rode in several point to points."

"You're a sly thing, Fay Trent, but go on."

"As Father got older, the more he got mixed up with women. Grandmother made it a rule, no women to be brought to the house. Mother couldn't have cared less if he had; she'd made her own life. One night I went for a walk around the grounds, which are extensive, and as I came towards the summer house, which is quite large and furnished, I heard laughter; I opened the door and walked in. The sight that met my eyes was a huge shock. Two naked women and Father, naked as the day he was born, entwined on the couch, beer bottles were strewn around. He looked up and saw me, 'Ha, my darling daughter'; he laughed, then pulled one of the women on top of him. For a moment I stood, rooted to the spot, disgusted, I was seventeen, maidenly pure."

"Then what did you do?" April asked.

"I ran to Grandmother. She could see I was in a state of shock. When she calmed me down and I'd told her what I'd seen, she sent for Mother. When Mother had been told, she said that she wasn't the least bit surprised. 'Right', Grandmother said, 'I'm going to send for Mr Bates, my solicitor, and change my will, I must protect you both against this man. From tomorrow I want you both in my office every morning at ten o'clock. You, Francis, will have to know about my money and properties.' She did as she said she would, changed her will, explained to Mother and me what had to be done, left everything to me, the whole lot, I had to take care of Mother and make sure she would want for nothing. 'That creature of a Father of yours will get an allowance every week. The sum will be no more or less during his lifetime, let's hope that it'll not be a long one', she said. We all agreed on that, and Mr Bates sat me down and explained how things worked. I soon realised that I was a millionaire, but money didn't mean a thing to me as my Grandmother always said good health and happiness came first. She died two years ago, she was ninety, I still miss her. So, here I am in the Land Army, happy, Mother is enjoying her life, Father is still alive and hating me more than ever. You see, he thought Mother was going to get everything then could bully her into getting what he wanted. I keep getting begging letters from him; every time I do, I knock his allowance down. Soon he'll have nothing left, then I shall kick him out of the house, it'll give me the greatest of pleasure."

"And you say that *I'm* hard," April laughed. "Well, that's quite a story; it would make a good film! But why did you join the WLA?"

"I wanted to do my bit; Mother was upset but soon came around to it. She's happy for me."

"It was you who helped get rid of Topp, wasn't it?" April asked.

"Yes, Mother knows the right people, she was outraged when I told her about Miss Topp, and she wants to meet you, April."

"One day she shall, but I have to ask this, Fay and don't be angry. Larry and you, have you told him about your money?"

"No, and I don't intend to."

"Is it serious between you two?"

"Yes, very."

"Will you marry?"

"I hope so, it's what we both want."
"It's all very sudden, are you sure?"
"Very sure, as soon as I saw him, I knew."
"Did he?"
"Yes, he did."
"You won't be able to keep your money a secret from him forever."
"I know, I'll face that when I have to."
"You do know that you have to leave the Land Army when you get married, don't you?"
"So I understand."
"I thought you loved the life?"
"I do."
"When will you get married?"
"As soon as possible."
"Where will you live?"
"Larry lives in a rented cottage."
"You'd be happy with that?"
"Yes, as long as I'm with him."
April sighed.
"Loves young dream."
"One day it'll be your turn, April."
"I'm already in love with the land."
Fay turned to Tina, who had not said a word.
"What do you think about things, Tina?"
"Think?" Tina said bewildered. "It's like someone was reading a book! You're so lucky to be rich, and have the man you love too."
"I'd take the man over the money any day."
Tina closed her eyes and said ardently.
"Oh, I wish it were me."
"I want you both to give me your solemn promise that you won't tell another soul about all this, do you promise?"
"Yes, I promise," both girls said.
"And you won't treat me any differently?"
"We won't, having money doesn't make you any better than us," April said gruffly. "You're still our Fay, okay."
"Okay."

12

The next day as the girls hurried noisily into the farmhouse kitchen, Mrs Bellows looked up from her task of slicing a large homemade loaf.

"Hello, girls, an extra one again I see, there's plenty of sandwiches ready for you." She swung round to the range and picked up a large dinner plate which was piled high with bacon sandwiches. "There you are, a bit of my best bacon, enjoy."

The girls ate quickly, and hastily gulped down a cup of tea.

"They were lovely, Mrs Bellows, we must be off, Mr Bellows will be waiting," April said as she slammed her cup down hurriedly onto the table.

Mr Bellows was waiting for them, and upon seeing them, called.

"Come on, girls, the lads have already..." when he saw Tina, he called, "ho, ho, another one of you again, eh."

"Yes, aren't you lucky, three for the price of two. I know you didn't ask for extra help, but Tina's new so wanted to come with us, she still hasn't been told where to go," Fay explained.

"Alright by me," Mr Bellows said. He turned to Tina and asked. "You've milked before, lass, haven't you?"

"Only once or twice on a dummy," Tina stammered.

"Only once or twice on a dummy?" Mr Bellows repeated. "Well, there's no dummies here, lass, this is a nice how-de-do isn't it."

"Be fair, Mr Bellows," April pleaded. "You *have* got extra help; Fay and I will put Tina through her paces." She turned to Tina and asked. "You're willing to learn, aren't you, Tina?"

Tina looked nervous but nodded her head.

"To be fair, she wasn't given hardly any training," Fay explained.

"No, it seems not. Anyway, she's a little un like you, April, and you're a good worker, so, let's hope, Tina is too," Mr Bellows said.

"There's good stuff in little parcels," April answered pertly.

"Aye, let's hope there's good stuff in this one."

"Everyone has to learn, and it's not easy is it, land work, so much to do and remember. When I first started, I was feather-legged, and unfortunately I had a bad farm, well, not exactly bad, it was the farmer who was the fly in the ointment. He expected way too much, but you, Mr Bellows aren't like him, you're a fair man." April said this calculatingly.

"I like to think that I am," Mr Bellows said proudly.

"Good, now we'd better get on with the milking," Fay said firmly.

Tina gritted her teeth, gave a sigh, and felt her heart thudding in her chest and ears as she took hold of the cow's udders and began pulling at elastic feeling teats. She felt clumsy, but the cow didn't seem to mind, she stood quietly swishing her tail as Tina got into a rhythm, and the rich, creamy milk pinged into the pail.

April had started to sing 'As Time Goes By', and soon the boys began to whistle along with her.

I could get used to this, Tina thought, it's pleasant, April has a lovely voice, some training there I'll bet, how lucky I am to have met April and Fay, they're two nice girls. I wish I could be more like April though, *she* was afraid of no one, or anything, but, that Miss Topp was something else again, she put the fear of God up me the first time I saw her.

Her thoughts were cut off as April called over to her.

"How are you doing, Tina?"

"Alright, I think that I've got the hang of it," she called back.

"Good-o," April answered.

This gave Tina more confidence, and she was able to work a little faster. April had stopped singing, and for a while there was silence in the shed, except for the bellowing of the cattle, and the ping of milk hitting the sides of the buckets.

Tina's bucket was now full, so she decided to empty it into the churn as she had seen the others do. She rose, picked up the bucket carefully, and walked up the sides of the channel. Suddenly her foot slipped sideways, throwing her to one side, she dropped the bucket with a clang, and the milk flowed merrily away down the channel. As she righted herself, she gave a loud cry of horror and screamed.

"Oh, dear! Oh no! No, no, oh, dear! The milk, the milk!"

April and Fay raced up to her.

"Are you alright?" April cried.

Fay took hold of her arm.

"Calm down, it's not the end of the world."

"But the milk, look, it's all gone down the channel, oh dear, what shall I do? What will Mr Bellows say?"

"It's unfortunate, but these things happen," April said firmly. "Don't worry, Tina, I'll tell Mr Bellows."

"I can't let you do that," Tina cried, tears running down her face. "It wouldn't be fair."

"Stop crying, Tina, you're not the first to spill a bucket of milk, I did it myself at my first milking didn't I, Fay." she winked at Fay.

"Oh, yes, I remember," Fay replied, playing along. "You were upset, but not for long."

"As much as I could be upset, which isn't much; all kinds of things can go wrong on a farm as you'll learn, Tina as you go along," April said firmly.

"I was really enjoying the milking too," Tina said sadly. "Next time, I'll watch where I'm putting my feet."

"You'll toughen up, life's going to get harder, sometimes the fieldwork is hefty going, working in the rain with it trickling down your neck isn't very pleasant, *and* we've harvest time coming up, now *that's* demanding work, *and* long hours. While we're on the subject, some, only *some* of the farmer's wives belittle us and say we're common ungrateful brats. If we hear them, we try to ignore them, but one day I won't be able to, and they'll be sorry." April nodded her head, then repeated. "Yes, sorry."

Fay raised her eyes to heaven, sighed heavily, then said under her breath.

"Oh, God." Then aloud. "I hope I'm not around when that happens."

"If you are, I'm quite sure you'd support me," April said with confidence.

"Of course I would. Now, let's finish the milking and get down to the fields, we've a drystone wall to build up remember, part of it's come down, we don't want the bull getting out, Mr Bellows is putting him out tomorrow."

"A bull?" Tina's face paled.

"Yes, a bull," April laughed. "Mr Bellows hires him to impregnate his cows, hopefully."

"Oh," Tina said uncertainly.

"We'll be seeing some action then," April laughed again.

"Some action? He can't get out, can he?" Tina gasped.

"He'll be too busy to try and get out," April said loudly, winking at Fay.

"Too busy? What do you mean?" Tina asked.

"The birds and the bees, Tina, you know, man and woman make a baby, well, bull and cow make calve."

"Oh," Tina said in embarrassment.

"If we have time, we'll bring you down and let you watch," April smiled mischievously.

"No, I don't want to; I'd most likely faint again."

"You can't go fainting every time you see nature take its course."

"Oh, dear, I'll try not to."

"That's, my girl."

"If only I could be more like you, April."

"I hope you never are."

"I second that," Fay cried.

* * *

After lunch found the girls happily sorting different sized stones ready to build up the broken wall in the bottom field near the wood. The cows were happily munching, swishing their tales to keep off the hordes of flies that hovered around them, now and again raising their heads and giving a loud moo, which echoed across the fields.

"It won't be as peaceful as this tomorrow when Mr Bull arrives, the cows will be skittering around trying to get away from him," April pointed out.

"They'll be lucky if they do," Fay said. "Poor things, I feel sorry for them."

"When you see how well hung some of those bulls are, I don't blame any cow for taking to their heels, do you?!"

Tina looked puzzled and asked uncertainly.

"What do you mean, well hung?"

Fay raised her eyebrows and said to April.

"You take that one."

April raised her eyes back at Fay.

"Okay," she said with a mischievous smile. "Well, Tina," she began. "We call bull's private parts his tackle; you know what private parts are, don't you?"

Tina nodded her head.

"A bulls tackle, especially his balls, are huge, so, the other bit which has to go inside the cow is also large, which is why one feels sorry for the poor cow."

Tina began to look green.

"If the bull can manage to get the cow to stand still, he heaves himself onto her back, puts his large organ inside her, and gives a couple of heaves and thrusts. The poor cow can be nearly on her knees, and when the bull leaves her, hopefully she'll be pregnant. The bull will catch all the cows in the end, that's his job, that's what Mr Bellows is paying for him to do, the bull would be no good at his job if he didn't breed. Do you understand?"

Tina swallowed loudly, then said.

"I think so, but I feel sick."

"You'd better not be. I think we should bring you down here tomorrow and let you watch," April said firmly.

"No, I don't want to," Tina moaned.

"Didn't they teach or tell you anything of that nature in the home?" Fay asked Tina gently.

"No, there was never time, we were always so busy looking after the little ones," Tina replied.

"I may as well tell you the whole lot about bulls while we're on the subject," April went on. "Sometimes a cow has to be fastened to a wall in the cowshed and held still by someone, a stable hand or a Land Girl, so that the bull can mount her. Sometimes he misses, and his lot shoots all over the place, sometimes onto the person holding the cow still. I always feel sorry for the poor cow having to be false mated."

Tina gulped, white-faced.

"His lot? What do you mean? His lot," she asked.

April had to hold her laughter in, she wanted to scream hysterically, and on seeing the look on Fay's face, she didn't think that she could contain herself.

"Do *you* want to answer that one?" she asked Fay hopefully.

Fay had anticipated this but shook her head.

"No," she said abruptly. "You're doing alright, go ahead."

April grinned, then asked Tina.

"Do you know what sperm is?"

Tina shook her head.

"No."

Fay grinned.

"No, I thought not," April said.

She was saved from giving an answer as Fay held up her hand, saying.

"Listen, a plane, sounds pretty close, *and* low."

The three girls shaded their eyes with their hands as they looked to the sky.

"It's coming this way, and you're right, Fay, it *is* flying low, he's maybe in trouble," April cried anxiously.

"We don't know that it's one of ours, it could be a German flyer, I don't like this," Fay said.

As the plane came closer, it was hedgehopping.

"Quick, all underneath the hedge!" April cried.

Tina stood, locked in shock, Fay started to run, and April grabbed Tina's arm and dragged her along. They threw themselves under the nearest hedge, sending birds squawking and flapping into the air. The plane swooped over where they had been stood, and a hail of bullets hit the ground. Stones, soil, and clumps of grass flew into the air. The girls lay mesmerised, holding on to one another as the plane flew on, slowing.

"God!" April said. "He's not going to land, is he?!"

As Fay caught her breath, she managed to get out.

"It wasn't one of ours."

"No," April said breathlessly. She shook Tina by her arm. "Are you okay, Tina girl?" When there was no answer, she looked closely at Tina who lay with closed eyes. "She's passed out."

"I don't blame her; I thought I was going to," Fay replied. "If we hadn't had our wits about us, he would have killed us."

"Yes, it was a close shave," April replied as she rose to her feet.

Suddenly a loud bang rent the air.

"Listen," Fay cried. "He's crashed!"

April set off running, with Fay screaming after her.

"No, April, come back!"

April carried on running and covered two fields in record time. When she reached the plane, its nose was deeply embedded in the earth, and she saw a small flame glowing from within. The body of a young man had been thrown clear, he lay spread-eagled, breathing in difficulty, he was obviously dying, but April dragged him clear of the plane, knowing that it could explode into flames at any moment.

He was dressed in a German uniform, but German or English, no one should be burned to death.

Fay ran up to join April and knelt by her side. She took hold of a name tag which hung around his neck, it glinted in the sun.

"He's German, it *was* a German plane, he's dying, April."

Fay began to say The Lord's Prayer, then suddenly the man's eyes opened, then closed, then his breathing stopped.

"He's gone," April said softly.

"Yes, and we'll be gone too if we don't get away from that plane, it's going to explode," Fay cried in panic. "Come on, move it."

As the girls sprinted across the field, there was a loud explosion, it threw them into the air, and they landed on their backs winded, but all in one piece.

"Wow," April felt herself all over. "I think I'm okay, are you?"

"Yes, thank goodness," Fay replied shakily.

The lane was suddenly full of villagers, jeeps, ambulances and police cars.

Mr and Mrs Bellows, Barry, Dennis and Larry ran up to the girls.

"My God! What a thing to happen! Are you both alright?" Mrs Bellows asked, white-faced.

"What were you doing so near to the bloody plane is what I want to know?" Mr Bellows roared.

"It's a long story," April said quietly. "And, for your information, we were *not* near the plane, we ran to it when we heard it crash, it had flown over our heads."

"Wow, you saw it before it crashed," Dennis said in amazement.

"Yes, we did, we saw the whites of his bloody eyes," April said sarcastically.

"Gerr-away," Barry said, shaking his head in disbelief.

Larry had taken Fay into his arms, murmuring words of comfort to her as the tears rained down her face.

An ambulance man hurried up.

"Now you people, I need you all to move away from here, these two girls could be in shock." He turned to April. "How do you feel, love?"

"Alright, but I could do with a strong cup of tea."

Mrs Bellows stepped forward, glowering at Mr Bellows as she did so; she pushed him out of the way.

"Ted," she said firmly. "I don't want to hear one more word from you, these girls have had a very nasty shock, I'm getting them up to the farmhouse, giving them a strong cup of tea laced with a slug of brandy, *and* the day off."

"The day off?!" he repeated.

"That's right, the day off," Mrs Bellows repeated.

"But what about the work?"

"I'm sure the boys will manage along with you."

"It's a bit much."

"Nonsense, we have *less* help at Christmas and get through, so shut up, go away, and make a start, all of you." She waved the boys away, saying. "Off you go. Come up to the house in a couple of hours and I'll give you something to eat." She turned to Larry, who was still holding Fay. "Put Fay down and be off with you, lad."

Suddenly April turned to Fay, panic in her voice.

"My God, where's Tina?!"

Fay looked confused, then said horrified.

"Tina! I left her lying under the hedge, she passed out cold when that plane went over. When we heard it come down, I just ran after you and left her. Well, we both did, didn't we."

"If she's come around, she'll be in a panic wondering where we are!" April cried.

"Don't worry," Larry said. "I'll find her and take her to the farmhouse."

"Would you? That's good of you, Larry, thanks," April said in relief.

As Larry hurried away, PC Humble called to them.

"Hey, you two, girls, just a moment."

"Oh no, not PC Plod! I'm not in the mood for him," April groaned.

Fay raised her eyes to heaven and made the sign of the cross on her chest. Seeing this, Mrs Bellows asked.

"Why Fay, why on earth did you do that?"

Fay closed her eyes as she said.

"You'll see, just wait."

As PC Humble joined them, notebook in hand, he said abruptly.

"Well, the Land Army, in the thick of it again, I see." He looked pointedly at April, who glared at him, narrowed her eyes, then asked quietly.

"What did you say?"

Fay began to breathe in and out slowly as she said, 'Oh God' twice.

Mrs Bellows asked angrily.

"What do you mean? I don't like your sarcastic tone of voice, Mr Humble."

April raised her hand for silence, then said.

"Leave this to me, Mrs Bellows."

"Do as she says," Fay whispered.

April went on haughtily, her head held high.

"Yes, *Mr Bumble*, the Land Army in the thick of it again, trying to save a life would you believe! Have you been told all the story?"

The PC shook his head.

"Not really no, a plane had come down, on fire, and two Land Girls were involved was what I was told. And by the way, my name is Humble, not Bumble."

"That's a shame, because Bumble suits you much better, you're bumbling along with no facts, we've committed no crime, only helped a dying man on his way out. So put your bloody notepad away, we've no need to tell you anything. If we do need to talk, it'll be to the press. We risked our lives going near that burning plane to pull the pilot out, so shut your gob, go away, and let us go about our business!"

"I can see why some of the lads in the village call you, Miss Trouble," the PC blustered.

"Do they? I'm flattered," April said.

"No need to be flattered, you should be ashamed. The day will come when I'll be able to arrest you, we'll see how brave you are when you're cooling your heels in a police cell."

"If that day ever comes it'll take more than you to arrest me, I'd have you on your back in one second."

"Are you threatening a police officer?"

"No, a bloody fool and idiot."

"*April!*" Fay cried.

Mrs Bellows stepped forward and spoke.

"I don't know what's going on here, but you, PC Humble must have better things to do than standing here harassing poor April, when all she's guilty of is serving her King and country."

"Yes!" April said angrily. "Go and sort out those village nutters you seem so proud of. And let me tell you this, one of those 'troublesome Land Girls', Fay here," she pointed to Fay. "Said The Lord's Prayer over the dying man, one hundred yards from a blazing plane, how's *that* for troublesome?! So, don't forget to spread *that* around your village!"

The PC stood speechless.

"Go on then you, fool," April said quietly.

"That's enough, April," Mrs Bellows said as she took both girls by the arm. "Come along, let's get you up to the farm and give you a drink of tea, then I'll run you back to the hostel in the van.

* * *

As April and Fay got wearily out of the Bellows' van on rubber-like legs, they called their thanks to Mrs Bellows.

"Have a good rest for the remainder of the day. See you both tomorrow, and Tina of course," Mrs Bellows called back.

Tina had been brought back earlier by Larry, having been in an uncontrollable state.

April and Fay had taken to calling her Mouse.

"Mouse will be tucked up in bed, still in shock I expect," Fay said as they walked into an empty kitchen.

"Yes, it's certainly kicked her into the Land Army the hard way," April replied. "Look, an empty kitchen, isn't this nice."

As April finished her comment, a tall, slender, dark-haired lady with beautiful brown eyes and a beaming smile showing brilliant white teeth, walked into the kitchen from the hall. On seeing the two girls, she said in a deep voice.

"At last, two more humans! I was beginning to think I was the only inhabitant of the house, but I must introduce myself. I'm Mrs Keir, your new housekeeper."

"Hello, I'm Fay, and this is April."

"Pleased to meet you both. I say, this is a lovely house isn't it, I think I'll be incredibly happy here, it has a lovely feel to it. I arrived this morning at eleven, of course all you girls had gone to work, so I wandered around exploring. I'm very impressed and can't wait to meet the rest of the girls."

April looked puzzled.

"So, you haven't seen Mouse I take it?"

"Mouse? Who's that?"

"She's supposed to be in bed, resting."

"Is she ill?"

"Not in the normal sense of the term, but she had a terrible shock earlier today, as did Fay and I, which is why we're back early."

April launched into the crashing plane story.

"My dear's, how awful for you all, you must both go upstairs and rest, I'll not disturb you. I'm going to prepare an evening meal for you all."

"An evening meal, I can't remember when we last had anything decent here," Fay cried.

"I know all about Miss Topp, she was a very foolish and cruel woman, but I can assure you that I'm a different kettle of fish."

"She was the kind of woman that you wanted to pour a bowl of soup down her neck. She was lucky I didn't," April said.

Mrs Keir suddenly realised that April was the person involved in all the episodes of trouble with Miss Topp. She gave April a beaming smile, then said.

"Yes, April, the one who stood up to Miss Topp, she had stupid house rules I understand."

"Yes, too true, she had no idea of management, had no understanding of girls, and it was a continuing round of rows, although sometimes she was a worthy opponent, but she couldn't best me," April finished with a laugh

Mrs Keir laughed also.

"All that is over now, April, this is going to be a happy house, farm work shared out as it should be, good food whenever possible and sensible house rules. Boyfriends will be allowed in at certain times, and an odd party or two. I knew about the G.I camp before I came here, and you girls work hard and need to let your hair down from time to time. I have two girls of my own, so I know how girls feel."

"I'm going to like you, Mrs Keir," Fay said happily. "And so will the other girls."

"I second that," April said, then. "Do you mind if I ask how old you are?"

"April!" Fay cried in horror.

Mrs Keir laughed.

"I can see that you're a straightforward kind of a girl, April. No, I don't mind in the least. I'm forty-five, and before you ask, my husband died when my girls were very small. They're now twenty-one and twenty-three, both nurses. Wendy, the eldest, is engaged. Norma, single and fancy-free, which is how she likes it, so she says. So, you see, I'll maybe find *myself* a boyfriend."

Both girls laughed with delight.

"It's not out of the question; you're a good-looking woman, Mrs Keir if I may say so," April said softly. "But me, my love is the land, it's here forever, it'll never deceive or leave you, and will do its best for you if you do your best for it."

Mrs Keir smiled in understanding.

"You have a point there, April." She turned to Fay. "How do *you* feel about men Fay?"

There was a dreamy, tender, radiant look in Fay's eyes.

This girl has already fallen in love; you could tell by the radiance of her face; it made her personality shine through, Mrs Keir thought as Fay said happily.

"Too late for me, Mrs Keir, I've fallen hook line and sinker for all time with the best, most handsome man in the world. I hope to be married soon, so, if you hear me break into song around the house, don't be surprised."

"I like my girls to be happy, I won't mind you singing," Mrs Keir said.

April giggled.

"Believe me; she's got a terrible voice."

"Well at least I try, we can't all be as good as you, April," Fay said honestly.

Mrs Keir looked at April with interest.

"Oh, you sing, do you, April?" she asked.

"Yes, I love singing, I had lessons when I was younger, and these days I only sing to the cows, they seem to like it."

"The cows?!" Mrs Keir exclaimed.

"Yes, the cows like the boogie-woogie stuff, you know, songs with a swing to them. But I *can* sing the serious stuff."

"Most interesting, I'd like to hear you sometime," Mrs Keir said as she rose to her feet. "But now, you, girls should go to your room and rest, I have to get on with tea."

"Yes, we should," Fay agreed. "And, welcome to Whitmore, we hope that you'll be happy here, don't we, April."

"Of course, and I'm sure the rest of the girls will love you," April replied.

"Thank you, what nice girls you are. I'll see you at teatime, and I'm very much looking forward to meeting the others," Mrs Keir said happily.

As the two girls walked into the hall, April suddenly came to a standstill and looked up at the highly polished bannister.

She said determinedly with a mischievous gleam in her eyes.

"In the morning that's my route down, I've been dying to slide down it, and now that Topp's gone there's nothing to stop me."

"I'm with you, me too," Fay cried.

They ran lightly up the stairs and into their bedroom. Tina was laid on her bed, gazing into space; she did not turn her head to look at the girls.

April nudged Fay, then nodded towards Tina.

"Well," she said loudly. "Look at you, laid there, malingering."

Without turning her head, Tina said angrily.

"You left me, you both left me!"

April narrowed her eyes, then said.

"Yes, we did, you fainted, and *we* had a shock too."

"You left me lying there," Tina repeated.

"Oh, shut up, Mouse, I'll bet you don't know what really happened out there, do you?" April shouted angrily. "Well, do you?!"

Tina ignored this.

She marched up to Tina, took her by the shoulders and sat her on the edge of the bed. "You silly little, fool," she said cuttingly, her eyes flashing with anger. "That plane went down in flames in the next field."

Tina gasped loudly.

"Yes, in flames, the pilot was flung out, he was only a young man, he died in my arms, and Fay said The Lord's Prayer to him while he was dying. The plane exploded and flung us into the air, luckily, we weren't injured, only shook up. And you're laid there moaning because we left you. You're luckier than that boy who died, you're here, he isn't." She shook Tina, causing her head to bobble from side to side.

Fay took hold of April and said.

"Steady on, that's enough."

"That's enough?!" April cried. "That's enough?!" she repeated. "She's in the real world now. Grow up or go home!"

Tina began to cry loudly, so Fay sat by her side, put her arm around her shoulders and tried to offer comfort.

"That's right, mollycoddle her why don't you," April said disgustedly.

"Well, it was a shock for her, April, be fair," Fay pleaded.

"Rubbish, how could it have been a shock for her? She was out bloody cold *before* we left the hedge."

Tina let out a loud wail.

"Oh, shut up, Mouse, my patience is fast running out with you!" April cried.

"Oh, please, April, don't fall out with me, I couldn't bear it. I'm so sorry to be a bother to you, and I'll try not to faint again, I promise you, but that plane was so low, I thought it was going to hit us and that we were going to die. I'm so sorry about that young lad, but how brave of you both to do what you did."

"We're at war, Mouse, you don't think about what you're going to do, you just do it," April said authoritatively. "Now dry your eyes, get into bed and shut up, we're all going to have a rest before tea." April winked at Fay as if to say, Mouse needed that.

Fay winked back in agreement.

* * *

The next day's weather did not look promising, low cloud forecasting rain, and the three girl's faces looked grim.

"Threshing, it's a dusty mucky job; remember it at the last farm, Fay?" April asked.

"How could I forget, I'd just started, remember. It was Barley and made my eyes itch something awful, that night I had to bathe them in warm milk, but let's hope we don't have a wet harvest," Fay finished.

"We each have to have a stick, a big one remember," April reminded.

"Why do we have to have a stick?" Mouse asked curiously.

"Because there's always rats about and you have to belt them one, hard," April said firmly. "If we're stacking, we sometimes put wire netting around the stack so the rats can't escape, then the dogs have a whale of a time killing them."

"Oh no, that's cruel!" Mouse wailed.

"If one ran up your trouser leg you wouldn't think it cruel, would you."

Mouse shuddered.

"I don't think that I could hit them with a stick."

"You will, believe me," April laughed.

"Yes, you'll learn," Fay said. "Just pray for a dry harvest, if it's wet, we have to go into the fields and re-stook the stooks."

"What does that mean, re-stook?" asked Mouse.

"You've to turn each sheaf of Corn round, outside to inside. They never seem to stand right, and there's always a lot of green at the bottom of a sheaf, like cloves or grapes. They don't dry out, so, on a fine day you've to pull stooks over so the wind can blow them dry."

"Oh, dear, that sounds hard," Mouse cried.

"All in a day's work," April replied airily.

"We'll have more help, won't we?" Mouse asked anxiously.

"Yes, we have help from the village, maybe more Land Girls, young lads and older men. It can be a fun time, but hard work," April replied. "And, here come the lads, along with some extra help." She looked up at the sky. "The cloud's breaking up and the sun trying to shine, it could be a nice day."

"Let's hope so," Fay said. "And here comes Larry with the tractor." Fay's eyes lit up at the sound of Larry's name.

"I may as well tell you, if the weather holds, Mouse, it's going to be a long day, maybe until nine o'clock," April said.

"Gosh, nine o'clock," Mouse cried.

"Yes, nine o'clock," April repeated. "There's nothing easy about harvest time, we've to get stuck in, all hands to the pump, and here comes more help." She shielded her eyes with her hands. "And Mr Bellows is with them, he'll get the gang working."

"What do we do?" Mouse asked anxiously.

"You and Fay will most likely be pitching with Mr Bellows; I'll be on the wagon to build the load, as I've done it before. Us three and Mr Bellows work as a team, as will the others. There's nothing to be anxious about; you'll soon get into the swing of it."

"I think that I'll like the spring best when the furrows have the tiny green shoot showing," Mouse said quietly.

"There's the threshing machine starting up, old Jack from the village operates that. You'll be pitching up, that means feeding the threshing machine, you'll have muscles like Sampson at the end of the summer."

The work went on all morning; April sometimes breaking out into song, and the lads whistling all the war songs.

The teams worked hard and methodically all morning, with a short break for lunch, eating and chatting about the rest of the day's hard work to come, then it was back to the grindstone.

As they trooped back to the wagons, April asked.

"How are you feeling, Mouse?"

"Don't ask, I'm fagged out."

"No good being fagged out, there's a good eight hours to get through yet."

"I'll never do it."

"You will."

"They don't pay us enough."

"I agree, but ours is a safe job."

"I suppose it is."

"Now come on, don't flag, you're doing well."

"Do you think so, April?"

"Most definitely."

"Thanks, that's cheered me up," Mouse plastered a smile across her face and strode on revitalised.

The day wore on, sunny and warm, and evening crept upon them, bringing with it Mrs Bellows with a picnic supper, helped by one of the village girls. Thick sandwiches of homemade bread, scones, cakes, buns, and jugs of sweet cocoa, all ate with enjoyment until not a single crumb was left.

"I can't remember when I enjoyed food as much as that," Fay said happily.

"I'm so full; I don't think I can do anymore work," April laughed.

"It's cheered me up I can tell you," Mouse said happily. "Given me the heart to go on."

"Mrs Bellows is a marvellous cook, isn't she," Fay said.

"She's a marvellous woman altogether," April said.

"I hope we never have to be moved on," Mouse said sadly.

"We may be, there's nothing definite in this life."

"I don't want to be moved away from you and Fay; I would die if that happened."

"You wouldn't at all, now don't be silly, Mouse."

"I'd leave the Land Army."

"Now, that's enough of the daft talk, back to work."

Everyone worked through the evening as the shadows fell, and a beautiful, glorious harvest moon rose higher in the star-spangled sky.

At last, the loads were finished and secured with ropes, and everyone made their way home.

Mr Bellows asked if the three girls wanted a ride back to the farm and they accepted gratefully. They climbed onto the wagon and lay down on the warm corn, tired, happy and relaxed. Fay and Mouse lay with closed eyes, while April lay looking up at the sky filled with skittering twinkling stars. The night was warm with a slight breeze, and April pulled off her turban, feeling it gently ruffle her hair. The wagon was jolting beneath her, and could have rocked her to sleep, but she was much too happy to sleep, and realised how absolutely contented she was in this life. This was an excellent way to live, and she would never leave it, she loved her life and the land, and one day, by hook or by crook, she would have her own farm. She turned her head to look at Fay and Mouse, both seemed to be asleep.

She nudged Fay with her elbow, and Fay opened her eyes.

"What's wrong? Why have you nudged me?"

"How can you lay with your eyes closed? Look at that sky, that moon, did you ever see anything as beautiful?"

"Yes, many a time at home."

"But not in the country."

Fay chose to ignore this and closed her eyes as April went on.

"How can you not appreciate such a beauty? It's like the world's stood still."

"The world will stand still for me when I'm in my nice warm bed; we've to bike back to the hostel yet, so please shut up and let me have five minutes kip."

"No kip for you, kiddo, we're nearly at the farm." She shook Mouse. "Come on, Mouse, climb down, get your bike and let's be off."

Mouse looked confused as if she didn't know where she was.

"Oh, are we there? At the farm?"

"Yes, we are, what a silly, girl *you* are too."

"Me? Why?"

"Missing all the beauty of the night sky."

Mouse raised her eyes heavenwards.

"It is rather nice, isn't it."

"Rather nice? Is that it? It's *beautiful*."

"If you say so, April, can we go now? I'm so weary I don't think that I can put one foot in front of the other."

"You can, and you will, now come on, get on your bike and let's be away to our beds, and remember, we've to go in quietly, some of the others will be in bed."

"Not a lot of them I don't think, some of them will have been working late like us," Fay commented.

"Yes, I expect so," April agreed.

* * *

"That's another day over, thank goodness," Mouse moaned as she sat in the hostel kitchen with some of the other girls.

"Listen to moaning Minnie, we *all* feel the same," Nancy said angrily. "Anyway, forget work for a moment, what about Mrs Keir?" She glanced around at all the girls. "Do you like her? I do, she's smashing!"

"She is," Connie agreed. "We're lucky to get her."

"We certainly are, she's a corker," Belinda said happily.

"A good-looking corker too," Anita said, nodding her head. "How I wish I had her looks."

"It's inside a person that counts, and you're a nice person inside," Belinda comforted.

"I can tell you that she's young at heart, this Mrs Keir," April said seriously. "Although she's a widow and has been for years, she told Fay and me she'd consider going to a dance with us."

"Did she? She'd attract all the good-looking men, especially the G.I's," Belinda said. "That would be hysterical, wouldn't it?"

"She doesn't look her age," Fay said loudly.

"How old is she? Did she tell you?" Nancy asked curiously.

"I believe she said forty-five," Fay replied.

"Getaway, never!" Belinda cried.

"I hope I look as good as she does when I'm forty-five," Connie said, hopefully.

"I know for a fact *I* won't, nothing is going to alter *my* face, I've got it for life haven't I, so I think that you should all consider yourselves lucky and be happy with what nature gave you," Anita ended aggressively.

"We should all consider ourselves told off, Anita," Fay said abruptly. "*And I am* happy with my looks."

"Sorry, Fay, I didn't mean to sound nasty," Anita said apologetically.

"Oh, take no notice of Fay; she's the hump because she's not seeing her precious Larry tonight," April said mischievously.

Fay pulled a face then stuck her tongue out at April.

"To change the subject," Belinda said loudly. "I don't know if anyone has realized, but there's a notice on the board in the hall, saying that there's to be a meeting for us all tomorrow night at eight, and could some of us be kind enough to take half a dozen of the kitchen chairs through to the sitting room. Mrs Keir wants everyone to have a seat; she's going to talk to us about the new rules. Any girl who can't attend will be informed of the rules later."

"I think that she's going to be very fair," Anita said softly. "Tons better than that horrid Miss Topp."

"She as good as said that we'd be allowed to have boyfriends in on certain days when we were talking to her the first day she was here," April informed them.

A chorus of voices cried.

"Oh, good!"

"Well," Connie exclaimed, "that's a turn up for the book."

"It is if you *have* a boyfriend," Mouse said shyly.

April shrugged.

"It doesn't affect me; I've no wish to have a boyfriend at this moment in time."

"Ah, April my love, you won't remain single for long, a pretty girl like you," Connie said with a twinkle in her eye.

"I say, maybe we can ask some of the G.I's from the base to come one night, have a singsong round the piano," Belinda cried excitedly.

"Just imagine, we could practice our jitterbugging!" Connie said.

All the girls laughed.

"Pity I've no sense of rhythm," Mouse said.

"We'll get you going; I've been told that I'm quite good at it," April said seriously.

Mouse chuckled with quiet amusement.

"We'll see," she said.

Fay nodded her head.

"If April says she'll teach you, she will, you can be sure of that. She'll be like a dog with a bone until you're as good as her," Fay warned.

Mouse looked uncertain.

"I don't know if it'll be a comedy or a farce, I'm always so tired at the end of a working day. Where I'll get the energy from, I don't know."

"Now, I don't want to hear that defeatist attitude from you, Mouse before we even start," April said angrily.

Interest was flickering in Anita's eyes.

"Would you teach me, April? I'd love to learn, I know that I'll never go out dancing, but I could jitterbug here with you girls."

"Of course," April smiled. "I'd love to."

"Oh, April, you're a treasure!" Anita cried, clapping her hands together, her disfigured face lighting up. "I'll look forward to it."

All the girls fell silent as a persistent knocking came at the kitchen door.

"Now, who can this be I wonder?" Connie said puzzled. "It can't be one of the girls, they wouldn't knock."

"Only one way to find out, I'll open the door," Belinda said firmly. She stood and pushed back her chair as the knocking resumed louder than ever. She hurried to the door and threw it open to reveal two boys clutching a bunch of flowers each. They stared at Belinda with wide, startled eyes. "Hello," she said kindly. "What have we here? Are you boys lost?"

"Who is it?" Connie called.

"Two young lads, I think they may be lost," Belinda called back. She smiled at the boys. "What's the matter? Can't you speak? Don't be afraid. Can I help you?" she asked kindly.

The taller of the two boys said determinedly.

"We want to see Miss April and Miss Fay."

Belinda laughed heartily, then called over her shoulder.

"April and, Fay, two boyfriends here to see you."

"Boyfriends?!" both girls exclaimed as they rose to their feet.

"You'd better come in, boys; I see you come bearing gifts," Belinda laughed.

"Not gifts, Miss, flowers," the bigger boy said, wondering if this Land Girl was blind.

They stumbled into the kitchen holding the flowers out at arm's length, as they wore a terrible smell.

"Norman!" April cried. "How nice to see you! And who is your little friend?"

The little friend blushed a fiery red.

"He's Titch, that's what we call him on account of him being so little."

"Does he have a proper name?" April asked.

Norman turned to the small boy.

"Do you have a proper name, Titch?" he asked.

The boy shook his head.

"If he has, he doesn't know it, he's always been called Titch. He doesn't talk much, he's kind of shy, so me and my mates look out for him, don't let anybody bully him if you know what I mean."

"I know what you mean, Norman; you're a lad after my own heart," April said softly.

Norman grinned, then held out the flowers to April. He nudged Titch as April took them.

"Go on, dummy," he said. "Give yer flowers to Miss Fay."

Titch looked blank, not knowing who Miss Fay was. She stepped toward him and took the flowers.

Both girls looked surprised and mystified.

"Well thank you, boys, they're lovely, but it's not our birthdays," April said.

"All the lads gave their pocket money to buy them, Miss April, because you were so brave going to that burning plane and helping that pilot to die."

April smiled at his choice of words.

"Bless you and your pals, Norman; it's a very kind thing to do," April said softly.

"Yes, Norman, a lovely kind thought," Fay agreed.

"Give the flowers to me and I'll put them in water," Connie offered.

"Thank you, Connie, we'd like them in our bedroom, wouldn't we, Fay?" April asked.

"Oh, yes, where we can see them," Fay said.

"Now, you, lads sit down, and we'll give you a glass of milk and find you a biscuit," April said. She turned to Anita. "Could you do that while I have a chat to Norman, please Anita?"

"Yes, sure I can." She gave her lop-sided smile at the boys, and Titch stared mesmerised at her disfigured face until she turned away in embarrassment.

"Do your parents' know that you've come here?" Connie asked. "It's seven-thirty, and quite away from the village."

"No, they don't worry about us; they know we won't come to any harm around here. We cut across the fields and through the woods, it only takes twenty minutes."

"Really? We'll have to remember that," April said, nodding her head. "But how do you know so quickly about the plane crash?"

"Oh, you get to know everything in our village, jungle drums, you know," Norman said wisely. "You're better known than the milk-man, Miss April, and everyone knows him."

"Am I really?" April said with a grin.

"You can say that again," Fay said behind her hand.

Anita put a glass of milk and a plate of broken biscuits before each boy.

"Tuck in," she said.

"You're a hero to us village lads, Miss April," Norman said, his mouth full of biscuit.

"Heroine is a woman, Norman; a man is a hero," April corrected.

"And," Norman went on. "Our teacher, Mr Simms, knows about you, he heard us talking in the playground, and in-class he was sounding me out about you."

"What do you mean, sounding you out?" Mouse asked.

"Asking me questions about Miss April and me, how I came to know her. I told him about the bus and Miss April sorting out Perkins."

"Who's Perkins?" Connie asked.

April sat back and let Norman get on with his tale.

"He's the bus conductor, he's a clever bugger."

"Norman, no swearing if you please," April said firmly.

"Sorry, Miss April, but he is, as you know yourself."

"Back to this teacher of yours, Norman."

"He wanted to know all about you, and when I said that you'd thrown Perkins onto his arse, he called me a liar, and said that was impossible as Perkins was a big man, and that he wanted to meet you. Then, in his 'I'm going to cane you voice', he said 'McMasters, come here.' I knew what was coming as he picked up his cane and swished it around."

"Cane you?!" April broke in, horrified.

"Yes Miss, three lashes."

"Where?"

"On my arse."

"Oh, the brute!"

"It hurts, but I'm learning to hold my breath, you don't feel it as much then."

"The bully, *he* wants sorting out!"

"He loves it when you cry out."

"Does he now?"

"I never do."

"Do your parents' know about this?"

"Yes."

"Didn't they go and see this Simms?"

"No, Miss."

"Why not?"

"Mum says I must deserve it, and Dad says it'll make a man of me."

"Do they now."

There were cries of concern from the girls sat around the table.

"So really, you got a caning because of me," April said with a gleam in her eye.

"Oh, I didn't mind, Miss April; I'd do anything for you."

"I mind, Norman, I mind very much. This Simms, he doesn't cane little Titch, does he?"

"No, Miss, he wouldn't dare, Titch's Dad's as big as a house side."

"Right, I think I'll have to pay this Simms a visit seeing as he wants to meet me."

Fay gasped loudly.

"No, April you can't."

"Watch me."

"Oh, God, you can't."

"I can, and I shall, I'm not having that Simms cane my friend Norman for telling the truth."

"But it's not up to you; his parents' should sort it out."

"It sounds as if his parents' are half-soaked."

"What does half-soaked mean?" Mouse asked nervously.

"Oh, shut up, Mouse!" April snapped angrily.

"Don't speak to her when she's in that mood, Mouse, you'll get no change," Fay said firmly.

"No change? What does that mean?" Mouse pleaded.

"Sometimes I think that you pretend not to know," April said, her patience beginning to run out.

Norman began to look concerned.

"You don't have to go see Simms on my account, Miss April, I can take whatever he dishes out, and he knows it."

"For now, Norman love, forget it, finish your milk, it's time you were both getting home, it's past eight o'clock. I'll come part of the way with you."

"No need, Miss April, we'll run some of the way, Titch only has little legs you see."

April patted Titch on the head, who nodded and said.

"Goodnight, Miss April."

"You both go straight home now," April said.

"We will, Miss April, we go back through the woods, it's a short cut," Norman said, nodding his head at Titch.

"Oh, I don't know about going through the woods at this time of night, I'd rather you went a long way around on the road," April cried, concerned.

"We know the woods like the backs of our hands, we've climbed every tree, haven't we, Titch?"

Titch nodded.

"If we wanted to hide in there, the *Army* wouldn't find us, would they, Titch?"

"No," mumbled Titch.

"Alright then, off you go, and thank you once again for the lovely flowers," April said softly.

As the two boys passed her, she pulled them to her and gave each boy a kiss on his cheek.

Titch flushed to the roots of his hair, and Norman's eyes lit up like Christmas tree lights.

"Cor," he said. "Wait till I tell the lads that Miss April kissed me, they'll be green with envy."

April laughed merrily.

"Don't tell them, Norman, or *they'll* be queuing up for one. Now on your way, I'll see you soon." As April closed the door, she saw the boys darting off across the lawn.

"What nice boys they are," Mouse commented.

"They certainly worship April," Fay said. "But seriously, April, you're not going to see Simms, are you?"

"I sure am."

"How are you going to manage that? We start work at six in a morning, school starts at nine."

"I know that, Fay, I'll ask Mr Bellows for an hour off."

"He'll want to know what for."

"I know that too."

"What will you say? Don't ask me to back you up; I'm not getting involved in this."

"Have I asked you to?"

"Not yet."

"I won't, so put your mind at rest. Now, I'm going up for a bath before the others get back, so, I'll say good night."

She walked quickly to the door and closed it quietly behind her.

There, that will give them something to talk about, but there was no way she was going to let young Norman take a caning because of her. She would go along to that school and see that sadistic Simms; he wouldn't beat another kid when she had finished with him. Unbeknown to Fay she had her story all ready for Mr Bellows, he was an alright kind of man, and she was sure he would give her an hour off.

The next day dawned fair, clear and bright, and saw the girls repairing broken fencing which the cows had managed to trample down.

"I'm not keen on this job," Fay grumbled.

"It is a *man's* job I suppose, but we can do anything a man can do don't forget it," April said as she hammered nails happily into the fence post. She bent down and picked up a long narrow plank of wood. "Here you two, hold this at each end and I'll hammer it on." She put two or three nails into her mouth as Fay and Mouse set the wood into position.

"Right," Fay said. "Ready."

April set a nail into the middle of the wood and began hammering; she did the same at each end, then said.

"Right, you can let go now, it's secure enough, I'll just put more nails along its length, then we'll move further along. I wonder what the next job will be?"

Fay took her watch out of her overall pocket.

"Eleven o'clock," she said. "How time does fly." Then. "Listen, a plane's coming, it sounds to be low."

As it passed overhead, April waved her hammer. A few minutes later, they heard it returning, and the three girls looked at each other apprehensively.

"It's one of ours. I'm sure of it," Fay said firmly. "So, let's not panic."

"My God, it's going to land, look, in the corner of the field!" April cried. She took a firm grip of the hammer.

"Look, two men are climbing out," Mouse gasped.

The men were dressed in leather gear and walked towards the girls.

"They're not German's, I can see that," Fay said, relieved.

April and Fay ran towards them, Mouse stood still where she was, shocked and frightened.

As the girls reached them, April thought, wow, they're G.I's, how handsome!

One said with a charming smile.

"Pleasure to meet you, I hope we didn't frighten you when we flew low over your heads."

"We could see that it wasn't a German plane," Fay said. "So, we weren't scared."

April held up the hammer which she still held.

"If you had been German, I would've laid you out with this," she waved it menacingly.

Both men laughed.

"Thank goodness we're not then. As you gals can see, we're G.I's, out on a practice run, and what luck to have found two such pretty gals out here in the country. I'm Orry, and this here is my brother, Bix. As you can see, we're twins, and are inseparable."

Alike as two peas in a pod, both had classic features and were of medium height. They shook the hand of both girls as Fay said.

"Hello, I'm Fay, and this is April."

Orry pointed across the field toward where Mouse still stood immobile.

"Who's the little one over there? Why doesn't she join us?"

"That's Mouse, her name's really Tina, but she's so shy and quiet we nicknamed her Mouse."

Orry made as if to walk towards Mouse, but April pulled him back.

"No, don't, I'll fetch her," she said quietly. She beckoned to Mouse as she hurried towards her. "Come on, Mouse, they're not Germans, they're G.I's, and very nice."

Mouse sat down on the grass.

"I'll just wait here for you."

"Okay, it's your choice," April said as she walked back to Fay and the G.I's.

"I didn't think that she'd join us," Fay said.

"How old is your little friend?" Bix asked.

"Seventeen, and still only a baby. She was brought up in a children's home from birth and didn't know anything of the outside world until she joined the Land Army. She's very wary of men, and some women, but Fay and I look after her."

"I'll bet you do too," Bix laughed. "You seem like a very capable gal, the way you waved that hammer around."

"Oh, she's capable alright," Fay exclaimed.

"What do you gals do on your nights off?" Orry asked.

"We don't get many of those, we work late when the weather's good, we've just finished the harvest, and that *was* hard work," Fay explained.

"Well, it's certainly given you good looks, you're two pretty girls," Orry said with a twinkle in his eye. "You'll both have a boyfriend?"

"I've just gotten engaged," Fay said.

"I'm fancy-free and intend to stay that way," April said firmly.

"That's a pity," Orry said to Bix. "But that shouldn't stop you expecting an invite to a dance we're putting on at the base next Friday. It's going to be in our largest hanger with a big dance band, food laid on, drinks and a jitterbug contest. Bring your other Land Girl mates, the more the merrier. I understand girls from the surrounding villages are coming, so it's going to be quite a turnout. Please say that you'll come," Orry finished.

April's eyes began to shine.

"I'll come! A jitterbug contest, that's right up my street."

"You jitterbug do you, April?" Bix asked. "I do too, you must be my partner."

"Yes, I will, don't forget now."

"How could I? A gal like you is unforgettable, April," Bix laughed.

"You Yanks and your flattery," April said with a toss of her head. "But you haven't told me where your base is."

"The one just outside of Tiptree, we'll send a wagon to pick you up at seven-thirty." He took a pencil and small notebook out of his leather jacket pocket. "Here, write your address down, we'll find you, no problem."

As April wrote down the hostel address, she asked.

"You will bring us back, of course?"

"We sure will, April my dove, don't you worry about that."

"How do we dress? Is it informal?" April pressed.

"We G.I's love to see you Land Girls in uniform, but it's up to you," Orry answered.

"I'll give it much thought," April said seriously.

"And now, girls, we must be off back to base, we're late. It's been good to meet you both, sorry about your little friend though, we'll see you next Friday."

As they ran across the field, April called.

"Ta-ra, see you, boys."

They watched as the G.I's climbed into the plane, taxied down the field and took off noisily. It wasn't until the aircraft was a speck in the sky that the girls turned away and hurried back to Mouse, who still sat unmoving on the grass.

April looked at her in disgust.

"You know, Mouse; you should make an effort to meet people."

"I know, but it just frightens me."

"I don't know what I'm going to do with you when the war's over, I don't know *where* you'll end up."

"Back at the home, I'll feel safe there," Mouse said sadly as she rose to her feet. "Are we going to finish the fencing?"

"Yes, if we don't, Mr Bellows will have something to say," April snapped.

As the girls began work once more, April asked Fay inquiringly.

"You are going to the dance at the base, aren't you, Fay?"

"No, I don't think that Larry would want me to," Fay replied.

April turned, then laid her hammer onto the grass and put her hands onto her hips.

"It's what *you* want to do, Fay, Larry doesn't own you."

"Larry *does* own me in a way, we love each other, we're bonded."

"You do have a right to a say in your own life."

"I'm delighted with my life the way it is."

"Are you happy with the way the village girls flock around him?"

"I don't mind, I know he loves me, and I trust him."

"I should be embarrassed to admit that a man owned me."

"Well, April, I am not, so you go to the dance and enjoy it, I'm happy with my life, and I'll stay in and keep Mouse company."

April gave a loud sigh.

"You won't change your mind and go?" April persisted.

"No, and that's my last word on the subject," Fay said. "End of story."

April pursed her lips.

"Okay, have it your way, I just hope that you don't come back to earth with a bump."

"I won't, Larry and I are perfectly happy," Fay said angrily. "Now, can we change the subject?!"

"I know that I look on the black side, but I do wish you luck, you'll need it," April said, determined to have the last word. "And look, here comes Mr Bellows, I rather think that he's going to chew our ears off for taking so long on this job."

As he joined the girls, he was breathing heavily, he bent down, put his hands on his knees and breathed slowly in and out.

As he straightened up, he said.

"That's better. Now you, girls, you should've finished this job an hour ago, all the eggs need packing ready for the pickup truck in the morning, I'll be busy with the sheep."

"Sheep?" April and Fay echoed.

Mr Bellows nodded his head with a big grin spread across his face.

"I've bought a dozen sheep, the wife doesn't know yet, she's not going to like it, hates sheep, says they're nasty smelly things, and that the only thing they're good for is cooked and eaten with mint sauce."

"I must say that I agree with her," Fay said.

The grin left Mr Bellows' face as he continued.

"Also, I've treated myself to a stallion."

"A stallion?" Fay repeated.

"We haven't seen the *other* two horses you have yet," April said surprised.

"Yes, I know, my nephew has those up in Yorkshire at the moment, his two girls are learning to ride."

"Lucky nephew, being loaned two horses instead of buying two," April said incredulously.

Mr Bellows began to laugh.

"I never thought of it like that. My stallion is a beauty; his name is Trigger-Me."

"I like the name, it's very catchy, did you choose it?" Fay asked.

"No, it's always been his name," Mr Bellows said.

Curious, April asked.

"Why has he been sold on?"

Mr Bellows narrowed his eyes as he answered April.

"He was becoming a bit of a handful; the lady who owned him has ill health, so decided to let him go. He's a lively one and has a bit of a roguish eye."

"I don't like the sound of that," April said dubiously. "Are you going to be able to handle him, Mr Bellows?"

"Oh, I think so, lass," he replied with confidence.

April looked at Fay with a mischievous look in her eyes, then bent down and picked up the hammer and tin of nails. Turning, she said.

"I'm sure that Fay here would lend a hand to Trigger-me, she's a professional horsewoman, very skilled, and won lots of prizes and cups when younger haven't you, Fay?"

Fay glared at April furiously.

"Well, can you beat that! Am I not a lucky man?!" Mr Bellows cried. "Is that right, Fay? Are you a horsewoman?"

"I've not sat on a horse for two years, Mr Bellows, so please don't rely on me."

"Riding a horse is like riding a bike, you never forget," Mr Bellows laughed. "Anyway, come on and meet him, you girls jump in the wagon, I'll run you up to the farm."

As the group walked across the field, to get her own back, Fay shouted.

"April's remarks are very flattering, but she's no mean hand with horses herself, at our last farm she very bravely detangled a harness from around a horse's neck, the horse was terrified, but April talked him into being calm. It was a courageous thing to do, she could've been trampled to death, she deserved all the praise she got."

April stared at Fay with a look in her eyes that said, 'just you wait.'

"Well blow me; you girls never fail to surprise me! Anything else you've done that I should know about?"

"Believe me, Mr Bellows, you don't know the half of it. And don't want to know," Fay said grimly.

As they came up to the stable, a loud whinnying, snorting and thumping could be heard.

"He's noisy, isn't he?" Mr Bellows said matter of factly.

"I want to see what's behind all that noise," April said firmly.

Mouse gripped Fay firmly by the arm, she was trembling uncontrollably.

"I'm going in last. In fact, I think that I'll wait outside for you."

"Oh no you're not, you're coming in, it's only a horse, he's making a lot of noise because he's in a stable he doesn't know and wants to be in the one he's used to," April said matter of factly.

Fay removed Mouse's hand from around her arm.

"Calm down and come on."

As the four entered the stable and stood around the stall that held Trigger-me, he ceased to prance around and swung his head round to stare at the four people he did not know. He snorted loudly as if in disgust, then tossed his head from side to side as he pawed the floor with his left hoof.

"He's upset because he's in a strange stable. You three stand back and let me nearer to him. Do you have anything handy that I can offer him to eat, Mr Bellows?" Fay asked.

Mr Bellows turned to Mouse.

"You, girl, run over to the house and ask Mrs Bellows for a couple of carrots, and an apple if she has one."

Mouse looked startled.

"Well, go on, girl, what are you waiting for?" He gave her a push. "Go on, girl," he shouted.

His raised voice upset the horse still more.

"Don't shout," Fay pleaded. "You'll upset the horse, just stand still until Mouse gets back."

"I told you that she's an expert, didn't I," April said authoritatively to Mr Bellows.

"Aye, you did. I've got myself a good girl here," Mr Bellows replied, his face glowing with pride.

"What about me?" April asked indignantly. "You couldn't get a better worker than me, not that I want to blow my own trumpet."

"I'll give you that, April, you're a worker," Mr Bellows laughed.

Fay had been talking quietly to the horse.

"Now," she said to Mr Bellows. "He is a handsome horse, just look at his coat, black with a healthy sheen, he's been looked after, very well looked after. I hope that you'll carry on the good work, Mr Bellows."

"Of course I shall, he's a present to myself, I hope he'll settle down here and let me ride him," Mr Bellows said hopefully.

At the sound of running footsteps, Fay said.

"Here comes Mouse."

Mouse ran pell-mell into the stable, with a carrot clutched in one hand, and an apple in the other.

"I haven't been long, have I?" she cried loudly.

The horse began to prance around.

"Keep your voice down, shouting seems to upset him," Fay warned.

"It's a good job he's not a racehorse and has to face a crowd on the racecourse," April said, stepping nearer to the stall.

"Keep back," Fay warned. "Let me settle him. Give me the apple please, Mouse." She held out her hand, and Mouse handed her a large red apple.

Fay held the apple in both hands, pulled, and the apple broke into clean halves.

"Gosh, I've never seen that done before," Mouse said in amazement.

"It's a knack I have," Fay laughed.

"A knack? What's a knack?" Mouse asked curiously.

"Don't start with your questions just now, Mouse, we'll explain later," April said sharply.

Mouse looked contrite, then fell silent.

Fay put one half of the apple onto the palm of her hand and held it out to the horse.

"Come on boy," she said softly. "You'll like this."

The horse snuffled round it, then took it, chomping loudly as if in enjoyment. He nudged Fay on her shoulder as if asking for more.

"This is an intelligent horse," Fay whispered as she held out the other half of the apple. "You've got yourself a prize, Mr Bellows." Then turning to Mouse, she asked, "do you want to give him the carrot, Mouse?"

"No, I'll pass if you don't mind; I'd like to keep my fingers," she said, shuddering.

"There's a way of holding things to an animal," April said firmly. "It always has to be on the flat of the hand, if you hold it between your fingers, he'll take them too."

"Oh dear," Mouse moaned.

"Watch, I'll give him the carrot." She took the carrot from Mouse and held it out to the horse who took it quickly. "See, nothing to it," April bragged.

Fay began to pat the horse gently on his neck, he liked this, so she started to murmur softly to him, and with her other hand, she opened the stall door.

"You three keep quiet, don't say a word."

She stepped into the stall; the horse began to back away from her. She continued to speak softly while moving nearer to him, and he became still as if surprised at her daring, then tossed his head high into the air with a loud whinny. Fay stood her ground and did not back away; he became still and looked curiously at her. She moved forward and put her hand onto his nose, stroking it gently, all the while speaking quietly, words the others could not understand. Then slowly she put her mouth close to his nostrils and began to gently breathe and blow, pause, breathe and blow, she continued to do this for a few minutes. When she moved her head away from him, he stood as if mesmerised, docile, now to be easily managed, at least by Fay.

"Well, I've never seen anything like that," Mr Bellows said amazed.

"Nor me," April said. "Fay, you're a marvel."

"Not really," Fay answered modestly. "It's a trick the Irish Tinkers taught me; Mother befriended them once when they were in trouble with the law. They used to let me ride their horses and ponies, taught me all the tricks. They taught me how to ride bareback too, how to grip a horse's back on a special place, especially over jumps."

"Over jumps? Bareback?" April exclaimed.

"You grip with your knees, not your hands?" Mouse asked.

"Of course, silly, you have to sit upright, it's easy when you and the horse know what you're doing," Fay said matter of factly. "I always enjoyed it."

Mr Bellows had not spoken a word and stood immobile in shock at Fay's words.

"Fay, you never fail to amaze me. What else can you do that we lesser mortals can't?" April asked.

"There's no need to be sarcastic, April."

"Sorry, I didn't mean to be sarcastic," April apologised.

"I think you're marvellous," Mouse said loudly. "And brave."

"Yes, give me a medal, but now, I'd better get myself out of here, or Trigger-Me will think that I'm moving in with him."

Just as she opened the stall door, Dennis entered the stable and shouted.

"Here you all are. What's going on?"

The horse reared in fright, and Fay threw herself out of the stall just as the horse bolted forward. Everyone flattened themselves against the wall as he galloped by, making for the open stable door.

"You bloody fool!" Mr Bellows shouted. "After him, everybody."

Fay calmly took a halter and bridle that was hanging by the stall and walked unhurriedly out of the stable. She saw that Mr Bellows and Dennis were running across the field after the horse, who, coming to a closed five-barred gate, cleared it with ease, then raced across the field where he jumped a high hedge with a ditch running alongside. This continued for two or three fields, in one, cows with calves scattered in fright as Trigger-Me charged like an express train through them.

Winded and his legs feeling like lead, Mr Bellows drew to a halt. Dennis slowed down and looked back at his Boss.

"Are you alright, Boss?"

"No, I'm not, that bugger seems to know where he's going, and if we *do* catch up with him, which I doubt, how are we going to hold him?" Mr Bellows said.

Dennis looked across the fields.

"Here comes Fay, she's carrying something, looks like horse equipment. Sensible girl," Dennis said in relief. "And," he said hesitantly. "I know where he's heading. Mr Seaton's mare's on heat, he's going for a bit of how's yer father."

"Oh my God he can't, that mare is Seaton's pride and joy, he's talking of getting her into racing, she can't be put in foal."

"I'm afraid it may be too late."

"You bloody, fool, this is your fault, coming into the stable shouting and bawling, panicking the horse!"

"I didn't know you were all in there looking at him did I."

"If old Seaton gets on to me, *and* he will, I shall blame you!" Mr Bellows shouted, waving his hands in the air.

As Fay joined them, Mr Bellows garbled out what Dennis had said.

"Don't jump the gun, it may not happen. But talking of jumping, did you see how he cleared that five-barred gate and those hedges?! He can really jump, it was superb!" Fay cried.

"I'm not interested in the gate or hedges he jumped, only the jumping he's going to do on that bloody mare!" Mr Bellows shouted, nearly tearing out his hair.

Fay seemed not to hear this; she went on.

"Unless I'm not very much mistaken, he's a National horse; you should find a good trainer for him, Mr Bellows."

"Have you lost your mind? He's on his way to get in foal an expensive mare that the owner will shoot him for, me as well!"

"Now calm down," Dennis put in.

"Maybe no one will see the hanky-panky, if so, Seaton wouldn't be any the wiser, would he?" Mr Bellows asked, hopefully.

Fay smiled.

"How many stallions are there around here?" she asked.

"I haven't a clue," Dennis answered.

"I don't think that anyone knows I have Trigger-Me yet," Mr Bellows said.

"I'd suggest we get moving and get the horse back into the stable," Fay said. "I can manage on my own, you two go back and tell April and Mouse what's happening." She paused, then said. "I'd be interested to see the paperwork for Trigger-Me, you know, find out about his sire. You do have the paperwork on him don't you, Mr Bellows?" She asked, hopefully.

"Yes, I do, but I haven't looked at it yet."

"Then, may I?"

"Yes, with pleasure."

"I love his name."

"It's alright."

"Oh, please don't change it."

"You like it so much, do you?"

"I love it, it sounds posh!"

"You'd better go and find this horse with the bloody posh name then hadn't you."

"Yes, I'd better."

Fay jogged across the field, with Mr Bellows and Dennis watching after her until she was out of sight.

"She's quite a girl isn't she," Dennis said affectionately.

"Aye, you could do with a girl like that. You'd have to watch your P's and Q's with her," Mr Bellows laughed.

"She's not my type, too posh for me, she needs a gentleman farmer, but she's fallen for Larry."

"Larry?" Mr Bellows said incredulously, "gerr-away!"

"It's true, he's fallen for her too, be a wedding soon I'd say."

"Is it that serious?"

"It is, they're engaged."

"Wait until I tell the wife."

"Oh, she knows."

"Does she, I wonder why she didn't tell me?"

"Probably waiting to see if it lasts."

"My own farm and I don't know what's going on; I hope that they're not canoodling on my time," Mr Bellows fumed.

"Larry's too much pride in his work to do that," Dennis defended.

"I hope so. Anyway, let's get on, soon be milking time, and we've to round up the cows. I hope April had the good sense to get on with the fruit picking, I don't know about that Tina, Mouse as they call her, she seems a bit slow to me," Mr Bellows remarked as he hurried along. "I hope we can keep April and Fay though; these Land Girls get moved around every week."

"We must keep our fingers crossed," Dennis said, hopefully. "I wouldn't like to see them go; April's a scream, the things she comes out with!"

"I bet she *is* good to work with," Mr Bellows said. "I've heard her singing to the cows, she's a lovely voice. Any road, the cows like it."

"Oh, they do, they stand really still as if listening with enjoyment," Dennis laughed.

"You know the old saying, 'if music be the food of love, play on'; there must be something in that."

13

Most of the girls were sitting in the living room waiting for Mrs Keir to appear with her new set of rules.

"She did say eight, didn't she?" Connie asked the room in general.

"It's only just five to, give her a chance," Belinda said impatiently.

"I hope that she isn't going to be late, I'm worn out and need my bed," Jane said.

"Don't we all," Anita agreed.

"Well, I can tell you, none of you will have had the day that me Fay and Mouse have had," April put in firmly.

There were cries of.

"Here we go!" from the other girls.

Fay shook her head at April and mouthed.

"No."

"*I've* been dealing with blinking rats all day, all I want to do is jump into a bath full of hopefully, hot water," Nancy cried.

"I think that you should rephrase that Nancy, no full bath remember, only six inches, we have to remember the rule," Jane reminded.

"I know, but I can dream, can't I," Nancy sighed.

"The first thing I'm going to do when this war's over is fill a bath to the top, empty a bottle of scented bath oil into it, take a good book, and soak for an hour. Heaven!" Belinda said.

"We all have dreams of what we'll do when the war's over. Mine is to own my own little farm, that's my dream of heaven. To lean on my own five-barred gate and look at all the land I shall own," April said dreamily, her mind far away.

"That's a nice dream *and* hope, but it'll cost money, where will you get that?" Connie asked.

April shook her head, then said.

"Something will turn up."

"A man, a rich farmer whom you will marry," Anita laughed.

"Me? Marry? Not on your life! I love the land too much; no man could compare. Besides, what's mine will be my own; I'm not prepared to share it with any man," April said with flashing determined eyes.

"But don't you want children?" Jane asked.

"No, I never want kids, I'll be too busy on my farm. Besides, you have to have a husband to have kids, and as I just said, no marriage for me."

"Oh, you're only young; you'll change your mind," Anita said knowingly.

April shook her head.

"No, I won't."

"She means it," Fay said firmly.

Just then the door opened to admit Mrs Keir.

"Sorry if I'm a little late, but an important telephone call came through, of which I'll tell you later. Now, how many of you are they?" She looked around the room and counted. "Eight I see, the others are still at work, but not to worry, I'll see them later. The first thing I have to say is that The Ministry of Labour and Works, plus your Local Representative, send their heartfelt apologies for the treatment you all received at the hands of Miss Topp. They don't understand how you put up with it for so long. However, Miss Topp's in serious trouble for her wrongdoing, and is being dealt with I can assure you. She stole your rations, we cannot replace those, but from now on you will be fed edible food I promise you, no more beetroot sandwiches."

Loud cheers rang around the room at this.

Mrs Keir went on.

"From now on, there'll be a signing in and out book by the door for the simple reason, that the last girl in can check the *in* list against the *out* list, and if she sees that she's the last in, she can lock and bolt the door for the night."

There were cries of agreement to this.

"I should like you to be in by ten-thirty on weekdays, of course at weekends I realise you go dancing or are out with boyfriends. So, sensible times, please. I trust you all to be sensible, don't abuse the rules. At my mention of boyfriends, you're going to be able to bring them in on Tuesdays and Sundays. Entertaining them can be done in the large sitting room where the piano is. I intend to have the piano tuned, I play a little myself, so dancing is on the cards, we can roll the carpet back."

There were calls of 'good-o' and whistles.

"I don't have to tell you that boys are not allowed in bedrooms."

"Of course not, Mrs Keir," Jane said firmly.

There were nods of agreement from the others.

"Parties are allowed, if I have notice. Birthday's will be celebrated, and a special tea laid on."

"Oh, how lovely!" Fay said.

"I hope that all girls will keep their bedrooms tidy, the days of Miss Topp when you had to clean your own rooms are gone, I'll be employing a cleaner to do that. You girls work hard enough on the land without being expected to clean your rooms, so hence tidiness. Now we've got that out of the way, this next bit concerns April." She looked down at the papers she held in her hands, then looked at April with a smile. "April, I've heard from The Agricultural Committee that you're to be given your own hostel, which means 'in charge of'. They think that you're imaginative and original, and able to control. It's a great honour, April; you're so young."

"You've got to be kidding me!" April was stunned.

"Yes, you, April."

"But I'm always in trouble."

"The point is you always get out of it."

"Not always by fair means. Do they know that?"

"They must do."

The other girls began to clap and cheer, Fay looked knowing, and on April seeing this, a suspicion began to form in her mind.

Could Fay's Mam have had a hand in this with a word put in her ear by Fay who was getting married very soon? Fay would want to see her settled until the end of the war.

Fay, seeing the look on April's face, shook her head and mouthed.

"Not me."

But April's mind was quickly made up, she turned to Mrs Keir.

"It's a very kind offer, but one I must turn down, it's not for me, it would put me apart from the other girls and I want to be one of them. Jane would be much better suited to the job than I ever would. So please thank The Agricultural Committee for me, it's a great honour, but one I must turn down."

Mrs Keir looked crestfallen.

"April, won't you think about it?" she asked.

"No, I'm sorry, Mrs Keir, I won't change my mind."

"Mrs Keir is right, April, you should think about it at least, and it'll be more money," Fay pleaded.

"I don't wish to discuss it, Fay, the matters closed, they'll find someone else for the job, I'm sure."

"Well, I think that you're a fool, April, I wish *I* had the offer, it would get me away from all those blooming rats," Nancy said, shaking her head.

"Me too, I wish I'd had the offer," Jane said. "Actually, I was in charge of a group of girls in my last job."

"It wouldn't do for me, I'm too short-tempered," Anita laughed.

Mrs Keir looked curiously at Jane.

"Would you really like the job? If so, I would recommend you."

"Would you, Mrs Keir? That would be kind of you. Where is this hostel?" Jane asked.

"Cornwall, in a lovely spot, so I've been told," Mrs Keir replied.

"Not too far away from home, I'm from Paignton you know. I'll keep my fingers crossed."

"I'll do my best for you, Jane, you may be sure. Now for some good news that I know you're all going to like. I had a telephone call from a Captain Silverton of Bomber Command."

There was a gasp from April as Mrs Keir went on.

"You're all cordially invited to a dance at the G.I base, it's being held in their most massive hanger with a big dance band, next Friday from seven-thirty onwards. He hopes that all you girls will be there. Food is supplied, and there's a jitterbug contest.

April gasped again as she looked knowingly at Fay.

Mrs Keir smiled, then went on.

"The G.I's are expecting villagers from round about to attend, so it sounds like it's going to be a big do."

"I can't wait!" Belinda cried. "But I only have one good dress, so it'll have to do."

"I'll worry about what to wear nearer the time," Binnie said firmly. "If I've to go in my nightgown I'm going."

"That'll get you lots of partners anyway," Belinda said with raised eyebrows.

"Have you seen her nightgowns, they're like bloody tents, the G.I's won't be able to find her!" Katrina cried, laughing uproariously.

Everyone laughed at this.

"If I may finish girls, the Captain also said that if you wished, you could go in your uniforms, it's up to you."

"We couldn't very well go in our uniforms with dancing shoes, high heels at that, we'd look silly, and I'm certainly not dancing round in our Land Army lace-up shoes," April declared in a loud voice.

"Yes, we should all go in a dress," Nancy replied.

"I agree," Joan said, raising her hand.

"Girls," Mrs Keir called. "One more thing, would you mind if I came with you?"

There was a surprised silence for a moment as a look of amazement came over every girl's face.

April was the first to find her voice.

"I'd love you to; as I'm sure the other girls would too." Then abruptly. "Wouldn't you girls?" April hoped that she would not sound patronising to Mrs Keir. "All the girls and I consider you a friend as well as being in charge of us, Mrs Keir." She turned her head and looked at everyone, then said, "don't we girls."

"Oh yes, of course we do!" the girls said.

"I don't want any of you to be on your best behaviour, you must let your hair down. I shall, and I want us all to have a good time."

Fay nudged April in the ribs and whispered.

"That's interesting."

Mrs Keir surprised them further.

"If anyone wants to borrow a dress, I've quite a good wardrobe, so please come to me."

Fay nudged April again.

"Yes, I heard," April said softly.

"We're going to be picked up at eight o'clock, and I would like a list of girls names who wish to go. Captain Silverton also assured me that we would be brought safely back home. So, girls, that seems to be all, I'll leave you to talk amongst yourselves, you'll be excited, I'm sure. I know I am; I can't remember when I last went to a dance."

"Can you dance, Mrs Keir?" Fay asked.

"Oh yes, I used to be quite good on the dance floor, although I'm likely to be a little rusty."

"You'll be okay after the first dance," Connie said. "I'm not very good, but who will be looking at me."

"Don't put yourself down, Connie; the G.I's will be looking at your figure, not your face," April said.

"Will they?" Connie said, dubiously. She stood, pushed back her chair, took hold of her generous breasts, then said in a Mae West voice, "come up and see me sometime, big boy."

There was hysterical laughter at this, and Mouse, who so far had not spoken a word, asked.

"Why did Connie do that?"

"Oh, Mouse my love, you're unbelievable," April said as she took hold of Mouse's hand and patted it gently.

"Connie was doing an imitation of someone, wasn't she?" Mouse asked curiously.

"Yes, love, she was," April answered softly. "An actress called Mae West who has a well-shaped generous figure with a large bust. She's well known for her rude remarks about men. Have you never seen any of her films?"

"No, I haven't, but I'd like to," Mouse said eagerly.

Connie was still doing a take-off of Mae West, which was bringing forth gales of laughter from the girls. She was swaying her shoulders seductively and nodding her head as she said in a deep southern drawl, one hand on her hip.

"It's not the men in my life; it's the life in my men." Then putting her hand on her chin, and with a naughty twinkle in her eye. "Is that a gun in your pocket, or are you just pleased to see me?"

Joan had tears of laughter running down her face.

"Stop, Connie stop, I'm going to wet my knickers!" she shouted as she ran from the room.

"You're really funny," Fay gasped. "You should be on the stage, Connie."

"Should I? Scrubbing it do you mean?" Connie asked.

There were further gales of laughter at this, and Fay took a hankie and wiped her eyes as Mouse looked on in bewilderment.

"We should put a concert on for the G.I's, you'd be the star, Connie, all the Yanks love Mae West, and you know, her big bust," April said as she made two large round circles with her hands.

"Well, my boobs aren't as big as hers," Connie declared. "You'd have to stuff balloons up my sweater."

"That could be done, that's what they do with men playing a woman in a film," Belinda responded, nodding her head.

"Oh, it won't come to that, we haven't time to be putting concerts on, we're too busy working," Jane said firmly. "Anyway, if everyone has settled down after Connie's act, there seems to be post for someone." She picked up two letters from the table. She handed one to April, who looked at the writing on the envelope and said.

"From Mam, I'll read it later, she never writes much."

"One for you, Connie, Newcastle postmark," Jane said as she handed the letter to her.

"This is from *my* Mam as well. If you want another good laugh stay where you are, Mam writes as she speaks. Her spelling's atrocious, she's hilarious and doesn't realise it. I'll read it to you." She opened the envelope with her thumbnail, cleared her throat loudly, then began to read.

"Dear Connie,

Hi girl, hope you're okay and that Land Army ain't working you too hard. I'll tell you what's been happening in this neck of the woods. Your Dad is sending me mad with his bloody pigeons, nasty, dirty, noisy, smelly things. They shit all over mi washing on Monday, one day he'll get pigeon pie for his bloody dinner. He thinks more of them bloody birds than he does of me. You know our young Billy is coggy-handed, I ad to trail up to that school of his last week, you should've seen his hand, red raw it was. His teacher ad been belting it with a ruler to mek him use his right hand. I telled her if she did it again, I'd brek the bloody ruler and mek her eat the pieces. Our little Mary has broken her arm, she has a pot on, she wer falling out with little Stanley next door, hit him with her pot arm and broke his nose. His Mam came around like a raging bull, but what could I do. Aunty Ada has had a fall out with Aunty Jean, a right punch up it wer, they both had a black eye, and Jean ended up with half her hair missing, she doesn't half look funny with those bald patches. Old Tommy Roe still gets sken-eyed drunk, he staggered down the street with no trousers on, our little Mary saw him and wer fascinated at what hung between his legs. What could I tell her, a kid of nine? He was arrested for indecent behaviour. Mrs Benny still scrubs the pavement outside her house and won't let nobody walk on it. The other day she ad just finished when a ton of coal wer delivered, serves her right. Gent Butler as got another lady friend just like all the others. War painted up, all fur coat and no knickers, but that suits him, saves him having to get em off when he wants a bit of how's yer father, he tells all his mates in the pub about it. Before I forget, Uncle Amos is over from Irish land for a couple of weeks', our Billy thinks the sun shines out of his arse. I wer just going through the door to church when I heard him telling our Billy about rude Irish titty's. Eye-eye I thought, I'll tell the Father about that. Any road, after the service, I told Father O'Shea about this titty business, and I thought he wer going to swallow his false teeth. He clacked them together and couldn't speak. His face went brick red and he shooed me away. Fancy doing that. Any road, I found out later that I'd got it wrong, it was ditty's, not titty's, I must be going deaf. Any road, your Uncle's going back to Irish land tomorrow thank God, you wouldn't believe the smell he meks in the bathroom, it's like a brass band when he's in there. Must end here love, I've to get your Dad's tripe and onions on.

Love from your Mam X"

During the reading of the letter, there had been screams of laughter.

"We know who you take after now, Connie, your Mam without a doubt," April cried.

"That's a very funny letter, does she always write like that?" Fay asked. "How I'd like to meet her."

"She certainly has a way with words; does she want to join the Land Army?" Anita wondered.

"I enjoyed listening to your letter, Connie; your Mam's a Catholic I take it?" Mouse asked softly.

"Yes, so am I, but not a practising one, never have been, I don't hold with all this church stuff. Mam gave us the choice of going to church or not when I was a kid, once was enough, all of them hymns and swinging that horrible smelly stuff around, it made me feel ill. And all that claptrap about confessing your sins, I'll bet a few of the old boys sat listening in the confessional have a few sins they could confess."

"Each to his own," Jane rendered.

"You've to be clever to be able to sit down and write a letter saying that, there must be something to the saying 'write as you talk,'" April said, nodding her head.

"I agree with that, April, Connie does have a very clever Mother, she has a way with words," Jane smiled, then turned to Connie. "I hope that you'll read your Mum's next letter to us Connie?"

"I certainly will," replied a proud Connie. "And in my next letter home, I'll tell Mam everything you've said, she'll be so pleased. My Dad always says that she has cornflakes for brains."

"It sounds as if your Dad has the cornflake brain; I'd like to read *his* letters," April said disgustedly.

"He's put my Mam down all of her life," Connie said softly as she put her letter back into its envelope.

"Men are such pigs aren't they," Anita said.

"Not all of them, but one is lucky if one gets a good one," Jane said as she stood, stretched and said with a yawn. "I'm going to bed, so I'll say goodnight, and thanks for the entertainment, Connie, you're a star."

"I like to see people laughing, especially in these war-torn days, although the war seems very far away to me, it's like we're cut off from the rest of the world. I only learn about what's happening from the farmworkers, and they don't know much. We really should listen to the wireless shouldn't we, or buy a paper now and again."

"That's alright in theory," Fay broke in. "But when do *we* get time to listen to a wireless or read a paper. Miss Topp always had the wireless in her office when really it belonged to us."

"She most likely made off with it, I wouldn't put anything past her, we must ask Mrs Keir," Anita said firmly.

"And on that note, I'm off to bed," April said, yawning loudly, she covered her mouth with her hand. "Are you coming, Fay and, Mouse?"

The two girls nodded in agreement as they stood and carried their chairs back into the kitchen and placed them neatly around the table, the other girls following suit.

"I'll put the lights off in here; the girls who are still out will put off the hall lights," Anita said. "So, goodnight girls, sleep well."

14

It was a mild, fresh, sunny morning, but with a hint of autumn in the air as Fay and Larry stole a few moments together behind the small barn.

"I can only stay a few moments; I'm supposed to be on my way to the toilet," Fay said anxiously.

"I'm supposed to be looking for the new hoe," Larry laughed as he pulled Fay into his arms and kissed her lingeringly, she moved closer to him.

"Oh, Larry, I love you so much," she whispered.

"I should hope so," he said, and drew her even closer.

Fay relaxed against him and sighed in contentment.

"Don't let's get too comfy, sweetheart. We're supposed to be working."

"Don't remind me," Fay said unhappily.

He held her at arm's length and asked.

"Are you going to the G.I dance at the base on Friday, my love?"

"No, I didn't think that you'd want me to go," Fay replied, surprised.

"Are the others going? April will be, won't she?"

"Yes, and three or four others."

"Then you must go too."

"Oh, I couldn't, not without you, Larry."

"Don't be silly, you go and enjoy yourself, you work hard and deserve a night out. I'm sorry I can't take you out more, but my hours are long."

"I know that, so are mine, it's a shame we don't get to spend more time together, alone I mean," Fay said sadly.

"Plenty of time for that when we're married," Larry said suggestively.

"I'll look forward to that," Fay said coyly.

"To be honest, I don't want to wait until the end of the war to get married; I don't think that you do either, do you, my love?" Larry asked.

"No, I don't, we'll have to talk about it, but I must go now, the others will think that I've gotten lost. See you tonight, same place and time all being well." She kissed him hurriedly then walked quickly away, calling over her shoulder, "love you lots."

Larry turned away and went into the barn for a further search of the lost hoe.

The three girls had been pulling swedes for two days and were finding it a toiling back-breaking job, luckily the weather was holding well, in the rain it would be thoroughly miserable they agreed with one another.

"Sorry to take so long you two," Fay said. "You must have thought I'd fallen down the loo."

"We *were* beginning to wonder, or is the truth of the matter that you'd bumped into Larry and were kissing and canoodling?" April asked sternly.

Fay chose not to answer and bent to the job in hand.

"It's a good job you're back because here comes Mr Bellows; he would've wanted to know where you were wouldn't he," April said, a mischievous note in her voice. "Anyway, I want a word with him."

Fay stood upright.

"Why do you want a word with him?" she asked in alarm.

"You'll see soon enough," April replied.

Mr Bellows strode up to them and asked.

"How's it going, girls? I want this field cleared by tomorrow, the wagon will be here to take the load to the station at dinnertime remember, you'll have to stay longer tonight if necessary."

April pulled a face, then said apologetically.

"I'm so sorry to put a spanner in the works, Mr Bellows, but I've to have an hour off, as from now."

"What the hell for?!" he shouted.

Fay and Mouse looked astonished.

"Well, it's rather embarrassing, Mr Bellows," April said gingerly, casting her eyes down, putting on, she hoped, a shy air.

"Embarrassing? What do you mean, girl?! When you work on a farm, nothing's embarrassing."

There was a short silence.

Fay wondered what the hell April was up to now. She hadn't long to wait, as Mr Bellows shouted.

"Spit it out, girl!"

"It's women's trouble. You know," April said as she raised her head and looked at Mr Bellows.

"No, I don't know, explain yourself," Mr Bellows said aggressively.

Fay breathed slowly out as she realised what was coming.

"It's my monthly's, and I've to have pads, so. I've to go into the village, please don't be embarrassed, Mr Bellows, you *did* ask. And you're quite right, no need at all to be embarrassed when you work on a farm."

Fay and Mouse stared at April unbelievingly, unable to look at Mr Bellows, who felt that he had been put very firmly in his place. He had flushed beetroot-red, and for a moment could not utter a word. He had never come across anything like this, not ever, but he quickly pulled himself together.

He looked at his watch.

"Half-past ten, you've one hour. I want you back here at half-past eleven, the bloody swedes won't pull themselves up. Have you got that, girl?"

"Yes, Mr Bellows, I'll be as quick as I can, and thank you for understanding," April said meekly.

He stormed off after growling out.

"Never heard the like of it."

"Well, what's all this about?" Fay asked, her face like thunder. "That was one big outrageous lie you told there – monthly's indeed. I know for a fact that you had that last week. What are you up to, April? I hope this doesn't mean trouble. But, knowing you, that's a foregone conclusion, so *what* I ask myself, are you going into the village for?" She paused for a moment, deep in thought, then said. "Oh no, you can't be going to the school?!"

"Clever girl, go to the top of the class," April said as she clapped her hands. "But I haven't time to stand here listening to you, Fay, I must be off."

"Don't go, April, leave it," Fay begged.

"Simms can't be allowed to cane Norman because of me, he's nothing but a bully and I shall tell him so. Don't worry, Fay, I know what I'm about," April said firmly. "And I don't expect you and Mouse to do my share of picking out the swedes, I'll stay behind tonight, not you two, it'll be worth it to put Simms in his place."

"You'd better go then and get on with it," Fay retorted as she turned and bent once more to her task.

* * *

As April walked through the school hall, she heard the chanting of girls voices coming from the classroom on the left.

Learning their six times tables, I used to hate that, always got it wrong, still am a dud at adding up, but was always the top of the class in English and spelling, you can't beat having the use of words.

She walked to the classroom on the right, knowing it to be the boy's room. What a shock Norman was going to get.

She pushed open the door without knocking and walked boldly in. All heads swivelled towards the door, complete amazement on every face, each knowing who she was, all except Simms, who had turned towards her and stood glaring at her over his spectacles.

"Yes, what do you want?!" he snapped.

"You!" April snapped back.

He took off his spectacles.

"I don't know you, who are you?" he asked.

"You may not know me, but you've certainly heard of me, actually from one of your pupils," April replied firmly.

All the boys were sat as if electrified, on April's words a ripple swept through the class, and Norman punched the air with his fist. Titch sank lower down onto his chair, his eyes like saucers.

"From one of my pupils?" Simms repeated. "You still have not told me who you are, but from the way you are dressed, you are one of those Land Girls who have brought so much trouble to the village."

"I beg your pardon, trouble to the village?" April asked politely.

"I do not intend to go into that in front of my class, I am not interested in why you want to see me, or in you, so please leave."

"No, I'm sorry, but I can't do that," April said quietly, having gotten the measure of Simms.

"What?!" Simms shouted.

"Kindly do not shout, you'll make me angry, and you don't want to see me angry."

"Get out of my classroom, you stupid, girl!"

"Oh dear, you *are* going to make me angry, poor you."

"How dare you speak to me like that!"

"Oh, I dare, wait until I *really* get started."

Norman leant across to Titch and dug him in the ribs.

"This is gonna be good, Miss April's getting mad," he said under his breath.

Titch's eyes opened wider as he gulped deep in his throat, in fright *or* excitement, he did not know. But he *did* know that he wanted to go to the lav, so, he must be frightened – for Miss April, not Simms.

The rest of the class were all agog. This was better than crappy lessons; this was great, Simms getting his comeuppance.

Meanwhile, the white-faced Simms was digging his toes in.

"Before I assist you out," he said threateningly. "Why in particular do you wish to see me?"

"By assist, I hope that you don't mean what I think you mean," April exclaimed.

"Oh, no, no, no," Norman said loudly.

Titch clenched his legs together, willing himself not to wet his pants as Simms went on.

"Surely you know what assist means, but still, what can you expect from a girl who grubs about on the land for a living."

"Oh gosh, he's done it now," Norman muttered.

April bit her bottom lip and told herself to keep her temper, when all she wanted to do was to wring Simms scrawny neck.

"I anticipated you bringing the Land Army into disrepute." She walked past him to his desk chair, hooked her foot around it and pushed it towards him. "Sit down!" she snapped.

"What?!" Simms thundered.

"You heard," April said quietly. "Sit down."

"I'd sit down if I were you, Sir," Norman called.

"Kindly keep your mouth shut, McMasters!" Simms shouted angrily.

April pushed him down onto the chair, and Simms gasped like a fish caught on a hook. She bent down and stared into Simms's face.

"Don't call that lad McMasters, he has a first name, it's Norman." She stood upright, turned to the class, and with a beaming smile said. "Hello class, good morning."

"Good morning, Miss April," the class responded.

April went on.

"I hope you don't mind me interrupting your lesson, but *I* am going to give you one in the English language. You don't mind, do you?"

"No, Miss April," the boys cried out.

"First of all, boys, I've to make myself known to Simms here." She turned to Simms who was sat stony-faced but listening keenly. "I'm April Thornton."

A look of understanding crossed Simms's dour face.

"Ha!" April cried. "I see that you recognise the name."

"I do," Simms said smugly. "The one who is supposed to throw grown men around like a sack of potatoes."

"That's the one, and, I am she," April said.

"So, what has *that* got to do with me?" Simms asked as he crossed his arms on his chest.

"Oh, it has a *lot* to do with you, Simms, you see, young Norman was on the bus when I demonstrated my daring to accept Perkins' bet, or should I say dare. I couldn't let Perkins, a mere man, get away with saying he could put *me* off the bus. He had the shock of his life when I lifted him like a sack of spuds and threw him onto his arse."

"That's quite enough," Simms chipped out.

The class tittered loudly.

"I want you to leave now," Simms said authoritatively. "*Now*," he repeated.

"Oh, I couldn't leave yet, Simms; I haven't told you why I'm here, have I?"

Simms sniffed and looked bored.

"I understand from my friend Norman, that when he told you about my bit of bother on the bus, you called him a liar, and that you'd like to meet this so-called Herculean Land Girl. But what I *don't* understand is, why you caned the lad for using the word arse."

There was loud laughter from the class, and Simms looked round with a scowl.

"I'd like to specify that the word arse, *is* in the English Dictionary, it's the Kings English," April said with a flourish.

Simms looked mortified as April continued.

"Well?" April said.

"If you say so," Simms conceded.

"I haven't time for stupid men, especially bullies, and you, Simms are both."

"A bully?! I certainly am not!" he shouted.

"Do you know what gets me about men like you, Simms, silly men who comb the few strands of hair which they have left over their balding patch to conceal it. It gives away the fact that they're getting old. It isn't so bad if you have the right shaped head, but you, Simms don't, yours is shaped like an egg."

This brought a roar of laughter from the class, and Simms squirmed in embarrassment.

"You see, Simms, I look at it this way, poor Norman got a caning because of me. Now, I don't like that, the lad was telling the truth as I see it, so *what* if he used the word arse, it's no crime, no lad should get a caning for using a word that's in the dictionary. And by the way, you marked him. You're a bully, Simms; do you enjoy bullying people smaller than yourself? How I would like to lash you with a bullwhip."

There were muttered words from around the classroom of.

"I'd like to see that."

"Serve him right the bugger."

"I've not forgotten when he caned me, he really enjoyed doing it."

Norman had a beaming self-satisfied smile on his face, and poor Titch was sat uncomfortably in wet trousers as the class hung onto April's every word. This was the best school day that they had ever had.

"Did you hear about that fight at the local hop a couple of weeks' ago, Simms?" April asked.

Simms nodded.

"I was there, and involved, those girls made me angry, they were bullying my friend who's a timid, shy little thing, they terrified her. I couldn't let that go on, so, I had to stick my oar in as they say."

"From what I have seen of you so far, I can't say that I am surprised," Simms said.

"If you cane any of these boys ever again, I'll be back, Simms."

"Really, am I supposed to tremble in my boots? This has gone on long enough; I want you to leave right now."

"If I don't, will you assist me?"

"No, but the police will," Simms said cockily. He pointed to a fair-haired boy in the front row. "Silverton, go and fetch PC Humble."

The boy shook his head and said.

"No."

"You heard me, boy, go and get PC Humble!" Simms thundered.

April swung round to face the class.

"Does *anyone* want to fetch PC Humble?" she asked.

There was a chorus of.

"No's."

"Seems you're out of luck, Simms, see how your class respects you. I've said all I came to say, so this land grubbing Land Girl must depart. I can't say how nice to meet you it was, I find you a poor specimen of a man, you should be in the army with a few bullets shot up your arse, how I'd love to do the firing. Before I go, there's something I must do." She turned to the class and asked. "Boys, where does Simms keep his canes?" she asked with a twinkle in her eye.

Titch looked apprehensively at Norman as he thought oh gosh; she isn't going to cane Simms, is she? Then promptly wet himself again.

All the class pointed to a corner behind Simms' desk. Leant against the wall were two canes, one longer and thicker than the other. April picked them both up and weighed them in her hand.

"Oh, I see," she said loudly, casting a steely look at Simms. "Depends how hard and long the punishment is to be as to what cane is used, interesting. You, Simms, are a sadistic bully." She walked to where Simms stood by his desk and whacked it as hard as she could with each cane in turn. Pens and pencils flew into the air and Simms jumped back in shock. "Ha!" April said angrily. "That made you jump didn't it, Simms. How would you like to feel blows like that across the palm of *your* hand?! That's what you administer to these boys. Do you enjoy their pain? I'll bet you do. If I did it to you, you'd squeal like one of our pigs, wouldn't you, Simms."

Simms chose not to answer.

"You go too far, get out!" Simms yelled.

"Will you stop telling me to get out, I'll go when I'm ready, but first there's one thing that I have to do." She laid each cane in turn across her knee and pulled hard backwards, they snapped in two with a loud crack. She put the pieces gently on the desk. "How I wish that had been your neck, Simms, what satisfaction that would give me."

"I shall report you to PC Humble," Simms threatened.

"Let's have no theatricals, Simms, I've done what I came to do, give you a dressing down, don't let me have to do it all over again. And as to your threat of reporting me to Humble, please do, I've some reporting of my own to do."

"Really, and what pray do *you* have to report?" Simms asked sarcastically.

"Your assault on these boys of course, that's punishable by law."

"Rubbish."

"I'm sure that the Judge will agree with me."

"I don't think so."

"A sensible man is the Judge; I know him very well."

"Do you now? So do I."

"Good, that evens it up then doesn't it." The lunch bell ringing loudly stopped all conversation. "Class dismissed," April called cheekily.

"How dare you!" Simms roared.

The boys ran out of the classroom, pushing and shoving each other while laughing merrily, carrying April along with them. Once in the playground, the boys surrounded her.

"Miss April, you were bloody great!" Norman shouted, jumping up and punching the air.

"No swearing, Norman if you please," April admonished.

"I never thought I'd see Simms brought down a peg or two!" a tall boy said happily. "He won't dare cane us again."

"I wouldn't bet on it; Simms is an old bugger," a small fat boy said dubiously.

A pimpled-faced boy with a runny nose said loudly.

"Simms is a cantankerous sod, my Dad says so, and my Dad drinks with Simms in the pub."

"Simms is a beer swiller *my* Dad says," another lad piped up.

"Your Dad ought to know because he's one as well," a ginger-haired lad laughed. "Anyway, thanks to Miss April, things will be better in the classroom."

"It was brilliant when you broke them canes in two, Miss April," Norman said.

April had been listening to all the comments, and now she said sternly as she held up her hand.

"Listen to me, boys, I don't want you to be slack-set-up, that means not attend to your lessons, cheek Simms or misbehave. If you do, you'll be letting me down, do you understand?"

The replies of "yes, Miss April," came slowly.

"I mean it now," she said sternly. She looked around at the boys. "Where's little Titch?" she asked.

"He's gone home for his lunch; he only lives around the corner," Norman replied.

Just at that moment, little Titch was feeling through the letterbox for the key to the front door which hung on a string. As he let himself into the hall, he called nervously.

"Mum?"

Only silence greeted him, good, his Mum had gone to work, he could go upstairs and change out of his wet trousers, he could feel that he had also wet halfway up to his vest. Thank goodness the other kids hadn't noticed; they would've tormented the life out of him. Norman knew about his accidents, but he wouldn't say anything, he was a good mate Norman, the best. His Mum had taken him to the doctors a couple of times, but only when he had started to wet himself more often. The doctor had said that he had a nervous disposition whatever that was; Mum had said that the doctor didn't know what he was talking about. She knew as well as himself that it had started after his Dad had died, that was two years ago. We shall just have to put up with it until you grow out of it, which you will, I'm sure, Mum had said. It didn't happen at school, but today had been an exception, he had been petrified for Miss April, and Simms put the fear of God into him. Thank goodness he never had to be caned, he would really wet himself then, that would be awful in front of the whole class.

He went into the bathroom and ran some water into the washbasin, then, taking off his wet clothes; he pressed them into the water until they were completely submerged. Mum would be pleased that he had put them in to soak, she worked hard up at the G.I base, but it had its compensations, she brought tins of fruit, chocolates and chewing gum home which the G.I's had given her. They had even sent him a cake for his birthday last year, and Mum had given him a party.

He went into his bedroom whose walls were covered with pictures of Roy Rogers, his cowboy hero, and rummaged through draws until he found clean underwear and trousers. He put them on quickly, then went downstairs into the kitchen and opened the pantry door. Good, there was a bit of potted meat. He would have a sandwich, have a read of his Dandy, then head back to school.

He wondered what kind of a mood Simms would be in, he did not want to wet himself again.

15

"Ha, the wanderer returns!" Dennis called out as April hurried breathlessly up to join the group.

"What, not cleared this field of swedes yet?" April said jokingly. "I'd better get cracking, hadn't I?"

"You do know you've been gone for two hours, don't you?!" Fay said angrily.

"Yes, I know," April replied. "Things took longer than I thought they would."

"I hope you kept your temper?" Fay asked anxiously.

"I just about managed to."

"Thank goodness for that," Fay said, relieved.

"What happened? Fay told us where you'd gone," Dennis said.

"I'm not going into it now, but there was quite a row, which I'll tell you about later. The kids loved it!"

Fay frowned and exclaimed.

"Oh, God."

"I think that we should drop the subject for now and get on with the work," Tina said bravely.

"Mr Bellows has been down twice to see if you were back, the second time he was as mad as a hatter," Barry exclaimed. "He's really going to chew you out."

"I expect him to," April answered. "But I can handle him, whatever he says I won't care. It was bloody marvellous confronting that creature Simms, what a slug he is."

"I don't like the sound of this," Fay said.

"You may as well know that he's going to report me," April said cockily.

"Report you? What for?" Dennis asked, surprised.
"Trespass and disruption of a class."
"You've got to be kidding."
"Can't be helped."
"It's not all that serious, is it?" Fay broke in.
"I'll most likely get a caution from Humble," April said unconcerned. She waved her hand as if brushing the matter aside. "It doesn't worry me; it'll all be worth it."
"Well, here comes Bellows, he *is* something to worry about," Dennis cried.
Mr Bellows was stamping across the field, waving his arms in the air.
Mouse jerked her head up and said nervously.
"Oh dear."
He came to a slithering halt in front of April.
"Mr Bellows," April began, then stopped, uncertain as to whether to go on.
"So, you've decided to honour us with your presence have you, Miss Thornton, where the hell have you been? I said one hour, you've been missing for two. I run a farm, not a bloody holiday camp!" Mr Bellows yelled purple-faced.
April was amused, she would stop him in full flow, she knew that his bark was worse than his bite, she would tell him the truth and to hell with it.
She held up her hand, and Mr Bellows was so surprised that he fell silent.
April launched into her story.
"And that's the whole truth," she finished.
The others had remained silent, amazed at April's daring.
"You really did that?" Mr Bellows asked.
"Yes, I did, Simms deserved it, and I only wish I could've set about *him* with that cane."
"So, all that malarkey about monthly's was hot air?"
"Yes, I had to tell you something didn't I."
"I admit, it was a bloody good un," Mr Bellows said.
"So, am I forgiven?"
"Because I can't stand Simms, *and* because you were standing up for those boys, yes."
"If I'd told you the truth in the beginning you wouldn't have let me go, would you?"
"No."
"I've always believed that honesty is the best policy, it's the first time I've strayed from that, but it was worth it, those boys thought that all their birthdays had come at once. Simms being bullied, makes a change doesn't it – a bully being bullied."
As Mouse listened, she was worried that they may be trouble over this, she hoped not, April was a champion of the underdog as she knew.

"I have to tell you, Mr Bellows," April went on. "I'm expecting a visit from PC Humble, but I don't think that he'd come here to the farm where I'm working, most likely the hostel."

"I wonder if he'll bring his handcuffs?" Barry laughed.

"It'll be a first time, me in handcuffs," April cried.

"I don't think it's anything to joke about, what if Humble reports you to the War Agg? You could have a visit from her," Fay cried.

"So be it," April said saucily. "Let Humble bring it on."

Mr Bellows took April by the shoulder and gently shook her.

"I don't know what you'll do next, my girl, the mind boggles, but now, get stuck into clearing this field. Mrs Bellows will be amazed when she hears about this." He tramped off, then turned and called to April. "You, April, are in the delivery shed in the morning."

"Delivery shed?" April said surprised.

"I know what that means," Dennis said with a massive grin on his face. "One of the cows is due to drop tomorrow, and Bellows is expecting it to be a difficult birth. He's going to test your metal, April. Have you ever put your arm up to the elbow in a cow's arse and had a feel around?"

"Is he now?" April replied straight-faced. "Let me let you into a little secret, Dennis, I *have* done it before and enjoyed it, so Bellows is in for a shock, isn't he."

"What *haven't* you done?" Dennis asked in amazement.

At April's words, Mouse went white and swayed on her feet.

"Oh, dear, I feel sick."

* * *

The next day the weather had changed, the rain was lashing down, flooding the farmyard. April was dressed in her long black raincoat and wellies, she splashed from the barn carrying the bucket of eggs which she had just collected, and, spying the narrow wall which ran alongside the midden heap, decided to walk along it instead of splashing through the yard. She climbed slowly and carefully onto the wall, holding the bucket of eggs tightly. She began to walk slowly taking short steps, but suddenly a gust of wind caught her, she lost her balance and fell feet first in the midden up to her waist. She was stuck fast. She started to wriggle her feet out of her wellingtons and heaved herself out. What an awful smell, pig droppings were sweeter than this! She would have to strip off and get washed down in the trough and hopefully borrow a jumper and weralls from Mr Bellows. She had lost all the eggs and the basket, but oh, horror of horror, what if she had fallen in headfirst?! It did not bear thinking about. There were gales of laughter from the boys and Fay and Mouse.

Mrs Bellows found her clean clothes and told her not to ever walk on the midden wall ever again.

If you had gone in headfirst, we wouldn't have heard you, you could have died she had said.

By dinnertime, the rain had stopped, and after a meal of shepherd's pie and peas, the gang were back digging out potatoes. It was dirty muddy work but had to be done, the weather waited for no man. The field was near to the farm, and the pigs could be heard making a right racket, squealing loudly.

"Goodness me, what a loud noise the pigs are making today!" Mouse exclaimed.

April and Fay looked at each other.

"The farmer's having one killed for his own use," Fay replied gently. "And the other pigs probably sense what's to happen."

"Oh," Mouse looked apprehensive. "How will they kill it? That's so cruel, poor thing."

"Well, the butcher and one of the lads tie wires around its neck and pull at each end," April said, matter of factly.

Mouse looked ready to pass out.

"Why are you telling her that?!" Fay protested furiously. She laid down her spade and put her arm around Mouse. "Don't listen to her, Mouse, she's having you on, April's showing her sadistic streak."

"I would've reported it to the RSPCA," Mouse said, in tears.

"Toughen up, Mouse, you eat meat, don't you? How do you think lambs, sheep and cows are killed?!" April cried exasperated.

"We won't go into that if you don't mind, you've frightened her enough," Fay said disgustedly.

April threw down her spade.

"Okay, I stand corrected," she said. "But Mouse must realise that girls play jokes on each other, it's part of being all girls together. Jane told me of one girl at a farm she was at was always saying that she wanted twins when she got married, so the farmer's wife said one way to achieve this was by having a double-yolked egg every day. The girl did this for two weeks' before she was told that it didn't work that way.

Get Nancy to tell you about when she had to have a pee behind a bush when working with the POW. She undid her buttons on her trousers but couldn't do them up again, her fingers were frozen, one of the POW's had to do them up for her, how about that. If you stay in the WLA long enough, Mouse, you'll see and do lots of things that you never thought you would."

"Oh," Mouse said humbly.

"And on that note, here comes Mr Bellows with the horse and cart to collect the swedes. Thank goodness this job's done; I wonder what the next job will be?"

"An easy one, I hope," Fay said glumly.

"Bellows is still stunned from when I shoved my arm up that cow's arse without a qualm, his eyes nearly popped out of his head! The calf arrived fifteen minutes later."

"April, couldn't you put things more delicately?" Fay asked, pulling a face of distaste.

"Why? It's the Kings English, and don't get me on about the word arse again, I had enough of that with Simms."

"I've no intention of doing that," Fay muttered.

Mr Bellows pulled up alongside the group.

"Come on you lot, start throwing those swedes onto the cart, be quick about it, we're late as it is. I'll move alongside you, be easier."

"Supposed to be athletes now as well as farm workers," Barry grumbled.

"What was that?" the sharp-eared Mr Bellows asked.

"Just wondering if the weather's going to hold, Boss," Barry said, hopefully.

"You'd better hope that it does, you're cleaning out the pigsties next," Mr Bellows laughed. "You as well, Dennis," he finished.

Dennis made to throw a large swede onto the cart but deliberately missed so that it clonked Mr Bellows on his head.

"Here! Watch what you're doing you clumsy, sod, that hurt!" Mr Bellows yelled. He rubbed his head then shook it from side to side. "Must weigh a ton that swede, I'll have to put the price of them up," he said complacently. "I'll have a word with the Mrs, see what she thinks."

"What are we girls doing next, Mr Bellows?" Fay asked.

"I want little Mouse in the stables cleaning the horse brass, it needs a good clean, so mind you put some elbow grease into it, Mouse," Mr Bellows said, looking at Mouse piercingly.

"Oh, I will, Mr Bellows," Mouse replied bewildered. She had never worked on her own before.

"And you other two girls, Mrs Bellows wants you with her in the kitchen wrapping up the apples to go into storage."

Fay looked pleased.

"We'll enjoy that won't we, April?" she asked.

"Not half! We'll be able to have a natter with Mrs Bellows; she'll want to know all about my dustup with Simms."

"The less said about that, the better, it'll be all around the village by now. The more sensible villagers will be wondering what the hell I was thinking of giving you time off to heckle Simms. He's not going to let you get away with it you know, April, so watch for the law knocking on your door," Mr Bellows said, shaking his head.

"Humble knocking on my door, he couldn't knock over a jelly!" April laughed.

"He *is* the law around here," Fay said quietly.

"Oh well, let him bring it on," April said gallantly. "I can run rings round Humble with words and well he knows it."

As she began to throw swedes quickly onto the cart, she began to sing 'I'll Be Seeing You.' Her voice rang beautifully around the field.

"Look at her, not a care in the world," Dennis said admiringly.

* * *

Most of the girls were sat in the kitchen enjoying a cup of tea, and supposedly listening to the news on the wireless, but their chatter blanked the announcer's voice out.

Nancy suddenly announced.

"I'm not going to the G.I dance on Friday."

April stared at her in disbelief.

"But you were so looking forward to it."

"Yes, I was, but I've nothing decent to wear."

"Mrs Keir will fix you up, she said so, and you're about her size."

"It's not only the dress, what about shoes? I take an eight, who else takes an eight?"

"I take seven," Fay broke in. "Maybe they'll do?"

"I can't squeeze an eight foot into a seven shoe, and I'm not going to try," Nancy said firmly.

"You're going to that dance, *even* if you go barefooted," April cried determinedly. "Something will turn up."

"Like the good fairy in Cinderella, I suppose," Nancy said dejectedly.

"Look on the bright side; you are going to that dance. We want as many of the Land Girls there as possible to hold our side up," Fay cried. She turned away from Nancy and winked at April.

Joan nodded in agreement, then said.

"I'm not going to look like the bee's knees, my dress is old and my sandals shabby, my hair will go its own way, but who cares, I'm going to enjoy myself."

"That's the spirit, that's just how *I* feel!" Belinda exclaimed.

"A proper dance band, it'll be heaven! The Yanks know about music, look at Glen Miller, Harry James, Benny Goodman, Tommy Dorsey and Gene Krupa! Oh, it's going to be wonderful!" Katrina said as she clasped her hands together in delight.

"I'm not such a good dancer; I hope I get some partners," Joan said hopefully.

"I'm not bad on the dance floor," Belinda said. "Actually, I was considered one of the best in our village, so I expect not to sit one dance out."

"I hope it works out that way for you," Fay said. "I hope we all enjoy ourselves."

"I understand that you're going now, Fay. That Larry doesn't mind?" Nancy asked.

"No, he's told me I've to go and enjoy myself, so I shall. I'd rather be with him of course, but we're not joined at the hip, as he pointed out," Fay said quietly.

"That's sensible of him, of you both," Nancy said.

"You think so?" There was a sceptical expression on April's face. "I hope you're right."

Fay rose to her feet.

"I'm going to turn in; it's been a long, harrowing day, as I'm sure April will agree. Mouse will be hard on, so come in quietly please, April."

"I will," April said.

When Fay had left the kitchen, Nancy said.

"Your words are very flippant about her and Larry; she turned a blind eye, didn't she. I take it that you don't approve, April. But really, it's none of your business is it."

"Fay's my best friend, I look out for her, this has happened too quickly with her and Larry, all this talk of getting married so soon, she's only known him for three weeks', what does she know about him? It's what *he* knows about her that worries me."

"What do you mean, what *he* knows about her?" Nancy probed.

"Like you said, Nancy, it's not my or your business is it," April snapped. "So, let's change the subject... But all the same, I *am* worried. Larry was too good to be true, there's something about him I don't like. There must be a way of checking his past out, maybe the Judge could help? Yes, that's what I'll do, have a word with the Judge."

Nancy seemed anxious to continue the conversation.

"Well," she said dubiously, looking at April apprehensively. "Maybe I'll be talking out of turn, but, when I was leaving the village shop yesterday evening, Larry was stood outside with one of the village girls, a pretty one too. They were laughing and talking, when Larry saw me, he looked taken aback, surprised like. I said, 'hi Larry', and he didn't answer me, just nodded his head."

"That's interesting, but do me a favour, Nancy, don't mention this to Fay," April asked.

"Of course not. Do you think she'll be upset?"

"I couldn't honestly answer that."

"My lips are sealed, but I wonder what he does with his time when Fay's working and he isn't?" Nancy wondered.

"That's an interesting question. I'll have a word with Barry, maybe he'll know," April said.

"If Larry *is* up to something and Barry knows, he may not want to say, after all, they are mates," Nancy said cautiously.

"I have my own way of obtaining information," April laughed, touching the side of her nose. "If there's anything to find out, I'll find it."

* * *

Eight of the girls and Mrs Keir were stood outside the hostel waiting for the G.I transport taking them to the dance at the G.I base.

"Look at us, don't we all look beautiful in our frocks, best shoes and elaborate hairdo's!" Belinda remarked, smiling around at everyone. "Those G.I's had better look out!"

"Count *me* out of the elaborate hairdo. I've just scraped mine back into a ponytail," Joan said.

Jane had brushed her hair into the Veronica Lake style, hung straight down, obscuring one eye.

"I don't know if I feel right with my hair like this," she said anxiously.

"Well, I don't think it suits you," April commented hotly. "Tie it back and let people take you as they find you."

"I've a yellow ribbon in my handbag you can have, Jane. We'll fix it for you when we get to the dance," Fay offered.

"Thanks, I'll feel better," Jane said.

"Well, I think we look like a rainbow, all the different colour dresses we're wearing, and all flared skirts as well," Connie commented.

"They'll be some knickers shown tonight," April said with a twinkle in her eye. "All that jitterbugging."

"Trust you to come out with that," Fay said disgustedly. "And what are you taking a carrier-bag for? What have you got in there?"

"None of your business," April snapped.

Mrs Keir, who so far had been stood silent, clapped her hands.

"Now, girls, behave yourselves. This transport is a little late, I do hope they haven't forgotten us."

"They wouldn't dare, not the Land Army!" Nancy said angrily.

"Something's coming now, look, it's a truck!" Joan cried in excitement.

"A bloody truck?!" April cried in dismay. "It'll have a high back, not easy to get in; it'll be jump up, cock your leg over and hope for the best."

"I hope that you're joking about, April?" Mrs Keir said in dismay. "But I'll sit in the front with the driver."

April smiled mischievously as she said.

"If you do, Mrs Keir, watch the driver's hand, he might like to let it wander."

Mrs Keir looked apprehensive, then said firmly.

"If he does, I'll slap it, and hard."

All the girls laughed as the wagon was stopping slowly.

A small thick-set G.I jumped out and walked round to join the girls.

"Hi there, gals, sorry I'm a bit late, let's get you to the base. Don't you all look dandy! Hollywood style too! The guys are waiting for you; the Land Army Gals are famous."

"Famous, what for?" Connie mumbled.

"We're not in our uniforms so they won't know we're the Land Army, will they." April said sarcastically.

"All the guys have had strict instructions to be polite and act like Gentlemen to all visiting gals. My name's Simon, my buddies call me Si."

"Hello, Si," the girls called out.

Mrs Keir decided to take control.

"Would you help the girls into the wagon please, Si? April seems to think it's going to be difficult to climb in."

"That's no problem, Ma'am, I'll help." He walked to the back of the wagon, then called out. "Who's going to be first?"

April stepped forward, then said.

"I shall, and mind where you're putting your hands."

Si smiled.

"Of course, Ma'am." He grabbed her around the waist, swung her around and up, then said, "there we are, sweetheart."

April landed on her back, legs in the air and dress around her waist; she heard Si give a loud laugh as she scrambled to her feet and straightened her dress. As she leaned over the tailgate to bawl him out, she noticed a bolt each side, she slid them back, and the tailgate dropped down. She could have walked into the truck!

Si looked apprehensive as if knowing what was coming.

April was furious as she shot out of the truck like a rocket and pushed Si hard in his chest. He staggered backwards, white-faced.

"You bloody clever, bugger! You threw me into that truck on purpose!" She thumped him hard in his chest again, and he retreated backwards. "You were going to do it to the other girls, weren't you?! Hands full-on, eh!"

Si opened his mouth to speak.

"Don't you say one word, or I'll smack you in the mouth and you'll be picking your teeth up off the bloody floor!"

Si drained of all colour.

"You knew that tailgate let down, didn't you? But thought you'd have a bit of fun at our expense!" She gave him a forceful punch in his chest, and he fell gasping to the ground. She stood over him like an avenging angel, then put her foot onto his chest. "If I weren't going on this night out, I'd set about you. Think yourself lucky! Now stay exactly where you are."

All the girls stood in silence, looking on in amazement, except Fay who said.

"Oh God, I hope for his sake he does as she says and doesn't move."

Mrs Keir hurried round to face April, who looked at her inquiringly.

"What on earth is wrong, April? Why is that man on the ground?"

"I put him there, and there he had better stay if he knows what's good for him," April answered coolly.

The other girls had joined Mrs Keir, but it was April who took charge.

"Girls, get into the truck, there are wooden benches down each side, room for you all, sit tight and hold on."

The girls looked bewildered but trooped onto the truck. Only Fay hung back.

"You are getting in, April, are you not?" Fay queried.

"Yes, I am, in the front with Mrs Keir," April said shortly. "Get yourself in." She gave Fay a push, saying, "go on." She turned to Mrs Keir and said, "please get into the front of the truck." Mrs Keir stood undecided, so April took her by the arm. "Come along, I'll help you up, it's quite a high step."

When Mrs Keir was seated, she looked round to where April was stood looking up at her.

"Is that man going to get up and take the wheel?" she asked.

"No, he isn't, we don't need him," April replied shortly. She went to the back of the truck and called out. "Fay, bolt the tailgate please." She heaved it up into place and heard Fay slam the bolts into position.

"Are you climbing in, April?"

Her answer was a shake of the head.

A look of dawning crossed Fay's face, which had lost its colour suddenly.

"Oh no, please tell me you're not."

"Yes, I am. I'll get us there all in one piece, so don't worry."

"But you can't drive," Fay said frantically.

"I drive the bloody tractor don't I, so I can drive this truck."

"You don't know where the base is."

"It can't be so far away; I can always ask directions. Besides, Mrs Keir may know."

"I've been through some escapades with you, April, but this beats the lot!"

"Shut up, Fay and go sit down, you worry too much, and don't say anything to the other girls; I don't want to have to deal with their hysteria."

"Mrs Keir won't let you drive."

"Mrs Keir won't stop me."

April ran around and pulled open the truck door, heaved herself up behind the steering wheel and started the engine pulsing into life. Out of the corner of her eye, she saw Si running towards the truck waving his arms wildly in the air. With a clashing of gears, she was off, tearing down the drive where she saw the stone gate towers looming up quickly. She rose what she hoped was the correct foot, and the truck slowed down and went through the gates safely.

Good, she thought, a piece of cake, nothing to it, all she had to do now was get them to the base, and she would, or her name was not April Thornton.

So far Mrs Keir had sat silently in shock, unable to speak, but she now found her voice.

"I take it that you've not driven before, April?"

"Only tractors."

"I'm trying to keep cool, but what you're doing is wrong."

"We're moving, aren't we?"

"You could be placing all our lives in danger."

"Land Girls don't place other Land Girls in danger, Mrs Keir, we trust each other. Do you hear any screams from the back?"

"No."

"Fay will have told the others that I'm driving, although I told her not to."

Mrs Keir breathed slowly out.

"I shall have to trust you too then."

"Do you happen to know where the base is?" April asked calmly.

"It's practically a straight road, around another six miles," Mrs Keir said.

"I'd better put my foot down then," April said gaily.

"No, don't do that," Mrs Keir said anxiously. "The pace we're going at is quite fast enough thank you."

April started to whistle, unconcerned.

Mrs Keir listened in amazement; did nothing frighten this girl? She had such confidence in herself, if she oversaw the army, we would have won the war long since. She would put April up against Hitler any day, he would soon take to his heels. She wasn't doing too badly at the driving either, give the girl credit!

"How much further?" April asked.

"Actually, we're just coming to it," Mrs Keir answered. "As you can see, almost no lights, not allowed, unless planes are taking off, but once inside it'll be all lit up, as you know, G.I's are extravagant in everything. A hundred yards on your left, turn in then pull up. I hope you know how to stop this thing, and there'll be guards on the gates."

There was, and one of them stepped forward, holding up his hand.

"Pass, please," he said.

Mrs Keir wound down the window and put her head out.

"Don't need one, only this." She held out the invitation card, then said, "Land Army."

"A real welcome to you all, Ma'am." He waved them on, saying, "third hanger on your left."

April leant over Mrs Keir and winked at the G.I.

"Are they all as good looking as you in there, friend? Are you dancing tonight?"

"I'm the best looker around the base, honey, but I'm on duty tonight, it's a pity, you and I could have tripped the light fantastic."

"Oh, what a shame. You and I will trip it another time," April laughed.

As she drove off the G.I called.

"What's your name, honey?"

"Tell him it's Fanny, Mrs Keir."

"I'll do no such thing, don't be rude, April."

"I've a feeling I'm really going to enjoy myself tonight, there's going to be a real hotchpotch of talent inside that hanger."

"Just remember half of the G.I's are married men, and I trust you to behave yourself, all of you," Mrs Keir said sternly.

April pulled up outside the hanger; two G.I's were stood each side of the door.

They look as if they could handle trouble if there were to be any; April thought as she jumped lightly from the truck and slammed the door behind her.

One of the G.I's was helping Mrs Keir to alight, so April went to the back of the truck and called happily.

"We're here, girls, let them out, Fay."

She heard the bolts being drawn, and the tailgate dropped with a heavy clang. The girls trooped out in single file, silent and white-faced.

"Well, look at you miserable lot, I've never heard you so quiet, what's up?" April cried.

"What's up?" Connie said. "We've all been paralysed with fright knowing you were driving. We thought Mrs Keir was doing it until Fay told us differently."

"It didn't bother me," Nancy said cheerfully. "Once you've done my job dealing with rats, riding with an untrained driver is nothing."

"Well, I for one am glad to be in one piece," Joan muttered.

"We're here now, so no good going on about it," Jane said firmly.

"Riding on a ferry in a storm is a lot worse," Belinda joined in.

"If you all want to stand here moaning about my driving you can, I'm going inside," April said abruptly.

"Now just a moment, April, we must all go in together, we are the Land Army, no going in alone," Mrs Keir said. "Actually, I hold the invite; you wouldn't get in without this." She waved it around in the air. "Are we all ready?"

"As we will ever be," Nancy replied.

Fay tapped April on her shoulder.

"Yours, I believe," she said as she handed a carrier bag to April.

"Thanks," April acknowledged as she took it from Fay. "I'd forgotten it in all the excitement, you didn't peek inside did you, Fay?"

"No, I didn't," Fay replied angrily.

One of the G.I's looked at the invite card Mrs Keir held out to him.

"Oh, the Land Army Girls, glad you could make it. There's plenty to eat and drink, feel free, as you English say." He held the door open as he waved them inside.

The girls trooped in, chattering amongst themselves. The sight that met their eyes brought them to a full stop in amazement; they stood mesmerised, speechless, even April for once. The hanger they stood in was enormous, with every wall covered in American flags. Bunting and coloured trimmings were hung from one side of the hanger to another. Toy aeroplanes dangled from the roof, swaying and twirling in the draft. It was glorious, colourful and alive. Spotlights were dotted here and there, and a few small tables set neatly around three sides of the dance floor, the fourth held the band that was placed on a raised platform.

"I say, what marvellous organisation," Jane gasped.

The band was playing a quickstep, and the floor was a dazzling whirling array of colour, mixed in with the uniforms of the G.I's.

Joan was entranced, while Nancy stood with her hands clasped together, eyes shining with wonder.

"I think we should move away from the door," said April.

"Yes, I think so too," Connie agreed. "But I'll say this for the Yanks, they know how to entertain."

"Don't they just, but remember, they have the money, our boys don't," Fay pointed out.

As they made their way down a crowded floor, Belinda said.

"We haven't seen the food, that's going to be a real spread if the rest of the room is anything to go on."

"I wonder where it is?" Connie said.

Mrs Keir, who had been leading the way, came to a sudden halt, causing all the girls to cannon into one another. She held up her hand.

"If you can hear me above the music and chatter, you'll see that we're stood under a photograph of the American White House. This will be our meeting place in case we get split up. After the dance we return here, do you all agree?"

Heads were nodded.

"A sensible idea," Fay agreed.

"Trust Mrs Keir to think of that," Connie said.

"I don't expect to see the rest of you all night; I hope to be dancing every dance," Belinda said, hopefully.

"So do we all," April said, giving Belinda a push.

"My feet are killing me now before I even start!" Nancy moaned.

The quickstep had ended, and a waltz was announced by the bandleader.

A voice behind Jane asked.

"Do you want to dance, honey?"

Jane turned to see a tall handsome G.I looking down at her.

Oh boy, do I, she said to herself, then she smiled as she said aloud.

"Yes, thank you."

April was watching the couples dancing, wishing someone would ask her. Joan and Connie had already been whisked off when suddenly her hand was grabbed by a small broad-shouldered G.I who bellowed.

"Come on you red-haired dream, can't have you stood there like a fairy on a wedding cake." He pulled her onto the floor, clasped her tightly in his arms and whirled her round and round.

April put her face close to his and said.

"Slow down, it's supposed to be a waltz, not a race."

"Is it? I do the same to every dance," the G.I bellowed.

"Do you," April shouted back. "Well, I won't be dancing with you again, so kindly do not ask me."

The G.I looked taken aback.

"You English gals are funny cold fish."

April pulled a face.

"Cold fish, are we? That's our way of cooling down you red-hot Yanks."

The dance ended, and April walked off without saying thank you. When she joined the other girls, she said hopefully.

"I hope a get a better partner than my last one, he was the pits."

"Mine was a darling; I hope to dance with him again," Jane said happily.

"I just hope to get anyone," Connie added.

"The band is good, isn't it? What you call 'sweet', the trumpet player's good," Fay said, beginning to enjoy herself.

"Just wait until they play the jazz and boogie-woogie numbers," April said. "You'll really hear something then."

"I hope that you're not going to be throwing yourself around the dance floor?" Mrs Keir asked apprehensively.

"Now, would *I* do anything like that?" April asked mischievously.

Under her breath, Fay said.

"Oh, she would."

"Listen, they're playing a foxtrot, I love it. I hope someone asks me to dance!" Belinda cried.

Her hope bore fruit as a black-haired Italian looking G.I sauntered up to her and said.

"Hi, honey, wanna dance? I'm not a good dancer so I'll try not to tread on your toes, wanna risk it?"

"I'll risk it," Belinda laughed, taking his hand.

"Mrs Keir seems to be doing alright for partners, doesn't she?" April said to Fay.

"Yes, better than me," Fay replied shortly.

"You'd do better if you took that miserable expression off your face and stopped thinking of your precious Larry," April said angrily. "Take my advice, enjoy yourself." She broke off her words as a G.I asked her to dance. He guided her onto the floor and led her smoothly round in time to the music, which was 'Begin the Beguine.'

"Ha," April commented. "Artie Shaw, isn't it?" she asked her silent partner.

"Yes, Miss, it is, it's my wife's favourite."

"You must miss her very much," April said softly.

"I do, and my two children."

"This war's a bloody mess, tearing families apart."

"It is, but necessary."

"We will win."

"Of course, Miss, no question."

The music came to an end, and they thanked each other politely and walked away.

As the girls joined, Nancy asked.

"Is everyone enjoying themselves? Because I am. I like catching rats, but this beats it!"

"I am!" Connie cried with shining eyes. "It's wonderful; I've had some good partners."

April laughed loudly.

"It's that Mae West figure of yours, Connie."

"Do you think so?" Connie said seriously. She stuck out her chest and held her breath, let it out slowly, then said, "Yanks, come and get me."

"It's packed in here; I'm beginning to sweat," Belinda complained.

"I say, where's Mrs Keir by the way? The band finished the last number a few minutes ago," Fay asked.

"She won't be far; she has to keep her beady eye on us," April pointed out.

"Here she comes now," Nancy said, then as Mrs Keir joined them. "You're enjoying yourself, Mrs Keir, aren't you?"

"Do you know, Nancy, I am, more than I thought I would," she replied.

"We all are except Fay, who can't forget Larry's universal charm for one night," April said sarcastically.

"Oh, shut up, April, let it rest. Now if you'll excuse me, I'm going to find a toilet." Fay glared at April then stormed angrily away.

"I don't think that you should mention Larry, April, the girl's in love and doesn't really want to be here," Mrs Keir said firmly.

"Fay may be, but is Larry?" April asked questioningly. "There's more to him than meets the eye." She nodded her head. "A lot more."

"I like Larry, he's nice," Joan put in.

"We'll see, I for one don't trust him," April said determinedly. "And that's my last word on the subject, for now." As the band struck again, April cried. "Oh listen, they're playing 'Woodchopper's Ball', I love this number, it's a quickstep."

She was suddenly unceremoniously dragged onto the floor by a tall white-haired G.I, and danced madly around the floor, her feet hardly touching the floor as they bumped and barged their way around, her partner giving no apologies. As the dance ended, the G.I raced her back to the other girls, who had been screaming with laughter at the sight of April being danced around like a rag doll. The G.I sped off with not a single word having been spoken.

"Well, that was a sight to behold, April Thornton not in control," Jane said as she wiped her streaming eyes. "It was so funny, April."

"I can't remember breathing, the room was a blur, and I don't think I even put my feet on the floor. The man's a bloody robot, he'd better not come for me again!" April said aggressively as she wiped the sweat from her brow with the back of her hand. "This is more like it, a waltz, restful, just what the doctor ordered."

A smooth looking G.I with a twinkle in his eye sauntered up to April.

"Hi, baby, could I please have this dance?"

I've got a right one here, thinks a lot of himself this one, April thought as he led her onto the floor. She wasn't wrong.

"Well, babe, what's your name? Mine's Brett, all the girls love dancing with me. They love being held close to my athletic body, gives them a thrill. Of course, they've got to be good looking chicks. You English gals aren't used to men like me; they can't believe how muscular I am in a certain department."

April rolled her eyes towards heaven as he went on.

"How about you coming outside and let me show you."

April managed to get a word in.

"You really don't want to go outside with me, buddy, it would be a mistake."

"Hmm, now you've really got things moving," he muttered as he pulled her roughly closer to his body until she could feel the large bulge in his trousers.

"I didn't know you were allowed to carry guns around, that could be very dangerous," she said as she lowered her arm from his shoulder. She moved her body slowly away from his, put her hand between his legs, grasped his testicles roughly, then gave a slight twist. He jumped away from her, wide-eyed with shock, while she stood still, other dancers waltzing past her. She smiled calmly, then weaved her way across the floor, thinking it takes all kinds to make a world, her Mam was always saying that; it was too true.

She had a self-satisfied smile on her face as Fay asked her why.

"Oh, nothing, that Yank and I were just sharing a joke."

"I know that look of yours, April."

"I'll tell you later."

"And you left him standing on the floor!"

"Had to, he couldn't walk."

"Oh, God, what did you do?"

Connie, who had been listening, said.

"I get the picture," and burst out laughing.

The band struck up a tango, Mrs Keir sighed lovingly, then said.

"My favourite dance."

"This will sort the men from the boys; the floor will be practically empty," April said, looking around for would-be tango dancers.

"I can do the tango, but it looks like no takers," Jane moaned.

"I can do it, in a fashion," Connie commented.

"I get my legs in a twist when I try," Nancy said.

A tall man in the uniform of a Captain approached Mrs Keir and held out his hand.

"Mrs Keir, would you like to?" he asked.

She gave him a beaming happy smile, then replied.

"I would love to, Captain."

April was astounded as she watched Mrs Keir being led onto the floor by no less than Captain Silverton of Bomber Command. It was him, Captain Silverton, here, dancing with Mrs Keir.

Fay, who was stood next to April, dug her in the ribs.

"Have you seen who it is?" she asked.

"Yes, I'm gob-smacked, and look at them dance, they're wonderful."

"They look professional."

Everyone fell silent as other couples left the floor, realising that they were no match for Mrs Keir and the Captain. Their turns, flicks, twists and kicks were done in unison with each other. Sharp, neat and controlled; they were a delight to watch. It was a beautiful exhibition of how the tango should be danced. As the music ended, wild applause and cheering broke out. The Land Girls ecstatic and proud of their Mrs Keir.

Instead of joining the girls, the Captain led her towards a group of prominent looking top brass at the other side of the room.

"I'd like to tell you, girls that Fay and I know Captain Silverton," April said proudly.

"She's right, we do," Fay added.

"How do you know him?" the other girls asked.

"We'll tell you all about it later," April promised.

She looked over to where Mrs Keir seemed to be making a good impression on the Captain's friends, and to her amazement saw Tony stood with them; he looked directly at April, smiled, waved his hand, then turned and walked away.

"Oh no," she groaned.

"What's wrong?" Fay asked.

"Tony is what's wrong, he was stood near Mrs Keir and the Captain, I hope I'm not going to be pestered by him all night telling me I'm going to marry him!"

Fay laughed.

"Oh, he's harmless, a bit of a laugh really."

"It's not funny to me, he's a bloody pest."

"He can't help being in love with you, what does he call you? His April morning, wasn't it?"

"I hope he's gone; he waved then walked away in the other direction."

"He maybe had a girl waiting for him outside."

"I hope so."

As a samba was announced, a small middle-aged bow-legged G.I ambled up to the girls and said in a high quivering voice.

"Here's a bunch of dewy-eyed maidens waiting for my good self to ask one of them to dance, now, which one will it be?" He looked at Joan and held out his hand. "How about you, sweetheart?"

April tried to hold back a laugh, then said firmly with a smile.

"Sorry, but my friend isn't dancing, neither are any of us, it's our rest time you see."

"Oh," the little man said, scratching his almost bald head. As he turned away, he could be heard saying. "These young gals have no stamina."

"Did you hear what he said?!" Nancy cried enraged. "No stamina, us, the Land Girls!"

"He wasn't to know, was he?" Connie replied.

"I'm going to tell everyone I dance with from now on that I'm a Land Girl," Nancy said firmly.

"That's a good idea, I think we all should," Joan agreed.

"It'll be passed around the room like wildfire," April said.

"Don't look now, girls, but there's a six-foot giant coming towards us, I hope he wants to dance," Belinda said hopefully. "Boy, is he my kind of man!"

The giant came to a halt in front of them, picked up April and swung her round and round in the air, the smaller man who was with him did the same to Fay.

"Tiny put me down you fool, everyone's looking," April cried. Tiny set her gently onto her feet. "I'm really pleased to see you, but do you have to be so boisterous?" April complained.

Tiny looked down at her.

"Little, April, I was hoping to see you, you're a sight for sore eyes, how you doing, gal?"

"I'm doing good, Tiny." She turned to Glenn who had set a breathless Fay onto her feet. "And, Glenn, nice to see you too." She gave him a hug. "How are you?" she asked.

"Great, April, still in one piece as you can see, nearly caught it a couple of times, but someone likes me up there." He raised his eyes towards heaven and made the sign of the cross on his chest.

Tiny looked around at all the girls.

"These are your friends I take it, April?" he asked. "Land Girls?"

"They are, let me introduce you."

When all introductions had been made, April said mischievously.

"Belinda here would love to dance with you, Tiny, she admires very tall men, don't you, Belinda." She pulled Belinda forwards. "Don't you Belinda?" she repeated teasingly.

"Yes, I do," she laughed as she dragged the unresisting Tiny unceremoniously onto the dance floor.

Glenn had already led Fay off.

"There's nothing shy and timid about Belinda is there," Jane commented.

"Best way to be. If you like a thing say so, never hide your light under a bushel," April laughed.

"Like you, you mean?" Connie said.

"Yes, exactly like me," April answered.

To change the subject, Nancy said.

"Look at that dance floor, talk about sardines packed in a tin, you can't really dance, just shuffle about and go with the flow."

"I love this number." The band was playing Glenn Miller's 'In the Mood'. "It'll be long remembered after the war's over, it means so much to lots of people, and Glenn Miller knows how to write music doesn't he, so nostalgic," Joan said softly.

"Well, I don't know about you lot, but I'm feeling peckish, I'm off to find the nosh," Nancy said firmly. "My tummy's rumbling something awful; I'd eat snails if I had to."

"Don't be cruel," Joan said in disgust.

Nancy laughed.

"Nothing cruel about it, they eat snails in France. I've tried hedgehog and various kinds of birds, I've yet to try badger." She turned away from Jane and winked at the others.

"She's only having you on, Jane, take no notice of her," Connie said kindly when she saw the sickly look on Jane's face.

"I hope she is," Jane said. "Poor little creatures, I don't think that I'm very hungry after all, I'll pass on the food."

"You don't mind being left on your own if we go, do you?" April asked.

"Not at all," Jane answered.

"We won't be long, after all, we should be dancing, not eating, shouldn't we."

There was a chorus of.

"No."

The girls piled into an extra-large office which had been turned into a supper room. They exclaimed loudly at the sight that met their eyes.

"Would you look at this!" April cried.

"I'm looking; I've died and gone to heaven!" Jane said, sighing in rapture. "Would someone pinch me, then I'll know that I'm really here."

"Look at those prawns."

"Never mind the prawns, look at the crabs."

"Keep your fish; look at the joints of pork, lamb, beef and ham."

"Keep your savouries and sandwiches; I'm getting stuck into the trifles, flans, fresh cream buns and gateau's, look at the decoration on them!"

"I'm going to have one small mouthful of everything," Belinda said happily.

"You'll make yourself ill."

"Who cares?"

"*You* will when you're being sick in the morning at four-thirty."

"I, for one, am not having a lot, just half a dozen mouthfuls," April said seriously. "Although it's going to be hard not making a pig of myself."

"You're kidding."

"I've my reasons for not partaking."

"Which are?"

"You'll all find out soon enough," April said mysteriously with a twinkle in her eye.

"I hope that doesn't mean trouble," Connie said with a worried look on her face.

"Oh no, I can put your mind at rest on that," April replied firmly. She pointed at Belinda. "Look at Belinda, stuffing her face, she lives to eat, not eats to live. I'm having a few bites then I'm off back to Jane."

As April left the room, Connie remarked.

"She's up to something."

"Yes, she is, and I think that it won't be long before we find out what," Joan said.

As April joined the other girls back in the dance hall, the music was just coming to an end to much applause from the dancers. The band leader stepped up to the mike and held up his hand for silence.

"Thank you everyone. After a great many requests, I would like to announce a jitterbug competition after the band has had a twenty-minute break."

April turned to the girls, her eyes sparkling with excitement.

"This is it," she said.

"Are you entering?" Jane asked curiously.

"Does the sun rise and set? Of course I am," April cried.

"But who with? What about a partner?" Jane asked.

"I have a partner, he's here and will come for me," April laughed with confidence, then she turned to Fay. "Remember the G.I plane landing in the field last week, the twins, Orry and Bix?"

"Oh yes, I'd almost forgotten that," Fay exclaimed.

"And remember Bix making me promise to jitterbug with him, he must have known there was going to be a contest."

"He must have done, but is he here? I haven't seen him," Fay asked.

"He's here," April answered with certainty. "He's with a girl, he's seen me, he'll be here to claim me as his partner."

"I'd laugh if he didn't," Fay said dubiously.

"Oh, he will. Before the band comes back, I've something to do, so if you'd please excuse me."

"I'm off to get Belinda and Connie; they're still in the food room," Jane cried.

"Yes, do that, Jane, they won't want to miss the contest, I'm jitterbugging for the Land Army!" She walked towards the outside door where the two G.I's were still stood on guard. "Hi," she said. "Could I have the bag I gave you to look after for me please?"

"Sure, sweetheart, here it is." He handed her the bag which had been hung on a nail by the door.

"Thanks," April said with a smile. "Now guys, would you do one more thing for me please? I need to get changed, could you stand together, forming a kind of screen? I'll get behind you; it won't take more than a couple of minutes."

"Sure, honey," they said together.

They were big men and stood side by side suited April's purpose admirably.

She pulled off her dress and underskirt, kicked off her high-heeled shoes, then took out of the bag her brown breeches and white aertex shirt. She pulled them on quickly, then bending, put on her feet a pair of white flat shoes. She rolled up her dress and underskirt and thrust them, along with the high heels into the bag, then, patting her hair into place, picked up the bag and stepped from behind the G.I's.

"Thanks, guys, all done. Would you retake charge of my bag?"

"Sure thing, sweetheart, say, you're Land Army," one of them said in admiration, they both wolf-whistled together.

"Sure think highly of you gals," one of the G.I's said.

"This is the first time I've met one of you, sure is a pleasure, honey," the other one said.

"Thanks, guys, pity you can't leave your post, I'm in the jitterbug contest and I'm going to win."

"Sure would like to see that, honey, some of our guys are real good."

"My partner's a guy called Bix, maybe you know him?"

"Bix, one of the twins, sure we know him, he's a great dancer, the best jitterbugger around. You'll have to be good, sweetheart to keep up with him."

"Oh, I'm good; we'll see how good *he* really is when he gets *me* on the floor."

"What I wouldn't give to see this," one of the G.I's said sorrowfully.

"Never mind, guys, you'll hear the music, hear people cheering and clapping and see it in your mind's eye. Now I must go, wish me luck."

"We do, and lots of it, sweetheart."

As April closed the door behind her, she saw people stood around the floor in groups, waiting for the band to return. She made her way towards where the girls were stood, as she did so, she heard the various comments about her uniform, she was the only girl in the room to wear trousers. As she joined the girls, they cried out in surprise at seeing her in uniform.

The penny slowly dropped for Fay.

"You're entering that competition, aren't you? You meant it, I thought you were kidding."

April shook her head.

"Why should I be kidding? I'm going to love it showing off and being the best."

"Is there anyone like you in the world?" Fay said, then began to laugh. "Why is it so important for you to be the best?"

April smiled at her.

"I could go on explaining forever, but you'd still never understand, anyway, this is for the Land Army, to show everyone that we're the best. We may not be classed as a fighting force, but by God, we're a force to be reckoned with, and I'm going out onto that floor to prove it."

All the girls started to clap, which drew inquiring stares in their direction.

"Good on yer, April!" Connie shouted as she clapped her on the back.

Then, to the girls in merriment.

"I had no intention of throwing myself all around and showing my knickers for everyone to see, and believe me, they do see, you end up with your frock around your waist. And of course, the men love that, hence why I'm wearing trousers, I *do* have a *bit* of decorum you know." She glanced down at herself. "Here's what everyone gets tonight; I only hope that Bix won't leave me standing like an idiot having forgotten our deal."

"We didn't know him from Adam until he stepped from that plane, did we?" Fay asked.

"No, we didn't, but here comes the band."

A loud buzz of expectancy ran around the room as the band members took their seats. The band leader walked to the front of the stage and pulled the mike towards him, then held up his hand.

"Would the gentlemen of the dancing pairs please come to the stage where they'll have a number pinned to their back. If the Judge touches the gentleman on the shoulder during the dance, would the couple please leave the floor. When we're left with one couple, they're obviously the winners."

April looked around the crowded room hoping to see Bix, but with not a sight of him, she began to feel anxious. Then suddenly there he was, striding towards her, waving and calling.

"April baby, are you ready to show them how it's done?" When he reached her side, he kissed her on her cheek. "I hope you didn't think that I'd forgotten, honey."

"As if I would, I hope you're going to prove to me how good you are."

"He doesn't know the half of it does he," Fay whispered to Connie.

"Sounds big-headed to me, this Bix," Connie whispered back.

Bix went on.

"April honey, I've some good moves, hope you're up to them."

April grinned.

"Bix buddy, there *isn't* a move that *I* am not up to."

"Good, sweetheart, but just remember, when I hold you straight up in the air, headfirst, keep your legs straight, then I'm gonna swing you through my legs twice."

"Bix sweetheart, if you don't go and get our number you won't be swinging me anywhere, so off you go." She gave him a push towards the stage.

When he was out of earshot, Nancy said sarcastically.

"Thinks he's a big shot that one, can't wait to show off."

"That makes two of us then because neither can I," April said smugly, hitching her breeches higher up her waist.

"Aren't you nervous?" Jane asked. "I would be."

"No, I'm not nervous," April laughed. "Why should I be? I know I'm good, our Bix is in for a shock."

Belinda rolled her eyes towards heaven, then said.
"The proof will be in the pudding."
Joan clapped her hands and cried.
"Oh, I can't wait! Sock it to 'em, April!"
"I shall, don't you worry. I only hope it's a good number the band plays."
"Everything always seems to go your way, so it will be," Joan agreed.
As Bix joined April, he put his arm across her shoulders and grinned down at her.
"We're gonna win, honey."
"Of course we are, buddy."
The band leader called for all competitors to take to the floor.
"Ready, honey?" he asked April.
"As I'll ever be," she answered confidently.
He took her hand firmly as they walked into the middle of the floor.
"Hope they're gonna play a good number," Bix said.
"We won't have long to wait before we find out, but how many couples are they?" April wondered.
"Nine," Bix replied. "We're number nine."
"My lucky number, my birthday's on the ninth, so that's a bit of luck!" April cried, rubbing her hands together.
The band leader's voice boomed out.
"Ladies and Gentlemen, 'Two O'Clock Jump'!" The band swung into the number, and all nine couples began to dance.
"'Two o'clock Jump', April's favourite swing number! That's a bit of luck!" Fay cried, hugging Joan and swinging her around. "Now we'll see some action."
"'Two o'clock Jump! Couldn't be better, come on, Bix honey, let's go!" April shouted aloud as she punched the air with a clenched fist.

They began moving around in a easy yet lively fashion, sashaying their hips, twisting on the balls of their feet, jumping to the side of each other and shaking and pointing their index finger in time to the music.

It's funny April thought, but I know every move he's going to make.

As she was pulled, thrown and twisted around, out of the corner of her eye, she caught flying glimpses of the other couples, it seemed to be a kaleidoscope of vibrant colours. She had been right; dresses were wrapped around waists and knickers were on full view. Thank goodness she had brought her breeches with her. Bix swung her around his hips twice, he was good, but she was matching him. Mr Cookson, the Judge, was walking towards them, oh no, he's not going to knock us out so soon, is he? But no, it was the couple to their right who left the floor. She felt an incredible feeling of exhilaration and cried out.

"Come on, Bix baby, another couple's left the floor!"

Bix gripped her underneath her arms and slid her between his legs, slid her back, then repeated the move, he then let her go and she leapt nimbly to her feet. She was then yanked up and levered around his back, then brought back. They were performing well; she didn't know that she was so kinetic. As she was brought upright once more, she saw only three couples besides themselves remaining.

Bix suddenly cried.

"This is it, baby, upside down in the air above my head."

Oh, bloody hell she thought as he bent down, upended her by grabbing her ankles, then lifted her body in the air, up and up until she was straight, her head touching his. He did two or three twirls as she thought thank God I didn't have any food, I would have uploaded it all over myself and him. He lowered her to the ground, as he did so she could hear shouting; whistling, stomping, clapping and cheering. Another two couples had left the floor, one other couple besides themselves left. She put more verve and energy into her legs as she was flung this way and that, and caught a glimpse of her mates jumping up and down screaming at the top of their voices, 'come on, April, come on, April, up the Land Army!', all the G.I's were shouting, 'come on the Land Girl, come on, Bix!'

The noise was deafening, she could hardly hear the band, and was that Mrs Keir jumping up and down? And Captain Silverton whistling through his fingers?

She could feel sweat dripping down her face and trickling down her back, then, she saw the Judge walking across the floor towards them and the other couple. The music stopped, and a pin could be heard to drop as all noise ceased. April tried to get her breath; her legs felt like jelly. Bix had put his arm around her and pulled her around to stand in front of him.

He whispered confidently.

"Don't worry, sweetheart, we've got it."

As the Judge reached them, he said, "sorry," and touched the boy of the other couple on the shoulder. Bix swung her high in the air as a great cheer filled the room.

"We did it, baby, we did it! Gosh, you were the greatest, the best I ever danced with!" He gave her a smacking kiss on the lips.

The room was going wild as all the Land Girls ran to surround April, hugging and kissing her. Joan and Jane had tears raining down their face.

Nancy was brick red with pride as she said.

"You were wonderful, bloody wonderful, girl; I'll never forget that till the day I die!"

"Didn't I see it in the cards?!" Belinda was shouting to anyone who would listen.

"Oh man, you were the greatest, I'm so proud of you," Connie said, choked.

"We knew right from the start she'd win; she's our April isn't she," Fay said to everyone in general.

Then suddenly, they were surrounded by G.I's all wanting to kiss or shake April's hand, which, most of them did, and all talking at once.

"Wow, England sure has something to be proud of, baby!"

"You were great, honey!"

"You were the goods, doll, the very best!"

"Gee, what a gal, look out Ginger Rogers!"

"Where did you learn to dance like that?!"

"Sweetheart, you were a wow, the way you swung your rear!"

"I'd take you home any day to meet my Mom!"

"Honey, the best bit of jitterbugging I ever saw!"

At last April managed to get out.

"Thanks, girls, thanks, fellows."

Then Mrs Keir and Captain Silverton were pushing their way forward, and as they reached April, Mrs Keir said.

"April I'm so proud of you, and so are the Land Army. I've never been so thrilled or excited in my life, never have I cheered or clapped as much! What a clever girl you are!"

"May I add my congratulations please?" Captain Silverton interrupted. "April you were magnificent and deserve to win." He bent and kissed her on the cheek, then turned and shook Bix's hand, saying, "well done, lad."

"Could the winners come onto the stage to collect their prize please?" the band leader's voice suddenly rang out.

Bix swung April up into his arms as he strode to the stage.

"Put me down you fool, I can walk," April said with laughter.

Bix looked down at her and grinned as he lifted her onto the stage and set her gently onto her feet. He leapt nimbly up to stand beside her.

"Congratulations!" the band leader said as he shook Bix's hand and pecked April on the cheek. "What a display you put on; you're worthy winners."

Loud cheering and clapping rang around the room once more, April acknowledged this by bowing from the waist. As she straightened up, she caught sight of Tony once more, he gave her the victory sign, then was gone.

The thought went through her mind he's not a pest tonight, must have found himself a girl.

Then, she was being handed a packet of silk stockings and the largest box of chocolates she had ever seen. As she looked down at the packet of stockings, she saw that it had the number six on it in gold. Golly, six pairs, was *she* going to be popular! Bix was given a large bottle of whiskey and a box of cigars.

"Well earned," the band leader said. "May I ask your name, little lady?"

"April Thornton, Land Girl," she answered loudly, speaking directly into the microphone.

He turned to Bix.

"And you, young man?"

"Bix Stevens, Bomber Command."

"Let's hear it for these two wonderful dancers once again!" the band leader cried.

Cheering, clapping and whistling raised the roof once more, then, it was all over.

April was helped down from the stage by Bix.

"Must get back to my gal now, April, we'll have a waltz later on."

"We'll have to find somewhere to put our prizes first, can't spend the rest of the night hugging them can we."

The band leader saw their dilemma, so bent down and suggested that they leave their prizes on the stage where they would be quite safe.

"Thanks," April said in relief as she held them up to the bandleader.

Bix did likewise then kissed April on the cheek before hurrying off, anxious to get back to his girl.

As April re-joined her friends, she was met with laughing comments.

"You'll never eat all those chocs by yourself, I'll help you love."

"I've never seen a box as big."

"Must be from the good old U.S.of A."

"You can't buy one as big in England."

"Couldn't anyway, wouldn't get the coupons."

"What a way to die, stuffing yourself with chocolate."

"What a way to put on weight too."

"Bugger the weight; at least you'd die happy."

"They're April's chocolates; she'll do as she wants with them, so all of you shut up," Jane shouted.

"I'll have the last word on this," April said firmly. "I'll share them with all of you one night when we're all in together, sat by a cosy fire and telling ghost stories while a storm rages outside."

"I've plenty of ghost stories, having the second sight, you know," Belinda said seriously.

"Oh, shut up, you and your bloody second sight!" Connie snapped. "It's all in your mind."

"Listen, the bands starting up again, and here comes the G.I's stamping across the floor as if they can't wait to get to us," Nancy said delightedly.

"I don't know if my legs will hold out, I could do with a sit-down," April said. "Actually, I'd appreciate a chair just now." She realised that hope was gone as she saw Tiny coming towards her.

"Come on, April my love."

She sighed inwardly then took his hand.

They moved slowly around the floor as she thought thank goodness Tiny isn't a clodhopper for his size; he was a surprisingly good dancer.

He looked down at her.

"You were great out there, April."

"Thanks, Tiny, but I wouldn't like to do it every night."

"Pity, you'd be a champion."

"A much worn out one." She paused. "I only did it for the Land Army, to prove we're the best."

"You certainly did that, oh boy you did. Do you have a boyfriend yet?"

"No, and I don't want one, I'm quite happy on my own. When a boy kisses you, he thinks he's giving you a thrill, when it's entirely the opposite. Boys at home at the village dances walk you home, then give you a sloppy, clumsy kiss on the cheek, then hurry away thinking he's God's gift. I can do without the experience; life has more to offer than that if approached at a moderate pace. Silly young girls rushing headlong into a courtship with overbearing boys who think they know it all isn't for me, Tiny."

"*You* are a very smart gal, April."

"I'm not a serious, sober, sad-faced English girl, Tiny, I live for the moment, I enjoy life. I love my job, I respect my friends, I believe in fairness in all things, and I love to stand up for the underdog."

Tiny bent and kissed her on the cheek.

"April, if you ever change your mind, I'd marry you in a heartbeat."

"Not another one," she said dubiously.

"So, you have someone wanting to marry you?" Tiny laughed.

"Yes, you could say that, one of your lot actually. A proper pest he is, whenever our paths cross, he shouts out and calls me his April morning, tells everyone I'm going to marry him when the war's over, most embarrassing. I only had a couple of dances with him, he never shut up, Tiny. He's not a bad looking lad, but what an imagination, saying that I was going to marry him. I count myself lucky tonight, I've seen him twice around the edge of the dance floor, he just waved then moved on. He's maybe got a girlfriend, I hope so, then he won't pester me."

"One of our boys you say, Bomber Command, was he?" Tiny asked curiously.

"Yes, but I don't know what his job is, he never said," April replied.

"What's his name?" Tiny inquired.

"Tony, very black hair, a bit on the short side."

"That rings a bell, I knew him, but not very well, I used to see him around the base a lot, cheerful, always cracking jokes and really loved England."

April came to a halt as she asked.

"You say *knew* and *loved*. Has anything happened to him?"

He looked at her apprehensively, then said.

"His plane was shot down over Germany last week, he was a rear gunner, they all died. I'm sorry, April."

"Last week?" April repeated.

Tiny nodded his head.

"Are you alright? You've gone very white."

April stared at him wide-eyed, then said.

"Let me get this straight, you say Tony died last week?"

Tiny nodded unhappily.

"Yes, there were no survivors, absolutely impossible; the plane went down in flames."

"Then tell me how the hell I've seen him here twice tonight?"

"You couldn't have done, April; it must have been someone like him."

"I'm telling you, Tiny, it was Tony, there's nothing wrong with my eyes."

Tiny could have kicked himself for telling her in such a clumsy way, it had evidently given her a shock.

He took her arm.

"Come on, let's get out of here, the fresh air will make you feel better. Shall I get you a whiskey?"

"No, I'll be alright."

They made their way around the dance floor towards the outside door, April feeling slightly wobbly as if her legs didn't belong to her. She could not believe what Tiny had just told her, it was impossible, Tony could not be dead, she had seen him, twice, and he had waved to her.

As they were going through the door, one of the two G.I's who were still on guard duty said.

"Hello, here's our little Land Girl again. How did you do in the jitterbug contest, honey?"

"She won," Tiny said shortly. "But at the moment, buddy, she isn't feeling so good and has to have some air."

"Poor little thing, bet it's hotter than an oven in there, glad you won, honey, now out you go." He held the door open for them, then closed it after them with a bang.

April thankfully took great gulps of fresh air, then began to feel better and gather her wits about her. She turned to the silent Tiny, then said softly.

"You don't believe me do you, Tiny? That I saw Tony, but I did you know. I'm not the type to imagine things. I don't care what you believe, I saw him as clearly as I'm seeing you now."

"You've had a shock, honey, which can do weird things to the mind."

"Shock has nothing to do with it."

"One of our guys says that he's always seeing his Ma – she's been dead for ten years. Most of us laugh at him, we think that he takes in too much oxygen when flying, it's odourless and tasteless you see."

"So, before you'll believe the man you pass it off as that?"

Tiny shrugged.

"No other explanation is there?"

"How very uneducated of you all. I believe him. After my experience tonight, I'll believe that the moon is made of green cheese."

"Aww, come on, April honey."

"I'm not daft, nor blind, I saw Tony." She paused for a moment, then said with certainty. "A lot of people believe in life after death, my Mam does. All my life she's talked about it, and as I grew older, I said that I'd believe it when it was proved to me. Well, it now has been. You say that Tony was killed last week?"

"Yes," Tiny said firmly.

"You are sure it was last week?" April probed.

"Absolutely, we have guys on duty whose job it is to count and markdown planes as they come back to base. We lost three last week. I know that Tony's didn't make it, I'm sorry, April."

"Tony wasn't a friend, just a pest, but I feel awful about the way I used to talk to him, my lack of patience, but he took it and would just say with a grin, *you* are going to marry me when this war's over April morning, never just April, always April morning. I'd tell him to swan off, to go and pester someone else, but when I turned around, there he would be again."

"He must have been very much in love with you, honey."

"No, he just had a fixation about me, he didn't even know me."

"You can meet someone just once, and bang, the spark is there," Tiny said softly.

"I don't think that can happen, not so suddenly," April said with certainty.

"You'd be surprised," Tiny laughed.

"After tonight I wouldn't be surprised at anything. But now I should get back, the girls will be wondering what's happened to me, and, Tiny, not a word to them about my experience."

"Sure thing, honey, not a word," Tiny said as he took her arm and led her to the door.

They edged their way around the dance floor towards the girls.

"I'll leave you, honey; the girls will look out for you. See you later, chin up as you English say."

"April, where on earth have you been?!" Fay cried. "You've missed the hokey-cokey." She looked more closely at April's face. "You're very pale; don't you feel well?"

"I'm alright, I just had to have a breath of fresh air, Tiny took me outside and we've had a chat, nice fellow Tiny."

"Oh, outside with Tiny eh, was it a chat you were having or a kiss and a cuddle?" Nancy said mischievously. "I wouldn't mind a wrap-around with him, he's all man."

"Don't be daft, Tiny's not my type," April said. "Anyhow, have any of you got yourselves a man yet?"

"I think *I* might have," Connie said.

"I've had four dances with the same G.I," Joan said. "So, I'm hopeful."

"There's one I like, but I've a feeling he's married," Belinda said with a shrug.

"There's one I like; he likes animals as much as me, he works in a pet shop in New York," Jane put in.

"Well, it seems as if you're nearly all fixed up," April laughed. "No one's taken my eye in here, I'm still fancy-free and loving it. Has anyone seen our Mrs Keir?"

Belinda nodded her head.

"Yes, she's around and having a ball. Her and Captain Silverton are glued together, have been all night. Something's going on there, I'm sure."

"I hope there is, good luck to her," Fay said.

"I don't want to burst everyone's happiness bubble, but has anyone given a thought as to how we're going to get back?" April asked.

They all looked at each other until Nancy said.

"In the truck, the way we got here."

"April drove us here," Joan said.

"Yes, she did, is she going to drive us back?" Belinda said. "And where's the bloody truck? It won't be parked outside waiting for us, will it?"

"I think we've a problem here," April said.

"There isn't a problem that can't be solved," Fay said firmly. "We must see Mrs Keir; after all, she's in charge, isn't she."

"I'll bet the Captain is taking her home," Connie said matter of factly.

"We could all walk home. Cut across the fields?" Jane suggested.

There was an outcry of.

"You've got to be kidding; I wouldn't make it in these shoes!" Joan cried, nearly in tears.

"Are you bloody mad, Jane?!" Katrina shot her an angry glance. "You walk if you want, and good luck to you."

"I'm game, I'll walk," April said.

"So am I," Fay agreed. "As the Crow flies, it should only be about five miles."

"Five miles? At night? No lights, you've got to be crackers!" Nancy shouted.

"We walk more than that in the course of our working day I would think," Fay said.

"No wonder I'm always worn out at the end of the day then," Joan said, puffing out her cheeks. "You don't think about it like that, do you? Who's going to see Mrs Keir then? There's no way I'm walking back."

"We're Land Girls, not a bunch of namby-pamby village girls. You lot do what you like, Fay and I are walking," April said, making up her mind.

"But what if you have to drive us back?" Connie asked.

"I won't be here, will I," April laughed. "One of you lot can have the pleasure." She looked, then laughed at the looks on their faces. "You can all drive a tractor, can't you?" There was silence. "A truck isn't so very different."

"But you can't go yet, what about the last waltz?" Joan asked.

"I'm not bothered about the last waltz, are you, Fay?" April asked.

"No, let's be off, maybe we'll be back before the others if we put our best foot forward," Fay laughed.

April looked at the other girls, then asked.

"Anyone else coming? It's a nice healthy walk over the fields."

Only Jane stepped forward.

"I'm game," she said.

"Just us three then, come on you two, let's be off," April said, then, as she looked down at the feet of the other two girls she said. "Good job you both have comfortable wedge heels on and me in my flatties."

As they walked through the outside door chattering happily about the evening, the door guard asked.

"Had enough girls? Going home, are you? But not on your own surely, where are the boyfriends?"

"Don't have one, don't want one," April said pertly.

"What a shame, I'd see you home if I weren't on duty, I'd be honoured, three good-looking dames like you, and I could manage the three of you, kissing you all good night in your turn."

"Really?" Jane said sarcastically.

"The only thing you'd be kissing good night is a cow's arse, a four-legged one," April said.

The G.I gaped at her in bewilderment.

"Really, Ma'am, I was only joking."

"So was I," April replied with a laugh. "Goodnight, buddy."

The three girls walked out into a moon drenched night with a myriad of stars sparkling in a velvet black sky.

"Look at that moon, isn't it beautiful," Fay said. "And it's a full one."

Jane took in some deep breaths, then said.

"You can taste and smell the night."

"A full moon, when the werewolves prowl," April said impishly.

Jane clutched hold of her.

"Oh, shut up, April, there's no such thing," she said nervously.

"Ghouls, ghosts and spirits roam at midnight," April went on in a deep sonorous voice.

"Pack it in, April, or you'll be walking on your own," Fay said angrily. "Take no notice of her, Jane, she's winding you up."

"Of course I am, Jane, sorry," April said as they came to a stone wall. "We have to climb over this, then head to our right."

"Why our right?" Fay asked.

"Because the hostel is on our right."

"How do you know?"

"I just do, trust me."

"We look like having to, don't we."

"If you remember, it was a straight road coming, that is to our left. We did a mile down to that from the hostel. So, if we cut across the fields a mile from the main road, it should work out right."

"You sound confident."

"I am."

"Alright, lead on, you're the leader."

"I'm not going through any woods, you and your talk of werewolves," Jane whispered.

"Don't worry, if we meet one, I'll let him take me," April laughed.

Once they had scrambled over the wall and set off across the first field, the wind began to sigh gently, and from the direction of the road, a motorbike could be heard rattling along. When its noise had died away, there was a dense silence. Jane broke it by saying worriedly.

"I do hope we're going the right way, how many fields will we have to cross?"

"Don't worry about that, worry about not stepping into cow plops, watch where you're putting your feet. I don't think werewolves like smelly victims," April said warningly, quickening her stride.

"In that case, I'll tread in every one I see," Jane said defiantly.

"That won't take much doing, the moon's so bright it's like daylight, it's a good job too, without it we wouldn't be able to see a hand in front of us," Fay said. "But I'm really enjoying this, I've never walked under a full moon at this time of night, it's like magic, isn't it?"

"Yes," April agreed. "The little people and the fairies in their dells will be dancing to their miniature violins and harps, having a ball."

Jane came to a standstill, wide-eyed.

"Oh, I hope I don't tread on them."

"Don't listen to her, Jane, she's a fool. The moon's gone to her head," Fay cried. "Come on; get moving, and look, a five-barred gate ahead."

"We don't have to open it, we can climb over, the three of us are nimble enough," April said. Then her eyes sparkled with amusement. "Pick yer frocks up, cock yer leg over, then bob's yer uncle," she said this in a country yokel voice.

As the other two girls complied, she said.

"That's the way, I could jump over I feel so fit!"

"You'll do no such thing; we don't want to have to carry you back with a broken leg," Fay said angrily. "And another thing, we're not impressed with your sense of direction, where the hell are we?"

"Your faith in me isn't very flattering, Fay, but I can reassure you that we're on the right track," April said, then burst into loud song.

Jane started to giggle, which increased Fay's anger.

"Shut up, April!" she cried.

"Why? No one can hear me, only the nightlife." She fell silent as the other two girls looked at her. They stood still as if waiting for something to happen, then it did, a long-drawn-out howl.

Jane jumped onto Fay and clung to her.

"Oh, my God! It's a werewolf!"

"Don't be bloody stupid, it's a dog howling," April said confidently.

"I don't wonder what with you bellowing out in song like that!" Fay said disgustedly.

"We must be near a farm."

"Must be, I'm going to run over the field to the next wall, climb up and have a look around," April shouted as she began to run.

Jane began to cry.

"Oh, don't leave us, April, what if it's not a dog?"

April by this time was out of earshot.

"Now don't be silly, Jane, leave go of me. We'll go and join April," Fay gently disengaged herself from Jane's clinging arms and set off at a steady pace across the fields, Jane trotting along behind her.

April had clambered onto the top of the wall and was looking around the countryside in awe. It was incredible; she could see for miles; the moon was so bright it lit up everything. She heard a short, sharp bark, and a fox streaked away across the field.

As the girls joined her, she said excitedly, pointing around her in a circle.

"This is wonderful; the whole countryside is lit up for miles."

"Good!" Fay snapped. "But does it tell us where we are?"

"No!" April snapped back. "So, we just keep on going."

"Maybe we should head for the road, find a phone box, and phone Mrs Keir to pick us up?" Fay suggested. "It's a sure thing that she'll be waiting up for us."

"She's going to be very angry," Jane said. "But I don't care, I just want to get back, I don't like the night."

April clasped her hands together ecstatically.

"Don't like the night, Jane? But it's wonderful! Listen to them, the children of the night, how they sing!"

"What are you talking about, April? The moon's gone to your head," Fay said worryingly.

"Just listen," April pressed. "If one listens to the sounds of the night, it seems to hum and sing." She pointed to a huge Oak Tree across the field, it stood in majestic splendour, its leaves rustling gently, creating a low humming sound within the hush of the slight breeze. There came the squeak of low flying bats, the hoot of a barn owl, the bark of a fox, the cry of a night hawk, the scream of a stoat, the scampering of field mice, the scurrying of rabbits, and the call of a nightjar. "Can't you hear all that? I can, put it all together and it's their music, nature's music. The night doesn't belong to us, but to them, the creatures of the night, and I wouldn't have wanted to miss this for anything."

"Maybe I should feel a little bit ashamed, but no, I don't hear that," Fay said.

"I don't either," Jane replied.

"Well, that proves that I'm a child of the land once and for all," April said happily. She jumped down from the wall, straightened her breeches, and set off in a brisk walk across the field.

The other two girls looked at one another, shook their heads, then set off in pursuit.

"We seem to have been walking for hours," Jane grumbled. "I don't think she has a clue where she's going."

Fay gave her a slightly contorted smile, then said.

"Neither do I."

They walked in silence for a while, then climbed a style into a smaller field. After a moment or two, Fay said.

"Something's following us, listen."

"Yes, I heard that," April said. "Only one thing to do – confront. We all turn around, put our hands on our hips, and wait. I'll do the talking."

"I don't like this," Jane said nervously as she turned with the other two. "I'm scared."

They waited as the footsteps came on, then a small black horse ambled in to view.

They all laughed.

"A horse!" April cried.

"Thank God it's only a horse," Jane said, thankfully.

Fay walked up to it and stroked its neck as she said softly.

"Hello, boy, are we in your field? We'll soon be out of your way, sorry I don't have an apple or carrot to give you, but you mustn't follow us, we have to go, and you must stay in your field."

April pulled his ears softly.

"Sorry, old boy," she patted his flank.

"He's well looked after."

"Yes, quite plump in fact."

"Wait a minute," Fay said as she bent down and looked at the horse's back legs. "It's not he, but she, and I think, in fact, I know, she's in foal."

"Aww, you're going to be a Mummy," April crooned. "Isn't that lovely."

"Yes, it is," Jane said, angrily. "But could we please get home."

"Alright, keep your hair on, we'll go," April cried. She turned to the horse that looked at her with gentle eyes and said to it. "Goodbye, little Mother, good luck, I hope you have a lovely little foal."

Jane sighed in relief.

"I'll never forget this night; I'll remember it when I'm an old lady, what with climbing walls, gates and being scared out of my wits with talk of werewolves, being followed by a pregnant horse, having my head filled with fairy folk dancing and singing. What else can happen."

"You never know, always expect the unexpected," Fay said. Then colour swept her face as she realised that she had used one of April's sayings.

Another field was crossed.

"How many fields have we walked do you think? I've lost count," Jane asked. "And what time will it be?"

"I don't know to *both* questions," Fay replied. "Better ask our leader here."

"I really don't care," April said, shrugging her shoulders.

"You should care; you got us into this mess!" Jane cried, angrily. "I'm just about fed up; if I were near a river, I'd throw myself into it!"

"There's one in the village, it's small, would that do?" April inquired sarcastically.

"Not funny, April," Fay said angrily.

"And," April added. "It could be dirty, but if you're going to drown yourself, does it matter?"

"That's not a nice thing to say," Fay cried, coming to a standstill.

"No, it's not, but I hate to hear people say things like that."

"I was only kidding," Jane cried, bursting into tears. "I wouldn't do such a thing."

Fay pulled a face at April.

"Now look what you've done, upset Jane all over again." She put her arm around Jane's shoulders.

April tutted, then whispered.

"Hush now. You will disturb the children of the night."

Jane howled louder.

"I'm only kidding," April laughed.

"I just want to get back to the hostel," Jane sobbed. "I'm tired out, and we're lost, why don't we admit it."

"We can't be far from the main road, listen, that's a motorbike. We'll soon find a phone-box, I promise you, Jane," Fay said, trying to console her. "Won't we, April."

"No, we won't, all phone-boxes were removed or painted black. No lights allowed; the phone-box light comes on automatically when the door's opened remember. The only phone-boxes around are either in towns or villages, not the country, and even then, you can only use them during the day because it's useless at night with having no lights, you can't see a thing."

"Oh, gosh, I forgot," Fay said.

"So, I suggest we get on and hope for the best," April said determinedly. "No good standing here weeping and lamenting is it." She strode on with the other two girls following behind.

Another field was crossed.

"Look, another style to help us, better than a wall," April said cheerfully.

She was enjoying herself and did not feel a bit tired. She could understand the tramps, or one should call them 'Gentlemen of the Road', loving the life that they led. Great in summer, but grim in winter.

As she drew closer to the style, she narrowed her eyes.

What have we here? Three figures were stood, watching them approach.

"Oh no, I hope this isn't trouble," she said loudly. Turning to Fay and Jane, who had almost reached her, she said carefully. "Actually, we're not alone in the night, girls; we seem to have more full moon roamers."

Fay gasped as she saw the three men, and Jane stepped behind April and grasped a handful of her sweater.

"Now keep calm, they're probably harmless," April said softly, not wanting to panic Jane again.

She strode boldly on, the other two girls more slowly and apprehensively. The three men stood deliberately in front of the style, blocking the girls progress. April noticed that they were well-built, two of them stocky with it. The tallest of the three had a mean, crafty look about him, and wore a flat cap back to front. They were strangers to her, probably on their way home, just like us she thought, but why block our way to the style? This could be trouble.

"Hello, girls, on your way home, are we?" the crafty looking one said.

"Yes, we are, would you mind moving and letting us pass?" April asked politely.

"What's your hurry?" he asked, just as politely. "And where are you heading for?"

"I don't think that's any of your business," April replied, still politely.

"Let's say I'm making it my business."

"Are you? Let's say I'm making it *my* business to get myself and friends over that style, so if you'd all move out of the way please."

The crafty-faced one turned to the other two men who had been stood silent, then asked.

"We don't want to move out of the way do we, lads?"

The shortest of the three men, who had shoulder-length hair and overly broad shoulders, said uneasily.

"Don't be a fool, Jake, let the girls pass, we don't want no trouble, I don't. I'm off," he turned to the other man at his side. "You coming, Lefty?" he asked.

"No," Lefty replied. "It's only a bit of fun; I'll stick around with Jake."

His pal shrugged his shoulders and strode off.

One down, two to go, April thought, she would take the bull by the horns as the saying goes.

"Your friend's sensible, why don't you both go with him?" she asked. "I'd appreciate it, then we could be on our way."

Fay raised her eyes heavenwards, please let them go. April's beginning to get mad, that's a bad sign.

"No, we're not going with him, we're going to stay and entertain you," said Jake as he took a step closer to the style. "It's not often we get three girls to ourselves, is it, Lefty?"

"I should think never with your ugly mugs," April said aggressively.

"Well, you've a right mouth on you," he snarled, taking a step closer to April.

Fay dug April in her arm and said.

"Please, April."

Jane moaned softly.

"Like I said," Jake went on. "A bit of fun never hurt anyone."

"A bit of fun? What do *you* call a bit of fun, shit face?!" April ground out.

"Now that's not very nice, is it? Not lady-like at all is it, Lefty?" he asked.

Lefty stepped forward to stand closer to April. He had a nervous twitch in one eye, then, he bent down and looked at Jane.

"I'll have this one," he leered.

Jane screamed and clutched April tighter.

"Yes, I'll do that one, Jake, I like her."

April pushed him in the chest.

"The only thing *you'll* be doing is picking your teeth up from the floor!" she cried.

Fay stood silent, knowing what was to come, it was a foregone conclusion, April was angry, with justification. This was going to be spectacular under a full moon, and all that was needed was a werewolf.

"So, Jake isn't it," April was saying. "You think that you're going to have some shenanigans with us, is that right?"

"That's right, starting with you."

"What may I ask, do you have in mind?"

"Do I have to spell it out?"

"Yes, you do."

"If I say a bit of slap and tickle, you know what that means, you're not dumb."

"No, I'm not *that* dumb," she smiled smugly, then said scathingly. "I'll do the slapping; you do the tickling."

Oh my God, here it comes, Fay thought.

Jake looked at Fay.

"You're a quiet one, you'll have to wait your turn, quiet ones are the best, they like it good and hard."

"What an absolutely disgusting creature you are!" Fay said loudly.

"I am, as you'll find out," Jake laughed.

April decided to be crude.

"Okay, if you want us on our backs, let's see what you've got *Jake*."

Jane moaned loudly and Fay gasped in amazement.

Jake was taken by surprise.

"What?" he said.

"You heard, let's see what you've got, drop the trousers, hurry it up, I'm getting fed up with your claptrap."

"*APRIL!*" Fay cried.

"Do shut up, Fay, I'll handle this moron!" April said angrily. "Unless you want to stand here all night?" She stared piercingly at Jake, then asked. "Well, what are you waiting for?!" She paused. "Ashamed of what you've got in there are you?"

Jake's face registered shock at April's boldness, all the aggressiveness slowly draining away.

Lefty too, could not believe his ears, this had been a big mistake stopping these girls, Jake and his big ideas, well, he had had enough, he was off, but first, he moved closer to April and said.

"I think I know who you are, I saw you in the pub when you had a go at my Uncle Joe."

"You're Uncle Joe?" April said inquiringly.

"Yes, Joe Smedley."

"Oh yes, I remember him, I had to put him in his place for calling the Land Girls," April said, shrugging her shoulders.

Lefty turned to the still speechless Jake and said.

"You don't want to mess with *her* Jake, she's the one who threw Perkins around the bus, the one all the village talks about, she went and sorted out Simms as well. I tell you, leave it."

Jake pulled himself together and found his voice.

"What, her?!" he cried. "She's no bigger than a pennyworth of copper!"

"I tell you, it's her," Lefty insisted. "And I'm off; she's not getting her hands on me."

As he turned to leave, Jake cried.

"Go on yer great soft pob, take off!"

"Yes, you go, Lefty, save yourself a lot of trouble, because that's what your mate's going to get any moment now," April said brusquely. Then she glared at Jake. "Go with him, but then, I knew the minute I clapped eyes on you that you had no brains."

As Lefty hurried away, he muttered under his breath.

"You're right."

Jake sat down on the style, grinned, then said.

"Sorry to disappoint you, Land Girl, but my pants stay up."

"Thank God for that, I thought we were about to see the eighth wonder of the world."

"April!" Fay said in disgust.

"I want to go home," Jane moaned. "I'm beginning to feel cold."

"Okay, this is where the game ends!" April cried as she bent down and grasped Jake by his hair, then swung him off the style. He landed on his back; the breath knocked out of him. "Fay, Jane, over the style, quickly!" she shouted.

The two girls climbed swiftly over, and once on the other side; Fay called.

"Come on, April."

"I'm coming, but first." she put her foot on Jake's chest and stamped once. "Think yourself lucky that you've got away with no injuries, you really should have listened to your pal, don't ever mess with the Land Army again." She stamped once more on Jake's chest. "Understood?!"

Still winded, he nodded.

"Good," April said. "We understand each other." She turned and jumped lightly over the style.

Suddenly the moon was obscured by cloud.

"Stand still for a moment, wait till we see the moon, it's only masked by a drifting cloud so won't be long till it's clear again," Fay said.

Sure enough, its bright light shone down on them once again, and the girls strode briskly on.

"We're going to get into terrible trouble, being so late back, especially if Mrs Keir's waited up for us," Jane said apprehensively.

"We'll face that when we come to it," April said authoritatively. "No use worrying about it now."

"I wonder what time it is," Fay said.

"I'd guess half-past-two," April replied.

"Oh gosh, we're in for it," Jane moaned.

April suddenly came to a halt and pointed straight in front of her.

"Look!" she cried. "Isn't that the back of the hostel?"

Fay ran forward, then came to a halt.

"I do believe it is, a couple more fields to cross and we're home and dry," she said thankfully.

"I've never been gladder to see anything in all my life," Jane said. "I'm worn out and shall fall into bed fully clothed."

"Me too," April agreed. "But have you noticed, one of the fields has a herd of young bullocks in it?"

"They won't bother us; we'll skirt around them," Fay said. "Come on, before the moon's blotted out again."

The sight of the hostel had put new strength into their legs, and they ran forward eagerly. As they approached the back door, Fay gently turned the handle and pushed, it opened with a loud squeak. April tutted, and as Fay crept in, herself and Jane followed.

A small lamp was lit, Mrs Keir was sat by it knitting, she laid it down onto her knees.

"Ah, the wanderer's return. I don't wish to hear any explanations at this hour, it's twenty-to-three. Go to bed, you have work tomorrow. That's wrong isn't it, it's now today. Off you go, lock the door please, Jane."

16

April handed a cup of tea to Fay.

"What a day, I don't know where I got the energy from to work today after only two hours sleep! Old Bellows is in a right mood, Tinkerbelle lashing out at me with her tail, knocking over a pail of milk, and it's been chucking it down for over an hour. I got wet through before I got my oilskins on, and the King of spiders was crawling all over my hat, oh how I *hate* bloody spiders!" April moaned. "I feel half dead; I'm off to bed before I go to sleep on my feet."

"It was your idea to walk back may I say, and look at the trouble it caused us. But wasn't Mrs Keir a brick, she didn't get angry with us, just listened to our explanations, and said not to let it happen again. Though she's no need to worry about that, it'll be a long time before I go to another G.I dance! A long time," Fay repeated.

April sighed, then said.

"You don't mean that, Fay, you'll be there with bells on, you enjoyed it, you know you did, Larry or no Larry."

Fay hesitated before replying with.

"Yes, I did enjoy it, especially you winning the contest and us all being together! And don't forget, when all the girls are in, you'll have to give a demonstration."

"Oh no I won't, not tonight, I'm too buggered."

"You'd better get yourself up to bed then, but first we've to look at the working list in the hall, it's all change on Monday. I'll be sorry to leave the Bellows, won't you?"

"Yes, I shall," April replied sadly. "I liked both Mr and Mrs Bellows, they fed us well didn't they, and they had a lot of time for Mouse. I think she was their favourite wasn't she. I hope Mouse's still with you or me, we're bound to be split up sooner or later, Fay."

"I can't see Mouse being happy to go on her own to a different farm, can you?" Fay asked.

"She's to grow up some time, she can't always be with us. Come on, let's look at the list," April urged.

As she ran her finger down the list, she said disappointedly. "Look here; I'm at Willows End Farm, to be picked up at the end of the lane at four-thirty, bloody four-thirty! That's a joke is that, how far away can it be? Sounds like a milking farm," she continued to run her finger down the list. "Here's you, Fay, Knighton Hall, sounds posh. Lucky you, you're to be picked up at five."

"I've never heard of that; still, a change is as good as a rest as they say. I'm happy with that, although it'll be funny not working with you, April. How about Mouse?"

"Here she is, still with the Bellows, I'm glad about that for her sake," April cried.

"So am I, but she's going to be upset not being with us," Fay said sadly.

"She'll get over it," April said firmly.

* * *

April climbed down thankfully from the ramshackle dirty pickup truck, which had been her mode of transport to her new farm. Its driver had spoken to her in grunts and seemed not to be able to string a sentence together amid spasms of coughing; besides that, he stunk, she wrinkled her nose in disgust, he badly needed a shave too, and God alone knew when he had last had a bath.

She slammed the pickup door as hard as she could. Something told her that things were not going to work out here. This oaf had a Father; she hoped that he was not a carbon copy of the son. As she glanced around the yard, her heart sank. Mrs Keir tried to be fair allocating rotten farms in rotation because some of them were putrid, but this looked hardly civilised, she should clap her eyes on this! Junk and bits of rusty machinery were thrown haphazardly around the yard which was strewn with cow dung, hen droppings and old food bones, also, she would bet her life on there being no sanitation if the smell were anything to go by. She looked at the small, dilapidated farmhouse; it was nearly falling to pieces and seemed to have had no repairs done for years. With its peeling paintwork, filthy windows covered with bird muck, and ramshackle door, it was a sorry sight, then, its door opened to reveal a tall, once handsome elderly man, who was dressed like a tramp. This must be the Father, Mr Boss man April groaned to herself, the son walked around the pickup to stand at her side; she took a deep breath, then let it out slowly.

"Hi there," she called to the Father. "I'm Miss Thornton." No way was she going to allow these two morons to call her by her first name.

"Hmm," the old man grunted.

"Hmm yourself," she said under her breath.

These two were illiterate and had the manners of pigs, they were hardly civilised, and she had never come across anyone like them before and could not see herself lasting a day here.

She walked towards the old man, who had not moved out of the doorway, she saw at once that he was unspeakably filthy, he had not been washed for weeks' by the look of him, and she shuddered to think what state the house must be in. Then suddenly, she had that feeling deep in her bones that things were going to get nasty. She raised her eyes to look at the roof of the house, no telephone wires, which meant no phone, and she realised how very isolated this place was. Oh well, she would jump in feet first.

In her no-nonsense voice, she asked.

"What would you like me to do?"

"In here," he grunted.

"Why?" she asked.

"You'll clean the house, it's a mess."

"I'm a Land Girl, not a cleaner."

"You'll do what I tell you."

April recognised the steel in his voice, well, he didn't know April Thornton did he, but he was about to. Her hackles had risen.

"Are you deaf?!" she snapped. "I just told you that I don't clean."

The son moved to stand behind her.

"I pay you, so do what I say. Get inside." He stood to one side to allow her to enter.

"Excuse me, but you don't pay me, the government does, and we the Land Army do what *they* tell us."

"You were sent to help us."

"Yes, on the land, we're *not* allowed to clean."

"Bloody rubbish, stop wasting time and get in here."

"I'll ask you once more," she said quietly. "What do you want doing outside?"

"Bloody women!" the old man ground out. "Only fit for one thing."

April's cocky nature came to the force.

"I can guess what you *think* that is."

"Yes, on your back taking it!"

April turned around and looked at the son, then turned back to the old man with a grin on her face, saying.

"Looking at what *you* have produced, you weren't very good at it were you."

The old man turned brick red.

"Don't listen to her, Pa!" the son cried.

"Shut up, I'll handle her!" the old man snarled as he took a step forward. "Are you going to do some work?"

"No, I'm going back to the hostel, I'll be sure to report your uncouth behaviour to the War Agg, also the state of this farm."

"Oh, you are, are you, that's if you ever get off it."

"That sounds rather threatening."

The old man leered at her as the son gave her a push in the small of her back, which sent her nearer to the old man. Suddenly, she moved back a step and jabbed her elbow into the son's stomach, throwing him off balance.

"Look what she did, Pa!" he yelled.

"I see," the old man said calmly. "Come here and stand by me, lad."

The son did as he was bid.

"Interesting," April said aloud.

They both stood looking at her, the son touching himself between his legs with a lecherous look on his face and grinning, showing a mouth full of rotten blackened teeth.

April waited.

"Let's get her inside, Pa, have some fun," the son said.

"What's your name, pig face?" she asked the son.

"Leo," he replied proudly.

"Well, Leo," she said quietly. "You'll rue the day you ever dragged me in there because I take some dragging. I have fight in me, lots of it. I'd love to break your head, so don't tempt me."

The old man pushed the son inside and closed the door; he turned to April and said.

"Get yourself off my land, I don't want any trouble. The postman tells me all the village news, he's my brother, he told me about this fighting Land Girl. I think you're her, aren't you?"

"Yes, I'm her, and nothing will give me the greatest of pleasure than to get off your land, and by the way, I'll see to it that no other Land Girl is sent here."

The old man grunted, stepped into the house, and banged the door shut behind him.

Well, that's the shortest job I've ever had, also the nastiest.

Eight o'clock saw April sat in Mrs Keir's office repeating to her all the mornings happenings.

Mrs Keir was horrified.

"That's shocking! How did you get back April?"

"I was lucky; I got a lift on a G.I motorbike."

"You had a lucky escape; I shudder to think what would've happened if they'd got you inside that house," Mrs Keir said.

"Nothing would've happened, as you know, I can take care of myself."

"*You* can yes, but it could quite easily have been some other poor Land Girl."

"Yes, it could," April agreed. "That's why you have to ring the War Agg right away; tell them about the situation at that horrible farm."

"Yes, I'll do that, they will most likely send out an inspector," Mrs Keir said.

"If they do, I hope it's a male one," April said firmly.

Mrs Keir nodded her head in agreement, then said.

"Off you go, April, I'll get on the phone, they may have another job for you for the rest of the day."

"I hope so; I should be bored out of my mind having to spend the rest of the day here." She wandered into the kitchen where Mrs Wilkinson, the cook, was peeling potatoes.

"Hello," she greeted April. "What are you doing here this time of day? Are you ill?"

"No," April replied with a smile. "I got a crappy farm, had trouble with the two men there and walked out."

"Which farm would that be then?"

"Willows End Farm, although there was no Willow Trees in sight."

"God, they didn't send you there, did they?!"

"They did indeed."

"Them two there are heathens, the dregs of humanity, not to be trusted as far as they could be thrown. A few years ago, the son was arrested on suspected rape, but it was his word against the girl's, who happened to be a bit backwards."

"That wouldn't surprise me, about the son, I mean."

"The Father's just as bad; some folks say he had a hand in it as well. No one around here bothers with them, they don't come into the village, they have food left at the end of the lane."

"Hmm, they were ready to drag me into that filthy house until I made a stand, then suddenly he realised that he'd heard of me, the Father that is, said that I must be that fighting Land Girl he'd heard of. When I said that I was, he backed off."

"That settled his ash didn't it," Mrs Wilkinson laughed. "I should've liked to have seen his face. But you know, in his youth he was a good-looking lad, but he got into the wrong company, married the wrong girl and had a lout for a son, but these things happen."

"Mrs Kier's on the phone now, he won't be getting any more Land Girls, thank goodness."

"I don't know how he makes a living."

"From the state of the place, neither do I."

Mrs Keir hurried into the kitchen and said.

"Right, April, all done and dusted. The War Agg's horrified and is going straight out there, along with a male inspector, *and* I've got you another job for the rest of the day, to which I'll take you in my car, and bring you back. It isn't far, and a smallholding, owned by two sisters, they deal in hens and pigs, very nice ladies, so you should be okay there. One is a little scatty, Ada, the young one, but Doris has things in hand, although she's finding it a little hard now as Ada's hurt her back, so I'm sure you'll be a good help to her."

"Fallen on your feet there, April, I know the two ladies, adorable they are," Mrs Wilkinson called as April left the kitchen with Mrs Keir.

Once on their way, Mrs Keir decided that this was as good a time as any to have a chat to April.

"What are you going to do with the rest of your life when the war's over, April?"

"Do? I'll stay around here, I love it. There'll be plenty of work on the farms. I've no intention of going back to South Yorkshire; I couldn't bear it after having lived here."

"But what about your family?" Mrs Keir asked.

"As long as I'm happy, they won't mind."

"I have to agree with you, April, it is lovely around here, I wouldn't mind staying myself."

"You never know, Mrs Keir; you could get married again."

"What makes you say that?"

"Any fool could see that you and Captain Silverton go for each other."

"Why, April, what on earth do you mean?"

"I mean that you two more than like each other."

Mrs Keir chose not to answer this; instead, she said.

"April, I've been meaning to ask you and have been very curious, how did you manage to learn all about self-defence? The way you handle yourself is awe-inspiring."

"When I was a kid, being small, the school bullies loved to knock me around, two, sometimes three at a time. Every week saw me going home with a black eye, cut lips and torn dress. Mam always wanted to go up to the school, but I wouldn't let her, it would've made things worse you see. One day my twin brothers, who are very tough lads, said, enough is enough; we're going to teach you how to fight back, the proper way. Every day they took me into the fields, punched and threw me around, and made me fight back their way. I still went home bloodied with torn clothes, but slowly I learnt, the feeling was wonderful."

"But who taught your brothers?" Mrs Keir asked.

"My Mams eldest brother was a Commando, need I say more. He taught my brothers; hence, it was passed on to me. I hate to see anyone being bullied, I know just how they feel, and I'll always champion the underdog."

"It's all very well, April, but hardly ladylike is it."

"I don't profess to be a lady, never have, never shall. People must take me as I am or not at all."

"Well said, April. And here we are, just round the bend. This place is well hidden, isn't it?"

April caught her breath. Before her was a large, pretty farmhouse, or it *could* be called a cottage, ivy-covered, which stood in a yard as clean and neat as a new pin. On each side stood two large barns in immaculate condition, and on the right of one of these was a huge hen pound which contained at least a hundred hens and a dozen ducks. Somewhere there was a pig enclosure as the grunting of pigs could be heard, and surprise surprise, a large Great Dane dog.

"Wow, this is something!" April cried, "I love it!"

"This is my first time here; it *is* really something isn't it," Mrs Keir said.

April jumped from the car and ran to the fence which enclosed the hens and dog. Suddenly a loud voice called out.

"Do not touch the dog."

April turned, startled to see a tall white-haired old lady hurrying across to her.

"Sorry I had to shout, my dear, but until you have been introduced to Cain and told that you are a friend, he could take off your hand if you tried to pet him."

"Gosh, I was just about to stroke him, he looks harmless."

"Looks can be deceiving, my dear."

The old lady stared at her with the bluest of eyes that April had ever seen on a woman her age, she must be eighty, or am I insulting her.

Mrs Keir introduced herself and April to Miss Doris Mannering, then said apologetically.

"I must rush off back to the hostel, I've to take delivery of groceries. So nice to have met you, Miss Mannering, maybe we can have a little chat when I pick April up tonight, say at about six o'clock? Is that alright?"

"That will be fine, my dear, off you go."

As Mrs Keir hurried away, Miss Mannering took April's arm and led her towards the house.

"Come along, my dear," she said kindly. "You must have a cup of tea and meet my sister Ada, she had trouble with her back last week but is feeling much better, but we still thought we should have a helping hand. Although we do things ourselves, keeps one young you know, and I can't tell you how much I admire you girls of the Land Army, you are simply marvellous. What a wonderful idea putting women to work on the land. I wonder whose brainchild it was. Women are much tougher than men make us out to be. Don't you think some men are silly, look at that stupid man Hitler; thinking he can take over the world, I ask you, take over the world indeed." As they arrived at the farmhouse door, she opened it with a flourish and said, "please come in, April, and welcome to Kincaid House and farm."

The smell of beeswax and Lavender met April as she stepped into a kitchen which sparkled with cleanliness, one would never think that this was a farm kitchen. Everything had a place, and everything was in its place, these two sisters believed in tidiness without a doubt.

"Sit yourself down, my dear, the kettle is on the boil on the range, then we shall have a chat over a nice cup of tea."

Miss Mannering bustled about putting cups, saucers, milk jug, sugar bowl and a plate of biscuits onto the large round wooden table.

It's the first time I've seen a round wooden table, it looks as if it's been scrubbed within an inch of its life, April thought as Miss Mannering set a large white teapot onto it.

"Do you like a strong cup, April dear?"

"As it comes, Miss Mannering."

"Oh, please call me Miss Doris; Mannering is such a mouthful isn't it, dear."

"If that's what you prefer, of course," April said. "How long have you been at Kincaid?" April asked. "It's a very nice little farm."

"We like to call it a smallholding, it belonged to our parents', and of course on their deaths it came to my sister Ada and me. My Father bought it when we were just schoolgirls, and we all loved it on sight. My sister and I were brought up as farmers you see; we always worked the land and reared poultry and pigs. We don't have much land now. As Father got older, he sold a lot off. We just have the four fields, we grow potatoes, carrots, parsnips, sprouts, and of course we have help from the village boys when it's time to pull. We have lots of eggs, four cows for milk, and of course the pigs. A lot of produce including eggs and milk goes to help the nation as you'll know."

"Yes, that's where the Land Army comes in," April agreed.

"And what would we do without you!" Miss Doris cried.

"Do you ever leave the farm?" April asked.

"No, not for years, don't have to, the village shop delivers what we need once a week, it's an arrangement that works very well. People come to us, the doctor keeps an eye on my sister Ada, she is going a little vague, thinks she is a young girl still. So, I can't always rely on her to lend a hand."

"Would you think me very rude if I asked how old you both are?" April said quietly.

"I am the eldest at eighty-four, and Ada is eighty-one."

April was astounded.

"In your eighties and still running a farm, I think you're bloody marvellous!"

Miss Doris smiled proudly.

"Yes, we are, my dear, but all good things come to an end, it's the winters you see, they are getting hard for us. I have given lots of thought lately to selling up and the two of us retiring to the coast. Ada is not going to get any better, and these days I have my work cut out looking after her."

"Oh dear, I'm sorry," April said sadly.

Suddenly, a voice could be heard calling.

"Is anyone here? Doris? Where are you? Oh, where are you?"

"In the kitchen, dear," Miss Doris called.

The door opened, and a tall, skinny woman with long white hair flowing around her shoulders, which partly hid her light blue eyes, hurried in. She gave a hop, skip, and a jump.

"Oh, Doris, I can't find my alice-band, do you think the maid has taken it?" She turned to April. "I shall see that you are dismissed, my girl, give me back my alice-band at once."

Miss Doris stood and took hold of Ada's hand as she spoke gently to her.

"We do not wear alice-bands anymore, dear, and this is not the maid. We do not have maids either, this is April, she has come to help us."

"I don't like her, send her away, and where's Mother? I want Mother."

Miss Doris looked at April apologetically.

"I'm sorry about this; she is having a bad day."

Ada pulled herself away from Miss Doris, smiled at April, then said.

"Hello, you are pretty, who are you?"

"I'm April."

Ada walked to her and touched her face.

"I like you; you are pretty. Will you walk to school with me?"

April smiled and nodded her head.

"Yes, of course I will."

"Goody, I shall go and get ready." She ran out of the kitchen, laughing happily.

Miss Doris sighed sadly.

"I see what you mean," April said. "It must be very hard for you."

"It is, but she is my sister, she would do the same for me."

"You've both been close all your lives haven't you," April asked.

"Yes, we never married, never had time for boys, *or* do the things girls used to do when we were young. Mother and Father were our worlds you see, and the farm of course."

"Will Miss Ada be okay on her own while you show me around?" April asked. "I really should be working you know."

"Yes, Ada will be fine, she tidies her sewing box a hundred times a day, it keeps her amused, there is not a lot that she can do. She collects eggs, feeds the pigs, and sometimes milks one of the cows, but, April dear, you must meet Cain. I must tell him that you are a friend, he's a lovely dog and guards my sister and me with his life. He has the run of the house at night, if anyone broke in, he would kill them, but, that's unlikely to happen, we are so out of the way here."

April shuddered.

"But come," Miss Doris went on. "I shall show you around the house, I am enormously proud of it, it's just as it was when we were girls, we haven't changed a thing. Mother and Father would not have wanted us to."

She led the way into a dark wood-panelled hall which had a light highly polished wooden floor. Throwing open a door on the right, she said.

"The dining room which we never use."

Its walls were covered with heavily embossed gold wallpaper, no pictures were hung. It contained only an oak table with six chairs set around it. April was then led into the sitting room where she stood in amazement, to her eyes it was splendid, sumptuous, and if she had to describe it to someone, she would not have been able to find the words. Thick royal blue carpet into which the feet sank. Low slung pink silk chairs and sofa, which held royal blue silk cushions. Small round mahogany tables set here and there, a large mahogany sideboard set against one wall, all holding priceless looking figurines. But it was the enormous white wooden fireplace which stood out from the rest of the room, giving its character. It was gothic, its architecture magnificent, characterized with dancing figures, mixed in with cherubs, angels and bunches of grapes and cherries. It was a work of art, its most outstanding feature being the two life-like figures stood to each side, which was holding the fireplace on their shoulders, their arms raised, unclothed, except for a fig leaf covering their private parts, it was beautiful. April could only stand speechless, gazing with wonder and awe.

"It is rather wonderful, isn't it?" Miss Doris said quietly. "It was Father's pride and joy."

"Was it here when you bought the house?" April asked.

"Oh no, dear, Father bought it from a friend who was pulling down an old house. Mother hated it, she thought it graceless and inelegant, and she did not want it at all but was overruled by Father. I like it, and so does Ada, do you, dear?"

April took a deep breath, then said.

"I think it's stunning, I've never seen anything like it. Whoever did all the carving was an artist indeed, I could stand and look at it all day. I see that you have no ornaments on its shelf, they would spoil it."

"Mother got her own way with that, she said it was an eyesore enough without putting her precious china on it," Miss Doris laughed. "If you only knew the row there was about that."

"Well," April said with a toss of her head. "I think it's magnificent, imposing and a work of art."

"Thank you, dear," Miss Doris said. "And now we must get on, come on and meet Cain. Don't be afraid, he will show his teeth to you at first, but when I have told him you are a friend and helper, he will lick you to death."

April pulled a face as Miss Doris led the way out of the house and across the yard to be greeted by the loud barking of Cain, the distant sound of grunting pigs and a chorus of clucking hens.

"It sounds as if the pigs want feeding, but they can wait a little while longer," Miss Doris called over her shoulder to April.

As they reached the hen enclosure the noise reached a crescendo, it was deafening.

Cain bounded up to the fence barking.

"Shut up you silly dog," Miss Doris said in a stern voice. "Or I will not let you out."

The dog looked at April, then began to growl deep in his throat.

Miss Doris put her hand onto his great head, she stroked him several times, murmuring soothing words to him, then opened the gate. He stood silently by her side, still looking at April.

"Now, Cain," Miss Doris began. "This is April, she is a friend." She repeated loudly. "Friend. Now, put out your paw and shake April's hand. Put out your hand, April."

April did, and the dog put his paw into it, he moved it gently up and down, while April did likewise.

"You see, April, he is your friend for life now, and will protect you with his," Miss Doris said. "Isn't he a lovely dog?"

"Yes, he is," April said as she petted him.

She had never really been keen on dogs and did not make a fuss of the farm dogs, but they did not seem to mind. Cain, you had to treat with respect because of his enormous size.

Suddenly Miss Ada's voice could be heard calling across the yard.

"Doris, I can't find Mother, I want a cup of tea, is that Mother with you?"

"Oh dear, I had better go, there is nothing wrong with my sister's body clock, she always has tea at eleven. Come along, April, *we* may as well have one."

"But don't you think I should do some work, Miss Doris? Maybe feed the pigs, collect the eggs?" April asked.

"Later, dear, later, plenty of time for that. Now come along, you too, Cain," Miss Doris said.

The dog bounded happily toward the house, skidding to a sudden halt to stand before Miss Ada, who shouted.

"You silly dog, careful now, don't knock me down. Why are you not with Father? And I can't find Mother, I want my tea," she turned into the house, calling. "Mother, I can't find you, where are you?"

Miss Doris hurried up to her and said pacifyingly.

"Now, dear, Mother and Father are no longer here, have you forgotten? Come along and I shall make you some tea, you sit up in your room and I shall bring it to you."

Miss Ada smiled happily, then said.

"Alright, Mother." She ran lightly up the stairs, with no evidence of a bad back.

"You see what I mean, she is becoming a handful and challenging work, but I love her dearly," Miss Doris said quietly.

"I know you do, but she's going to get worse, not better. You do know that don't you?" April said kindly.

"Yes, I know, dear, that is why I must sell up, move to the coast, find a good retirement home for us both and look after her full time. Money is not a problem, no matter what I get for this farm."

"Money doesn't go far these days, Miss Doris."

"I know that too, April, but I want to show you something. We will take Ada her tea, then I'll show you something that will shock you."

Oh gosh, April thought, I hope she hasn't got a mummified Mam and Dad stashed away somewhere.

Miss Doris took her into a small back bedroom and walked to a four-drawer chest of draws.

She turned and beckoned to April.

"Come here, my dear."

April went forward uncertainly, and when she stood beside Miss Doris, she asked.

"What am I supposed to be looking at?"

Miss Doris pulled open the top drawer; it was packed with banknotes laid neatly in rows. She closed the drawer with a bang, then opened the other three in turn, all were packed with banknotes.

April stood with her hand clapped to her throat, astounded, she had lost all power of speech, and she could not believe what her eyes had just seen.

Miss Doris stood watching her, a smile hovering about her lips, then she asked.

"What do you think of that, my dear? A lot of money isn't there; you will never have seen as much before, have you?"

April shook her head, wordlessly.

"So," Miss Doris went on. "You see why money is no problem."

April nodded, then pulling herself together, she stammered.

"There must be thousands."

Miss Doris shook her head, then said firmly.

"Hundreds of thousands."

"But why isn't it in a bank?" April asked.

"I don't believe in banks, never did, neither did Father, that's how we were brought up."

"Amassing all that money must have taken years of saving," April responded.

"Yes, it did, but also Father sold off land before he died and got a decent price. He always insisted on being paid in cash, as he did with everything he sold, as I also do."

"Aren't you afraid of anyone breaking in?" April asked apprehensively.

Miss Doris narrowed her eyes as she said.

"*If* anyone got in, as I said, Cain has the run of the house at night, and would chew off the face of anyone who *did* get in."

"I assume no one else knows of all this money?" April asked.

"No," Miss Doris replied. "Just my sister, who, as you have seen, does not know what day it is. So, she will have forgotten all about it; and now yourself of course."

"I'll not speak of this to anyone, I wouldn't dream of it, you can trust me, Miss Doris, but I wish that you hadn't shown me, I'll worry about you both. Although, I believe what you say about Cain."

"We let him in at night, lock up, and he's happy roaming from room to room, so please do not worry, there's a dear."

"Could I ask you something, Miss Doris, and please don't think me rude. Have you ever counted all that money?"

"No, dear, not in the way that you mean, it would take an age. Every penny is written down and accounted for; Father taught me how to do it as my sister never had a head for figures. I have always kept the books up to date, so, I know to the pound how much is in those drawers."

"Very commendable, you're a very smart lady, Miss Doris, I take my hat off to you, but if I were in your place, I wouldn't rest easy at night," April said cautiously.

"Listen," Miss Doris cocked her head to one side. "Sounds like a car pulling up, I'm not expecting anyone, and we don't have visitors."

April shrugged her shoulders.

"It won't be anyone for me."

"Well, we had better go and see hadn't we."

Miss Doris hurried from the room, April following at a more leisurely pace; as she reached the top of the stairs, she recognised Mrs Keir's voice. That was odd, it wasn't time for her to leave yet, and Mrs Keir was supposed to pick her up at six. She hurried down the stairs and into the kitchen to see a white-face trembling Mrs Keir asking to see her at once.

As April ran up to her alarmed, she cried.

"Mrs Keir, what on earth's wrong?"

Mrs Keir started to cry and babble inaudibly, Miss Doris looked apprehensive and took Mrs Keir's hands.

"Now, now, dear, we can't tell what you're saying, sit down," she pulled out a chair and lowered Mrs Keir onto it. "I'm going to get you a tot of brandy; you certainly look as if you need it."

April knelt in front of Mrs Keir.

"What is it?" she asked.

Mrs Keir gazed at her ashen-faced, then said.

"Oh, April, Anita's dead, she's been killed." She broke out into fresh sobs. "Killed, she's dead, I had to come and tell you at once."

April stared at her in shock for a moment, stunned.

"Anita, dead? Anita killed?" she repeated like a parrot. "But how? When? I don't believe it."

Mrs Keir tried to pull herself together, took a hankie out of her pocket and dried her eyes. She hesitated as Miss Doris handed her a small glass of brandy.

"Don't say another word until you have emptied that glass, go on now," she commanded.

Mrs Keir put the glass to her lips with a trembling hand and gulped down the brandy. She handed the glass back to Miss Doris.

"Thank you, I needed that, I feel a little better, but maybe April's going to need one too."

Miss Doris hurried away to comply.

"Now," said a deeply shocked April. "Tell me what happened. Anita killed, it's unbelievable."

"I haven't been told the full facts by the police, but I understand that she tried to help a man who was trying to cross a field full of cows and their calves. He had a dog which wasn't on a lead and was barking and chasing around the herd. To cut a long story short, they crowded him and got him to the ground. Anita went to help him and got trampled to death, the man did too. A field hand heard all the commotion and went for help, too late of course." She paused, then started to sob loudly. "They had to shovel the bodies up, imagine, shovel the bodies up; they'd been mangled to a pulp."

Miss Doris handed April a glass of brandy.

"Drink," she said gently.

April emptied the glass, then said.

"We have to get back to the hostel, Miss Doris, you don't mind, do you?"

"Mind, of course not, my dear, off you go. I am so sorry about your friend, it's terrible."

"Thank you, Miss Doris. I'll see you again soon," April replied.

"I do hope so, but don't rush back to work," Miss Doris said firmly.

Work, that's a laugh, I haven't done a stroke all day, but that's not important. She could not take it in about poor Anita, to have her life cut short in such a terrible way after all she had been through – her face disfigured, a family who did not care a jot, and no hope of a better future. To die hemmed in by a herd of cows that were determined to protect their young, no matter the cost, was awful.

Cows were especially excellent Mothers, and on seeing a threat to their young will put a stop to it right away. Its only means of protecting its young are its legs and feet, hence, being trampled to death. That bloody stupid man who had also lost his life, could not have been countrified; otherwise, he would not have been in that field with a dog.

Once back at the hostel, they found Mrs Wilkinson stood at the kitchen sink, red-eyed, her tears falling among the potatoes she was peeling.

When she saw April, she cried.

"April, can you believe it, poor Anita dead as a doornail, just like that!" She slapped the potato water with her hand; it flew up and dripped down her face along with her tears. "I'll never eat beef again, how could anyone, them killing Anita like that. Great clodhopping things, PC Humble said she had to be scraped off the ground with a shovel," she bent over the sink and sobbed loudly.

April was furious.

"That bloody PC Bumble hasn't the brains of a louse, fancy saying that to you! Just wait until I see him!" she cried.

She took hold of Mrs Wilkinson and hugged her.

"Take no notice of what anyone tells you, we don't know the full facts yet. I suppose it's going to be all around the village by now."

"Mrs Wilkinson, you're terribly upset, I think you should go home, take the day off," Mrs Keir said. "I'll see to the evening meal. Although I don't think any of the girls will want to eat when they hear about Anita."

"Oh, thank you, Mrs Keir, I *am* all at six's and sevens. I'll go home and lay on the bed for a couple of hours, get myself together. All my neighbours will be coming in wanting to know about everything."

"Lock your door, Mrs Wilkinson, let them wonder," Mrs Keir said. "Now come along, I'll take you home in the car; you're in no fit state to walk. Unless you want to stay here in your bed-sit?"

"No, it's my day to go home and I'd like to, Mrs Keir."

"Very well, let's go." She turned to April. "Will you be alright on your own, April?"

"Of course, I take things in my stride. I'm going to make a cup of tea, then sit and think about the reactions of the other girls on hearing the sad news. Nancy was awfully close to Anita and is going to take it hard."

Mrs Keir nodded her head.

"Very wise, April. I won't be longer than twenty minutes."

She ushered Mrs Wilkinson out of the door and closed it quietly behind them.

When April was sat with a cup of tea in front of her, she thought about Anita, she would have had a brilliant career, but had to shut herself away from life and people. How she must have suffered inside herself. But it had not broken her spirit, not entirely, she had become interested in the land on joining the Land Army and enjoyed the company of the girls. She had no ties, would never have had a boyfriend, and when the war was over had talked of being a typist.

April stood as she felt anger welling up inside her. What was done was done and could not be undone; she would have to help Mrs Keir tell the other girls. She was not looking forward to that, neither would Mrs Keir be. Someone would have the unenviable task of getting Anita's things together; she hoped it would not have to be herself.

She walked slowly upstairs and into Anita's bedroom, which she shared with Nancy and Katrina. Anita and Nancy had been very close; Nancy was going to be very upset.

She stood by Anita's chest of drawers, on top of which was Anita's Land Army hat. She had gone to work in her turban.

April picked it up and held it to her chest, her eyes filled with tears. She gulped back a sob, poor Anita would never wear it again, but the Land Army would not get it back, this was going to rest on top of Anita's coffin, she would have wanted that.

"This will be with you Anita; I shall see to that," April said aloud. She paused, then walked out of the room and into her own where she placed the hat inside her wardrobe.

She sighed, then going to her bed, she lay down and closed her eyes. She did not expect to sleep but did, deep and dreamless until she was gently shaken awake by Mrs Keir, who held a cup of tea to her.

"Sorry to wake you, April, but it's six o'clock, the girls are going to be back soon. Here, drink this tea, I've put just a drop of brandy in it to fortify you before breaking the news of Anita's death to the girls."

April sat up and took the tea from Mrs Keir.

"Thanks, I think I'm going to need it, unless I miss my guess, Joan will go into hysterics, one or two of the others will faint with the shock, and Nancy, well, Nancy will take it very badly, Anita and she were firm friends. And as for Mouse, she'll be in floods of tears."

Mrs Keir's face changed, she looked apprehensive. April noticed this, and she asked.

"What's wrong? Is there something you're not telling me which I should know?"

Mrs Keir sat down onto Fay's bed, facing April.

"Oh, April," she began. "I'm so sorry to give you more bad news, but it's Mouse."

"Mouse?!" she cried. She jumped up and slammed the cup of tea onto the bedside cabinet. "Is she alright? What's happened to Mouse?"

"Nothing's happened to Mouse, nothing bad that is. Sit down, April and I'll explain."

"Where is she? Isn't she at work?"

"No, she's not at work."

"Then where the bloody hell is she? She's not in the house!"

"I know, April, calm down."

"Tell me where the hell she is."

Mrs Keir took a deep breath.

"Mouse has left the WLA, and by now is on her way to Ireland."

"Ireland?!" April cried, amazed.

"Yes, my dear. There's no easy way to say this, but listen to me, and don't interrupt. Mouse is going to be a nun."

"A nun?!" April exploded. "A bloody nun?! Has she taken leave of her senses?!"

"No," Mrs Keir said gently. "She's just come to them." She folded her hands in her lap. "Mouse thought very carefully before she made up her mind, once she had, she was determined to do it. This life was not for her, she knew that from day one, but hoped that she would grow to like it. She realised that she never would, so came to me and talked about what she wanted to do. I tried to change her mind, but I couldn't."

"Why didn't she speak to Fay and me about it, the little fool. Does she not know how it's going to be shutting herself away for life in a convent?" April asked.

"Yes, she knows," Mrs Keir answered gently. "And she didn't speak to you or Fay because she knew how upset you'd be. Which you are, are you not?"

"I don't know about upset, more like mad!" April said angrily.

"When you seriously think about it, you'll see that Mouse has done the right thing. You taught her a lot about life in the brief time she's been here, April. She's never going to forget it, or you. She's left a letter for you and Fay explaining."

"That's nice of her," April said sarcastically. "When did she go? When we'd all gone to work evidently, and how did she go? How's she getting to this convent, where is it in Ireland?"

"So many questions all at once," Mrs Keir said tiredly.

"I'm sorry about that, but I need to know, and so will Fay. She was like a sister to us. That's funny isn't it, she's going to be Sister Tina, unless they change her name, as I believe they sometimes do in these religious madhouses. These nuns have a rule of obedience and monastic vows you know, and are on their knees praying twenty times a day, what, and to whom ? Nobody *they've* seen *or* ever will see. Does Mouse know all this?"

"Of course she does. Mouse isn't a fool, and the children's home she was brought up in had nuns going in and out all the time."

"She never told me that."

"Of course she didn't, she knows you're an atheist and would've pulled her to pieces."

"It sounds as if our Mouse told us only what she wanted us to know."

"Of course she did. She wasn't proud of being brought up in a children's home, never knowing who her parents' were, but she was happy enough and remembers the nuns and how kind they were to the children, the good they did, the kind deeds to the poor."

"Our little Mouse was deeper than we thought."

"Not deep, April, but private within herself."

"You haven't told me where this church is in Ireland, or how she's getting there."

"Two of the nuns are over here visiting Canterbury, they go back today. Mouse has gone with them, Dennis took them to the ferry and the church is in County Wicklow, a lovely part of Ireland."

"But how's all this been arranged so quickly?"

"A few phone calls during the last two weeks'."

"And Mouse never said a word."

"Because, April, she knew that you'd try to talk her out of it."

"I would've."

"I rest my case," Mrs Keir said quietly.

"Fay's going to be gobsmacked," April said. "About Anita also."

The sound of the kitchen door being slammed shut rang through the house.

"And so, it begins," Mrs Keir said nervously.

* * *

"Well, I'm glad that's over," April said thankfully. "What a day. I hope I never have another one like it." She was sat hugging her knees as she watched Fay brushing her hair.

"It hasn't sunk in with me yet, Anita dying. What a horrible way to die. And Mouse, who would've thought she'd plan her leaving like that and not tell us," Fay retorted. "I thought she'd settled down and was getting used to the work."

"If I had her here, I'd shake her until her head rolled off," April said angrily.

"That wouldn't do any good would it. Her mind was made up, and by the sound of things for a long time," Fay replied. "And what about this letter she's left for us, shall we read it now?"

"Not tonight if you don't mind, I'm rather tired, it's been a very distressing day. You read it if you want."

"No, we'll read it together tomorrow."

"She must be in Ireland by now."

"Yes, and trying to sleep on a hard bunk bed I'll bet," Fay laughed as she climbed into bed. "Just listen to me laughing and poor Anita dead. If I didn't, I'd cry and wouldn't be able to stop. What else can happen, April, it always comes in threes."

"Yes, that's true," April sighed. "Anyhow, do you like being at Knighton Hall?"

"Oh yes, Lord and Lady Knighton are very nice, no airs and graces about them, and they're so grateful for the Land Army's help. It's a beautiful estate, such a shame the grounds have had to be given over to growing crops. I would've loved to have seen it as it stood." As Fay ended, she sighed deeply, then asked. "What about you, how was your day?"

"Do you really want to know?"

"Of course, I wouldn't have asked otherwise."

"It's been a bugger, well, the morning was."

"I don't like the sound of that."

April launched into the story of the hour spent with the two lecherous farmers.

"Oh God, you didn't set about them, did you?" Fay cried.

"I didn't have to; the old one knew of me and so backed off."

Fay laughed as April continued.

"He didn't know how lucky he was, did he. I walked away, came back to the hostel where Mrs Keir found me another job to go to, and what a job, it was made in heaven as the saying goes. I didn't do a stroke of work, although I wanted to. The farm's only small, run by two sisters, one of which has gone soft in the head, gone back to her childhood, and Miss Doris is coping with things on her own. You should see the inside of that place, Fay, it's lovely! How I'd love to own something like that, but, the sad thing is, Miss Doris is putting it up for sale, her and her sister are going to retire to the coast."

"How old are they?" Fay asked curiously.

"In their eighties," April replied.

"It's time they packed it in then," Fay said.

"There's a lot more to tell you, but not tonight, I'm whacked, I have to sleep." April lay down, pulled the covers over her and put out her bedside lamp. "Good night, kiddo," she said to Fay.

"You haven't called me kiddo for a while," Fay said softly.

The only answer she got was.

"Hmm..."

17

As Miss Doris had given April the day off to help Mrs Keir with Anita's funeral arrangements, she was on her way to the village flower shop to order a wreath. The day was dull with a grey heavy sky forecasting rain, and the wind had suddenly sprung up.

"Could've done with my raincoat and wellingtons by the look of it," she said aloud.

Tightening the cord on her hat, she put her head down and jogged smartly along the road. As she came to the beginning of the village, the first person she saw was Norman.

"Hi young, Norman, why aren't you at school?"

"Got a bad throat, Miss April. I'm just going to the shop for some Fisherman's Friends."

"Oh, poor you. How's little Titch? He'll be lost without you."

"Oh, he's off too, he always says he has what I have, and his Mam believes him."

April laughed, then said.

"The little bugger."

Norman also laughed at April's words, then said seriously.

"I'm glad I've seen you, Miss April, I wanted to, and little Titch said I should tell you too."

"Tell me what, Norman?"

"You're not going to like it, Miss April. But you see, we, that is, little Titch and me, like Miss Fay, she's awful nice, just like you."

"I'm getting worried, Norman, tell me, what's wrong?"

"Well, Miss April, it's about Larry."

"Larry, what's he done?"

"We don't, that's little Titch and me, don't want to see the dirty done on Miss Fay, she's too nice, and Larry isn't."

"My sentiments exactly, Norman, and before you go on, I must tell you that I didn't like Larry the moment I clapped eyes on him. So, don't be afraid to tell me what you know about him."

"Well, we know that he's courting Miss Fay, or supposed to be, and that Miss Fay's crackers on him," he rolled his eyes upwards, "but he's messing about with Sue Morton, has been for weeks', she's crackers about him too." He rolled his eyes upwards again.

April had to smile as she thought, this lad is a pearl, then asked.

"How do you know about this Sue and Larry?"

"Me and little Titch can trust you not to say anything, we trust you with our lives, Miss April."

"You can, Norman, go on."

"Me and little Titch hang around in the park at night, hide up trees and watch what's going on below, and we see a lot, Miss April. Little Titch doesn't understand a lot of it, but I do."

"Get to the point," April said eagerly.

"There's a little grassed space behind some young saplings where no one can see you as they walk past, but up a tree, you can see everything, and boy, do little Titch and me see everything. Larry and Sue go there often and have it off, if you know what I mean, Miss April."

"Oh yes, Norman, I know what you mean."

"So, you see, Miss April, it isn't fair to Miss Fay is it. So, will you tell her?"

"I will, Norman, but do you think that you should be up trees watching things like that?"

"Why not? The animals do it, and *you* see it happening on the farms all the time, don't you?" Norman queried innocently.

It was now April's turn to roll her eyes heavenwards. How could she answer that?

"Some grownups act like animals don't they, Miss April, my Mam says Mr Smedley acts like an animal, *and* looks like one."

"Ha, Smedley, with the bald head and goatee beard, I have to agree with your Mam on that one, Norman."

"Miss Fay has had a lucky escape, Miss April because Larry has a right big donger, you should see it."

April thought she would fall at Norman's feet in hysterics, and suddenly felt that she had to go to the loo.

Trying to hold her mirth in, she said.

"Norman, you've quite a way with words, but don't say to anyone else what you've just said to me."

"About Larry's donger? Oh, I won't, Miss April. I'd better get to the shop; Mam will be wondering where I am. You'll tell Miss Fay about Larry? Tell her he's no good, he's a right rat-arse, little Titch will tell you an all."

"I'll tell her, now off you go, Norman, you're a good lad."

As he ran down the road, April watched him, then gave way to her laughter. That lad was priceless, the way he had come out with Larry's big donger! She had never heard it called that before, but she did not think that Fay would want to listen to that bit of the story. Poor Fay was in for a rude awakening, but would she be that upset? She hadn't talked of Larry for the past couple of weeks'; maybe the first flush of love had worn thin? The bastard had been stringing her along, with, it seemed, this Sue, and maybe two or three more. So, I was not wrong about him, first opinions are always the best and most accurate. She had better tell Fay as soon as possible, but now she had to go to the flower shop and see about some flowers for Anita, also tonight they would read Mouse's letter. Little Mouse a nun, it was unbelievable, it had not sunk in yet, neither had Anita's passing, what *else* could happen?! Fay had said that bad news came in threes, let's hope she is wrong.

In the flower shop, she had to stand and listen to the owner, Mrs Holt's commiserations.

"Thank you for your commiserations, Mrs Holt. I'd like to order three wreaths please, one red, one white, one blue, in the shape of WLA."

Mrs Holt pulled a notepad and pencil towards her and wrote down April's instructions, then looked up at April.

"You'll want the W in red of course, the L in white, and the A in blue, have I got it right?" she asked.

"You've got it in one, Mrs Holt, that's right."

"When will you want them?"

"I don't know yet, but in the next two or three days. We don't have a date for the funeral, or where it's going to be, but carry out the order, Mrs Keir will pick them up and pay you."

"Thank you, Miss Thornton."

April raised her eyebrows, she had been given her full title, now that was unusual, and it was like a mark of respect.

Mrs Holt cleared her throat, then said.

"I must say, it's a novel idea having WLA in flowers, and in the colours of our flag."

"Why not," April asked. "We work under the flag for King and country, where would we be without the Land Army?"

"You do a good job, Miss Thornton, an outstanding job; I wouldn't like to do it, working with nasty smelly animals." She laid down her pen. "Talking of nasty animals, one's about to enter my shop. Thank you for your order, Miss Thornton."

Now that sounded like a dismissal, April thought as she turned to leave, then, on seeing who had entered the shop, she understood why. It was the goatee beard man, Smedley. She hoped he would not start any trouble because she was just in the mood to take him on, but on reflection she would ignore him, not let him light her fires. She marched smartly out of the shop without looking at him, but could feel his eyes boring into her back. He followed her out, and Mrs Holt, sensing trouble, followed him. He stopped and lit a cigarette, then called after April.

"All this trouble because a bloody Land Girl got herself trampled to mush by a bunch of cows." He laughed at his own words, then turned in the opposite direction to April and sauntered away.

Mrs Holt had heard him clearly and was shocked to the core.

April had also heard him clearly and felt a wave of white-hot anger rising inside her, so hot that it consumed her whole body. She turned and saw Smedley walking away, his shoulders shaking with laughter.

Mrs Holt saw April running like grease lightening after Smedley, a look of pure murder on her face, and knew what was going to happen. Norman was just coming away from the chemist, and she shouted, almost screamed at him.

"Norman, go get PC Humble, quick!"

As he stood staring at her open-mouthed, she cried.

"Move, boy, move!"

He looked around him startled, then, took in immediately April flying down the street towards Smedley.

"Bloody hell!" he muttered, then set off running to the police station.

April launched herself at Smedley's back, her weight knocking him to the floor face down. The lit cigarette was pushed into his mouth, burning his gums as April sat astride his back, her hand feeling for his goatee beard. She grasped it, then with all her strength, pulled back his head until it almost rested between his shoulder blades. The pain to him was indescribable as he coughed out the now damp cigarette. As April held his head in that position, she put her head towards his; they were now eyeball to eyeball.

"You nasty dirty pile of shit! You want exterminating from the face of the earth! How dare you say that about our Anita who was giving her all for you and your type you bastard! I'm going to make you suffer!" She pulled his head a little further back, and he gave a loud scream of pain. "Go on, scream, that's what our Anita did as she died!" She balled her hand into a fist and punched him between the eyes. "That's for our Anita!" Then again. "That's for me." Then again. "That's for all the boys who've died for scum like you!"

Mrs Holt was screaming hysterically.

"Stop, stop, you're killing him!" Then she saw PC Humble flying down the road, Norman behind him.

PC Humble's police coat was unbuttoned and flying open as he ran, his police helmet was set at a cock-eyed angle, its strap under his nose, it wobbled as he ran, and in his hand, he clutched a cosh.

Norman ran to the side of PC Humble, and on seeing the cosh he carried, thought, he isn't going to use that on Miss April, so quickly snatched it out of the PC's hand and threw it down an alleyway that separated the Post Office from the bread shop. He heard it clang against a dustbin and gave a smile of satisfaction as he ran.

When PC Humble reached April, he took hold of her by her arms and yanked her away from the now semi-conscious Smedley.

"I'm going to throw the book at you for this, my girl!" he ground out; his breath almost gone.

April started to kick backwards, she had her hob-nailed boots on and caught him smartly across his shins. He dropped her with a cry of pain, then bent to rub his throbbing legs, as he did so, she brought her right arm up, and with the flat of her hand, knocked his helmet from his head where it rolled slowly into the mud-filled gutter.

Norman screamed with laughter, oh if little Titch were here! This was better than the Key Stone Cops!

Mrs Holt could not believe her eyes; she clacked her false teeth together nervously. What Humble would do she dreaded to think, he could be a bit slow on the uptake sometimes.

PC Humble was at a loss as to what to do now, so he tried to pull himself together, then saw out of the corner of his eye; his police helmet laid in the gutter covered with mud. He shuddered at the thought of the Inspector finding out about this. This bloody girl was the bane of his life, there could not be another like her in England. He would have to arrest her, which was going to be a trial.

As he straightened to his full height, his pounding heart sank to his boots as he saw Judge Bentley bearing down on him.

Norman chuckled with glee; this was going to be good! Thunderous Bentley was on the scene to see the PC half-dressed, April dancing around in a paddy like the wicked witch of the west, and Smedley laid out cold. If only little Titch were here!

"Just what the hell is going on here?!" the Judge bellowed.

April stood still with her hands on her hips, looking at him defiantly as she said.

"Same old story, Judge. I've been defending the good old Land Girls again."

The Judge looked down at Smedley.

"So I see, and you look to have done a good job by the looks of him. You've gone too far this time young, lady."

"I couldn't care less, he's lucky he's breathing after what he said."

"You can tell me that later." Then he looked disgustedly at PC Humble. "What the hell are you doing half-dressed Humble?! You look a sight man; fasten your coat, and where the hell is your helmet?! A police officer is not a police officer without his helmet!"

PC Humble's eyes went apprehensively to the helmet laid in the gutter.

Judge Bentley saw this.

"In the bloody gutter! How the hell did it get there?!"

PC Humble's face turned fiery red as he pointed at April.

"She knocked it off my head deliberately."

"Don't be bloody stupid, Humble, you're six-three, she's five foot nothing. Did she suddenly grow expanding arms?!"

Norman giggled.

Mrs Holt began to enjoy herself and switched her false teeth from one side of her mouth to the other.

PC Humble shuffled his large feet in embarrassment.

"Well, Judge, it was like this," he began.

April broke in.

"I caught him bending, Judge, and as I was so mad, and it was half off his head to begin with, I knocked it off."

That was clever Miss April, Norman thought. Mrs Holt grinned at him as the same thought went through her head.

"I've always thought you an idiot, Humble; this debacle has not changed my mind. Get back to the station where you belong." The Judge shook his head, "I've a lot to say to you."

PC Humble put a stubborn expression on his moon-like face.

"I have to arrest this female, it's my duty, and also Smedley."

"How the hell are you going to arrest Smedley when he's lain sleeping like a baby?! And on what charge are you arresting Miss Thornton?"

"Causing an affray, disturbing the peace, grievous bodily harm, *and* assaulting an officer of the law," PC Humble reeled off. "It's my duty."

"Hmm," the Judge said. He rocked back on his heels, staring at PC Humble, then said. "Get back to the station now, Humble, and if you know what's good for you, you'll do as I say." He paused for a moment. "You should be looking for and arresting them poachers who are running around Lord Knighton's land pinching his game stock. Need I say more?"

PC Humble put his head down, then turned, making to obey the Judge.

"Have you forgotten something? Your bloody helmet, man, pick it up!" the Judge roared.

Norman jumped forward and picked it up before PC Humble could do so, he handed it to the PC with a cheeky grin.

"Bit mucky, sir," he said.

PC Humble snatched it from him and said out of the corner of his mouth.

"Watch it, kid."

Norman smirked and thought again, oh little Titch, you should be here. He turned and watched to see what would happen next. Miss April was in a heap of trouble this time; would she get out of it?

The Judge began.

"Mrs Holt, would you mind going to the pub and asking two of the men in there to come and remove this heap of slime lying on the floor, he needs taking to the doctors."

Mrs Holt would do anything for the Judge, she liked him a lot.

"Of course, Judge, I'll go right away." She took off in full sail.

"And you, Norman, why are you here?"

April answered for him.

"Oh, Norman is my knight in shining armour, Judge."

"Is he now. Why isn't your knight in shining armour at school?"

Norman looked down at his feet.

"Away with you, boy, go on now, off you go."

Norman looked sheepish as he walked away slowly.

The Judge looked sternly at April.

"Now, my girl, let's have it."

"Could we step into Mrs Holt's shop please, Judge?"

"If you wish." He took hold of her arm as they walked into the shop.

April pulled herself free, then closed the door behind them; she turned to face the Judge, her eyes blazing.

"Don't say one word until you hear what that heap of dog poo had to say about our Anita. He said, 'all this fuss about a bloody Land Girl being trampled to mush by a herd of bloody cows.' I wanted to trample *him* into mush and put what was left of him into the coffin with Anita. I would've done too if PC Plod hadn't stopped me. I don't regret what I've done, and I'd do it again." She glared at Judge Bentley defiantly.

He stood looking back at her in silence, then said.

"That was a truly terrible thing that Smedley said. I can understand you doing what you did. But, April, you can't keep taking the law into your own hands, one day it's going to land you in a whole heap of trouble."

"There's no law around here, Judge. So far nothing's been done about Smedley and his malicious mouth, everyone seems to be afraid of him, but I'm not. I hope I've broken his neck."

"I don't think it'll come to that, April; I'll be having words with Humble."

"That man's a waste of space, Judge; how he holds down his job, I don't know."

"Ours is not to know the reason why."

The shop door was pushed open, and Mrs Holt hurried in.

"All seen to, Judge, Smedley's been carted off to the doctors moaning and crying out what he's going to do to 'that bloody Land Girl'," Mrs Holt said importantly.

"See, Judge, see what I mean!" April cried.

The Judge looked at her sternly.

"Yes, I see what you mean, leave Smedley to me. I want you to go back to the hostel, April, straight back, and *don't* find any trouble on the way, you hear me now."

"I'll go, *and I* don't find trouble, *it* finds *me*." She marched smartly to the door, turned, made a salute of respect, then closed the door quietly behind her.

The Judge sighed heavily.

"I don't know what I'm going to do with that girl."

"Do with her?" Mrs Holt said, putting her hands together. "I admire her spunk, they could do with her at the head of the army, Churchill wouldn't know what had hit him."

The Judge laughed.

"Knowing April, she would have a cigar in her mouth alongside him. I must go and sort out this mess her and Smedley have created between them. By the way, Mrs Holt, did you hear what Smedley said about that Land Girl's death?"

"I did, Judge, with my own ears."

"Thank you, Mrs Holt, I'll bid you a good day."

When the Judge had left the shop, Mrs Holt gave a coy smile, patted her hair, and smoothed down her apron. Had the Judge winked at her? She rather thought he had. She must ask him over for a meal sometime soon. He had been remarkably handsome as a young man, and was still presentable as an old one, you never know what could happen, maybe there was life in the old dog yet. There was undoubtedly life in her.

The Judge would have been horrified if he had known Mrs Holts thoughts about him, but, at that moment, he was facing PC Humble in the police station.

"Well, Humble?"

"Well what, Judge?"

"This is a right mish-mash isn't it, Humble."

"I don't see what you mean, Judge. The law's been broken, and I have my duty to do."

"Smedley's a no-good nowter and you know it, Humble, he gets away with what he wants to do and thinks we don't know about it."

PC Humble looked scandalised, then flashed the Judge a look of indignation.

"I wouldn't want any man to lose his job, even if it's only half done," the Judge went on.

"What do you mean?!" PC Humble cried.

"Let me put it this way," the Judge replied with a sardonic smile on his face. "The pork your wife was cooking last week smelled delicious, I could smell it in my house. Now, where would she get pork when food rations are in force? *And* she was overheard shooting off her mouth, in a stage whisper of course, in the Post Office about a grouse that she'd supposedly picked up in the lane, dead as a doornail of course, she said."

PC Humble's face had whitened.

The Judge went on.

"The smell of trout lingers, what I wouldn't give for a nice trout for my tea. Where do you think I could get one, Humble?"

"I don't know," PC Humble stammered.

"I had a furious Lord Knighton on at me in the pub when I hoped to have a quiet drink. You weren't on duty, Humble. He had an official complaint to make, two of his piglets had gone missing, and someone laid traps for his birds; also, poaching has been going on in his river. Do you see what I'm getting at, Humble? Your wife cooks pork, grouse and trout, which no doubt fell out of the sky. We both know Smedley's ways don't we, Humble."

PC Humble remained silent, but his hands had started to tremble.

Abruptly the Judge changed the subject.

"Whatever injuries Smedley suffered today he deserved. All charges against Miss April Thornton are to be dropped from as of this minute, do you understand, Humble?"

PC Humble nodded his head.

The Judge turned and walked out of the police station, banging the door behind him.

PC Humble dropped onto a chair, shaking like a leaf.

Things would have to change, and quick.

18

April knocked on Mrs Keir's office door, and as Mrs Keir called, "come in", April entered. Mrs Keir looked up from the paperwork she was engaged in, then laid down her pen.

"Ha, April," she said with a smile. "Come and sit down, I've lots to tell you."

"All good, I hope," April replied as she sat down.

"Depends which way you look at it," Mrs Keir said. "I've had three phone-calls today, the first one from The Ministry of Agriculture, to say that they and Agricultural Wages Board are going to pay for Anita's funeral because she died in the line of duty."

"So they should," April broke in.

Mrs Keir went on.

"I had a call from the Coroner's Office at the Court House to say that Anita's death had been recorded as accidental."

"We didn't expect anything else, did we?" April asked.

Mrs Keir nodded her head.

"The third call was from a family member saying that the family had all agreed that Anita's funeral should take place here. Maybe two of her family would come, depending on the day, and time. Trains must be considered, of course. They didn't mention payment of costs. I've to ring and tell them that the WLA is meeting that."

"Poor Anita, they didn't give a damn about her did they!" April cried outraged.

"It seems like it, but never mind, *we* were her family, and in her own way, she was happy here, so don't get upset about her supposed caring family. Now, I must think about the next job which is going to see the Vicar about the funeral arrangements. How did things go about flowers?"

"Mrs Holt wrote everything down, three wreaths in red, white and blue, spelling out WLA. She'll call you when they're ready," April replied. She decided not to mention her bit of trouble with Smedley, it would upset Mrs Keir, and she had enough on her plate. "I'm going up to have a wash, is that okay, Mrs Keir, or do you want anything doing?"

"No, April, you go, Mrs Wilkinson has things in hand in the kitchen, I hope. She still sheds a few tears about Anita, says she can't help it."

April smiled.

"She's a good soul is Mrs Wilkinson."

April had her wash and felt better for it, and as she brushed her hair, she caught sight of Mouse's letter. Putting down the hairbrush, she picked up the still unopened envelope. Fay had not read it yet. I'm sure that she won't mind if I do. She took a nail file from the dresser drawer and slit open the envelope, then she began to read.

April and Fay,

My two dearest friends in all the world, how much I love you both, and thank you from the bottom of my heart for looking after me and trying to teach me the work on the land. Thank you April, for fighting my corner when coward me stood by in fear and trembling. I knew in my heart and soul that I'd never like being in the Land Army, and for weeks' I gave it much thought about entering the church. I'll have to do a year as a Novice, then I'll be not Sister Mouse, but Sister Tina. Sounds nice, doesn't it. I'll love the peace and serenity of the church, all the singing and praying.

I know your feelings about the church April, but you're quite wrong you know, someday I think you'll know this.

Please forgive me for not waiting to say goodbye to you both, I couldn't, it would've broken my heart. Know that I'm doing what I know I'll enjoy, be happy for me. Don't ever change April, there'll only ever be one April. And dear Fay, please try to do some good with your money.

I'll miss you both every day of my life, and I'll pray for you. I'll write often and hope you'll write to me with all the news about the hostel. I look forward to telling the Sisters of your exploits April. Despite what you think, nuns are human and do have a little time to themselves.

So, my dear friends, keep well and be happy, as I shall be.

I love you. I always shall, and may God go with you.

Mouse.

X X X X

April had a lump in her throat as she folded Mouse's letter and put it back into its envelope. Dear Mouse, she hoped that she'd made the right decision, all that praying and singing she talked about. How boring, and weren't those churches cold miserable places with no heating?

Now Mouse's letter had been read, the next thing she had to deal with was telling Fay about that louse, Larry. She was not looking forward to that. She hoped that Fay would not be too upset. She had warned her right from the start, she had summed him up right, a good looking no good jumped up now't. It made her wonder if somehow, he had found out about Fay's money. But how could he have? Still, no use worrying about that, and she had better tell Fay about her trouble with Smedley just in case Humble came to arrest her. How he would love that, be a feather in his cap. He'd better have arrested Smedley for spewing out his malice. She ought to have mentioned it to Mrs Keir, she was going to be upset, but it could not be helped. The Judge hadn't been pleased either, maybe he was getting a little bit tired of her and her trouble, she knew he had a soft spot for her, and she had one for him, but he had a job to do, had to do his duty. He was also a wily old thing, and he could not stand Humble, and neither could she.

However, she would not think of all that now, she would look forward to going to Kincaid tomorrow and seeing Miss Doris, what a lovely old lady she was. Kincaid… Someday she would have one just like it, she did not know how, but she would.

She looked at the clock on her bedside cabinet, she was bored and would much rather be at work, but this was an opportunity to read her book, Edgar Rice Burroughs, Tarzan Lord of the Apes. She was enjoying it, all those animals and Tarzan swinging through the trees.

Out of my world and into his, she thought as she stretched out onto her bed.

* * *

It was evening, all the girls had been told of the funeral arrangements, and now April and Fay were sat on their beds enjoying a cup of tea.

"Fay, there's something I must tell you. Two things actually."

Fay shook her head.

"Oh no, not more trouble, what've you done now?"

April spoke seriously as she told Fay all that happened.

"That was an awful thing for him to say, I would've slapped him myself if I'd been there. But you took things too far, didn't you? What if you're arrested?"

"So be it, I've never known such anger. I didn't come to myself until Humble pulled me off him, then," she broke into laughter. "I don't know what made me do it, but I knocked his helmet off his head, and it rolled into the gutter."

Fay started to laugh, then gulped out.

"You didn't." Then her laughter got louder and louder until she sounded hysterical. Then she gave deep belly laughs.

She wiped her eyes on the bedsheet.

"I don't know why I'm laughing; I won't be laughing if Humble comes to arrest you."

"Forget that. Now, the second thing I've to tell you is about Larry, it'll upset you," April said.

Fay looked at her calmly; her head on one side, then said grimly.

"If you're going to tell me about his other women, don't bother, I know, and I'm not upset."

"You know? How?" April asked surprised.

"Barry told me two weeks' ago."

"And it didn't upset you?"

"No. I realised what Larry was when he started not turning up to see me."

"I did warn you."

"Yes, you did, April, but I had to find out for myself."

"He's a louse."

"Yes, that name fits him."

"You know about this Sue?"

"Oh yes, poor thing. She must think she's his one and only. But how did *you* know?"

"Norman told me, he asked me to tell you, he was very worried about you getting hurt."

"Oh, bless him!" Fay cried. "But how did *he* know?"

April grinned; she was going to enjoy the telling of this.

"It seems Norman and little Titch make a habit of sitting at the tops of trees in the park. They see who comes and who goes, and with whom."

Fay giggled, then said.

"The little devils, go on, April."

"Several times they saw Larry having it off with this Sue, that's exactly how Norman put it."

Fay giggled again.

"Go on, I'm enthralled."

"When I told him that he shouldn't have been watching, he said why not, and that I must see the animals on the farm doing it all the time. How could I answer that?"

"The little monkey," Fay laughed.

"Wait till you hear this," April said. She put her hand over her mouth to stop the laughter bursting out.

"What's wrong with you, go on," Fay cried.

"Wait until I get a hold of myself," April gasped. She took a deep breath, removed her hand from her mouth, then said. "Norman said that I ought to have seen the size of his donger."

"His what? His donger? Norman's or Larry's?"

"Larry's, you fool. He came out with it, just like that; you do know what a donger is? Although I've never heard it called that before," April asked.

"Of course I do, stupid." Then Fay began to laugh loudly and hysterically, tears pouring down her face until she began to turn red as she hysterically repeated Norman's words.

"Donger! Oh my God! Donger! What a big donger!!"

April joined in as she stammered out.

"Just think what an escape you have had, kiddo!"

They rolled about their beds unable to stop laughing, until Fay kicked off her boots, climbed into her bed and stuffed the sheet into her mouth.

Gradually their laughter stopped, then April said.

"Can you just imagine little Titch's eyes when he first saw that, it's a wonder he didn't fall out of the tree!"

"It didn't stop him going, did it?" Fay replied. "He never talks does he, little Titch. Norman talks for him, and he'll have told him to say nothing of what they see in that park."

"Yes, Norman has his wits about him. *And* now I come to think about it, kiddo, you haven't mentioned Larry for a couple of weeks'."

"You don't notice everything, April."

"Oh, but I do, I only let you *think* I don't."

"I feel a fool to have been taken in by Larry like that; however, that's a lesson learned."

"I'll never trust a man, Fay, the only thing I trust is the land. It's beautiful and plentiful in summer, mean and moody in winter. At least I know what to expect."

"Hmm, you have a point there. But I say, I hope the others haven't heard us laughing our heads off, you know, with Anita dying, it's hardly the thing to do, is it?"

"Oh, I don't think so, the walls and doors are pretty thick. And now I think it's time for bed."

"One more thing before we get tucked up for the night. I'll be late back from Knighton Hall tomorrow night; Lady Knighton has asked me to stay back and help her entertain some men from Bomber Command whom she's asked over for a late supper."

"Sounds interesting, rather you than me though," April laughed as she climbed into bed.

"I don't know what I'll talk to them about," Fay said anxiously.

"Just be yourself, although *I* think it'll be all war talk."

"That's just it," Fay moaned. "I'm ashamed to say that I know little about the war. Well, we don't do we, tucked away safely here. We never listen to the wireless, read a paper, *or* talk about it between ourselves. The little we *do* know is what Barry and Dennis tell us."

"We're doing our bit for the war, *more* than our bit, it's hard-working on the land, we're in November and it's going to be tough graft. Think of all those frozen cauliflowers, carrots, parsnips and beetroots we're going to have to dig out of the frozen ground, *and* our legs, feet and fingers. Can't say I'm looking forward to that, can you?"

"Don't remind me," Fay shuddered.

"Mouse wouldn't have stood up to that you know," April said seriously.

"No, Mouse wouldn't, she got out at the right time, she was wise." She climbed into bed. "It's going to be a hard day tomorrow, good night, April, sleep well."

"You too," April answered drowsily.

* * *

The funeral was over, it had been well attended by the people of the village and boys from the G.I base. Also, a member from each Farmers Union, The Ministry of Labour and Agricultural Worker's, including The Local Representative. Land Girls from around about came, and the Land Army filled nearly half of the church. The service had been short but telling and gathered around the graveside in the cold and mist had brought home to them all that life was short, and what a tragic way Anita had died. Many comments had been made about the beautiful red, white and blue wreaths in the shape of WLA which covered the top of the coffin lid. Mrs Holt, or whoever had put them together, was incredibly talented and must have had nimble fingers.

The girls were sat around the kitchen table in the hostel, after having discovered that no one in Anita's family had been present at the funeral.

"Disgusting!" Nancy was in full flow. "Not one member of her family could be bothered to come, poor Anita. If they had I would've given them a piece of my mind, they never wrote to her, didn't send her a birthday card, and she was upset about it, she told me. After her face was disfigured, they wrote her off, didn't want her on their hands, and were glad when she joined the Land Army. Underneath, Anita was extremely sensitive you know, she felt things very deeply."

"Well, at least she had some happy times with us, and some laughs," Connie said.

"We didn't see her face, you got used to it," Binnie said softly. "Anita was a lovely girl inside."

"Yes, she was," Joan commented.
"She enjoyed her job," Jane said firmly.
Joan gave a loud sigh.
"I'll be thinking of her all the time."
"We'll have to see that her grave has fresh flowers every week," Katrina said firmly.
"That would be lovely; we could put a few pennies in a jar every payday," Nancy suggested. "Do you all agree?"
"Oh, yes!" they all cried.
"Do you think Mrs Keir would too?" Jane asked.
"I'm sure she would," Fay said firmly.
"Well, girls, life has to go on, Anita wouldn't want us to sit around moping," April said.
"Anita really admired you, April, she always said she wished she could be like you," Nancy said sadly.
"Well," Belinda began. "It's a good job I didn't say what I had seen in the cards, you..."
She was interrupted by cries of.
"Shut up, Belinda!"
"You and those bloody cards!"
"One more word, Belinda and I swear I'll gag you."
"We should take them off her and throw them in the fire."
"You wouldn't dare!" Belinda cried in alarm.
"Watch me," April said mischievously.
Belinda jumped to her feet with a cry of alarm and shouted.
"You'll do no such thing," and ran out of the kitchen.
They all laughed.
Fay looked towards the window, then said.
"Look, the sun's trying to get through, bless it."
"It's a bit late; it should've been out when we were stood in that cemetery," Nancy said angrily. "And another thing, I hope Anita haunts that rotten family of hers."
"That's silly, there's no such thing as ghosts," Binnie said in scorn.
"How do *you* know? There are more things in Heaven and Earth than man ever dreamed of," Fay said.
"Well, I don't believe it; anyone who does must be a bit stupid," Binnie said abruptly.
"Would you say that *I* am a bit stupid, as you put it?" April said bitingly.
"I know that you're not stupid, April, I didn't say that you were. You're too level-headed to have imagined you've seen a ghost."

"Am I really?" April said sarcastically.

Mrs Keir popped her head around the door and called.

"Fay, phone call for you, it's your Mother."

Fay sprang to her feet.

"Mother?!" she said worryingly. "She never calls at this time of day; I hope that there's nothing wrong." She hurried away from the kitchen and into Mrs Keir's office, where she snatched up the phone. "Mother? Hello, why are you ringing? Are you alright?"

Her Mother's voice came over loud and clear.

"Hello, Fay darling, are *you* alright?"

"Yes, Mother I'm fine, did you get my letter?"

"No, dear, not yet."

"It's lovely to hear from you, Mother, but is anything wrong? I've a feeling that there is."

"Well, Fay dear, yes, and no."

"Spill it, Mother."

"The good news is that your Father has gone and absconded with one of his fancy women, he came and told me he was going, and that he didn't want any more of your pittance of allowance. I'm going to deck the house out with flags."

"Mother, I feel delirious with joy! Has this woman of his got money?"

"Lots of it, dear."

"He'll soon trot through it, poor woman, I feel sorry for her. I'll never allow him to come back," Fay said firmly.

"I should think not, dear. I hope that we've seen the last of him. Now for a bit of sad news, Ted, our manager, has handed in four weeks' notice, it was a real blow, he's been with us for years as you know. I shall feel that we're losing a member of our family. Your Grandmother thought very highly of him as you know, and I'm terribly upset. What are we going to do? I can't run this large estate on my own. Shall I advertise for a replacement?"

"Slow down, Mother, don't be upset, leave it to me. If I must, I'll come home and run things myself. Can you manage for a couple of weeks'?"

"Yes, dear, I think so. I'm sorry to bring you trouble."

"There's nothing to be sorry about, Mother. I'll ring you tomorrow night. Now, put down the phone and make yourself a cup of tea, or have a tot of brandy."

"Yes, dear, I'll do that. Good night, Fay darling."

There was a click as Fay heard the phone put down at her Mother's end. She laid hers gently down. It seemed as if her life was about to change. She would have to go home, but first there was something she had to do, just *had* to do, then, she would hand in her notice. April was going to be upset.

The next day was a little brighter and saw Fay on her way to see Miss Doris at Kincaid Farm after begging a couple of hours leave from Lady Knighton.

As she peddled up the lane and turned around the slight hill to Kincaid Farm, she came upon it suddenly. On first sight of it she stopped, got off her bike, and just stood looking in admiration. April was right, it was a little gem, and how could Miss Doris bear to part with it? But, according to April, Miss Doris had her reasons.

She did not mount her bike again, but pushed it up to the kitchen door, leant it against the wall, then glanced around her. She could see that everything was well kept and could hear the raucous cackling of lots of hens, the quacking of ducks, the grunting of pigs and the bellowing of cattle in the barn to her left. April had told her of the animals Miss Doris kept, but wait, what about this giant of a dog April had mentioned? She hoped that it would not come bounding up to her out of nowhere. She was not afraid of dogs, they had four at home, but a Great Dane was another matter. She had better knock on the door, but, before she could do so, it opened, and a startled Miss Doris said.

"Oh, my word, you gave me a fright seeing you stood there like that!" She put her hand onto her chest, then took a deep breath.

"I'm so sorry," Fay cried, dismayed. "I was just about to knock when the door opened."

"We are not expecting a Land Girl today; in any case, it should be April," Miss Doris said firmly.

"Oh, I've not come to work, but to talk to you. You are Miss Doris?"

"Yes, I am Miss Doris, but why do you want to talk to me?" she smiled, then said. "I am very rude, please come in."

Fay stepped inside and quickly glanced around the neat and tidy kitchen as Miss Doris led her toward a chair.

"Please sit down, dear, what is your name?"

"Fay Trent." She didn't think it necessary to give her full name.

"April's friend, she told me about you, she is alright? You haven't come to tell me that something has happened to her? You lost one of your friends last week, didn't you?"

"I'm so sorry if my appearing on your doorstep has alarmed you, Miss Doris, April's fine."

"If April is fine, and you are not here to work, why *are* you here?"

"Can you spare me half an hour of your time please, Miss Doris? I want to talk to you about Kincaid."

"Kincaid?" Miss Doris said with a puzzled expression on her face. "Yes, I can give you half an hour, but *only* half an hour, I have the hens and pigs to feed. We may not be a large farm, but there is still plenty to do."

"Yes, farm work isn't easy, as I know being a Land Girl," Fay said with a smile.

"Of course you do, dear, now, what did you want to talk to me about? But, before you begin, would you like a cup of tea?"

"No thank you, Miss Doris, I can't be too long, I'm working today but begged a couple of hours off to see you."

"Sounds important," Miss Doris said, surprised.

"It is to me, so I'll just come straight out with it. I want to buy Kincaid, no matter what the price."

"You want to buy Kincaid?" Miss Doris was astounded.

"Yes, that's right," Fay said determinedly.

"April must have told you that I am putting it up for sale."

"Yes, she did, and I wanted to see you right away before anyone else got it."

"But can you afford it? You are only a Land Girl."

"If I didn't have the money, I wouldn't be here, Miss Doris."

"It hasn't even gone up for sale yet."

"I know that, but it doesn't have to, I want it very badly," Fay declared passionately.

"Really?"

"Yes, really badly."

"But this is the first time you have seen it."

"Yes, and it's lovely, I love it."

"But you have not seen the inside of the house."

"I don't need to; I know what April told me."

"Ha, April, the little minx. Why do you want Kincaid so badly, Fay?"

"Firstly, what's your price?" Fay asked.

Miss Doris looked at Fay with a business eye as she thought, this girl knows what she is about, and she must have a tiptop reason for being so keen to buy Kincaid, but, if she could pay its price, so be it.

Miss Doris named her price, then added.

"That includes all the furniture throughout, pots, pans, all kitchenware, curtains and carpets; we will only be taking a few pieces of china."

Fay gasped.

"But that's not enough, you're robbing yourself!"

"Do you think so? I don't. We have money to start with, my sister and I, and where we are going, it's more than enough to last our lifetime, we are in our eighties you know. Now, can you meet my price?"

"Meet it, of course, I may be a Land Girl, but between you and I, Miss Doris, I'm a rich one, a very rich one."

"Really? You surprise me, Fay, does April know?"

"She does."

"Well, maybe she will come here with you and help run the farm."

"Oh, I'll not be doing that, you see, Miss Doris, due to circumstances beyond my control I have to return home to North Yorkshire and run my own estate."

"Oh," Miss Doris said, "I see."

But she didn't really.

"Is it a deal then, Miss Doris? Will you let me have Kincaid? I'll pay your price willingly."

"On one condition," Miss Doris said firmly. "If you are not going to be here, who is going to run things? I must know that Kincaid is in good hands. You know, we have lived here for a very long time, and the place is very precious to us."

"If I tell you, I'll need your promise not to tell a soul until I've told the person who is to own and run the place." Fay waited for Miss Doris to speak.

Miss Doris was thinking deeply, then she said.

"You said *own* the place, but *you* will own Kincaid, Fay."

"I think that I'd better come clean with you, Miss Doris."

"Yes, I think that you better had."

Fay came right out with it.

"It's for April."

Miss Doris looked stunned.

"April? Does she know?"

"No, that's why I've to have your promise."

"But I don't understand, Fay."

"It's a long story, but I'll cut it short. April's my dearest friend in all the world. I know that the thing she wants, her dream, which she thinks is never going to come true, is to own her own little farm. Not a big one, just a small one, just like Kincaid. She came back to the hostel raving about it, and when she said that you were going to put it up for sale, I had this thought in my head about buying Kincaid for her. I've more money than I know what to do with, and I want to do this for April. It won't be easy getting her to accept it as a gift; indeed, I'm going to have quite a fight on my hands, April's very independent you know, Miss Doris. So, I'm hoping that once she has the deeds and bill of sale in her hands, she'll accept Kincaid."

"Oh, I hope she does, I'll rest easy knowing it is in April's hands. She is a lovely girl isn't she, I liked her on sight, and as honest as the day is long," Miss Doris cried.

"Do the animals come in with the price?" Fay asked.

"Of course, my dear."

"You really aren't asking enough for the place you know, Miss Doris, please let me give you more."

"No, I *am* satisfied with the price I asked, now that I know April is going to own Kincaid, I would gladly have lowered it." Miss Doris smiled, then clapped her hands together. "Oh April, how lucky you are!"

"I hope that *she's* going to think that, it's not going to be easy getting her to accept it," Fay said anxiously. "How soon can you have the deeds and paperwork ready, Miss Doris? You'll have to see your solicitor, won't you?"

"Solicitor? Oh, no, I don't have a solicitor, nor do I hold with them, *or* banks for that matter. No, this is a straightforward sale between us for cash, Fay."

"Cash?" Fay said bewildered. "You want all that money in cash?"

"Sorry, my dear, I should have made it clear from the start, I only ever deal in cash," Miss Doris said apologetically.

"Cash?" Fay repeated.

"Will that be a problem, dear?" Miss Doris asked.

"I don't think so; I think that there's a branch of my bank in Tiptree."

"Good."

"The cashiers face is going to be a picture when I ask for all that money in cash."

"Isn't it," Miss Doris laughed.

"I'll have to sort out a bag big enough to put it in. Just imagine me with all that cash slung on the handlebars of my bike."

Miss Doris laughed, then said.

"Stranger things have happened, dear. Father once brought home a dead sheep across Cain's back."

"Speaking of Cain," Fay asked. "Where is he? I expected him to bound out when you opened the door to me."

"He's in the far barn with Len, one of my weekly helpers, he's whitewashing the walls in there, keeps him out of mischief. Cain I mean, not Len," Miss Doris laughed.

Fay laughed along with her, then said.

"I'd better be on my way; Lady Knighton will be wondering what's happened to me. I'll get things moving and see you in two or three days. Miss Doris, it's been lovely to meet you, you are everything April said you were."

"That is a lovely compliment; I hope to see April tomorrow?"

"You will, we're all back at work, noses to the grindstone. Goodbye, Miss Doris." Fay leant forward and kissed Miss Doris on her cheek.

Miss Doris looked pleased, and as Fay cycled quickly away, she thought what nice girls these Land Girls are, and how lucky she was to have sold Kincaid so fast, no fuss or bother, and it could not go to a nicer person than April! I shall have to start on with the packing, with a bit of luck we could be off in a couple of weeks'. But first she had to look out the deed, make out a bill of sale, everything had to be done correctly, then she had to try to explain to Ada that they were moving. That was not going to be easy, would she understand? It was doubtful.

19

Fay gave a sigh of relief as she left Mrs Keir's office, which was one hurdle over. She had given her notice to Mrs Keir, who had been very upset, but, when she had explained the situation to her, had understood. Mrs Keir would pass all that on to The War Agg, and no doubt she would come out to see her.

Yesterday had been grim but funny. She had been to the bank in Tiptree and gotten the money for Miss Doris. The cashiers face had been one of incredulous amazement, he had stood speechless, and she had to ask again for the amount she wanted. Without a word he had hurried off and brought forth the manager, who had taken her into his office and had wanted to know all the details. He had been a pompous man full of his own importance until she had produced her bank book, passport and birth certificate. When he had realised who she was and the amount of money she had in his bank, he had changed his manner entirely. Then, she had thought she would have a bit of fun with him...

"Any problem, Mr Benson? If so, I'll draw the lot out, which will be difficult for you would it not, I don't think that you'll have so much money in your bank. I'd need a police escort to get it all back to the hostel, and, we don't want that now, do we."

"Oh no, Miss Trent, no problem at all," he blustered. "I'll get what you've asked for right away, I'll do it myself immediately."

His fat face had been red like a turkey cock, and he had been sweating, with drops running down into his shirt collar. He had jumped up and almost ran out of the office. She had thought him an obnoxious little man.

All her business had been done in half an hour, and she had walked out of the bank carrying a large black suitcase, she had had the foresight to ask Dennis to pick her up in the van, which he had done, and the case was sat on top of her wardrobe waiting to be taken to Miss Doris. April had asked what it was doing there, and she had promised to give her some sort of an explanation tonight. She was dreading that; April would be unhappy to say the least.

* * *

Half a dozen of the girls was sat in the kitchen, their hands wrapped around hot cups of tea.

"I'll never be warm again; I thought the day would never end. That Thomas Farm was a nightmare, the farmer kept us at it, digging out parsnips as if our lives depended on it, 'keep yer warm' he kept saying. But to be fair, he got stuck in too," Binnie wailed.

"You should talk," Jane said, holding up her hands. "Look at my fingers, still white with cold."

"You're not on your own, mine are too," Joan said. "I'm dreading tomorrow, I'm on milking, and one of those cows is sadistic, or doesn't like me, she lashes me across my face with her tail every time. She got me in the eye last week, I couldn't see for hours."

"It's better than digging cauliflowers out of a stone-hard ground with fingers numb with cold I can tell you," Katrina shouted.

"Give me rat-catching any day," Nancy said loudly.

"Oh, I don't know, I couldn't bear the thought of killing them," animal mad Joan said softly.

"You'd kill them if they bit you on your arse when you're bending down at harvest time," Nancy said with a grin.

"Oh, shut up, Nancy, we're all not as hard-hearted as you," Joan replied crossly.

"I hate to break up the party, but April and I have something to discuss," Fay said. "So please excuse us, girls." She smiled at April, "come on, love."

"Oh, secrets, is it?" Connie said.

"No, just private business," Fay replied.

"Not for long, we always get to know what's going on around here," Belinda said, nodding her head.

"Do you see it in the cards?" Nancy asked sarcastically.

"Are you trying to be funny?!" Belinda said angrily.

"No," Nancy answered with a grin. "Just curious."

"You shouldn't mock the cards; they tell it true," Belinda said, pointing at Nancy.

"We'll leave you to it, girls," Fay cried, sensing an argument brewing.

As Fay and April went upstairs for privacy in their bedroom, April was wondering what Fay wanted to talk to her about; she hoped that Fay had not changed her mind about lover boy Larry. Surely, she could not be that stupid?

Her fears were laid to rest when Fay began.

"April, there's only one way to say this, and that's to come right out with it."

"Oh no!" April burst out. "You're not going to tell me that you're pregnant?!"

"Don't be stupid!" Fay cried, startled.

"Go on then, what is it?" April demanded.

"I'm leaving."

"What, the hostel?"

"No, the Land Army."

"*The Land Army?*" April repeated. "But why? You can't. I won't let you." She lost all the colour in her face, then cried. "Why are you leaving? What's happened?"

Fay launched into the phone call she had had from her Mother.

"So, you see, April, I don't have a choice, do I? Mother can't possibly run that huge estate by herself. I've given in my notice explaining things, Mrs Keir's upset, as I can see that you are."

"Of course I'm bloody well upset, you're like a sister to me. Can't you hire someone to run it for you?"

"No, there'd be too much to learn, and besides, you've to be able to trust someone in so important a job. I must do it myself, and I've already told Mother I'm going home."

"I can't take it in, it's a shock, Fay."

"It's a shock to me too, I don't want to leave the WLA. I've gotten to quite like it, but duty comes first, and I do own all the estate, besides farms, rented houses and lots of land. Some of which I'll sell when the war's over."

"More money than you know what to do with, lucky you."

"Oh, I know what I'm going to do with some of it."

"Don't tell me, I don't want to know. When are you going?"

"In about two weeks'."

"So soon?" April asked surprised.

"No use putting it off, is there?"

"I'll miss you, Fay, first Anita gone, then Mouse. I'll have to write and tell Mouse, she'll want your address, as will I."

"Of course, but we'll still see each other, April, I'm not going a million miles away. When the war's over it'll be a better train service, one hopes."

"I'm glad you can be so cheerful about it."

"I'm not cheerful, I'm about to have my life turned over."

"Well, one good thing has come out of this; you're no good Dad is out of your life."

"Yes, for good, I hope."

"Your Mam must be very pleased."

"She is, she's over the moon."

"Now I know what the suitcase on top of the wardrobe's for, it's rather large, isn't it?"

"Yes, for a reason. I'll be taking some gifts back for Mother and friends, after all, it's nearly Christmas isn't it."

"Yes, so it is. Not a very nice one for me without you, so I'll volunteer to stay and work at Christmas, some of us must."

"It's over in two days, April."

"Two days of hell if the weather turns bad."

"Oh, look on the bright side."

"I'm not very good at that."

"Of course you are, *you* are April Thornton."

"I don't feel like her at the moment, your news has knocked me for six."

Fay laughed.

"Just imagine, *me* knocking out April Thornton, that's the first time anyone has managed to do that!"

"Yes, do you want a medal?"

"Now, I think we should go down and break the news to the other girls, or do you think that Belinda has already seen it in her cards?"

"Knowing her, she'll say that she has," April replied, shaking her head.

"Seriously, do you think that she ever *does* see things?"

"No, *I* think that she gets carried away and *thinks* that she does; however, we'll see what she says."

* * *

The girls had been shocked at Fay's news, but when she had explained the situation, they had understood.

She was stood by the main gates at the front of the hostel, waiting for Dennis, who was taking her to Kincaid. All this had been arranged without April's knowledge. April would go into the hostel the back way from work around six, Dennis was due to pick Fay up at the front at the same time. She had to get the money to Miss Doris, get any loose ends tied up, then she could present April with Kincaid, and it was not going to be easy.

Here was Dennis, he pulled up in front of her in his battered old van, and it was looking to be a bit of a relic. I shall give the lad a nice little cheque or present him with a new van – the look on his face would be priceless, Fay thought with amusement as she climbed into the van, it even smelled old, and had a lingering smell of petrol.

"Alright, girl?" Dennis asked. "How long are you going to be? Do you want me to wait for you or go away and pick you up later? Only I promised to have a pint with the lads, and maybe a game of darts."

"I'd like you to wait, Dennis; I should only be half-an-hour. It's very good of you to take me."

"Glad to be of service, Fay. Sorry to hear you're leaving us; I've liked working with you."

"News travels fast, doesn't it?" Fay laughed.

"It's not because of Larry, is it?"

"Oh, no! He's a thing of the past, no Dennis, I'm needed at home, so, I've no choice but to leave. It'll be a wrench leaving this place, the girls and April; I've really enjoyed my time here. I'll come back and see you when the war's over."

"Do you think the war will *ever* be over? It's going on a long time, isn't it?"

"It will, we're slowly winning I understand."

"I hope so, some of my mates are in the thick of it. I lost one of them, his ship went down with all hands."

"Oh, how awful! I'm so sorry."

"His Mum was heartbroken; he was her only child."

"The poor woman," Fay said sadly.

As they turned the corner, Kincaid came into view, but only just, no lights were allowed to show, but a myriad of twinkling stars shone down on it. It looked so peaceful and serene.

Dennis drove into the yard, then pulled up.

"I'll sit here and have a smoke while you do your business."

"I'll be as quick as I can," she said as she picked up the suitcase, which she had held on to her knees. Dennis had not asked what she had in it, if he had, she would have been at a loss at what to say.

She knocked loudly on the kitchen door, and Cain began to bark loudly.

"Oh God, I forgot about the bloody dog," she cried, her heart thundering in her chest.

"Who is it?" Miss Doris's voice called out.

"Fay Trent, Miss Doris."

"One-minute, Fay, I'll just shut Cain away."

When she opened the door a few moments later, she said.

"Sorry about that, but I suddenly remembered that he hasn't been introduced to you, so he could have been nasty. But that is his job you know, to protect my sister and me."

"Of course, Miss Doris, he sounds as if he's a big dog."

"He is. Great Danes usually are, dear. Ha, I see you have a suitcase. Does it contain what I think it does?" Miss Doris asked.

"It does, every penny. Do you want to see it?"

"No, dear, I trust you. How did it go in the bank? But first, sit down; would you like a cup of tea?"

"No thanks, Miss Doris, I have Dennis waiting outside so I can't be long."

"Tell me about the bank," Miss Doris said eagerly.

"Well," Fay began. "It was like a comedy show, the bank manager himself saw to me. I thought he was going to pass out at the amount I asked for. He huffed and puffed until I laid my credentials in front of him; he soon changed his attitude and got moving."

Miss Doris looked puzzled.

"Are you someone of importance, Fay?" she asked.

"It doesn't really matter who I am," Fay replied kindly with a smile.

"In other words, mind my own business, eh," Miss Doris said. "So, I will."

Fay pointed at the suitcase, then said.

"It's heavy; can I carry it somewhere for you?"

"No, dear, I shall manage it, thank you." She walked to one of the kitchens draws, opened it, then took out a large manila envelope. She laid it on the table in front of Fay. "There you are, dear, the deeds for Kincaid, the bill of sale, and a letter stating that all monies have been paid in full, in cash. I shall need a note from you stating our agreement, as you have one from me. I have put April's name on all paperwork as is right and proper as she is going to be the new owner, is that right? Are you going to look over the paperwork in my presence?"

"No, not now, Miss Doris, I trust you."

"So you should, my dear, so you should," Miss Doris nodded her head.

"I don't want to sound pushy, but do you know when you're moving?" Fay asked gently.

"Within the week," Miss Doris replied happily.

"Really?" Fay said, surprised.

"Yes, dear, my original plans had to be changed, we won't be going into a home for maiden ladies, it's the dog you see, I can't bear to part with him, and these homes do not allow pets. I have a very dear friend of long-standing whom I went to school with, we are in touch every week, and she has told me of a cottage by the sea in Cornwall that is up for sale. It has a large sitting room, two large bedrooms, but a small kitchen and bathroom. The beauty of it is, it has a garden back and front for Cain."

"It sounds lovely, and by the sea too," Fay said.

"My friend has excellent taste; I trust her implicitly. If she says it is right for us, it will be. So, I have told her to go ahead and secure it."

"I'm so pleased for you, Miss Doris; I hope you'll be happy there. What about your sister, will she settle do you think?"

"Ada does not know where she is half the time, but she will love the sea, I am sure."

"How are you getting there?" Fay asked.

"My friend's son is going to take us; he has a large car."

"Is the house furnished, Miss Doris? You don't want to take anything from here? If you do, I won't mind."

"Oh, I don't want anything dear, this house where we are going is part furnished, it will do us until the war is over, then I shall buy what I need."

"I'm glad it's worked out so well for you, Miss Doris. I'll see you again before you go. But now, I have a momentous task in front of me getting April to accept Kincaid."

"Yes, I don't envy you, dear, I have had April here today as you know, she is distraught at your leaving, and she did tell me why, I hope you don't mind."

"No, it's bound to get around, isn't it."

"Yes, it's surprising how quickly news travels around the farms."

"Now, I really must go, Dennis will want to get back." She picked up the manila envelope from the table and waved it in the air. "Thanks for this, Miss Doris."

"Thank you for the money," Miss Doris replied.

As Fay hurried to the door, she said.

"Goodbye, see you soon."

20

It was Sunday the eighth of December, April and Fay were in their bedroom chatting about this and that. In the corner was a large, packed travelling bag. Fay was ready to go home tomorrow.

April looked at the bag sadly.

"I can't believe that you'll be gone tomorrow, I'll miss you terribly, kiddo," April said.

"Who else is going to call me kiddo?" Fay asked. "I'll ring you once a week; besides the letters we're going to write."

"I warn you, I'm not particularly good at letter writing, I never know what to put. Poor Mam and Dad are lucky if they get a small page." April pulled a face.

"I've a feeling that you're going to have lots to write about. I know I am."

"Why do you say that? Do you know something I don't?" April said, narrowing her eyes. "Well, do you?"

Fay's heart sounded like thunder in her ears. It was now or never. She stood, walked to her chest of drawers, opened the top one, then took out the manila envelope. She turned and faced April, smiled, then said.

"April my dear friend, I love you dearly, and I want you to have this." She held the large envelope out to April, who took it from her.

"An early Christmas card? Rather a large one, isn't it? Still, save you posting it, thanks, Fay, I'll open it at Christmas."

"No, April, I want you to open it now."

April looked puzzled.

"Why?" she asked.

"Just do it," Fay replied, her heart beating ten to the dozen.

"Alright, if that's what you want, but a small one would've done just as well."

She picked up a nail file from the top of her bedside cabinet and slit open the envelope with it, she laid the nail file back onto the cabinet, then looked inside the envelope.

"What's this?" she said. "It's not a card." She shook the contents onto her bed.

The papers were folded neatly together, Fay had checked them, and everything was in order.

"What the hell are these papers, Fay?"

Fay took a deep breath, had *anything* been as hard to give away.

"Look at them, April."

April picked them up and quietly read them all, her face whitening. She handed them back to Fay.

"From these papers, it would appear that Kincaid has been sold, but someone has made a mistake, they have *my* name on them, it should be yours, Fay, *you* have bought Kincaid, haven't you? But what use is it to you? You'll be in North Yorkshire running your estate. But wait, you're going to need someone to run it for you, and do you have me in mind, knowing I'd love my own farm? Running one for someone else will be the next best thing wouldn't it, is that why my name's on the papers?" She came to a halt, waiting for Fay to speak.

"Look again at the deeds, April."

April picked the deeds up and looked closely at them, then she stared at Fay fiercely.

"I hope this doesn't mean what I think it does."

In for a penny, in for a pound, Fay thought. She took a deep breath.

"It means that you own Kincaid, lock, stock and barrel. I bought it for you."

"I can't, I won't accept it," April said angrily. "What possessed you?"

Fay started to feel angry.

"I'll tell you shall I. It's a gem of a farm. You came back raving about it, saying how one day you'd have one just like it, *and* that it was for sale. Well, I went to see it and bought it for cash, yes, cash, and not to brag, but I've bought it for you because I know it's meant for you, you are my dearest friend in all the world. Remember what Mouse said in her letter? Use your money wisely? Well, I am, and I'll tell you something else, April Thornton, you're not the only one! Dennis is going to get a new van, but he doesn't know it yet. I'm sending a cheque for ten thousand pounds to Mouse for the nuns and their church. I'm sending money for the WLA to have a stone statue erected in memory of all the Land Army Girls. I'm going to buy a house in Scotland for holidays for Mother and me. I'm going to buy a couple of racehorses because I want to win a Grand National, and I'm going to help the blind. Is there anything else you need to know?! So, who are *you* to turn down a gift given from the heart? Tell me that. I want to share what I have with others; Mouse was right."

"Just shut your gob, Fay. Given what you've just spouted at me, I accept, but tell me one thing; did Miss Doris promise you not to tell me? Because she's been stamping around like a racehorse in heat all day, full of herself, she's been bursting out into songs I've never heard."

"Of course she did."

"And do you mean to tell me that I now own all that beautiful furniture in the sitting room? Don't you think it's lovely?"

"I haven't seen it."

"Haven't seen it?"

"No."

"You just took my word on it?"

"Of course."

"Well, that beats the band does that."

"If I can't trust you, April, who *can* I trust?"

"I can't begin to tell you what's in my heart. I can never thank you enough."

"You haven't heard the best bit yet, I wasn't going to tell you, but I've changed my mind; if something happens to me and I pop my clogs, you're my heir."

"What? Are you mad?"

"No. I've no relatives, only Mother, and she's lots of money of her own."

"But you will marry, Fay."

"No, I won't."

"You don't know what the future holds."

"My will stands, married or not."

"I'm not going to worry my head about that because nothing's going to happen to you."

"Anyway, once the war's over and no produce to give to the Government, what you make on Kincaid is yours."

"Oh, Fay, I can't believe it, Kincaid mine! It's a dream isn't it; I'm going to wake up any minute!" she said gleefully.

"It's no dream, Kincaid *is* yours. So, you see, dreams *can* come true."

"Are you absolutely sure about this, Fay?"

"Absolutely. I want to see you happy, April."

"I am, but you'll come and see me, won't you?"

"I shall, and I'll bring Mother. I've talked about you so much that she's dying to meet you."

"I'll look forward to meeting her."

"To change the subject, I think you should go down and see Mrs Keir, get your notice in and tell her of your changed circumstances."

"What, now?"

"Yes, the sooner the better. Miss Doris is hoping to move to Cornwall shortly, her friend down there has found her a lovely cottage."

"Cornwall?" April said in surprise. "That's nice for her and Miss Ada."

"I wonder how she'll get all that money down there. It's a lot to be shipping down to Cornwall," Fay said.

More than you know, April thought as she touched the side of her nose.

"She'll have a way; Miss Doris is a very clever lady."

* * *

It was now the twelfth of December, and April was living happily at Kincaid. She had seen Miss Doris and Miss Ada off to Cornwall, and Fay had returned to North Yorkshire last week. Some of the girls had been to see her and had *loved* Kincaid, how lucky she was they had said, and fancy Fay being so rich!

She strode to the kitchen window and looked out at the neat and tidy yard, it was so quiet now, something was missing, dogs, that was it. She was not a dog lover, but she would get two sheepdogs, Dennis would help her with that. She would get pups; bring them up to her ways, yes, that is what she would do.

She felt a new sense of freedom, and would run Kincaid on the old traditional methods like Miss Doris had done. She had borrowed a horse for the ploughing, milked the cows by hand, and there was a pump in the yard for swilling out the barns. She knew that she would have to work hard, harder than she thought possible, but she was April Thornton, she would make this farm pay, or die in the attempt! Thank goodness for her Land Army training; she could handle the pigs, poultry, dairy work and working the fields. Maybe she would get a few sheep next year? The Land Army she realised, had given her an escape route to a life of happiness, bred in her a love of the countryside which would never leave her. She would be contented forever!

For December, it was a bright and sunny day, she walked out of the house, across the yard and stood at the gate that led to the fields, *her* fields. She leant on the gate and looked around her with pleasure.

My own, my *very* own!

Kay Snow

'THE LAND ARMY GIRLS ARE HERE' BOOK SOUNDTRACK

Boogie Woogie Bugle Boy – The Andrews Sisters
Begin The Beguine – Artie Shaw
Jealousy – Vera Lynn
Moonlight Serenade – Glenn Miller
Beat Me Daddy, Eight To The Bar – The Andrews Sisters
Two O'clock Jump – Harry James
As Time Goes By – Vera Lynn
In The Mood – Glenn Miller
Woodchopper's Ball – Woody Herman
Don't Sit Under The Apple Tree – The Andrews Sisters
You Made Me Love You – Harry James
I'll Be Seeing You – Billie Holiday

Listen and enjoy for free on my YOUTUBE channel POETRY IN MOTION:
(link can be found via my website – kaysnow.co.uk on 'SOCIAL MEDIA LINKS')

A SPECIAL MENTION

Many thanks to Pauline Loven, from **Crow's Eye Productions** for allowing me to use the amazing photograph taken by Nicole Loven for use as my book cover. And to my book cover model, Bryony – you shall forever and always be my April Thornton. Lots of love to you all.

ABOUT THE AUTHOR

My place of birth is the small town of Bingley, England. For all lovers of history, it is known as 'The Throstles Nest of Old England' and mentioned in the formidable Doomsday Book. Bingley is also a stone's throw away from Haworth, home of the wonderful Brontë's. My most admired being Charlotte, who of course, wrote Jane Eyre – one of my favourite books – I love to read and watch anything that features dark, brooding, gothic Victorian mansions and spend many an evening escaping into the world of all things gothic, whether it be a book, movie or TV series.

As a child I wanted the ability to evoke emotion within people, so naturally what better way to do that than to become a Singer or Actress? The only problem was, (and still is), my innate shyness. So, the next best thing for me was becoming a writer. Over the years I dabbled, but never really took it seriously until I entered Yahoo's writing competition – a worldwide call for writers and authors. Their sole purpose to write a story to entertain children during the 2020 spring/summer lockdown of the Covid-19 pandemic. I had never written a children's story before, but nonetheless, I was up for the challenge. My self-belief resulted in my story, 'The Diary of Primrose Goldie Gold' being a winner, and is now featured in Yahoo's debut edition of the STOR14S 2020 podcast series, and narrated by Hollywood actress, Megalyn Echikunwoke.

My first book, **The Lyons** – a gothic novel published in 2021; my second, **The Land Army Girls Are Here** published in 2023 – a WW2 comedy-drama. So, for all intents and purposes I guess you should call me a multi-genre author – I write what I am passionate about at the time. So, expect the unexpected for my next book...

kaysnow.co.uk

OTHER TITLES BY KAY SNOW

The Lyons – a gothic novel.

Would you live in a house whose legendary curse preceded it?

When Kathryn White takes up residence of Lyon House – an imposing gothic Victorian mansion, a plethora of ghostly events encapsulate and propel her into the past – cementing her future.

If you're a fan of 'Second Sight' (The Two World's of Jennie Logan) by David Williams, 'Somewhere in Time' by Richard Matheson and 'The Haunting of Hill House' by Shirley Jackson, then you'll love 'The Lyons'!

Arc Reviews:
"A very atmospheric and greatly intriguing novel!"
"Tomorrow's classic!"
"One story, two intertwining worlds – one set in the present, the other in the past – AWESOME!"
"The Lyons is a cleverly constructed supernatural story that keeps you guessing till the end."

THE LAND ARMY GIRLS ARE HERE

Printed in Great Britain
by Amazon